The Regency

Lords & Ladies
COLLECTION

*Two Glittering Regency
Love Affairs*

One Night with a Rake
by Louise Allen

The Regency

LORDS & LADIES
COLLECTION

The Regency

LORDS & LADIES
COLLECTION

Louise Allen &
Elizabeth Rolls

*M&B™ and M&B™ with the Rose Device
are trademarks of the publisher.
Harlequin Mills & Boon Limited, Eton House,
18-24 Paradise Road, Richmond, Surrey TW9 1SR*

First published in Great Britain in 2003 and 2002

THE REGENCY LORDS & LADIES COLLECTION
© Harlequin Books S.A. 2008

The publisher acknowledges the copyright holders of the
individual works as follows:

One Night with a Rake © Louise Allen 2003
The Dutiful Rake © Elizabeth Rolls 2002

ISBN: 978 0 263 86598 1

052-0108

*Printed and bound in Spain
by Litografia Rosés S.A., Barcelona*

One Night with a Rake
by
Louise Allen

Louise Allen has been immersing herself in history, real and fictional, for as long as she can remember, and finds landscapes and places evoke powerful images of the past. She also writes for Mills & Boon as one half of the Historical writing partnership Francesca Shaw, and enjoys the contrast between the fun and stimulus of writing with a friend and the different but equally satisfying experience of conjuring stories entirely out of her own imagination. Louise lives in Bedfordshire and works as a property manager, but spends as much time as possible with her husband at the cottage they are renovating on the north Norfolk coast, or travelling abroad. Venice, Burgundy and the Greek islands are favourite atmospheric destinations.

For AJH with love and thanks
for all the constant inspiration

Chapter One

Mrs Clare floated gently up into a delicious state of half-sleep, half-waking and hovered there for a few moments, comfortably aware that there was no light from the window on her closed lids and that therefore there was no need to wake and get up from the deep and enveloping feather mattress. She snuggled down warmly and drifted back into slumber, lulled by the reassuring sound of deep, regular, male breathing from the other side of the bed.

Perhaps an hour later the sounds of the household rising intruded into her dreams without waking her. Faint riddling noises signified that grates were being readied for the day's fires, a cockerel crowed in the yard and a door downstairs banged. Mrs Clare frowned in her sleep, turned over and burrowed into the pillow. It seemed that the other sleeper had turned too, for her unconscious hand touched body-warmed linen and her body sank into the central dip of the bed, to touch his lightly.

Her dream turned from a pleasant scene in a draper's shop where multicoloured piles of silks and taffetas heaped from floor to ceiling, every one of them so dag-

ger-cheap that it would be a sin not to buy them all, to
a confused image of herself, tangled both in the silks
and in the arms of a man whose face she could not see.
She struggled, but half-heartedly, for his hands were
caressing her body and his mouth...

Amanda Clare moaned gently, wriggling closer to the
long form beside her, then sighed as a strong arm gathered her close in a comforting, sleepy embrace. She
began to wake again, to become conscious of his nearness and her own pleasurable anticipation. Her lids fluttered against the light and with wakefulness came an
awareness of a number of disturbing facts.

She had a headache. Indeed, as she turned her head
on the pillow she found that it was very sore indeed.
And this was not her bed, for her stretching feet encountered an unfamiliar solid bed board at the foot. Nor
was it her bedroom, or even, she realised as she stiffened into full awareness, her eyes still tight shut in
alarm, her house. The noises were all wrong, the light
was coming from the wrong side of the window and
the singing voice coming up faintly from the yard below
belonged to none of her servants.

But most frightening of all was the indisputable fact
that Mrs Clare was a widow and had been for two years.
And in those two years she had lived a life of blameless
respectability, which did not involve the slightest intimacy with men.

Very cautiously Amanda opened her eyes and found
herself looking into the sleepy green gaze of her bedmate. He was so close that their noses were almost
touching. At that range it was difficult to tell much
about him, but it was very obvious that he was a complete stranger. Amanda realised that she was holding

her breath and that her heart was banging so hard against her ribs that they felt bruised.

The man's eyes widened slightly, then crinkled into a smile as he leaned forward and kissed her firmly on the lips.

'Aagh!' Amanda shot backwards in a tangle of limbs and bedding and landed on her knees on the floor on the far side of the bed. 'Ouch!' She peered cautiously over the edge of the bed, easing her bruised knees and tugging at the sheet which was round her feet, ready to run for the door the moment the stranger made a move.

He made no threatening gestures however, merely easing himself upright against the pillows with a muffled oath. Her scramble for freedom had dragged all the bedding off, but he was quite decently clad in a somewhat voluminous linen nightshirt. She saw his right cheek was badly grazed and bruised and he was favouring his right arm. Dark brown, almost black hair, tumbled across his forehead and she was very aware that not only was he tall and long-limbed, but powerfully built.

'Who are you and what are you doing in my bed?' she demanded. She thought about getting to her feet, but the high side of the bed was a useful shield and although she was covered from head to foot in a nightgown, the amused green eyes were making her feel decidedly exposed.

'I could ask the same thing,' he remarked. Amanda registered a deep, cultured voice with a hint of mockery. 'Are you sure it *is* your bed?'

'No, I am not. In fact, I am sure it is not,' she replied honestly, cautiously getting to her feet and dragging the faded chintz bedcover around her shoulders. She lifted the rest of the bedding off the floor and tossed it towards him before making a strategic retreat to the far end of the room where a planked door stood under the eaves.

Her hurried steps were painfully jarring. 'Oh, my aching head! What on earth has happened, and where *am* I?'

'I haven't the slightest idea,' the man said unhelpfully. 'But you have the most magnificent black eye, I appear to have dislocated my shoulder although it is back in place now, and my jaw—' He broke off, wincing as he explored it with careful fingers. 'Do you think we have can have been throwing the furniture at each other?'

'I very much doubt it,' Amanda replied tartly, 'although at this moment I am most tempted.' She saw a mirror hanging over the washstand and inspected her face in it. 'Oh, my goodness! I look a complete fright!'

'I think you look delightful,' the man observed dispassionately, 'although I must say you do appear to have been dragged through a hedge backwards.'

'Hedge…hedge backwards… It is coming back now!' Amanda drew a deep breath of relief. 'It was the stagecoach, a few miles after you got on at Felthorpe. It seemed to be going rather fast and then it lurched and I fell across the seat, and you—' She broke off at the memory of him gathering her tightly in his arms as the coach tipped terrifyingly off the road and down the bank. 'You caught hold of me and the stage crashed down the bank and into the hedge and someone was pulling me out—through the quickthorn—and that is the last thing I remember.'

'Then it is no wonder the pair of us seem to be covered in bruises. We should count ourselves lucky nothing is broken. But that does not answer the question of

why—although, believe me, I am not complaining—
why we find ourselves in bed together.'

'We were the only people on the coach,' Amanda
said, thinking hard, too preoccupied to be embarrassed
at his blunt speaking. 'But surely the guard or the driver
remembered that we did not get on together?'

She had been pleasantly surprised to find she had the
coach to herself as they left Norwich, for although it
was not a market day at any of the towns along the
route she had expected to have to share with several
people. Finding herself alone when the coach took up
a handsome man with a decided air of rakish elegance
was also not what she had bargained for. Amanda's experience of stagecoaches was limited to this one, eventful, journey and her fears had been of finding herself
crowded in less than genteel company rather than hoping for the speedy arrival of several stout farmers' wives
to act as chaperons.

The man had, however, behaved with perfect propriety, doffing his hat as he entered. He had wished her
'Good morning,' in civil, but indifferent tones, politely
taken the seat in the corner diagonally across from her
and had settled back against the somewhat worn and
grubby upholstery with the air of a man expecting to
find the experience entertaining.

Amanda, whilst apparently keeping her gaze firmly
on the Norfolk countryside rolling past, watched him
from the corner of her eye. He was an intriguing puzzle
and there was nothing Amanda enjoyed more than a
puzzle. And, as her friends and well-wishers said, the
opportunity to helpfully set things to rights. Those who
were not so fond of the young widow, including her
late husband's cousin and heir Humphrey, called it be-

ing 'intolerably managing and far too self-assured for a young woman in her position'.

Why should a fashionably dressed man of…what… twenty-seven or eight…be doing on the common stage? He was too old to be coming home in disgrace from a university or town scrape, and far too well dressed to be too hard up to travel any other way, unless the financial embarrassment was of very recent date. And for some reason, he did appear to be enjoying himself, which would hardly be the case if destitution was forcing him to make the journey in this style.

He was in riding clothes: Amanda shot a glance at exquisitely made boots, smartly cut breeches and a riding coat that fitted to perfection. His linen showed the attention of a superior servant and there was a heavy gold signet on his finger. Clothes were an abiding, if reprehensibly frivolous, interest for Amanda and although her experience of men's outfitting was by now rather out of date, her mental arithmetic arrived at a sum that made her raise her eyebrows.

He was sitting back, legs crossed, arms negligently folded, also gazing out of the window beside him. Amanda felt very sure that he was perfectly well aware of her and could have described her just as accurately as she could describe him, from the lazily amused expression in his green eyes, to the long calves clad in expensive leather. She was itching to start a conversation and find out who he was and what he was doing, but even Amanda blanched at the impropriety of striking up a dialogue with a complete stranger in these circumstances.

The coach had lurched and abruptly speeded up, she recalled, remembering the stranger's sudden alertness and the way he had turned on the seat to try and look up at the box and the driver. The coach had gone out of control very fast and her memory became confused. He had reached across and taken her very firmly in his arms, she did know, realising now how that firm hold and the shield of his body had saved her from the worst of the jarring, cushioning her away from the door as the stage had finally hit the ground on its side. No wonder his injuries seemed more severe than hers.

'I must thank you, sir—' she was beginning to say, when there was a brisk knock on the door and it opened to reveal a cheerful-looking woman in a stuff gown of comfortable cut, a large white apron and a mob cap over greying curls.

'Well, and there you are up and about already, ma'am,' she said, beaming at them. 'I said to Clay— that's my husband, ma'am—that poor lady and her husband will be knocked to flinders and doubtless won't be able to stir from their bed all morning. I'll go right up and see if they can fancy a nice cup of tea, I said, and just look at you, ma'am, with your poor head and all.'

'Yes, well, thank you, Mrs Clay,' Amanda cut in on the flow. 'I am sure a cup of tea will be delightful in a minute. But can you please tell us where we are and how we came to be here? I can recall the stagecoach overturning…'

'Oh, ma'am! What a tragedy!' Mrs Clay twisted her hands in her apron at the thought of it. 'It looks as though Jenkins the driver had a seizure and died right there and then on the box, for his face was all swollen up and red when Clay found him. And poor young Johnson the guard has a broken leg, his head all cut open and he is wandering in his wits, though doctor says he'll be all right given a day or two in bed, Heavens be praised.'

'And my wife and I?' the stranger in the bed asked.

'Oh, sir, you were quite unconscious—and a good thing too, the doctor said, when he saw your arm. Your poor lady seemed to come to her senses when Clay and Bill pulled her out of the stage, but she soon went off into a swoon again.' She drew a deep breath and plunged on with her tale, which Amanda strongly suspected had already been told over and again to whoever was to hand to listen.

'It was a terrible scene, sir! There was poor old Jenkins, lying there dead as though the Almighty had struck him down, and young Johnson, bleeding like a stuck pig and making such a snorting noises I thought he'd lost his mind. And you, sir, with your shoulder all out of joint and your lady, lying there in the dust on the verge! Clay said he didn't know which way to turn what with the horses plunging about in their traces, half in the ditch and half out—'

'You have all done very well, it seems,' Amanda cut the saga short firmly. 'But where are we? Is this your house, Mrs Clay?'

'Why, in Saxthorpe, ma'am, and this is the Lamb and Flag inn, of which Clay has been the landlord these past twenty years. And a better flagon of ale you won't find north of Norwich,' she added, proudly.

'I'm sure not,' Amanda interrupted again. It appeared that the man on the bed was quite content to listen all morning to Mrs Clay's exciting tale, but she was far too anxious to discover just how she had ended up in bed with him. 'And you very kindly called the doctor to us?'

'Oh, yes, ma'am. Dr Pauling and his young dispenser

as well, seeing as there was the three of you in such a state and poor old Jenkins lying there like—'

'Yes, quite, it must have been terrible.' Amanda felt she had heard more than enough about the frightful appearance of the unfortunate driver. 'And you realised that we must be a married couple? How clever of you! How did you discover that?'

'Well, ma'am, you had your wedding ring on, and there were just the two of you, and you were clasped in your husband's arms—' she broke off to sniff sentimentally '—as though you would never be parted, Clay said.'

'Indeed—' Amanda shot a repressive look at the man on the bed who hastily converted a broad grin into a spasm of pain. 'And there was nothing in our belongings?' She tried to recall what she had in her reticule and what she had left with Kate in Norwich. She had changed her reticule for one better suited for travelling and could not recall whether she had transferred her card case.

'No, ma'am, it was a real puzzle. Not that Clay or I would have looked, of course, but Dr Pauling said he had better so we could send a message to your family, but there was nothing. Even the gentleman's card case was empty.'

A puzzle indeed, for what gentleman would be abroad without his card case? It seemed as much a mystery to the stranger, judging by his expression. 'And our baggage?' he asked abruptly.

'Just the two valises, sir.' She gestured to the brown leather bags in the corner of the room. They were very alike, possibly even the product of the same London luggage maker, and it was not hard to see why they had

contributed to the impression of a couple travelling together.

Well, at least neither of them had been identified, she
reflected thankfully. The news that the widowed Mrs
Clare of Upper Glaven House had been found clasped
in the arms of a strange man on a stagecoach would be
round the county like wildfire! The sooner she was
away from here the better.

'Thank you very much, Mrs Clay. Please can you
bring me some hot water directly? When I have finished, if you could arrange for one of the men to bring
water for my husband and help him to dress and shave,
that would be most helpful. I will breakfast in the parlour.'

'Yes, ma'am, of course. Your gown is all brushed
out and hanging here behind the screen. Could I be so
bold as to ask your name, ma'am?'

'Brown…'

'…Smith,' said the voice from the bed a second later.

'Brownsmith,' said Amanda repressively. 'Mr and
Mrs Augustus Brownsmith of London, on our way to
visit friends in Holt.'

Mrs Clay bustled out to fulfil her errands, leaving
Amanda glaring at the stranger. 'What are you laughing
about?' she demanded.

'You are a very forceful young woman, are you not?
And I must congratulate you on your quick thinking.
But do I really deserve *Augustus*? It was only a very
little kiss, if that was your revenge.'

'You…' Amanda knew she was blushing, something
which frequently happened despite her best efforts. She
had not thought about that swift kiss; the overall shock
of the situation had wiped it from her mind. Now it

came back with horrid clarity. 'You should be ashamed of yourself! It was quite uncalled for!'

'Under the circumstances, a lot more than a kiss was called for,' he said reminiscently. 'I think I showed admirable restraint.'

'Hah!' Amanda was about to say a good deal more, but the arrival of the landlady with a jug of hot water and a clean towel sent her into retreat behind the screen.

This was a somewhat crude arrangement of cotton panels stretched over a wooden frame and Amanda peered nervously through the gap at one hinge. But the man on the bed, far from taking any interest in what she was doing, had lain back against the pillows with his eyes shut. Angry with him as she was, she could not help but notice with concern the frown of pain as he tried to shift his arm into a more comfortable position. It was not fair to ask him to travel, but they could hardly stay where they were with discovery and scandal a constant danger.

She slipped hastily out of the nightgown, which she presumed belonged to the landlady, had a hasty wash and scrambled into her undergarments and gown, which fortunately she could fasten herself. Then, feeling decently clad at last, she re-examined herself in the mirror.

The face that looked back at her was certainly not that which either her friends or critics would have recognised at first glance. Her mass of dark blonde hair was given to tumbling out of nets, pins or ribbons and falling down her back, but even so, it was always shiny and brushed. Now she winced as she tugged the comb through the tangles, removing several twigs as she did so.

Her admirers maintained that no one could match Mrs Clare's large brown eyes for depth of expression or laughing humour. Her critics, chiefly the matrons of the area who were wary of her attraction for their sons, or her possible rivalry to their daughters, remarked that it was a pity that dear Amanda's nose should be so very straight and her mouth just a touch too wide. All agreed that her chin was determined, which showed either charming independence and courage, or wilfulness and an unfeminine mind, depending on one's point of view.

Amanda herself, although she had her moments of wishing for primrose blonde hair, blue eyes, a tip-tilted nose and a heart-shaped face, was generally neither vain of her looks, nor overly concerned about their failings. After all, her colouring allowed her to wear most shades now she was out of mourning again, her tall figure and long legs showed off gowns to perfection, and incidentally contributed to her excellent seat on a horse.

However, even the most unconcerned young lady of three and twenty could not ignore a reddened cheek and a rapidly purpling eye. But there was no disguising it, for she carried no rice powder in her valise: she would just have to hope that the parlour was truly private.

The stranger's eyes were open again when she emerged, and his expression as he watched her was appreciative. Amanda braced herself for more teasing flattery, but when he spoke it was to observe, 'The sooner we are away from here the better. Doubtless they can hire me a gig. Have you far to go?'

'Once I reach Holt I am close to home.' Amanda folded the borrowed nightgown.

'Will you trust me with your true name and direction, Mrs Brownsmith?' the man asked, the glint of amusement back in his eyes.

'Mrs Charles Clare, of Kelling House—Amanda

Clare,' she replied, fighting the temptation to smile back. 'And your name, sir?'

'Now there, Mrs Clare, you have the advantage of me. I have not the slightest idea.'

Chapter Two

Amanda stared at him aghast. 'You must know what your name is!'

'I assure you I do not. The blow to my head is responsible, I suppose—we must be thankful that, unlike the unfortunate guard, I am not wandering in my wits.'

'And you have realised this ever since you woke up?' she demanded.

'More or less.' The tall man grimaced. 'It came as an unpleasant shock to find you did not greet my presence in the bed with either delight or the faintest trace of recognition. Whilst it is the duty of any gentleman to remember the name of the lady with whom he has spent the night, I am sure it is even more incumbent upon him to remember his own…'

'Do stop rambling—you hardly seem to be taking this very seriously.' Amanda sat on the end of the bed and regarded him with critical eyes. She had no intention of rising to the bait on the subject of their night together. 'What are you going to do about it?'

'Wait until I have shaved, dressed and had my breakfast.' He rubbed a hand over his chin, grimacing at the rasp of stubble against his palm. 'I will think better then.'

Amanda's instinctive retort, that the sooner he began thinking and took their predicament seriously the better, was left unspoken as a tap at the door heralded the arrival of Mrs Clay with more hot water, a bashful-looking potboy at her heels.

'Your breakfast is all set out in the parlour, ma'am, and here's Jem to help Mr Brownsmith.'

Amanda took herself off downstairs, following the tantalising smell of bacon and eggs. Mrs Clay proved to keep a good house, for the neat little parlour shone in the morning sun, there was a fire crackling in the grate and the food was excellent. Although her bruised face made chewing painful, Amanda still managed to do justice to the bacon and eggs and several cups of tea and was just deciding between gooseberry jam or mar-malade for her toast when the stranger appeared in the doorway.

He was clean shaven and with his hair brushed, it was only the bruise on his face and the sling supporting his right arm that distinguished him from any other well-dressed gentleman relaxing in the country. Amanda, regarding him critically, saw that yesterday's impression of expensive tailoring was quite correct, and that, furthermore, he was an extremely good-looking man.

She had just arrived at this conclusion as he took a step forward from the threshold where he had halted and she saw he was limping slightly.

'You have hurt your leg!'

'My ankle is slightly twisted, that is all. May I join you?'

'Please do.' Amanda waved him towards the other

chair 'Just pull the bell for Mrs Clay: I can certainly recommend her breakfast.'

'From which I can assume you have suffered no worse hurt from yesterday's adventure than the bruise to you face?' he asked.

'No, none at all, thanks, I believe, to you,' Amanda responded warmly. 'And if you mean that I have a good appetite, you are quite correct: I have so little sensibility that I rarely find myself unable to eat. That was an *excellent* breakfast, Mrs Clay,' she added as the landlady came in. 'I am sure Mr Brownsmith would enjoy exactly the same, if you please. And I would like some more tea and toast.'

The silence that followed the landlady's departure seemed to last a long time. Eventually Amanda observed, 'And have you done any thinking about your predicament, sir?'

'Some about mine, and rather a lot about yours, Mrs Clare.' He seemed considerably more serious than she had seen him before and the twinkle had gone out of his eyes, despite the lightness of his tone. 'Your husband is hardly going to greet magnanimously the news that his wife has spent the night—however innocently—in another man's bed. Assured of my name and station in life, he might have been prepared to take my word for my motives and actions. What he is going to make of someone unable to provide him with so much as a calling card, I hate to think. He has not even the recourse of any affronted gentleman of knocking me down and will have to wait until I have recovered the full use of my arm before issuing a challenge.'

For one reprehensible moment Amanda toyed with the idea of creating a fire-breathing husband complete with horsewhip, before honesty and the sense of what she owed this man got the better of her.

'My husband would always have taken my word, sir, whatever the circumstances. I can assure you, all he would wish to do now would be to thank you for saving me from worse injury than I received.'

He raised an eyebrow. 'You speak in the past tense, Mrs Clare.'

'I am a widow, sir, and have been these past two years.'

'My regrets and sympathy, ma'am. To whom then should I present my explanations and apologies?'

'To no one, sir. I am my own mistress, with neither father nor brothers to thank you for your actions. My husband's cousin and heir, Mr Humphrey Clare, is my nearest male relative, and this need not concern him.' Her tone was crisper than she intended and the man's eyebrows rose, although he made no comment. Humphrey Clare would be delighted to catch out his cousin's widow in some scandalous indiscretion and she had absolutely no intention of giving him the opportunity.

'My situation is easily remedied,' she continued, 'provided I take a little care and have no further ill luck. Once I am in Holt I can make my way home easily enough. But what of yours? I very much regret having to ask you to travel this morning, but it would create a very odd impression if I were to leave without you.'

The stranger remained silent while Mrs Clay brought in his breakfast and Amanda's toast, then, as the door closed behind her, said, 'I have been looking at my boots and my coat.'

'Of course!' Amanda caught his drift at once. 'They are both by very fine makers, are they not? Presumably you plan to visit either your boot maker or tailor where doubtless you will be immediately greeted by name.'

'Exactly.' He seemed amused that her knowledge of men's fashion was so good. 'Then either the mention of my name will immediately bring me to full recollection, or I will at least be able to retreat to a lending library and look myself up!'

'And if they greet you at Weston's or Lobb's with cries of "Good morning, your lordship!", what will you do then?' Amanda enquired, buttering her toast. 'Ask them which lordship you are?'

'Hmm, I had not considered that. I wonder if I do have a title? It would be simpler if they call me "Your Grace", it would narrow the field. You are right, this is excellent ham.'

'I do wish you would be serious,' Amanda chided, although she was beginning to enjoy herself and could only be thankful she was not in the company of someone thrown into gloom or bad temper by their predicament. 'There may be fewer dukes than other classes of aristocracy, but I can assure you that you are not one of them. I believe I have seen all of those young enough to be you.' She pushed the mustard pot within his reach and added, 'Do you feel as though you have a title? Does being called plain "sir" sound odd?'

'How can I tell?' he asked bitterly. 'I am still recovering from being dubbed Mr Augustus Brownsmith.'

Amanda ignored this reproof. 'Of course, you could simply take lodgings in Holt and con the London papers in case your family places an advertisement for you. After all,' she added, glancing at him from under her lashes, 'your poor wife may be frantic with worry, even now.'

'*My wife!*'

'It is not so very improbable. You are old enough to be married. In fact, you may well be the father of a large and hopeful family.'

'I do not feel in the slightest degree married,' he said firmly. 'Surely I could tell that? Would I not feel some anxiety if that were the case?'

'You might be a very bad husband,' Amanda observed, then hastily added as his brows drew together, 'Do you truly not feel any anxiety about your present predicament?'

'Only for you. Otherwise I have to admit to finding it stimulating. I seem to recall being bored.'

'That is interesting,' Amanda observed. 'When you got on the stagecoach you did look as though you were enjoying yourself, almost as though you were on a spree, escaping from something onerous. I must admit to wondering why you should be travelling by stage.'

'That puzzles me too,' he admitted, pushing back his plate and accepting the toast she proffered. 'Something tells me the stage it is not my usual mode of transport. Well, I have no intention of continuing by one! I think our best scheme would be to hire a gig from this inn to take us to Holt. I will then hire a post chaise and go on to London. Once there I will put up at a hotel…'

'Grillon's?'

'No, the Clarendon, the food is better.'

They stared at each other hopefully. 'Does the fact that you know that mean your memory is coming back?' Amanda asked.

'I doubt it—I cannot even think what the Clarendon looks like. Still, there is every chance someone will recognise me and greet me by name.'

'If you do not cut half your acquaintance first!'

'You are a cheerful soul this morning, are you not?'

he teased. 'Still, let us see what my resources are: there is our shot here to be paid, the doctor's bill, the hire of a gig...'

He dug a purse from his pocket, tossed it on the table and reached into an inner pocket. 'I should have a roll of soft in here. Nothing, that is odd, I could swear these are honest people... Still, let us see what the coins add up to.'

But the purse, tipped out on the table, yielded one guinea coin, two shillings, a sixpence and a number of coppers.

Amanda, who knew exactly how little her own purse held, was able to contribute a further ten shillings and a handful of coppers.

They stared at each other aghast, then Amanda said, 'I suppose some passing person may have robbed us before Clay found us, but that is improbable if we had to be pulled from the wreckage. It would seem that the reason you were travelling by stage was because you could not afford to do anything else.' His face was so expressionless that she hurried on, 'But we have enough here to cover our immediate needs. Once we get to Holt I will lend you what you need to get to London.'

'Certainly not!' He got to his feet and limped across to the fireplace. 'Accept money from a lady, when I have not the slightest idea whether or not I can repay it? Under no circumstances!'

He struck the mantelshelf with his clenched fist, the gold signet ring catching the light and Amanda cried, 'Your ring! Perhaps it has your crest on it.'

He came back to the table, holding out his hand and twisting the ring it so she could see the bold single letter engraved on it.

'J,' she said flatly. 'That could be anything: your Christian name, your surname…'

'An ancestor's Christian name,' he finished for her.

'Never mind.' With a good breakfast inside her, her headache clearing and the sun shining, Amanda was in the mood to be optimistic. 'At least I can call you something now! Come along, Mr Jay, I have a plan.'

She stood up and he came round to pull out her chair. As she turned he caught her hand in his and raised it to his lips in a brief, quixotic, salute. 'Just plain Jay, I think, Mrs Clare. You have both spirit and courage, have you not?'

'Nonsense.' Amanda laughed to cover the little *frisson* of pleasure both the caress and the compliment gave her. 'My friends will tell you that I am abominably managing and love nothing more than a mystery. Let us settle our debts with what we have and be on our way. I would have wanted to leave something for the families of the driver and guard, but I will have to send something once I get home.'

The landlord provided a gig and the brown cob to pull it, which proved plain but serviceable. There was a brief tussle for the reins before Jay surrendered and allowed an obviously competent Amanda to drive.

'Good bye, Mrs Clay, Mr Clay! Thank you so much!' she called, waving as the cob trotted out of the stable-yard and out of sight of the inn. 'Thank goodness we are away from there! The Clays are most excellent people, but the strain of remembering who I was supposed to be was giving me a headache.' Amanda regarded her silent passenger from the corner of her eye. He seemed remarkably serious: she hoped he was not going be plunged in gloom by his situation.

However, all he said when he did at last speak was to observe, 'You drive very well, Mrs Clare.'

'Why, anyone could with this solid old fellow.' She laughed. 'A single pair of reins, a quiet horse and a deserted road is no challenge.'

'You are used to more challenging driving then?'

'My husband taught me to drive his team—four beautiful Welsh bays. But since I have been on my own I only drive a pair in my phaeton, which, I regret to say, is a plain low-perch one. It does not do for a widow in a country district to seem to be too dashing, you know. People will talk so.'

'I can imagine that the sight of you driving a team in a sporting vehicle would indeed raise eyebrows! But tell me why—' He broke off and added apologetically, 'Forgive me, Mrs Clare, I should not pry into your affairs.'

'You wonder what a lady who can afford a carriage and pair is doing travelling on the common stage?' she asked.

'I confess, that had crossed my mind,' he admitted. 'Intolerably inquisitive of me.'

Amanda laughed, not noticing the appreciative gleam in his eye at her frank amusement and the way her smile lit up her face. 'Not at all! I am the most inquisitive person myself. The awful truth—and I would not confide this to just anyone, let me tell you—is that I spent all the money I took with me shopping in Norwich and could not afford to hire a chaise to bring me and my maid home again. Shocking, is it not?'

'Surely you could apply to your banker or man of business for additional funds?'

'Well, I *could* have done,' Amanda agreed, looping the rein neatly as they trotted round a bend. 'But Mr

Greenwich at the bank is such a Friday-faced person; whatever I do he disapproves of. I can hear him now. ''Very unconventional, Mrs Clare, if I may say so.'' Or, ''Are you sure that is quite prudent, Mrs Clare? So much money in two days, Mrs Clare?'' He makes me long to run out and do something really shocking, just to see his face, but I struggle against the impulse, for he means well.'

Jay observed, with a shake in his voice, 'I can quite understand that he would be the last person to confess to that you had outrun the bailiffs and spent your all on new gowns.'

'New gowns, a *killing* new hat, and the most wonderful taffeta for the drawing-room curtains. It was that material which did it, for it could hardly be called a bargain, but I do consider it a false economy to skimp on drapery, do you not agree?'

Jay considered this. 'I cannot recall ever having had to make a decision on drapery, but I am sure you are right.'

'Hmm…that may mean you *are* married and your wife makes all those decisions, or simply that you have a very good housekeeper.' She reined in the cob suddenly, then turned him into a narrow green lane running off the road. 'Listen, something is coming. We are getting near Holt and I do not want to be recognised.'

They waited while a chaise bowled past, apparently without seeing them, then Amanda concentrated on turning the cob in the tight space. 'I do worry about your wife, you know,' she said absently.

'That was neatly done,' he complimented her as they rejoined the road. 'Why do you worry about her—if she exists?'

'If she does, the poor woman must be in an agony of worry.'

'Oh, is that what you meant?' Jay enquired innocently. 'I am disappointed.' Amanda flushed slightly but made no rejoinder, so he continued. 'If I am a bad husband, as you suggested, she may be inured to my absence, or even glad of it. Or she may be expecting me to be away some time on my travels. But, you know, I really cannot believe myself to be married.'

'No female face presents itself in your memory?'

'Several,' he observed outrageously. 'But none of them seem likely candidates for respectable domesticity.' They passed a milestone and he added more seriously, 'We are nearly in Holt and you cannot risk being seen with me. Set me down soon, if you please.'

'And how do you propose getting back to London?' Amanda enquired, touching the whip to the cob who responded with a brisk trot.

'That is for me to worry about.'

'Nonsense.' She made no effort to rein in. 'You do not have enough money.'

'This is all very well, Mrs Clare, but I can see the tower of what I assume is Holt church and I really cannot allow you to risk being seen with me so close to the town. Please let me down—I can walk from here.'

'To what end, might I ask?' Amanda retorted. 'With a few coins in your pocket, how do you intend to get back to London? And if you fall ill on the journey, what then? You do not appear to be suffering from concussion, but we cannot be certain there will no delayed effects from the blow to your head.'

'That is my concern,' Jay replied with an amused smile at her vehemence. 'I cannot trouble you any further, nor risk your reputation. You have already done more than enough for a complete stranger.'

'Oh, poppycock!' Amanda turned neatly into a gateway that opened into a piece of rough pasture. Behind the tree tops of a spinney, a roof of red clay pantiles and several smoking chimneys were just visible. She turned the cob to face back towards the road and handed the reins to Jay, sticking the whip into its holder on the side of the gig. 'Now, I have a plan that will allow you to recover your strength and, let us hope, your memory also, in comfortable surroundings and without owing anyone a penny-piece.'

'Indeed?' He took the reins one-handed and regarded her quizzically. 'And just how are you going to achieve this? And what is more, why on earth should you?'

Amanda hopped down from the gig, catching up the skirts of her gown before they caught in the long grass. 'One should make every effort to help one's friends, Mr Jay.'

He said, 'Am I a friend? You hardly know me, and I behaved outrageously this morning, as well you know.'

She smiled up at him, a mischievous twinkle in her brown eyes. 'You saved me from severe injury or worse when the coach overturned, and as for this morning, I understand that many men cannot be held responsible for what they do before they have had their breakfast.

'Now, listen carefully, the roof you can see behind the trees is the Half Moon, which is owned by William Bream. He was our head groom, but he chose not to stay when my husband's cousin inherited and so bought this inn. It was in a terrible condition, and the worst kind of ale house, frequented by all the riff and raff of the neighbourhood. He has transformed it over the last few months and many respectable local people use it now. With three bedchambers and a small livery yard Will is attracting some of the passing carriage trade as well.'

'And you will recommend me for a potboy or an ostler?'

'Certainly not, I doubt you could escape notice for very long in either guise. No, Will is an excellent man, but he has always struggled with his figures and only the other day he was telling me he would have to employ a clerk from the town for several hours each week just to bring order to his book-keeping. My plan is for you to organise Will's accounts in return for your bed and board. In a few days either your memory will have returned or we will have thought of some plan to establish your identity.'

Jay steadied the cob, which was growing restive and trying to snatch a mouthful of grass. 'You, Mrs Clare, are a very managing young lady.'

'I know,' she said cheerfully. 'Mr Humphrey Clare—my husband's heir—says it is my besetting sin. Well, one of them,' she added frankly. 'Will you do it, though?'

'I will, and you have my thanks for it. Tell me, does Mr Humphrey Clare always feel so free to criticise you?'

'Yes, for he is now head of the family, and I am afraid I am a sad trial to him for he does not know what to do with me. If I would only show some feminine weakness and weep on his manly bosom, he would feel much better about it. But never mind Humphrey,' she added as Jay gave a snort of amusement. 'Allow me ten minutes to find Will and explain all to him, then drive into the inn yard. I will go in through the back door and wait inside in case anyone I know should pass.'

Amanda ran across the field, ducked between the two rails of the fence and began to thread her way through the spinney. Once she thought she was out of sight, she paused and looked back. The man she called Jay was sitting staring thoughtfully between the cob's pricked ears, his face impossible to read at that distance.

She stood for a moment, finally allowing the memory of waking up to come back to her, the warm, safe feeling of his body next to hers in the feather bed, the exciting pressure of his lips in that fleeting kiss. 'And that is more than enough of that, Amanda Clare!' she scolded herself out loud, turning to hurry on her way. 'He is probably married with several lovely children and a charming wife, or he is a rake who kisses three different women a day. Whoever he is, he will certainly be on his way and out of your life just as soon as his memory returns.'

Chapter Three

Will Bream was in the stableyard when Amanda emerged through the spinney gate. He came to meet her with a broad smile on his face, which faded as he took in her black eye and grazed cheek.

'Mrs Clare, ma'am! Have you had a fall? Come inside, do, and I'll send for Dr Hoskins this minute.'

Amanda allowed herself to be ushered into the inn but resisted the landlord's efforts to call a groom to fetch the doctor and a maid to bring lavender water. 'No, Will, I am quite all right, I had an accident on the stage yesterday and although it is sore, I do not need the doctor. Now listen, please, for there is not much time. In a few minutes a gentleman is going to drive into the yard and this is what I want you to do...'

At the end of her hasty recital Will, who had been listening with his mouth half-open, began, 'Now, Mrs Clare, this won't do and you know it! Taking up with some stranger when you don't know who he may be and then expecting me to employ a gentleman-born to do my clerking...'

'He saved me from being seriously hurt,' Amanda retorted hotly. 'And I am not asking you to employ him, merely to give him board and lodging in a charitable fashion in return for which he will cast your accounts into order.' He still looked mutinous, so she added coaxingly, 'And if I cannot rely on you to tell me whether he is a fit person for me to be acquainted with, I do not know who I could ask, for you know you are an excellent judge of character.'

'It's no good wheedling me with fine words, ma'am! What your poor husband would say I do not know.'

'He would thank you for taking such good care of me and for helping me fulfil my obligations to a gentleman who was hurt looking after me! Now, here he comes, Will, go out to him, do, before he encounters one of the grooms. Bring him in here.'

Will strode out to the gig, which had stopped under the newly painted inn sign of the half-moon partly hidden behind scudding clouds. Amanda watched his stocky figure, recognising the belligerent set of his shoulders, although his manner was polite enough. If he thought she had encountered a n'er-do-well, Jay would be on his way, never mind what she might say.

But it seemed he passed muster, for Will turned and shouted for the groom, then lifted the valises from the back of the gig himself. Jay climbed down with some care and Amanda saw his mouth tighten into a thin line as his injured ankle took his weight. He limped into the inn and met her in the shadowy hallway with a grin. 'Your faithful landlord is bristling like a bull terrier in case you have brought home an undesirable,' he remarked.

'I trust Will's judgement,' Amanda said primly as she led the way into the parlour. 'Naturally, being a mere woman, I could be sadly deceived in your character and must rely upon a male opinion.'

'You should not pay so much attention to your Cousin Humphrey!' was all that Jay could retort before the landlord joined them.

'The best bedchamber is free, sir, and this parlour is private, you will not be disturbed here. Are these all your bags? I will have them taken up.'

'Thank you. I would be obliged for the loan of some linen,' Jay said, ruefully regarding the state of his cuffs. 'No, not that bag, it belongs to Mrs Clare.'

'Will you lend me your gig, Will, and see that the one in the yard gets back to the inn at Saxthorpe?' Amanda asked. 'I would as soon not send it back from my own home. It was hired by Mr and Mrs Brownsmith, remember.'

'You leave it to me, Mrs Clare. And I'll drive you back home myself in a moment, just as soon as Mr Jay here is settled. I'm not having you gallivanting about the countryside by yourself with your poor face in that state. And not even a veil on your bonnet! What will people think?'

He marched out, shouting for the housekeeper and Amanda turned to peer into the rather dusty mirror hanging by the fireside. 'Oh my goodness, my eye is grown even blacker and more swollen! I look a complete fright!'

Jay's face appeared in the reflection over her shoulder. 'You are a very unusual young lady, Amanda. I sure there are none other of my acquaintance who would not be swooning away or having a tantrum or both despite the fact that the eye will soon subside and the graze is unlikely to mark your very pretty complexion. You are being both sensible and brave.'

'Nonsense.' She laughed, turning away from those penetrating green eyes to hide her pleasure. 'Beside the fact that you cannot recall any of your acquaintance to make a comparison, you forget I am not a young lady, I am an independent widow with no inclination to vapours.'

'Of course, you told me you had no sensibility, did you not?' Although she had turned from the mirror he had not stepped back and she found herself standing very close to him. The faint, warm male scent she remembered from the bed that morning filled her nostrils and she found it difficult to either step away, or make some light remark. She wished he would call her by her Christian name again, she liked the sound of it on his lips.

'You will promise me something?' he asked.

'What?' She kept her gaze fixed firmly on his top waistcoat button.

'Despite your lack of sensibility, your inability to have the vapours and your complete independence—you will go home, let your maid look after you, send for your doctor and rest.'

'I—'

'As you told me just now, you are a mere woman and must rely upon a male opinion.'

Will appeared in the doorway, his brows drawing together as he took in how close they were standing. 'All ready to go, Mrs Clare ma'am. I'll have one of the men take the gig back later. Let's be getting you home. What'll Miss Porter be thinking?'

'Nothing, except whether she should have transplanted the snowdrops under the beech hedge when they finished flowering and not have left them until now, if I know Jane.' She smiled at Jay. 'Miss Porter is my lady companion, but the garden is her abiding passion and unless she was expecting me to have returned with some new treasure for it, my absence is unlikely to have come to her notice.'

'An unusual companion,' Jay remarked drily.

'Indeed, and the perfect one to suit my temper! She gives the appearance of my observing every convention and yet causes me the least trouble in the world.' Amanda began to draw on her gloves and look for her reticule. 'You must not think her uncaring, for she is a dear friend. She is quite willing to accompany me, or help with entertaining if I ask, but if left in peace, she simply vanishes into the garden and terrorises the gardeners in the most pleasant way possible.' She retrieved her reticule and smiled at him. 'I will be off now. Do rest; I will come and see you tomorrow and find out how you get on.'

Jay took her proffered hand in both his. 'And you, too, take care. But do not come here, it would not do for you to be seen. I will give myself the pleasure of calling upon you in a day or so, if you will permit.'

Will helped her up into the carriage and watched her wave goodbye with a disapproving expression on his face. 'And just why did the gig have to be hired for Mr and Mrs Brownsmith?' he enquired ominously, turning into the High Street.

'Well, I could hardly leave Mr Jay there with no memory of who he was, and with barely a shilling to his name, and so we had to pretend to be married,' Amanda explained, reflecting that Will could be somewhat stricter than her governess ever was once he put his mind to it. She could tell he suspected he was getting only half the story, but there were limits to what even the most indulged family retainer might ask and he subsided into silence.

Fortunately Amanda saw no close acquaintance on

the streets and, thanks to Will's brisk driving, they were out of the little market town before her damaged face was remarked upon. The road rose and fell as they crossed the course of the River Glaven, wending its way to the sea a mile or so to the north. The wooded slopes gave way to arable fields with trim hedges and every now and again allowed a glimpse of the roofs and chimneys of Glaven Hall, Amanda's married home, now occupied by Mr Humphrey Clare and his mother.

Will turned the gig into a well-metalled driveway and soon the façade of Upper Glaven House came into view. Amanda's home for the past two years was a neat house of the local red brick with flint panels. Two windows on each side of the front door were balanced by a wing on either side, set slightly back from the façade, and with its restrained pediment the house sat with an air of unpretentious elegance amid its sweeping lawns and wide borders, now burgeoning into flower with the warmth of late spring.

The door burst open as they approached and Kate, Amanda's maid, ran out, down the steps and arrived breathless and red-eyed at the side of the gig.

'Oh, ma'am, I've been so worried,' she began, then gasped at the sight of her mistress's face. 'You are hurt, ma'am! What has happened?'

'I am quite all right, Kate, there is no need to fuss. Good morning, Jane,' she added as Miss Porter emerged from the side of the house, her inevitable garden trug in the crook of her arm. 'As you can see, I had a slight accident on the way so was forced to stay the night at an inn on the road, but it looks far worse than it is.'

'Goose grease,' was Miss Porter's response and she turned back towards the house. Amanda could hear her murmuring, 'And if there is any of my witch-hazel infusion left that will help the bruising.'

'Now, Kate, take my valise so as not to delay Mr Bream, he has enough to do without running me about the countryside! Thank you, Will,' she added quietly as she stood beside the gig. 'Please add the expenses of returning the other vehicle to Saxthorpe to my account, and if there is anything over and above Mr Jay's keep, be so kind as to add that too. There is no need to mention it to him.'

The innkeeper shot her a hard look. 'You take care now, Mrs Clare, and I don't just mean your face. Good day to you.'

Amanda followed Kate up to her room and submitted to having her bonnet strings untied and her pelisse removed. It was obvious that she was not going to escape without an explanation to satisfy both the maid and Miss Porter, who had produced a large pot of goose grease and a bottle of her own infallible witch-hazel remedy.

'The unfortunate stagecoach driver suffered a seizure and the coach ended up in the ditch,' she explained, wincing as Jane dabbed her cheek. 'We were all very knocked about,' she added, managing to give the impression that there were several passengers, 'and had to spend the night in an inn.'

Miss Porter gave a little gasp of horror. 'Then it is fortunate indeed that you have not suffered a worse injury! Was anyone else hurt?'

'The driver, I am sorry to say, seems to have died from his seizure, the groom was knocked unconscious and one gentleman suffered more serious, but not life-threatening, injuries.' That was all she was going to say about yesterday's mishap, now she must hope that such a spectacular accident did not reach the local newspaper or cause gossip in Holt.

'It was foolish of me to travel by stage,' she said. 'I do hope neither of you will say anything to anyone about it, I would be so embarrassed if it were to get out.' Embarrassment would be the least of her feelings if it were to become known that Mrs Clare had been staying at a country inn with a gentleman under an assumed name! 'Now, Kate, I would like a hot bath, a light luncheon and then I think I will rest this afternoon.'

Amanda's intention had been to refresh herself and then lie down to think seriously about what could be done to restore Jay's memory, or, if that could not be done, how she could persuade that stubborn gentleman to accept a loan to get to London to pursue his true identity there.

What happened, once she had emerged from a pleasant bath, eaten a slice of cold chicken with bread and butter, drunk a reviving cup of tea, submitted to being smeared once more with grease and dabbed, painfully, with witch hazel and was finally alone and in peace in her bed, was that she fell into a deep slumber.

Amanda woke when the setting sun streamed in through the west-facing, uncurtained, window of her chamber. Rubbing her eyes, she rang the bell for Kate and picked up the set of note tablets that she kept beside her bed in the hope that she might have woken at some point and jotted down a good idea.

She very often did, although sometimes the notes proved unintelligible in the morning. But the tablets revealed only the thoughts of the few days before her trip to Norwich: *Turnips and sheep—write to Mr Coke re pasture; elm trees, how long to reach felling size?; new gown—quilted hem?; point lace or Brussels? Speak to Cousin H. abt. Long End cottages.* And mysteriously, *Dried peas.* There was nothing to help with the problem of Jay.

And a problem it was, not least because one part of her did not want the riddle of his identity solved too soon, because then he would leave. Amanda was not given to self-deception, experience had proved it gave only a false sense of security. She knew she was attracted to Jay, to his expressive green eyes, to the long, lean body that moved with such grace, despite his injuries, to the humour in his voice and the courage with which he dealt with the loss of his identity.

She was just telling herself firmly to stop indulging in daydreams when Kate peeped round the door. 'Are you feeling better, ma'am? Will you be getting up for dinner? Mrs Howlett is roasting a nice joint of lamb, and she says to say there is a buttered crab and some almond tartlets if you could fancy a little of those.'

'That sounds excellent, Kate. Now, if you will just fetch my dark green gown, I will get up.'

The maid hastened about her work, but Amanda, more perceptive now she was rested, noticed that her eyes were still red, her face looked pinched and she showed slightly less then her usual energy.

When Amanda had made her decision not to apply for further funds from her banker in Norwich, she had intended purchasing tickets on the stage for both Kate and herself. But Kate had asked if she could not travel with the packages on the carrier's cart, which made its slow way from the county town up to Holt every week, laden with the orders dispatched by the housewives and yeomen of the market town for those goods that their local shops could not provide.

Kate was very friendly with the daughters of Thomas Green the carrier, and, Amanda suspected, increasingly with young Tom, his elder son and heir to the business. But they were a respectable family, and Kate could do worse than to take up with a well-set up young fellow who worked hard and had a good business to follow. She had agreed willingly enough, telling Kate she could stay and visit with the Greens if the offer was made and Mrs Green was at home. Perhaps there had been a falling-out with Tom.

'And what was your journey back like, Kate?' she asked as the girl stood holding the hair pins while Amanda twisted up her curls into a style suitable for evening wear. 'Did you stay with the Greens?'

'Yes, ma'am,' she said.

Glancing at her reflection in the mirror, Amanda saw Kate was blushing. 'Are they all well?' she persisted. 'Tom, and his sisters?'

'Yes, ma'am.'

As Kate could normally talk the hind leg off a donkey and needed very little encouragement to do so, this was worrying reticence indeed. Could she have fallen out with the young carrier? Perhaps he had found another girl. Amanda resolved to visit Mrs Green before many more days were past. The Greens were her tenants on a smallholding that supplemented the carrying business, and would not find a casual call from their landlady unusual.

'I didn't tell them you were coming back on the stage from Norwich, ma'am,' Kate added suddenly. 'I just said you had let me have a holiday. I didn't think you would want people knowing.'

'Thank you, Kate, that was discreet of you.'

'Well, you did say that if I was to be a proper lady's maid, I should learn never to gossip.' Kate looked so inexplicably depressed by this statement that it was as much as Amanda could do not to demand an explanation there and then.

But dinner needed ordering and she should join Miss Porter in the drawing room, so she contented herself with saying, 'Run along and tell Mrs Howlett that I would like dinner at half past six.'

Miss Porter was sitting by the fireside, perusing a letter when Amanda entered. Her companion, a tall, plain woman in her mid-thirties, had presented herself in answer to Amanda's advertisement for a lady companion just when the young widow was beginning to despair of finding anyone congenial to lend her countenance. She had already rejected two ladies of dubious gentility, another who had not stopped talking from the moment she had entered the room and several of undoubted good birth but with hardly an idea in their head.

Jane, who made no bones about her straitened circumstances, her desire to make her own way in the world and not be dependent on her relatives and her willingness to leave her employer to her own devices just as much as that lady wished to be left, was a breath of fresh air. Even Cousin Humphrey, who, at the instigation of his mother, had had his attorney cast a very sharp eye over Miss Porter's references, antecedents and family, had to confess he could find nothing to criticise.

'Are you feeling rested, my dear Amanda?' she enquired, setting aside her letter and getting to her feet. At all times she appeared cool and reserved, but Amanda knew her manner hid a warm and caring nature.

'Thank you, Jane, I am much better for the rest. Now, do not disturb yourself: tell me how you have been getting on while I have been away.'

The news was little enough: an altercation with the butcher over his account, an accident to the best teapot, some improvements in the new herbaceous border and a visit from Cousin Humphrey.

'Oh dear, I am sorry you had to entertain him alone, Jane. Was he very tiresome?'

'He just wanted to pry about why you had gone to Norwich,' Miss Porter said coolly. 'You may trust me that he got only the most vapid replies. I then asked him if he would give me his opinion as to the state of my compost heaps and he took himself away in great haste.'

Amanda snorted with amusement, then remembered her anxiety about Kate. 'When did Kate arrive home? I thought she was not looking her normal self.'

'Mid-morning today,' Jane replied. 'She said she had stayed the night with Mrs Green. She does look peaky—possibly they all sat up too late last night.'

'I think there may be more to it than that, but I will worry about it tomorrow. Now, let me tell you all about my shopping expedition—I have been quite delightfully extravagant.'

Chapter Four

Kate proved extremely difficult to speak to the next morning. She flitted in and out of Amanda's room performing her duties, but the minute Amanda put down her hair brush and turned to ask the girl to sit and talk she found she had vanished again.

Finally, after breakfast, Amanda tracked her down in the kitchen and bore her off to the back parlour. 'Now then, Kate, something is wrong, I can tell. Do you want to tell me about it?'

She was expecting some tale of a falling-out with Cook or perhaps a lover's tiff with Tom Green, certainly nothing very serious, and was startled when the maid buried her face in her apron and burst into noisy tears. The more Amanda tried to calm her, the worse the sobs became, so that all that was audible from the muffling white cotton was the occasional disjointed word, interspersed with weeping.

'I never should've…without a character…parish… wish I was dead…'

The volume was quite enough to disturb the rest of the household. Howlett the butler put his head around the door, his eyebrows raised in fastidious disapproval at the noise, and was waved away by Amanda. He had no sooner shut the door silently behind him than Miss Porter could be seen, peering anxiously through the window, obviously distracted from her gardening, for her bonnet was askew and there was a smudge of earth on the end of her nose. She too was waved away and Amanda, thrusting a clean handkerchief into Kate's hands, ran to the kitchen herself to fetch a glass of water: she had no intention of involving Cook or any of the maids in whatever was distressing Kate so much.

At last the sobs subsided into miserable hiccups and loud sniffs. Kate emerged from the sodden folds of her apron, her nose red, her eyes inflamed and the snail tracks of tears staining her cheeks. She gulped the water and eyed Amanda nervously.

'My dear Kate, whatever is this all about? How can I help?' Amanda asked gently.

'No one can help, ma'am. Wish I was dead,' Kate muttered again, drawing in her breath for a fresh onslaught.

Amanda decided sympathy would only make her worse. 'Now stop saying that, it is a wicked thing to say, even if you do not mean it! Have you fallen out with young Tom?' Kate drew in a deep, wavering breath, and Amanda said hastily, 'No! Do not try to speak until you have command of yourself, you will make yourself ill. Here, drink some more water.'

Finally, after much sniffing and twisting the handkerchief into knots, Kate blurted out, 'I'm pregnant! And now I'm ruined and you'll throw me out and I'll have to go on the parish, and I'll never be a lady's maid and go to London!'

'Oh, Kate!' Amanda gathered her in her arms and patted the heaving shoulders. 'Do not take on so, of course I will not throw you out! But in any case, Tom will marry you, and just think how happy you will be with your own baby and your own home...' Her voice trailed away. 'You have told him, haven't you?'

'No,' Kate said. 'I wasn't sure, you see, until we went to Norwich and then I went to see a midwife—one who doesn't know me—and she said I was a foolish girl and of course I was pregnant, and I'd better get the father to marry me before it started to show and I made a scandal.'

'You did not tell him last night?' Amanda pulled up a stool beside the girl and held her hands.

'No, because when I got there he was flirting with that Joan from the mill, and I thought, perhaps I'm mistaken in him, and he has lots of girls and he doesn't want to marry me. I won't marry him if he's unwilling,' she burst out with sudden vehemence. 'I don't care what anyone says!'

'Quite right,' Amanda agreed heartily. 'If he does not willingly offer for you, then we will have to think again, but, Kate, I am sure he will. And as for Joan Bridges, why, that girl flirts with every young man, and you can't expect them to behave like clergymen!' Kate began to look more cheerful, and she added, 'And you and Tom can have that little lodge at the south gate—it needs a bit of work, but it will soon be snug, and there's a garden, and a pigsty and room for hens. Why, you will soon be the complete housewife.'

'Thank you, ma'am,' the maid rejoined gratefully, but then added, with a little sniff, 'But I did so want to be a good lady's maid and go to London and work in a big house one day.'

Amanda got to her feet and said, not unkindly, 'Well, Kate, you have made your bed and now you must lie on it.' As have we all, she thought, her face suddenly expressionless. 'Now, go and wash your face, change your apron and you may run down and see Tom now. The sooner you tell him, the sooner we can make arrangements.'

The girl hurried out, already untying the ruined apron and Amanda stood where she was, the bleak look still in her eyes. What she would have given to have had Charles's child... She was jolted out of her reverie by a tap on the window: Jane Porter was peering in again. With a sharp shove Amanda raised the long sash window enough for her companion to bend and step over the low sill into the room.

'My dear! What was that all about? You could hear the girl as far away as the vegetable garden!'

Amanda checked that the door was closed, then said quietly, 'You will not speak of this to the staff, please, Jane, but Kate is with child.'

'Tom Green?'

'Yes, thank goodness, for they are a good, honest, family and he is a hard-working lad. No doubt he would rather have had a few years yet before having the responsibility of a wife and child, but he is no innocent, and he will not be surprised at the consequences of his actions!'

Jane pulled off the old gloves she used in the garden and tossed them on the table. 'Well, he will have to marry her, like it or not.'

'No! I will not have her forced into marriage with a man who does not love her, to someone who is only doing his duty. If he is not whole-hearted, I will just have to find her a respectable place somewhere and she must become a widow for the sake of appearances.'

Jane shot her a dubious look, but did not comment.

She had found Mrs Clare held strong opinions on marriage, and although she was not someone given to vulgar speculation about her acquaintance, she did sometimes wonder about the nature of her employer's own, short-lived, union.

'We will know soon enough if there is a problem,' she said calmly. 'Now, how do you feel, my dear? I am sure you should not be having these problems to wrestle with so soon after your accident.'

'Oh, I am well enough,' Amanda said, raising one hand to her grazed and bruised face. 'If only this would not stiffen up so as it heals—it is most uncomfortable and I must look a complete fright.'

'It is very fortunate that you did not suffer worse injury,' Jane commented. 'And the other passengers, with the exception of the one gentleman you mentioned—they were all unharmed, I think you said?'

Amanda felt awkward. By nature almost transparently honest, she disliked the subterfuge necessary on this occasion. Surely with Jane she could reduce the half-truths to the minimum? 'There was only the one other passenger,' she said, attempting to pass it off lightly.

'You were alone in the stage with a strange man?' Jane queried. 'That must have been most uncomfortable.'

'Why, no, he was a perfect gentleman, kept himself strictly to himself before the accident, and I do believe he saved me from worse injury by er...catching me when the coach left the road.'

'*Catching you!* My goodness, how very embarrassing for you.' Jane paused, then added, apparently inconsequentially, 'And is he a well-favoured gentleman?'

'What has that got to do with it?' Amanda demanded

hotly, then saw the twinkle in her companion's eyes and realised that her very vehemence had betrayed her. 'Yes, Jane,' she admitted with a smile, 'Mr Jay is a very well-favoured gentleman. Not, of course, that I expect to see him again.'

'Of course not,' agreed Miss Porter solemnly.

By the next day, with no word from Jay, Amanda found herself growing restless, whatever she might say to Jane. No news presumably meant that his memory was still a blank, but she was tormented by the desire to go into Holt and find out whether anything, however small, had come back to him.

That would be most unwise, of course, and any lady with a well-regulated mind would have the self-discipline to put him out of her thoughts entirely. No doubt she would eventually receive a note from him telling her that all was well again, or she would hear that he would had secured the resources to make his way back to London.

But Amanda knew well that whilst *she* might consider her mind was perfectly well regulated, Mr Humphrey Clare, his mama and many of the ladies who constituted society in the locality regarded her as headstrong, unbiddable and positively eccentric in the way she managed her life and the landholdings with which she had been so generously endowed by her husband.

Her instinct was to help people, to involve herself in the lives of her friends and those who were her dependents. It was only the fact that she owed Jay much and that he needed her help which made her so anxious, of course; there could be no other reason for wanting to see whether those green eyes still had that mocking twinkle.

At this point Amanda threw aside the quill with which she was casting her household accounts and looked irritably at the ledger in front of her. She had been working on this task since breakfast—a good hour and a half—and very little seemed to have been achieved except a column of figures, which at a second glance did not add up correctly, and a pile of bills from the tradespeople of Holt, still waiting her attention.

Normally this tiresome weekly task took her half an hour: perhaps the knock on her head had caused some ill effects after all. Her concentration was certainly not what it was, she decided, getting to her feet.

Kate, returning yesterday from her encounter with young Tom, had been in a glow of happiness, all her tears gone and full of wedding dreams. There was a great deal to do as a consequence—set the repairs to the lodge in train, speak to Tom to see what additional employment she might be able to put his way, and, not least, find a replacement lady's maid. But it all seemed difficult this morning.

Fresh air and exercise was what she needed, and if that did not clear her mind she would send for Dr Hoskins tomorrow. Amanda took an old bonnet from the chest in the hall where she kept it for when the urge to go for a walk took her, and looked around for Jane in case she wanted to accompany her. But there was no sign of her companion, and, when asked, the butler informed her that he rather fancied Miss Porter had taken the trap and the grey cob and gone into Wiveton immediately after breakfast with some cuttings for the Rector's garden.

Amanda stepped out into the garden, tying her bonnet

strings and trying to decide which way to go. The riverside path would be pretty, with the chance of seeing a kingfisher, but would probably be muddy. A stroll through the lanes risked too many meetings with neighbours, who would be shocked and curious at the sight of her bruised face, and the walk on to the Heath was too tiring given that the ache in her bruised limbs was still not yet responding to hot baths and Kate's vigorous rubbing with embrocation.

In fact, the garden looked very tempting, and even if she was not taking exercise, a stroll along the pathways would be pleasant in the sunshine. Despite the gardener's grumbles about 'wimmin' ordering him about in 'his' garden, he did do what Jane told him and the results of his manual labour and her knowledge and good taste was charming. The late-spring plantings were well advanced and the bees were droning and bumbling. The sunshine had encouraged the birds and several were in full song in the holly trees that edged the lane boundary of the garden.

Amanda finished her wanderings at the little summerhouse. It was screened from the wide gravel path that led round the side of the house from the stable yard by a small shrubbery of laurels. The ladies often took their reading or sewing there on a warm day and Amanda was just wondering whether, if she were to go back into the house for a book to read, she would be able to concentrate on it, when she heard the sound of hooves from behind the high brick wall of the yard and the sound of the groom running out to greet the arrival.

Who could that be? It might be Jane returning from Holt; it might equally be Cousin Humphrey. Amanda stayed where she was, just in case, peeping from between the branches. Booted feet crunched the gravel underfoot and Jay came round the side of the house.

Suddenly the day was perfect. Amanda felt her heart give a little skip of happiness, which she did not stop to analyse, and she turned and ran though the shrubbery to intercept him before he reached the front door.

'Jay!'

He turned and smiled at the sight of her, then came towards her with no sign of hesitation in his long stride. He had a riding crop tucked into his boot and his right hand was thrust into the breast of his jacket. As he took off his hat she saw his face more clearly and realised that, like her own, the bruising was changing colour, but the angry red soreness was disappearing.

'Good morning, Mrs Clare. How are you now?'

'Much better, I thank you, sir, except I still feel some effects from the jolting and I am afraid it will be some days yet before I feel brave enough to show my face in Holt. And yourself?' He had stopped a few steps away and was smiling at her in a way that made her feel pleasantly warm and not a little flustered.

'I too am feeling much better. My ankle is quite well again, but this wretched arm has no strength in it yet. My good landlord and employer gave me the most sluggish beast in his stables this morning, quite rightly judging I could not control anything with the slightest spirit.'

'Would you care to come inside and take a glass of wine?' Amanda wondered where Kate had got to—probably mooning over thoughts of Tom instead of mending hems. But with Jane out, she would have to be found to sit in one corner of the yellow salon and provide the required chaperonage.

'Thank you, no, but I would like to look around your

charming garden, if I may.' He offered Amanda his good arm and she allowed herself to be steered back along the path she had just taken.

'It is nice, is it not?' she agreed. 'But I can take no credit for it, my companion Miss Porter is the ruling spirit here. She cajoles miracles out of our curmudgeonly gardener, and is quite an expert horticulturist.' She hesitated as he paused to admire a forsythia's yellow blooms, then asked, 'Is your memory still failing you? Have any recollections come back to you?'

'No, nothing,' he replied. 'Yet I begin to detect some clues. I believe I must own land, for riding here I found myself judging the state of the farms as I passed. Many seem in very good heart and well kempt, and where there was a problem, I caught myself pondering the best solution for dealing with it—draining that flooded field half a mile up the road, for example.'

'That proves you are a good landlord,' Amanda conceded, 'but it does not help us, for most gentlemen will own some land—'

She broke off at the sound of another arrival in the stableyard. This time there was the distinct noise of wheels: perhaps Jane had returned.

But the person who came into view though the gaps in the laurels was not Miss Porter in the neat blue habit she wore when driving but a tall, rather portly young man with a dissatisfied expression.

'You will want to go to your—' Jay began but was cut off by Amanda's hand pressed firmly over his mouth.

'Hush!' she hissed.

He obediently stood still and made no attempt to speak, but under her palm she could feel his mouth curve into a smile. The sensation was disturbing and she whipped her hand away, conscious that she was blushing. Out of the corner of her eye she could see that Jay was still smiling slightly, although his gaze followed the other man until he vanished round the front of the house.

'Who is that?' There was the sound of the front door knocker and, after a moment, Howlett's voice informing the visitor that neither of the ladies was at home.

'Mr Clare—Cousin Humphrey,' she whispered back and they heard the butler assuring him that the ladies were not simply Not At Home, but were Away From Home, and unfortunately Howlett could not say when they might return. 'Oh, shh! Here he comes again.'

The two figures in the shrubbery remained still while Mr Clare strode past once more, this time looking decidedly put out. Amanda was just breathing a sigh of relief when a clear voice from the direction of the stableyard said, 'Why, Mr Clare! Good morning. Have you been calling on Mrs Clare?'

Amanda stood on tiptoe and whispered in Jay's ear, 'That is Miss Porter, my companion. Oh my goodness, he is coming back with her!'

'I am glad to see you, Miss Porter,' Cousin Humphrey was saying as they drew level with Amanda and Jay's hiding place. 'Last time we met, you promised me some snowdrops for the flowerbed outside my mama's parlour window, if you recall, and I believe you said they should be lifted while "in the green". Do I have the expression correct?'

'Quite correct, Mr Clare. If they are moved while the leaves are still fresh, they will grow again with no trouble. It is, however, rather late, but they should take well enough if you tell your gardener to water them in. Will you not wait here and choose a clump while I fetch a trowel and something to put them in?'

Humphrey Clare could be glimpsed through the laurels peering at the dying snowdrop foliage that carpeted the ground beneath the shrubs. He seemed to find the clumps deeper in of more merit, for after several moments' scrutiny he walked briskly down the path until he found the opening into the shrubbery and began to follow it back.

With silent, cat-like steps Jay began to back away, pulling Amanda gently with him into the shelter of the summerhouse. It was a quaint little structure, built around the trunk of a huge old oak that must have pre-dated the house by hundreds of years. A bench circled the trunk and rustic poles supported the eaves of a sloping thatched roof, which sheltered the bench all the way around. The whole was surrounded by a loop of the path and three tables stood at intervals under the shelter so the ladies could follow the sun around, whatever time of day they sat there.

Jay, avoiding the betraying gravel, moved softly over the grass until the great bulk of the trunk was between them and Humphrey. But he did not release her arm and Amanda found herself standing so close that she could feel the warmth of his body. She risked a glance up at him, but his eyes were looking straight ahead as though he could see Humphrey Clare's movements through the tree. She realised he was listening intently to the sound of booted feet crunching the gravel.

There was a pause. 'He has seen the summerhouse,' Jay whispered in her ear, so quietly that she felt, rather than heard, the words. 'Now, which way...?' She felt his muscles tense, his body balanced to move in either direction. The gravel crunched again and Jay began to edge around the trunk, still holding her to him.

The noise stopped again, and then resumed and paused. It is like Grandmother's Footsteps, Amanda thought wildly as they moved to maintain their distance. But this was no children's game, and, if Humphrey in his guise as Grandmother found them, they would be more than just 'out' of the game.

Jay cautiously took another step, glanced down just in time to prevent himself stepping on a dead branch and swayed to get his balance on one leg.

He caught her eye and grinned and Amanda suddenly found herself in the grip of helpless giggles. Desperately she stuffed her fist into her mouth to stifle the sound. How much longer could they maintain this ridiculous charade? They were almost round the trunk again, on the side nearest the house, when Miss Porter's voice called, 'Mr Clare?'

'Here, ma'am,' he called back. Amanda could hear Jane approaching from the house, and Humphrey walking round the tree to meet her. Suddenly Jay caught Amanda up in his good arm and with two long strides, heedless of broken boughs, swept her round to the far side of the summerhouse. The sound of Jane's approach masked any sound they made and Amanda found herself clinging to him, her face buried in his shirt front, shaking with laughter.

'Hush!' he hissed in her ear. Amanda looked up into his face, saw the answering laughter in it and shook her head despairingly. She simply could not suppress the giggles. It was hopeless—they would be discovered.

Chapter Five

The next thing she knew, Jay had bent his head and silenced her by the most effective method he could have thought of. He kissed her full on the mouth, turning the gasp of amusement into one of shock, then into a little moan of startled pleasure. His lips were warm and gentle but very insistent. She should have been scandalised; instead, she found herself kissing him back with shy responsiveness.

The entire household could have been meeting on the other side of the oak tree for all Amanda was aware as her arms reached up to his shoulders, but Jay, however much she was occupying his attention, had kept his wits about him. Suddenly he was gone. Amanda found herself sitting abruptly down on the rustic bench against the tree trunk, her knees shaking and one hand pressed to her parted lips.

For a moment she was disoriented, then indignant, then, with the sound of heavy footsteps approaching, alarmed. There was a glimpse of dark blue cloth, a rustle of laurel leaves and Jay had vanished entirely, just as Cousin Humphrey, Jane Porter at his heels, came into view. He was studying the ground at his feet and for a moment did not see her, but Jane, with one startled glance at her employer, began to pat her own bonnet in an exaggerated manner.

'Oh, look, Mr Clare,' she exclaimed brightly, causing him to turn while Amanda frantically straightened her own crooked hat and stuffed back several wayward locks of hair. 'That is a fine large clump, is it not? Would Mrs Clare also care for some aconites, do you think?'

Humphrey Clare agreed, holding open the hessian bag Miss Porter had brought while she carefully forked up a clump each of both plants with a hand trowel.

'There,' she said, straightening up and brushing the soil off her gloved hands, 'Now all you need to do is to have your gardener put them in at once before they dry out... Oh, Mrs Clare!' She gave an artistic start of surprise and Humphrey turned.

'My dear Cousin Amanda!' He sounded faintly affronted to find her here and his eyebrows rose at what she supposed must be her dishevelled appearance. Goodness knows what a sight she must present with her old bonnet all anyhow, her face flushed and the half-healed graze on her bruised cheek.

'Cousin Humphrey, good morning. A beautiful day, is it not? I see Miss Porter is finding you some snowdrops: you must be flattered you know, for the Rector declares there is no better strain in the district, and he is a good judge.'

Humphrey, however, was no longer interested in horticulture. 'Cousin, your face! Whatever has occurred?' As always he sounded as though he was more concerned with any potential for local gossip than with anxiety about her well-being.

'A fall,' Amanda replied coolly. 'It looks worse than

it is because of the bruising, but I do not anticipate any lasting damage.' Her mind was racing; should she tell him some thing of the true facts in case news of the stagecoach accident reached him and he put two and two together, or should she say no more? Instinct told her that the less she gave him to chew over the better.

'A fall?' Without asking, Humphrey seated himself beside her and peered at her face. Amanda edged backwards as unobtrusively as she could. At the best of times she disliked the company her husband's cousin and heir; now, fresh from Jay's embrace, his fleshy high-coloured face and staring eyes made her feel positively queasy. 'How did that occur?'

Humphrey Clare was in the invidious position of finding his late cousin's widow extremely attractive and at the same time of disapproving thoroughly of her independence, her intelligence and her spirit. He knew his mother shared his disapproval, but would fail to understand the attraction Amanda had for him, and he rarely did anything that displeased his mama. He also deeply resented the fact that Amanda's late husband had left her every acre of unentailed land—in consequence, she was a considerable landowner—and of acres that he jealously considered were rightfully his. The result was to make him even more judgemental of Amanda's actions and to leave him in a turmoil of suppressed desire whenever he was with her.

Now he leaned forward to peer at her damaged face, but could only look at her bright eyes and the red lips that seemed to him to be disturbingly swollen. The thought that she might have been pleasurably excited by his sudden arrival was so powerfully erotic that he hastily crossed his legs and leaned back, attempting to look nonchalant.

Amanda, who understood his ambivalent emotions towards her rather more clearly than he would have believed, saw nothing particularly odd in his manner. She found his pompous behaviour as head of the family ludicrous and resented deeply his assumption that he could question her actions, but she was far too well bred to show any of this on her face.

'As I said,' she responded, 'I had a fall. It was an accident.' She managed to assume a pious expression and added, 'Naturally, I am taking care not to go out where I might be seen until it is healed. I would not want to cause any comment—people will indulge in such ill-bred speculation and ask such impertinent questions.'

Miss Porter hastily stifled a snort of amusement, but Mr Clare did not appear to connect the comment with his own behaviour. 'Indeed,' he agreed gravely, 'I have often had occasion to remark so to Mama. Doubtless it is the restricted life of the countryside: in town, where society is so much more select, a greater restraint obtains.'

Humphrey liked to give the impression that he moved in the highest circles in London and that only his devotion to the estate kept him in the country. Amanda, who had experienced enough of the Season to have observed Society closely, rather doubted both his social standing and his vision of London life. She was saved from making any observation however by the sound of hooves on gravel, which faded away as the horse left the stableyard.

'Now, who could that be?' Humphrey enquired, with what Amanda regarded as an altogether too proprietorial manner.

'Um...' It would be Jay, of course. He must have

made his way silently out of the shrubbery, skirted the house and approached the yard from the opposite direction and was now riding away. To say she did not know would be a direct lie, and for the life of her she could not think of a convincing answer.

Miss Porter came to her rescue. 'It was the hack from the Half Moon. I noticed it when I came back. Doubtless one of Will Bream's people with a message.'

Amanda shot Jane a look of pure gratitude, but Humphrey had found another ground for disapproval. 'What has that man Bream to do here? If he is too puffed up with his more-than-generous legacy from your late husband to continue his previous employment at the Hall, he should mind his own business. It does you no credit, my dear Mrs Clare, to have dealings with a common alehouse keeper.'

Behind Humphrey's back Jane shook her head warningly and Amanda swallowed most of the retort she had been about to make, saying merely, 'He supplies the ale for the servants' hall here.' She got to her feet, relieved to find that her treacherous legs would support her once more. 'Would you care to take luncheon with us, Cousin?'

Humphrey, who caused both ladies much resigned irritation by always timing his visits to coincide with one meal or another, accepted with an alacrity that would have been flattering if Amanda did not know that Mrs Clare senior was finding keeping a good cook at Glaven Hall well nigh impossible.

'Has Mrs Clare been fortunate enough to find a new cook?' she enquired as they sat down at length in the small dining room. A hasty retreat to her room, a splash of water on her face and the vigorous application of a hairbrush had restored her appearance somewhat, but she could only be grateful that Humphrey had been distracted enough by her bruised face not to notice quite how dishevelled she had been.

'No,' he sighed, accepting a platter of cold meat and forking a more than generous portion on to his plate. 'Poor Mama has had to suffer a string of lazy, incompetent, unsatisfactory cooks since the Howletts saw fit to move here with you. But what should one expect in the country? It is not good for her health to be so troubled by these problems.'

Amanda knew perfectly well that it was nothing to do with the location and all to do with the endless nagging and interference that Mrs Clare senior considered to be essential in managing servants. Mrs Howlett's opinions on the subject had been entertaining, but in the interests of domestic discipline Amanda had had to repress her weekly bulletins from Glaven Hall where some of the old servants still continued, being unable to find alternative employment locally and unwilling to leave the neighbourhood.

'Perhaps you should take a wife, Cousin Humphrey,' she said sweetly. 'A younger lady to take the cares of domestic duties from your mother's shoulders.'

For a long moment Mr Clare made no response, apparently engrossed in the well-cooked beef, fine home-made relishes, excellent bread and freshly churned butter before him. Then he looked up, his gaze travelling round the well-kept, charming room until it rested on Amanda opposite him. 'Yes,' he said slowly, as though entertaining a completely fresh idea. 'Yes, perhaps I should.'

Amanda stared back, appalled at the results of what she had meant as a secret joke. Now, it appeared, she had made Humphrey realise that, in addition to the desire she knew he kept trying to suppress, she was an excellent housekeeper and would ensure the domestic comfort of any husband.

Jane had recognised this too and, as soon as they had managed to see him on his way at the end of the meal, she shut the parlour door firmly and exclaimed, 'My dear Amanda! What have you done?'

'Acquired a suitor, it seems, unless a little reflection reminds him just how very unsatisfactory I am in every other way than my housekeeping!'

'You will tell me if I overstep the mark,' Miss Porter said, taking the chair opposite Amanda's and reaching for her sewing, 'but we have discussed Mr Clare's apparent admiration of your…er…looks, before now. Can it be that you have modified your opinion of him?'

'Certainly not!' Amanda exclaimed, stabbing herself painfully in the thumb with her needle and getting a drop of blood on the hem of the nightdress she was hemming. 'Now look what I have done!'

'Then it was not the sight of Mr Clare that made you flush so when we found you in the garden?'

'No, it was not, as you well know, Jane. The only flush Cousin Humphrey brings to my cheeks is one of annoyance at the impertinence of his manner and questions. But I must thank you for your quick wits about the horse in the yard—I was quite lost for an explanation.'

'I assume the messenger was your mysterious fellow traveller, Mr Jay, is it not? Whatever had he said to make you blush so? And why is he using the Half Moon's hack?'

'He is staying at the inn,' Amanda answered, her head bent, apparently concentrating on binding her thumb with her handkerchief so as not to get any more blood on her sewing.

'At the Half Moon? A gentleman? Surely the Feathers would be more his style?'

'Um…' Amanda was not hesitating to tell the whole story because she did not trust Jane or her discretion but because she suddenly felt very shy indeed at the thought of talking about Jay. She bit her lip, then took a deep breath and said, 'He is staying there because he has no money. I suggested to Will Bream that he could earn his keep by bringing order into Will's accounts.'

'You did say he is a gentleman?' Jane queried, receiving a silent nod in return. 'Then why has he no money?'

'He does not know why—he lost his memory when he was struck on the head in the accident.' She met Jane's startled look and added, 'I could hardly abandon him after he saved me from much worse injury. I believe he could have prevented the blow to his head if he had had his hands free when the coach toppled into the ditch.'

'So…' Jane said thoughtfully. 'We have a brave, well-favoured and resourceful gentleman, who has no money, no memory but who causes you to blush and become flustered and who trysts with you in the shrubbery.' She waited for Amanda's rather rueful agreement, then added, 'But you know nothing about him! He could be married, he could be escaping from a scandal, from gaming debts… Has he been kissing you?'

'Yes,' Amanda said baldly, deciding she might as well be hanged for a sheep as a lamb. 'And I spent the night with him at the inn.'

'*What?*' Jane swallowed. 'You really should not say such things, Amanda—for one dreadful moment I thought you meant you spent the night in the same room as him.'

'I did, in the same bed.'

'But…but what is to be done?'

'Why, nothing, Jane dear.' Amanda did her best to look unconcerned and sophisticated. 'We were both unconscious. The landlady, a well-meaning soul, thought we must be man and wife. Naturally, when I awoke and discovered what had occurred I gave her a false name and we brushed through it well enough. But you can see, we had to leave the inn together or it would have had a very odd appearance.'

Jane was silent for a moment. 'Did he…did he take advantage of the situation in any way?'

'No! Not at all! Well,' Amanda, incurably honest, added, 'not once we had woken up. And it was only a kiss,' she hastened to explain at the sight of her companion's expression.

'Only a kiss—and he kissed you in the shrubbery?' She hardly waited for Amanda's nod. 'What can he be thinking of, to put you in such a position if he does not know whether he is married or betrothed, or in any way eligible?'

'Eligible for what?' Amanda demanded, flustered at this perfectly justifiable line of questioning. 'This is merely a flirtation, if that! And anyway, he says he does not feel married.'

'Oh, really?' Jane enquired darkly. 'Well, we will see about that!'

'Jane! What are you intending to do?' Amanda's sewing slid from her knees to the floor, quite unheeded.

'I hope I know my duty as your companion,' Miss Porter said firmly. 'I may be a spinster, but I am older than you and, grateful as I am for my position here, I cannot let it blind me to an unpleasant responsibility. I must talk to this man.'

'You cannot! Oh, how embarrassing! Please, Jane, do not think of it.' Amanda leaned forward and seized Miss Porter's hands in both of hers. 'Please!'

'Either I speak to him or I see no alternative but to seek the Rector's guidance. Or,' she added, a look of painful determination on her thin face, 'Mr Clare's.'

Amanda could see that her companion, hitherto entirely malleable to her wishes and tolerant of her oddest starts, had made up her mind. 'Very well, Jane,' she capitulated meekly. 'When will you go to the Half Moon?'

'Tomorrow at ten,' Miss Porter replied, apparently too anxious about the situation to be suspicious of Amanda's surrender. 'I must think carefully about how to approach this: I have never had to recollect a gentleman to his duty before. I shall go out into the garden, if you will excuse me.'

Amanda sat back in her chair, her brain spinning. She must prevent Jane from lecturing Jay at all costs. It would be dreadfully embarrassing and, even worse, could lead him to believe that she was attracted to him to such a degree that her companion found it necessary to intervene.

Hastily she got up and opened her writing desk. Her first three attempts at a note were torn up, at a great waste of hot pressed paper, before she managed a simple request that Jay call on her at a quarter to ten, *exactly*. On re-reading, she thought it seemed more like an agitated demand, but it would have to do. She added, *Do not tell Will where you have gone, only that you will be back about eleven o'clock, and do not, under*

*any circumstances, take the main road here—ask him
to show you the way across the fields.*

Goodness knows what he would make of that, but if
Will Bream told Jane she only had an hour to wait she
would not turn the gig around and come straight home.
Now all Amanda had to do was to think what she was
going to say to Jay when he did arrive. My companion
thinks you are flirting with me? My companion thinks
I am in moral danger from you? Miss Porter says you
are no doubt married? Jane thinks we should not meet
again, and I cannot bear that?

Well, the last was undoubtedly the truth, unpalatable
though it was. Not, of course, that this was anything
more than her anxiety to solve the problem of Jay's
identity! And, she added, the fact that I find him very
attractive, that I enjoy being kissed by him and that it
is wonderful to be flirted with again.

She wandered out into the hall where the late afternoon sunlight was slanting through the windows and
through into the yellow salon. She stood looking up at
the portrait of Charles Clare, which hung over the mantle facing the door. The artist had caught the essence of
the man, the decent, direct expression as he stared out
across the rolling acres he had loved so much, the humour in the eyes and in the turn of the lips, the line
that responsibility had set between his brows.

'When I'm gone,' he had said one afternoon, very
shortly before he died, waving aside her spontaneous
protest. 'When I am gone, you find yourself someone
to love you, someone who will give you happiness
again.' She had tried to speak, but his thin hand had
silenced her with a gesture so weak it had frozen her
heart. 'I have left you well provided for. Every acre that
is not entailed—and only this house and the Home Farm

are—I have left to you. There is no condition on this, no restriction. When you wish to remarry, I know I can trust your judgement, Amanda. Be happy again, that is all I wish for—promise me that.'

She had mourned him deeply, honestly, for a year; then, gradually, the sunlight had come back into her life, the demands of the land she had inherited and all its people ceased to be a burden and became a purpose that brought satisfaction and an ambition to learn more, do better, create something. She thought of Charles often, never forgot to raise her eyes to the portrait when she entered the room, but now it was a gentle grief, a regret, and she knew she was ready to do as he asked and to move on.

But she never found anyone who was more than a friend and as the months passed she began to think she was fated to be a widow all her life. She could have gone up to London, she knew. A wealthy, young, attractive widow would have no trouble finding beaux aplenty, but something in her revolted at the thought of setting out deliberately to find a husband.

And now it seemed she *had* met someone for whom she could feel the tug of something more than friendship. And he was most likely married, or engaged, and her duty was quite plain: to stop this before she began to feel anything more for him and before he stopped flirting and began to entertain the same sort of feelings.

Amanda bit her lip painfully, then tugged at the bell-pull until Howlett appeared. 'Please see this is delivered to the Half Moon this afternoon.' She handed him the letter and added, 'Is Mr Pococke still in the stableyard?'

Her estate manager had been there a while ago with a builder, deciding on repairs to the coach-house roof: a lengthy discussion with him about the merits of planting turnips—as the famous Mr Coke of Holkham, just along the coast, advised—would take her mind off her personal affairs if nothing would!

It proved so effective—for Mr Pococke was less convinced by the radical agriculturist's theories than his employer was and was prepared to put up a spirited argument—that Amanda was surprised to be handed a letter by Howlett just as she entered the hall for dinner that evening.

'Came by way of the stable lad up at the Half Moon,' the butler remarked. His face was as expressionless as usual, yet something in his tone alerted Amanda to the fact that her household staff were aware that something was afoot.

'Indeed, I wonder what it might be,' she replied coolly, slipping it into her reticule. 'Please serve in twenty minutes, Howlett.'

The letter, directed in a totally unfamiliar hand, seemed to burn through the reticule as dinner proceeded through its courses. Normally the two ladies had more than enough to talk about, whether or not they had company, and Amanda would have enjoyed recounting her battle over the turnips with Mr Pococke. Tonight, however, Jane was too distressed by the thought of the painful duty that lay ahead of her tomorrow and the fact that for the first time in their happy relationship she was disagreeing with her employer—and over such a matter!—to do more than talk in the most stilted manner.

Neither was sorry when the tea tray was removed and they could make their way to their chambers. As soon as she was alone Amanda slit the seal on the letter. As she had guessed from the black, arrogant hand, it was from Jay.

'*It will be my pleasure to do as you ask*' was all the note said and across the bottom of the sheet was scrawled the single letter *J*.

Chapter Six

Jane set off the next morning in the gig at half past nine, dressed as though for church. She had made a little speech after breakfast, much to Amanda's embarrassment, although she could not help but be touched by her companion's desire to protect her, at whatever cost to her own equilibrium.

'My dear Mrs Clare, I would not do anything to cause you distress, as I hope you know,' she had begun, her voice strained. 'But I cannot allow you to walk heedlessly—in your innocence—into a situation of the utmost peril to your reputation and your peace of mind. This man must be warned off, and it is my duty to do so.' She had hesitated, the tip of her nose pink with barely repressed emotion. 'And if you feel I have overstepped the mark, I quite understand if you wish to terminate my employment.'

'Oh, Jane!' Amanda hurried around the table to put her arms around her friend. 'As if I would do such a thing when I know you are only doing what you feel to be right!'

Her conscience pricked her at the thought of deceiving Jane, and she knew it showed exactly the sort of moral weakness that her companion was so anxious to save her from. Amanda waved Jane goodbye as she drove off with her face set in the solemn lines of someone carrying out an unpleasant duty, but the minute the gig was out of sight she called Kate and dispatched her on an errand to Cook at Glaven Hall.

'I have promised her the receipt for pickled walnuts and I keep forgetting to give it to her,' she said with perfect honesty. 'Mr Clare is very partial to them it seems. Here it is—and Kate, if you wish to call and see Mrs Green on your way back, that will be quite all right.'

The maid hurried off, only too happy to be sent on such a pleasant errand on a sunny morning and Amanda set herself to freshening the flower arrangement on the console table in the hall.

Her stratagem worked: she heard the sound of gravel crunching under booted feet and had whisked the door open before Jay had had a chance to raise his hand to the knocker.

'Good morning,' he said doffing his hat as he entered and looking around for the butler to hand it to.

'Good morning. Here let me take those,' Amanda responded, relieving him of his hat, gloves and whip. But instead of placing them on the chest in the hall which usually received callers' hats, she carried them with her into the yellow salon.

She turned, waiting for Jay to follow her and saw from his amused glance at her scattered flowers on the hall table that he knew she had deliberately let him in without the servants knowing.

'You are a notable strategist Amanda,' he remarked, smiling. He closed the door behind him as she put down his things. 'And no chaperon? Now what are you about? Your letter was very mysterious.'

'I needed to speak to you alone,' she admitted. She looked him firmly in the eye, then let her gaze drop, confused. She had known it was going to be difficult, but now, with him standing before her, watching her closely between narrowed green eyes it seemed impossible.

'It sounded urgent,' he said helpfully. 'Has any rumour of our accident reached the area?'

'Oh, no, nothing like that.'

'And you are quite well, not suffering any ill effects? Your face is healing well.'

'Oh, yes, quite well, thank you.' This was ridiculous. She walked to one of the wing chairs beside the fireplace and sat down, gesturing him to take the other.

Jay came towards her, and as he did so, saw the portrait hanging over the fire. 'That is a very fine piece of work,' he remarked, stopping to study it more closely, his head tipped back to take it in. 'I imagine it is very like—the artist has caught a considerable personality there, behind a quiet exterior.'

'Yes, indeed,' Amanda agreed warmly. Those who did not know Charles well had often mistaken his quiet, calm exterior for blandness or a lack of character. It pleased her that Jay should see through that at once.

'Your father? It has a place of honour.'

'My father? No, indeed not, that is my late husband.'

'Your husband!' He turned to stare at her, all the amusement gone from his face. 'But this man must be twice your age, at least.'

'Charles was thirty-three years my senior when we married,' she said quietly.

'And you were how old?' Jay demanded.

Shaken by his vehemence, Amanda stammered, 'Ni-nineteen.'

'Nineteen! And who was responsible for selling you into that bargain?'

'No one! I was not *sold*—how could you use such a term!' She was becoming angry now, but not as angry as Jay, whose voice and dark expression made her shrink back momentarily.

'Are you telling me you loved him?' He took an angry step away from her, then spun round to face her again.

'No…not at first…but I sincerely admired and liked him. He was a gentleman who could not help but command respect.'

'What possessed you to enter into such a marriage?' Jay was not compromising either tone or expression, despite her own pale face and shaking voice.

'I was in a position where… My situation was such… Mama…'

'So your mother forced you into it?' His tone was biting and his expression so bleak that she hardly recognised him.

Suddenly Amanda found her shock and alarm swept away by her own anger. 'No one forced me. I made a rational decision that led to a very happy, if short, marriage. It is none of your business and I will not be interrogated, shouted at and hectored!' She was on her feet now, confronting him across the width of the hearth, her hands clenched into fists at her side, tears of fury and distress starting to roll down her cheeks.

Jay was staring back at her and for a moment she could not tell whether he was about to take her by the shoulders and shake her or walk out of the room. But as she stood there she saw his eyes lose their focus; he raised one hand to shield them and with the other groped for the back of the chair to support himself.

'Jay!' She was at his side in an instant, steadying him, not knowing whether to leave him and call someone to go for the doctor or to try and get him to sit down.

But the weakness was over almost as soon as it had struck him. He lowered the hand from his eyes and looked at her, his pupils wide and dark. 'Amanda? What happened? You are crying.'

'You were shouting at me,' she said as prosaically as she could, rubbing her eyes with her free hand while trying to press him down into the chair with the other. But he was stronger than she and resisted, pulling her round to face him properly.

'Shouting at you?' He closed his eyes for a moment and when he opened them again his gaze was the lucid green she was used to. 'What on earth... Amanda, my darling, I am so sorry!'

Her lip trembled as reaction set in and with a muffled oath Jay pulled her tight into his arms, wrapping her in an embrace against his chest. Whatever had prompted that extraordinary outburst she did not know, but she felt safe again, only so shaky...so very shaky.

'I'm sorry,' she said, her voice muffled against his coat, 'but I think I am going to cry.' And she did. She could not remember the last time she had had this luxury, letting all her emotions out in the arms of someone who simply held her gently but firmly and did not tell her to control herself, or behave as befitted a lady. Nor did he seem embarrassed. And somewhere, behind the storm of tears, was the echo of his voice saying *my darling...*

Eventually she stopped with a little hiccup and simply stood, her face against the now damp broadcloth of Jay's coat, feeling strangely at peace.

She felt his grip slacken and he moved, turning her until he could press her down gently into the chair. He produced a large handkerchief from his pocket and handed it to her. 'Quite clean,' he said prosaically. 'The Half Moon has an excellent laundry maid.'

'I know, she used to work at the Hall,' Amanda said, blowing her nose vigorously into the white linen. 'I am sorry, I must look a fright, my nose always goes red when I cry.'

'*You* are sorry!' His vehemence made her jump. 'My word, Amanda—what happened, what did I say?'

'You do not remember?' She looked at him anxiously.

'Yes…no. I can remember being angry, but it was not with you, it was something in my past all mixed up with whatever it was that started this.' Jay rubbed his forehead and say down abruptly in the opposite chair. 'Can you bear to tell me about it—exactly what happened?'

'Yes, very well.' Amanda sat up straight, the handkerchief forgotten in her hands. 'Do you recall why you were here this morning?'

'Yes, you sent me a note last night.' Something of his old humour showed in his face as he added, 'A more mysterious mixture of precise instructions and vague intentions I have never read.'

'Jane—Miss Porter, my companion—is even now at the Half Moon, waiting to bring you to a sense of your duty. She feels she must warn you not to visit me again in case you compromise my reputation.' The words were out before she could feel any of the discomfort she had expected. Fortunately, Jay appeared to grasp the problem without further explanation.

'So, she considers me to be a shady cove, does she?'

'She fears it—if a shady cove is what I think. I had to tell her about your memory, you see, and what happened after the accident. She thinks you are doubtless either a rake or married, or both, and, whichever it is, I should not be seeing you.'

His mouth was twisted into a rueful smile. 'And I suppose if I tell her I do not feel in the slightest bit married, and that if I am a rake, which I feel is more likely, I promise to be on my best behaviour, she is unlikely to be convinced?'

'Exactly. And however unmarried you feel, you may well be wrong, or you may be betrothed. And in either case you ought not to be…to be…'

'Kissing you?'

Or calling me your darling, she thought, but said only, 'Yes.'

'Hmm.' He regarded her thoughtfully from under lowered brows. 'We can discuss that in a moment. But what did you expect to achieve by sending me the message? You can hardly hope to keep the pair of us shuttling back and forth across country every time she sets out to lecture me on my duty.'

'I was embarrassed—I thought I should explain in case you thought I had sent her.'

'Because you could not give me my marching orders yourself?'

'Yes. Not that I should not do so,' she added, then gave herself a little shake and continued more firmly, 'Anyway, you arrived, and I let you in without the servants knowing you were here, and you were going to sit down so that we could talk, when you saw the portrait over the mantle.'

Jay tipped his head back to look at it and his face darkened. 'It is coming back—but an old memory, not what has just happened.' He closed his eyes in an effort of concentration. 'There was a lady, a beautiful young lady with blonde hair. Very straight hair. And blue eyes, and the most lovely, gentle smile you have ever seen.' His voice seemed to be coming from a long way away and Amanda sat still as a mouse, terrified of breaking the spell. 'And she was going to marry an old man, an old, debauched man. And there was nothing I could do to stop it, and I was so angry...' His eyes snapped open. 'That is all I can recall and, what there is, is all distorted.'

'Then discovering I had married someone so much older than myself disturbed that memory, and all the anger came back,' she suggested eagerly. 'We just need to find some other clues that will trigger memories and sooner or later something you say will identify you.'

'You would risk another outburst like the one I appear to have subjected you to?' he asked incredulously.

'Yes, of course, if it helps. Now I know what to expect, I will not be frightened.'

'Did I frighten you?' Jay demanded, leaning forward and taking her hand.

'Yes, but only for a moment, then I was angry. And then...upset, because of Charles. But you are unlikely to hit on anything like that again.' She ought to tell him to let go of her hand, but the warm pressure of his fingers was so right, it was an effort to move her hand.

'You see, you suggested that I had been sold into marriage in some way, and that was far from the truth. Yet, if I am honest, my conscience did trouble me, for

I did not fall in love with Charles.' She bit her lip. 'But he knew why I married him and understood the circumstances, and I vowed I would make him a good wife, and I did.' Her voice softened and she almost forgot where she was, looking back. 'I began by truly valuing him and liking him, and I came to love him. And I do believe he was happy with me. He never reproached me for not giving him an heir.'

'How did you come to marry him?' Jay prompted.

'Mama was widowed when I was twelve. I have no brothers or sisters. I did not understand at first, but I think she must have been a very poor manager, and our trustees were not sympathetic. By the time I was seventeen it was obvious that there was no money for a come-out; in fact, we were hard put to maintain a respectable appearance. But by then I was old enough to take a hand, and whatever poor Mama's problems in handling money, I have not inherited them! I shocked the trustees by nagging them until they took more of an interest, and I introduced what economies I could and started to save.'

Jay released her hand and sat back, an expression of intense interest on his face. Amanda, still lost in the story, continued. 'I am, if nothing else, practical, and it seemed to me that our only hope was for me to make a respectable marriage. I could have supported myself by becoming a companion or a governess, but that would not have kept Mama as well. But to make a marriage I needed a Season, and it took me until I was just nineteen to save enough for the bare minimum of suitable clothes. Then I managed to persuade a distant cousin to sponsor me—her daughters were still too young, so I was no trouble to someone who loved parties—and there I was, launched on my first and only Season.'

'I wonder if I met you.'

'I think I would have remembered, but do not forget, this was a very muted come-out! No vouchers for Almack's, no fashionable parties.'

'But you were a success.' It was a statement, not a question.

'Goodness, no!' Amanda laughed. 'I was just a provincial nobody. And I soon realised that being practical about money did not mean that one was necessarily practical about life. Somehow I had imagined that there would be someone, and our eyes would meet, and that would be that. He would not worry about my lack of money for he would not be on the catch for a rich wife, and I would be sufficiently well born to satisfy his family.' She laughed again at the memory of the naïvely romantic girl she had been.

'It is not like that, of course, as you would know if you could remember London society and the Season. Prince Charming did not come along, I received two offers from men I thoroughly disliked, one from a gentleman who did not have marriage in mind but quite another arrangement, and I was beginning to despair, when along came Charles.'

'But you did not love him.' Jay's face, shadowed by the wings of the chair, was unreadable.

'No, but he loved me. He had been a childless widower for many years and told me he had had no thought of marrying again until he met me. I was honest with him about my circumstances, and my feelings, but he just brushed that aside. I did try to dissuade him, but in the end he convinced me that we could both be happy. And we were,' she ended simply.

'And your mama?'

'She died a year after we were married.'

Jay made no reply, but something in the quality of his silence made her blurt out, 'I would still have married him if I had known. Do not assume I was making some sort of sacrifice for her.'

'No, I can see that you did not. You made an honest bargain by all accounts, and it seems, from what I hear around about, that you repay his memory by being at least as good a landlord as he was.'

'Am I the subject of much gossip, then?' Amanda could not decide whether she was put out that she was talked about, or flattered that her reputation as a landowner appeared to be so good. 'I know I am much disapproved of by the older ladies for taking such an interest in farming and the tenants' housing.'

'Not gossip,' Jay corrected with a smile. 'Just interest.' He hesitated and Amanda saw his mouth twist wryly. 'I had the impression of a lady who had been much in the world, someone who was awake to all suits.'

'Well, and so I am—now,' she responded firmly. 'You should see me haggling at market when I take my corn to be sold, or my fleeces, and the quite brassy way I write to Mr Coke at Holkham for his advice on farming matters without going through my estate manager as a respectable lady should!'

Jay raised one eyebrow. 'I do not deny that you are a remarkable landlord, a highly practical manager and have scant regard for the conventions. But—'

'I knew there was going to be a *but*,' she interrupted ruefully. 'I ask you here to save you from a lecture and now you are going to lecture me!'

'I would not dream of it. No, what I am trying to say

is that your companion is quite right to want to warn me off. I had not realised I was dealing with someone so sheltered from the ways of the world—one quiet Season, then whisked off to the country by a doting older husband.'

'Are you trying to tell me that you thought I was the sort of dashing young widow—and yes, I did see enough of society in my one Season to know they exist—with whom you could enjoy a pleasant flirtation?' Amanda demanded.

Jay stood up and walked away to look out of the window. 'To start with, yes.'

'Indeed! And then?'

'I stopped thinking about flirtation.' He did not appear to be going to add anything to this.

'You *are* a rake, sir!' she said warmly to his unresponsive back.

'Very likely. I did warn you.'

'Well, I feel extremely sorry for your poor wife if you are apt to career around the countryside with hardly a penny piece in your pocket, looking for dashing widows to flirt with!'

That did make him turn. Jay strolled back to lean against the wing armchair, looking down at her. 'I hardly think setting out with my pockets to let would be a very satisfactory strategy if I wanted to attract a flirt! No, there is some other explanation behind the odd start that found me in that stagecoach.' He sat down again abruptly and looked across at her, his face serious. 'Before that extraordinary brainstorm just now, I could have sworn I was unattached and heart-free when I set out on this adventure.'

Amanda wished she could be as certain, but one thing from his flash of memory earlier did lend some credence to his feeling. 'Perhaps you have never recovered from losing the blonde young lady you were speaking of and never formed another attachment?' she suggested.

'Wearing the willow for years for my lost love?' he quizzed. 'I wonder just how long ago that was? I am left with the most extraordinary impression of powerlessness, which argues that I was very young. But this is beside the point: I now have no confidence at all in that certainty. If my mind can hide what was obviously such a powerful memory, there is no saying who I am or what my circumstances. Whether I am married with six children, or, as I believed, a single man not averse to the company of ladies, either way I am an unsuitable person to be associating with you. Especially when you consider the manner of our meeting.'

Amanda struggled to keep her feelings from showing on her face. Jay was rapidly becoming more than a chance-met stranger in need of help, more than a friend. Without her realising it, he had become essential to her happiness. What she knew was the right thing to be doing was becoming harder by the minute now that he was agreeing with her.

'What exactly are you saying?' she enquired, trying to sound unconcerned with his answer.

'That we see no more of each other,' Jay stated baldly. 'I am, of course, for ever in your debt for rescuing me, but I have allowed myself to become too attached to your company and too heedless of the risk to you.'

Amanda wondered if she could manage to see him to the door without bursting into tears. She did not dare think about what he had just said about her company but summoned up every ounce of self-discipline, fixed a social smile on her stiff lips and said calmly, 'You are no doubt correct, sir. But you know that curiosity is my besetting sin—you will write and tell me how you get on, will you not?'

'Of course.' He was gathering up his hat and whip, drawing on his gloves, readying himself to walk out of her life. From the deep, shared intimacy of their conversation only a moment ago they now seemed like strangers, formally bidding each other good day. Jane would be proud of her, for she had succeeded in everything her companion had desired. Jay was going out of her life.

Chapter Seven

Jay was standing to one side of the door, one hand on the handle ready to open it for her, when it swung inwards abruptly, causing him to step back.

'Well, Amanda, that was a morning wasted!' Miss Porter marched into the room and began untying her bonnet strings. 'I waited and waited at the Half Moon, with Will Bream assuring me that Mr Jay would be back directly, but there was no sign of the wretched man. Possibly he has recovered his memory and gone about whatever mysterious business brought him to the area, for I cannot disguise from you my grave doubts about his respectability, whatever you may say.'

She tossed her bonnet on to the chair and began to unbutton her pelisse, oblivious to Amanda's expression of mixed horror and amusement. Behind her back Jay also appeared to be struggling to keep his countenance. The strain of preparing herself for a delicate and embarrassing interview, heightened by the long wait, had obviously overcome Miss Porter's normally reserved nature and she was now thoroughly annoyed.

In a voice which shook, Amanda suggested, 'A shady cove, you mean, Jane?'

'Really! My dear Amanda, where did you hear such an expression?'

'From the *wretched man* in question.' Jay stepped forward, his hand held out as Jane spun round to confront him, her complexion turning from red to white in confusion. 'I do beg your pardon, ma'am, for inconveniencing you.'

'Inconveniencing me—' Jane began as Amanda hurried forward.

'Jane, may I introduce you to Mr Jay. Mr Jay, Miss Porter, my companion.'

The effect of the formal introduction was enough to restore Miss Porter to something approaching her normal reserved calm. She shook hands stiffly and observed, 'Good morning, sir. There is no need to apologise, you had no way of knowing I was seeking an interview with you.'

Amanda had the grace to blush, but Jay merely bowed and observed, 'However, I now know something of your intentions and I hope I may put your mind at rest by telling you that Mrs Clare and I have just been discussing the matter and agreeing that it would indeed be prudent if I avoided her company.'

'Oh!' Miss Porter was obviously taken aback by this immediate capitulation, but recovered swiftly. 'You had this discussion without a chaperon in the room?'

Amanda and Jay spoke together. 'On a matter of such delicacy, ma'am…' and 'Let me ring for tea, you must be fatigued, Jane. Mr Jay, will you not join us?'

To her obvious surprise, Miss Porter found herself seated by the hearth with Jay helpfully placing a small side table within her reach and Amanda making brisk social chit-chat.

'Mr Jay has been admiring the garden, Jane, and I

have told him it is entirely your creation. Ah, Howlett, tea, if you please.'

'Yes, ma'am.' The butler shot a glance at Jay. 'I beg your pardon, sir, I did not hear your arrival.' He bowed and went out, his expression as bland as usual, yet Amanda was left with the distinct impression that he knew more than he betrayed. The servants' hall were obviously well informed about their mistress's new acquaintance. She only hoped that they had no idea of the circumstances of their first meeting.

She turned back to find that Jane had been seduced—no other word seemed appropriate—into telling Jay all about her revival of the garden. He was leaning forward, all attention and encouraging nods as she recounted the problems of rampant brambles, neglected shrubberies and the constant battle with the cantankerous gardener.

Amanda made no attempt to interrupt. She suspected that Jane could not suspect a man who showed such an interest in mulch and black spot in roses of having evil designs upon her friend, and however much her head told her that she and Jay were right to keep their distance, she found it mattered very much that Jane should like him.

'You are very knowledgeable about horticulture, Mr Jay,' Jane observed after Howlett had deposited the tea tray and left.

'I fear I know nothing about it at all,' he replied, accepting a cup from Amanda. 'Thank you, Mrs Clare.'

'You seem so interested.'

'I can certainly admire the product of taste and hard work, Miss Porter, but I fear I can find no information in my brain beyond the merest commonplaces on the subject.'

'Oh, dear.' Jane sighed and offered him the plate of

biscuits. 'Will you not try one, sir? They are still warm from the range and Mrs Howlett is a fine cook. You must build up your strength,' she added.

'Bodily I am greatly recovered, ma'am, as I trust Mrs Clare is. But much as I have to agree with you on the excellence of the biscuits, I am afraid any amount of feeding is not going to assist my memory.'

'Well, what are we going to do about that?' Jane demanded.

Amanda's lips curved into a little smile. Even through the fog of unhappiness that seemed to be gathering around her heart, her irrepressible sense of humour could not but respond to the sight of Jane, fired up to help the very man she considered so dangerous.

'There is nothing you can do, Miss Porter. We have all agreed—have we not?—that my continued association with Mrs Clare may expose her to the possibility of associating with someone whom she is better off not knowing, and, at worst, the risk of the truth of the coach accident becoming known.'

'Hmm.' It was obvious to Amanda that, having met Jay and realised she was not confronting the lecherous, yet insinuating, adventurer she had been expecting, Jane was no longer so anxious to send him about his business. 'It would appear to me,' she said thoughtfully, 'that our best defence against the true story coming out is to restore your memory, sir, and to establish you where you ought to be, in your true character.'

'Restored to your family,' Amanda added firmly. She found that conjuring up a mental picture of a young wife with children clustered around her did nothing to help her aching heart, but did much to stiffen her resolution to do the right thing.

'Another blow to the head might help,' Jane pronounced, oblivious to the look of mock alarm on Jay's face. 'If I were a betting woman—which of course I am not—I would—'

She broke off as Jay said sharply, 'What did you just say? I beg your pardon, ma'am, but if you could just repeat that last sentence.'

Puzzled, Jane obliging repeated, 'If I were a betting woman—'

'That is it!' Jay turned triumphantly to Amanda, his face alight. 'A bet! That was why I was on the stage with my pockets to let.'

'But who made this bet with you? And where?' she demanded. 'If we can but find one of those two facts, surely the whole puzzle will unravel.'

'That is the devil of it,' he admitted, apparently not noticing Miss Porter's cluck of disapproval of his language. 'I suspect I had had a fair bit to drink at the time. All I can remember is a small group of men around a table and one of them saying, ''You wouldn't be so very superior about my shortcomings if you had to manage without your guineas, your servants and your calling cards for a week or two.'' I assume I had made some remark that had touched a raw nerve with him.'

'And he and his friends made a wager with you that you could live without any of the benefits of your station in life for a fortnight!' said Amanda delightedly. 'Surely we can gather some useful information from that?'

'We already knew that I could afford a good tailor and bootmaker and that I can support at least the appearance of a gentleman. All that this tells us is that I have been known to drink too much in male company and have made at least one foolish wager.'

'Oh,' said both ladies together in a joint sigh of disappointment.

'We must not be downhearted,' Miss Porter stated after a moment's reflection. 'We have agreed, have we not, that it would be imprudent for you and Mrs Clare to meet in circumstances that might present the slightest appearance of intimacy. But now that I am involved, I see no reason why we cannot continue to assist you, if only at a distance.'

Amanda did not know what to say. Jane had obviously forgotten any suspicions she might have had that Amanda's feelings were involved in any way beyond an eagerness to help someone in difficulties. She wanted to stay in touch with Jay so much, yet knew that it was wrong to do so. For a long minute she kept her gaze fixed on her hands, closed tightly on each other in her lap, then raised her eyes to find that Jay was watching her with an expression she could not fathom.

'Jane, I really do not—' she began, and the door opened.

'Mr Clare, ma'am,' Howlett announced. 'Shall I bring fresh tea?'

'Yes, please do,' Amanda said, fixing a smile on her lips. Why on earth had she not told Howlett she was not at home to visitors? Then she realised that Humphrey would have seen Jay's horse and it would have made him curious if he had been denied admission when another morning caller was already there.

'Please come in, Cousin. Mr Jay, allow me to present Mr Clare. Cousin Humphrey, Mr Jay, who is a visitor to these parts.'

The gentlemen shook hands and took their seats. She saw Humphrey's eyes narrow in calculation, for she had instinctively presented him to Jay and not the other way around, implying that Jay was of the higher status. Humphrey, who was particularly sensitive about his position in society, and would dearly have loved a title, however minor, was doubtless running through a mental list of county families in search of Jays.

'One of the Hampshire Jays?' he enquired, so obviously fishing that Amanda winced.

Jay leaned forward and, with an air of confiding in a gentleman likely to instantly comprehend, announced, 'I am travelling incognito, sir.'

'Indeed?' Cousin Humphrey looked surprised, as well he might at this revelation, but almost at once a smug glow came over him. Amanda recognised the signs. Humphrey liked to believe that he was awake upon every suit, and would have sooner have been seen on the dance floor in riding breeches as admit that he had not the slightest idea what Jay was talking about.

'As a man of substance, a notable local landowner,' Jay continued smoothly, keeping eye contact with a mesmerised Humphrey, 'you will understand how delicate these matters can be.'

'Of course, of course,' Mr Clare huffed. Amanda met Jane's horrified eye. What was Jay leading up to?

'The slightest rumour, and the price soars, as I am sure you are well aware,' Jay continued, his voice dropping slightly so Humphrey had to lean towards him as though sharing a secret.

'And you are acquainted with my cousin…'

'Mrs Clare is spoken of locally with great respect as a landlord well versed in the latest agricultural theories. I presumed to call and have been most kindly received. You too are spoken of widely in connection with land management.'

He was outrageous! Not a single word was an untruth, but the implication was that Jay had called upon her to discuss Mr Coke's theories and that local opinion had told him that Humphrey was an equally advanced landlord.

'So you are interested in acquiring agricultural land,' Humphrey ventured, light finally beginning to dawn, 'and such a considerable amount that you are viewing the area incognito so as not to force up the price!'

Jay simply leaned back in his chair, steepled his fingers and smiled a slight, saturnine smile. 'I can see, Mr Clare, that everything I have heard about your intellectual powers are nothing less than the truth.'

Amanda closed her eyes, quite unable to risk meeting Jane's. Just how much flattery would Humphrey accept without becoming suspicious? Apparently an unlimited amount, although thankfully Jay appeared to feel he had said enough.

'You may count upon my discretion, sir,' Humphrey announced, with the air of a High Court judge delivering a judgement.

'And now I must take my leave and not encroach upon Mrs Clare's kindness any longer.' Jay stood and turned to Amanda as Jane pulled the bell cord for the butler. 'Your thoughtfulness means a great deal, ma'am. Be assured I will communicate what success I have.'

'I wish you an early success, Mr Jay. Good day, sir.' She stood and held out her hand.

As he took it in his he met her gaze; something there seemed to arrest his attention, for he murmured, 'What is it?'

His back was turned to Jane and Cousin Humphrey, effectively shielding them as she replied, low-voiced, 'I wish you had left before Jane came back.'

She did not expect him to understand her—indeed,

she hardly understood herself—but his voice had a sudden edge as he said, 'So do I.' Then he had released her hand and was turning to the others. 'Good day, Miss Porter, Mr Clare.'

Howlett shut the door behind him and the exchange of words as the butler ushered him out of the house were distantly audible through the panels.

Amanda returned to her seat by the hearth wondering, with a strange feeling of detachment, whether she was about to faint.

Cousin Humphrey did not appear to notice anything amiss. 'Mysterious fellow, that,' he remarked, reaching for yet another ratafia biscuit. 'Obviously a gentleman. Spotted the incognito at once, of course—you noticed the way he admitted it the moment I began to probe, I am sure.'

Amanda watched him as he munched his way through the sweetmeat. It seemed everything was magnified and sharp, as though seen through the hand lens her father had let her play with once when she was a child.

And like the creatures under that lens, Jane and Cousin Humphrey and all the things in the room, although perfectly in focus, were remote and unreal: Humphrey with his rather too-shiny striped waistcoat was a fat beetle; Miss Porter, fastidiously dabbing her lips with a napkin, a crane fly, all angular limbs and muted colouring.

Amanda concentrated on them desperately, as though Cousin Humphrey's every word was a life-line to stop her from bursting into tears and exposing her feelings and her vulnerability.

Inside her chest everything seemed to hurt—as her heart beat, as she breathed, as she swallowed minute sips of tea. She understood now why she had told Jay she wished he had left immediately.

They had reached a moment of decision and were doing the sensible, right thing, however painful she found it and she had felt a merciful sense of numbness. That would wear off, of course, but she could bear that, keep it to herself and learn to live with it in private until the inevitable letter came telling her that he was restored to his true identify, to his real life—to his real family.

But now she had seen him with others for the first time without his attention focused on her alone, and it was as though she was catching a glimpse of that real self for the first time. Why did that make it so much more difficult?

'Yes, mysterious,' Humphrey was continuing, frowning. 'But sound, I felt, very sound.'

'Sound?' Miss Porter queried, raising an eyebrow at Amanda.

'Yes, obviously a progressive man, and recognised another when he met one. Advanced ideas of course, but no harm in that, none at all.'

Both Miss Porter's eyebrows rose, as much in surprise in Amanda's lack of response than at Humphrey's opinion. He was a disastrously conservative landowner at a time when life was changing rapidly for both landlord and agricultural worker and he had consistently deplored Amanda's interest in the reforms of Mr Coke of Holkham.

Seeing Jane's face, Amanda pulled herself together. She was not in the slightest surprised that Mr Clare was adopting this attitude: he had obviously been impressed by Jay, flattered by his words and was hastily aligning his *spoken* opinions to mirror the other man's. 'You feel his ideas have some merit?'

'Well, of course, with a male intellect applied to these questions there is much worth considering.' Humphrey was never happier than when his opinion was sought, and Amanda had never known a lack of knowledge of a subject inhibit him in giving an opinion. 'I know you have dabbled in this to some extent, my dear cousin, but you would do well to leave such matters to men of understanding such as Mr Jay and myself. A lady cannot be expected to understand the subtleties.'

Yesterday Amanda would have enquired sweetly as to his last year's corn yield or the weight of his wool clip, then artlessly let him know what her lands produced. Now she let his patronising comments slide by unanswered.

Miss Porter hastily enquired, 'So you do suppose Mr Jay's business to be the acquisition of agricultural land, Mr Clare, as you said?'

Humphrey regarded her solemnly. 'Of course—why, his confidence in me was such that you heard him admit as much. But there is more to it than that. I am convinced he is in search of a major estate. Why else such discretion? Why else the need to linger in these parts? There are one or two families hereabouts whose affairs are, shall we say, shaky.'

Miss Porter, apparently sensed the need to carry the burden of the conversation herself and spare Amanda, whom she could tell was not herself. 'But there have been no advertisements of sale, Mr Clare.'

He regarded her with a patronising smile. 'Of course not, Miss Porter. Mr Jay is testing out the land, gathering the opinion of informed persons such as myself and then will doubtless make a discreet call upon his chosen landowner and conclude a shrewd bargain with someone only too happy not to appear to be making a forced sale.'

Humphrey was happily constructing bricks out of the few straws that Jay had so carefully strewn in his path. Amanda let her mind wander and suddenly realised why watching Jay with Humphrey and Jane had been so revealing and so painful.

Jay had been someone quite out of the ordinary, almost a fantasy. But for Jane and Humphrey, he was a chance-met gentleman about whom they were forming an opinion as they might about any new acquaintance. Jane obviously found him intelligent, charming and sympathetic, for Amanda knew her reserved nature too well to mistake the signs of approval in her open manner towards him.

Humphrey, while approving him as a gentleman and a knowledgeable landowner, was unmistakeably somewhat jealous of him. To Amanda, Jay had been simply Jay—a man who had insidiously become important to her happiness.

Now through Humphrey's eyes she saw a tall, handsome man, one with assurance and breeding. Even without their shared secret and intimacy, this made him a dangerously attractive man—and one from whom she had just parted forever.

And a good thing too, she told herself firmly. *Or you'll find you have fallen in love with him—and then where will you be?* And a small voice seemed to whisper in response, *Too late, Amanda, too late...*

Chapter Eight

Quite how long Amanda sat there lost in these disturbing thoughts she had no idea, but a small cough from Jane recalled her to the fact that they had a guest, however unwelcome. Cousin Humphrey had apparently asked her a question and was waiting for an answer.

'Yes, of course,' she said at random, forcing a smile.

'Excellent, excellent,' Mr Clare responded heartily, getting to his feet in a small shower of biscuit crumbs. 'It is fortunate that it is fixed for Monday evening. Your face is healing very well, but I would not want dear Mama alarmed by the sight of such an unladylike disfigurement.'

It was an effort to keep the polite smile fixed as she tugged the bell-pull, but as soon as Humphrey had been ushered out Amanda exploded, 'Insufferable man!' She took an angry turn around the room and came to a halt in front of her companion. 'And what have I agreed to for Monday night, Jane?'

'I did think you were not quite attending to the conversation, dear,' Jane replied mildly. 'We have been invited to dinner at Glaven Hall.'

'Oh, no, I *am* sorry, Jane dear. It is bad enough to

endure an evening there without inflicting it upon you as well. I wonder why he included you on this occasion, you usually manage to escape.'

'I am afraid Mr Clare does not always have the, shall we say, imagination, to realise that by ignoring a paid companion he may be giving offence.' Jane's tone was dispassionate. 'However, now he is courting you, he obviously feels it is proper to include your companion as chaperon.'

'Do you truly think he is courting me, Jane?' Amanda plumped herself down in the chair again with rather more force than elegance. 'I did wonder when I saw that look in his eyes the other day. I fear my good housekeeping outweighs my other faults.'

'And your land.'

'How lowering to be admired by such a man and for such reasons.' Amanda cupped her chin in her hand and gazed dismally out into the garden where a light drizzle was beginning to fall. 'Just look at that weather! Would it be very unworthy to hope he catches a cold riding home?'

'Yes, most unworthy,' Jane agreed. 'However, I do not think Mr Jay admires you for either reason.'

'Please, Jane, do not speak of him so. We are all agreed, are we not, that it is better if he and I do not meet.'

'Well, as you know, I did think that would be best,' Miss Porter said thoughtfully. 'But that was before I met him. I flatter myself on being a good judge of character, and I cannot believe he is anything but a gentleman of breeding who wishes you only good.'

'That is as may be,' Amanda retorted, trying to convince herself as much as Jane. 'But he says himself he is probably a rake, and, although he is convinced he is not married, who knows what attachment he is bound by.'

Miss Porter inclined her head in silent agreement, but after a moment's thought remarked, 'It is interesting to meet a rake. I suppose he would naturally be a man of handsome appearance and charm, but I had expected to find such a man sadly dissipated in appearance.'

'Really, Jane! What an improper observation! He will probably *become* dissipated in appearance; after all, he is comparatively young.' They looked at each other for a moment, then Amanda was suddenly struck by a thought. 'What *do* you think he would say if he could hear us?' And with one accord they dissolved into giggles.

Amanda eventually emerged from her handkerchief, mopped her eyes and remarked, 'I feel better for that. It was doubtless what Mrs Clare senior would describe as an unseemly fit of hysterics, but I refuse to be down-hearted about the situation. I am sure we will find some way to restore Mr Jay to his true identity.'

Looking at her over-bright eyes and determined smile, Miss Porter thought, *All very well, but is it going to restore your heart, my dear?*

The next morning, Saturday, dawned bright and fresh with the air washed clear by the previous day's drizzle. Amanda lay in bed, firmly talking herself into the frame of mind usually associated with New Year's resolutions. She reached over for the tablets she kept beside the bed, turned to a fresh page and sucked the end of her pencil. *Number 1: No daydreaming.* Not, of course, that she would close her mind to thinking about ways of helping Jay, but these thoughts would be purely practical and directed towards helping a distant friend. *Number 2:*

Kate re. Wedding. Banns? Cottage. She must talk to Kate about arranging a wedding day as soon as possible before there was any sign of the baby, and early enough that curious neighbours would not start adding up dates when it did arrive. A special licence would hasten matters, but that in itself would cause speculation. She would see what the young couple thought.

Amanda chewed the end of the pencil some more then added *Number 3: New lady's maid. Local? Norwich agency? London.* London was a very tempting thought. It was a long time since she had stayed in town and it was common knowledge that a flurry of shopping and dances was exactly the remedy for an aching heart. But she could not go not knowing what was happening to Jay, and once he was recovered he would almost certainly be going there himself and she shrank from appearing to follow him. No, London would have to wait. She would make enquiries about suitable local girls and resort to the Norwich domestic agencies if necessary.

That left one more item for her list. *Number 4: What to do about H?* What to do about Humphrey indeed! To fall out with him would be most unseemly and would create local gossip and comment of a most undesirable sort. Much as she disliked him, he *was* the head of the family now and she owed him and his mother the respect owing to that position.

Would he believe her if she simply declined him politely when—if—he proposed? She suspected he would not take 'no' for an answer without very good reason. She had no other plausible suitors, for she had been in deep mourning for a year, half-mourning for a further six months and was only now beginning to take her place in the somewhat restricted local society. She suspected that once she began to attend more local assemblies and dinner parties again she would find some eligible suitors appearing from the ranks of the local landowners, for word of the young widow with her generous portion and good lands would soon spread.

Amanda might be unconcerned about her looks, but she was aware she was accounted handsome by even the most exacting critics, so there was nothing to stand in the way of her receiving the flattering proposals that had been so lacking when she had first come out.

But she could hardly throw herself into a social whirl simply to surround herself with enough suitors to keep Humphrey at a distance, especially when she had no intention of accepting any of these imaginary men. A pair of lazily amused green eyes came to mind at this point and Amanda tossed aside pencil and tablets and scrambled out of bed, tugging the bell-pull as she did so.

Kate appeared with the water ewer and observed her mistress as she walked across the room. 'You are moving so much more easily, ma'am. Are your bruises better now?'

'Do you know, I think they are, Kate. I feel hardly a twinge, and my face is almost better.' She pulled off her lacy nightcap and shook out her hair. 'Kate, I want to talk to you about your wedding plans. I think the banns had better be called as soon as possible—unless you were thinking of a special licence.'

Kate nodded vigorously as she poured steaming water. 'I was talking to Tom last night and he suggested a licence too, but I think it'll make folk talk, so we are going to see Vicar tomorrow so he can start the banns on Sunday, then we can be married in four Sundays' time.'

She chattered happily while Amanda washed and sat in her robe, brushing out her hair, then asked, 'What will you be wearing today, ma'am?'

The sunlight sparkled off the cut-glass bottles on the dressing table and Amanda decided she could not bear to be inside any longer. 'My riding habit, Kate. It must be well over a week since I was last riding—it will shake out the cobwebs.'

She pulled a face at the sight of her habit as Kate lifted it out of the clothes' press. 'Oh dear, I wish I had thought to bespeak a new one while I was in Norwich. That one really is the most depressing colour.' She had bought it when she had come out of full mourning and had begun to ride about again, but the kindest description she could think of for the colour was greyish mouse.

Kate helped her into the long skirt and tight jacket and she bundled her hair into a net. 'It will have to do for now, I can hardly make another trip to Norwich so soon just for a riding habit, and none of the local tailors is up to a really fashionable lady's habit. Perhaps I will wait until I next go to London.'

'Oh!' Kate's lip quivered at the thought of missing the long-dreamed-of trip to town, but she sniffed resolutely and picked up Amanda's hat, gloves and whip to take downstairs, ready for when she wanted to go out.

Over breakfast Amanda politely asked Jane if she wished to ride too, but, as she expected, Miss Porter declined. She was an excellent whip and an energetic walker, but always declared she felt off balance in the saddle. 'Where will you go, dear?'

'Down to the coast and across the marshes to the seashore,' Amanda decided. 'I have missed the sea this past week.' The butler came in with fresh toast. 'How-lett, please send round to the stable and ask them to saddle up Jupiter. I will be riding after breakfast.'

'Well, take care—and do take a groom,' Jane urged, more in hope than expectation. One of the things that caused eyebrows to rise locally, at least among the ma-trons who did not quite approve of Mrs Clare, was her habit of riding out alone.

'Nothing wrong with that,' their husbands would counter. 'Mrs Clare is a good landlord, and a good land-lord rides their lands.'

'She should take a groom with her,' their wives would argue. 'After all, she is a female.' At this the men's eyes would tend to take on a thoughtful look and their spouses would wisely change the subject.

Amanda laughed without answering her companion and reached for the cherry preserve.

Her bruises were rather more painful than she had thought when she began to trot out of the yard and she realised that at some point during the accident she must have sat down hard on her behind. However, her grey mare Jupiter had a beautifully even pace, and once the first stiffness had worn off Amanda was soon relaxing. This had been a good idea, for her mount was fresh enough to give her both exercise and something to con-centrate on and within a few minutes the nagging un-happiness about Jay, if not forgotten, was less over-whelming.

Jupiter trotted down the lane between high hedges and stretches of finely made cobble- and brick walls that marked the edges of some of her neighbours' parklands. Now and again she saw someone she recognised and waved, but did not stop until she met the Rector, off on some errand of mercy in his pony trap.

He pulled up and doffed his hat, obliging her to stop also. Jupiter sidled and snorted but Amanda held her with a firm hand and exchanged polite conversation about the weather and how improved the ring of bells was now the entire peel had been tuned and re-hung. 'And I believe I will be seeing you on Monday evening at Glaven Hall,' Mr Maddison added. 'I am sure it will be a most interesting gathering.'

Describing an evening at Glaven Hall with Mrs Clare senior presiding over the dinner table as 'interesting' was, Amanda felt, carrying charity too far, even for the Rector, but she smiled and agreed she was looking forward to it. At least the addition of the Maddisons to the party promised a more stimulating evening than she had feared, for Humphrey had probably invited several other couples while he was about it.

'Until Sunday service then, Rector.' She smiled as he shook the reins and the fat pony ambled on its way. They were almost at the village green in Wiveton; within a few minutes, she was trotting over the humped-back bridge spanning the Glaven and heading into the little port of Cley. Although all but the smallest craft now had deserted its wharf for Blakeney, it was still busy and Amanda enjoyed the change of scene as she wove her way slowly amongst fishermen, housewives out for the morning's provisions and small groups of labourers hanging around in the hope of a day's work.

Then she was clear of the village and was at last able to give Jupiter her head. The ruler-straight line of the grass bank stretched before them from the coast road to the great shingle ridge hiding the sea. Waders and ducks rose screeching and flapping from the marsh as the horse passed by, then settled in wheeling clouds behind them. All too soon Jupiter was plunging to a walk as her hooves met the deep, loose shingle of the ridge. Snorting, she laboured up the side, sliding as she did so and forcing Amanda to hold tight to the pommel to keep her seat. Then they were at the top and the sea stretched cold and grey before them.

'All the way to the North Pole', Charles had said when he first brought her here, and even on a warm day like today she imagined that she caught the sharp scent of snow on the wind. Ridiculous, of course, but the thought was romantic and she always enjoyed the sweeping views to the west where the shingle rose gradually into low cliffs and to the east where the great spit of Blakeney Point curved out from its root, where she stood, to its tip guarding the anchorage.

Amanda scanned the sea for seals, for one could often see their black heads looking like human swimmers bobbing in the shallows. Sometimes there was even the excitement of sighting the great fins of basking sharks, but today there was only the passing white gannets and flocks of gulls to enliven the waves.

Sitting still for a while reminded her of her bruises and she decided to walk a little to stretch her legs. Jupiter made her usual fuss about having to scramble down the shingle bank again, but was happy enough to be tied to a post near a patch of short grass and left to graze while Amanda swung the long skirt of her habit over her arm and set off at a fairly brisk pace along the path on the landward side of the bank.

The bulk of Blakeney church with its little lantern tower to guide the sailors slowly grew larger to her left as the marsh between the coast road and the spit grew wetter and wider and began to be broken up by muddy channels. The tide was out, but as she walked Amanda saw that it was turning and the water was rippling and running back to cover the mud.

At last, rather out of breath, she scrambled up the bank to the top again. In the distance she could see Jupiter, head down, cropping grass. Near the horizon she could make out sails and just along the beach in the shallows a black head was bobbing—a seal at last. Amanda had walked rather further than she had planned and was beginning to think a rest would be a good idea. Almost opposite the seal the sea had thrown up a tumble of something—an old net, perhaps—and she decided to walk that far, then sit down and have a rest. If she sat quietly, the seal might come quite close in.

The shingle made walking difficult and, head bent, she trudged on, the wind snatching at her hat until at last she sank down, just under the top of the ridge, and pulled off hat and veil. The seal had gone, but with the little protection of the ridge the sun was winning over the wind and she sat hugging her knees, gazing with unfocused eyes over the waves.

Now she had stopped moving, Jay filled her thoughts again. What was he going to do if his memory did not return soon? If only he would accept a loan from her, but she knew he never would. He had recalled playing cards: perhaps he was such a good player he could win enough to finance a trip to London. But he would still need a stake.

At this point the seal bobbed up again, then vanished almost at once. Vaguely wondering why it was so shy, Amanda relapsed into her thoughts again. Time passed and still she sat there, the wind stirring her hair, her mind anxiously running round schemes, none of which, on closer examination, proved practicable in the slightest.

There was the seal again…no! Not a seal, a swimmer, a man rising from the sea and beginning to walk out of it, the water sluicing down his shoulders and chest, down to his waist, down…

Amanda buried her face in her hands and sat hunched where she was, praying that her drab riding habit would afford her some invisibility. She risked a quick glimpse from between her fingers: he had reached the point where the seabed rose sharply to the shore and with a scrambling stride was almost clear of the water.

With an awful inevitability she recognised that the swimmer was Jay, and also, as she reburied her flaming face in her palms, that he was quite naked.

She heard his feet crunching through the stones, then they stopped and she realised that what she had vaguely assumed was a pile of old nets must be his discarded clothing. At least he was getting dressed! Amanda pressed her fingertips to her eyelids until she saw stars, but nothing could banish the image of that tall frame, the broad shoulders and muscular torso tapering into the narrow waist, the long legs darkened with wet hairs, the dark chest hair narrowing downwards…

She felt hot and cold and realised her breath was coming short. If the shingle had opened up and swallowed her she would have been glad of it, but all she could do was sit there, her ears straining until they caught the crunch of footsteps again. They gradually faded away and she realised that he was not going to approach her.

Hardly able to breathe, Amada raised her head and looked around her. Jay was walking as briskly as possible on the shifting surface, away from her and towards where she had left Jupiter. Had he seen her? It seemed too much to hope that he had not. Had he recognised her? That too seemed only too likely. He must have been treading water out there for many minutes, hoping she would walk on, or back, and let him get out of the water. Finally the cold must have driven him out.

Amanda crouched there, shivering with reaction, watching Jay's receding figure. After what seemed like an hour, but was probably only ten minutes, he cut up off the beach to climb the ridge and dropped from sight. He would make better time on the grassy strip on the landward side and would soon reach the marsh bank. Which meant she must walk back along the beach or he would see her as he walked inland.

With a heavy sigh Amanda got to her feet and picked her way down the beach, hoping for at least a ribbon of hard sand to make her going easier, but the rising tide had covered it and she trudged on, perversely grateful for the effort of walking. She focussed on each footstep, forcing herself to think of nothing else until at last she reached the log, bleached by the sea and tossed high and dry by the winter storms, which acted as a marker for the point where she had to turn her back on the sea.

Jupiter was waiting patiently, one hoof cocked, head drooping, but she whickered at the sight of her mistress and butted her gently with her soft muzzle when the usual caress and titbit was not forthcoming. Amanda led her over to the stile which made a convenient mounting block and turned her head inland. The long path on the top of the embankment was empty.

Amanda let her breath out in a long sigh and tried to think rationally about what had just occurred. 'Pull yourself together!' she admonished herself. 'What a fuss about nothing. You have been a married woman after

all. It was embarrassing of course, but nothing to get
into a state about.' Jupiter twitched her ears, enjoying
the sound of Amanda's voice. 'I am not going to see
him again, which is a blessing.'

Jupiter walked on, but there was nothing further from
her mistress who appeared rather depressed with the
effect of her thoughts, for her hands dropped to the
mare's withers and the reins slackened. Jupiter ambled
along and at the coast road, when there was no direction
from her rider, turned west instead of heading back into
the village. Sometimes Amanda went that way—it was
longer, but there was the opportunity of a good gallop
over the heath as a reward for the steeper climb up.

Amanda sat, hands unmoving, eyes focussed on
something entirely other than the passing countryside,
until Jupiter stopped at a gate. 'What!' She started as if
woken from sleep and realised that the mare had found
her own way almost to the heath. 'Oh, Jupiter, I am
sorry! Are you very bored? Never mind, we will go
through here and have a good gallop, it will do us both
good.'

Drawing up at the gate off the heath five minutes
later, Amanda reflected that the gallop might have done
Jupiter some good, but it had had the most extraordinary
effect on her. She had fallen into a rather hazy daydream of the morning when she had woken in the inn
bed beside Jay and her mind, shying away from the all-
too-naked reality of what had just occurred, had been
soothed by the memory of his warmth, his deep, slow
breathing and of the safety she had felt, drowsing beside
him.

The gallop had aroused an entirely different feeling
of urgency and restlessness. She felt hot and cold all at
once, wanted to gallop again, feel the wind in her hair,

the power of the horse carrying her along, muscles surging beneath the saddle. 'What is the matter with me?' she whispered as she trotted sedately back along the lane, ducking her head to avoid the blossom which was beginning to cover the hedges, bending the boughs low. Perhaps she was sickening for a fever. It would account for her ridiculous over-reaction to the encounter on the beach, her absence of mind, the strange feeling that still possessed her.

Jane was in the stableyard as she rode in and her expression as she greeted her confirmed Amanda's diagnosis. 'My dear, are you quite well? You are so flushed. I do hope you have not overdone things.'

Amanda slipped down gratefully from Jupiter's back and handed the reins to the groom. 'I think I must be developing a cold, Jane, I feel so very odd.'

Jane put her hand under one arm. 'Amanda, you are positively trembling. Come up to bed at once and I will make you a saline draught. Reaction to the shock of your accident, that will be it, mark my words. That sort of thing will lay even the healthiest person open to a cold. Let us hope it is nothing more serious.'

Chapter Nine

Tucked up in bed by Jane, a hot brick at her feet, a saline draught forced down, Amanda found herself curiously willing to play the invalid. She had never felt quite like this before: even when Charles had died she had not wanted to hide away. There had been people to see and to comfort, just as she had needed comfort. There had been tasks to carry out and she had done all of that without shirking anything, even coping calmly with the unwelcome arrival of Cousin Humphrey and his mother, indecently soon after the funeral, to take up residence.

Perhaps she really was going to be ill, and not hiding as her conscience kept telling her, whenever she allowed herself to listen to its promptings. *You do not want to think about him*, it nagged her. *You are in love with him and now you desire him.*

'I am not! I cannot be!' she said out loud so vehemently that Jane, who had popped her head around the door to enquire if she would like a little chicken broth for luncheon, was alarmed.

'Oh dear, you are delirious,' she gasped, hurrying

into the room and placing one cool hand on Amanda's hot brow. 'I shall send for Dr Hoskins.'

'No, please, do not do that.' Amanda caught her hand and forced herself to smile reassuringly. 'It is nothing more than a delayed reaction to all the excitement with the accident, and Jay's predicament and so on. And I am worried about Kate, and finding a replacement for her.' All of which was quite true and nothing at all to do with the state she was in. 'I am sure that a day resting will do me a power of good, Jane. I will have a little broth and spend the afternoon with one of the books I brought back from Norwich. After that, and a good night's sleep, I will be right as rain in the morning, Jane, just wait and see.'

The first part of her remedy worked perfectly. The broth was reviving, Miss Austen's *Pride and Prejudice*, which she had unaccountably missed when it was published, was engrossing and made her laugh out loud, and she was able to address the supper that an anxious Kate brought up with relish.

'You see, Kate, I will be perfectly all right in the morning and able to go to church. I would not want to miss hearing your banns read.'

But the good night's sleep which Amanda had predicted proved to be far from reality. She certainly slept, but it was a sleep full of dreams so vivid and explicit that she finally awoke as the clock chimed five with the bedclothes in a tangle around her limbs and her breath coming fast as though she had been running.

Even with returning consciousness the dreams did not fade, leaving Amanda staring wide-eyed into the dawn light, remembering images of her body clasped in Jay's arms, their limbs equally naked, his mouth hot and possessive on hers, kissing her with an intensity that neither of his previous kisses had achieved. Her breathing was still ragged, her body felt almost unbearably tense and she was filled with a deep, aching longing.

Amanda scrambled out of bed, poured cold water from the ewer into the basin and splashed her face, towelling it roughly until she felt fully awake and the trembling in her limbs stopped. Shaken, she got back into bed, plumped up the pillows and sat watching the brightening dawn.

Was this desire, then? She had been brought up to understand that ladies did not experience this sensation, that the physical act was, if one was fortunate, not too unpleasant, and was the price one paid for a happy marriage, children and the comfort of an affectionate husband.

Charles had treated her from the first as though she was infinitely fragile and as though he expected her to be deeply shocked by the whole physical side of marriage. She had never seen her husband naked, for he always spared her blushes by drawing the curtains and extinguishing the lamps before coming to bed. His love making had been gentle, and over sooner than she had expected. At first it had been every bit as painful and embarrassing as she had feared, but as she grew to trust him it became simply something that had to be gone through in order to achieve the companionable presence of a satisfied and kindly husband in her bed.

She enjoyed sleeping by his side, listening to him breathing, feeling safe and loved. She had enjoyed their early morning conversations, both of them in their nightgowns, sitting up against the pillows, sipping their chocolate and planning the day.

His kisses were pleasant, but she had felt none of the

more exciting sensations that occasionally she heard whispers of from her faster acquaintances. And she had no one to ask whether this really was all there was to the marriage bed.

The sight of Jay's raw physicality had shaken her to the core and had brought into focus all the feelings that being with him had stirred in her, made the remembered touch of his lips something infinitely dangerous and exciting, full of longing and desire.

I told you so, jeered that inner voice she had so vehemently denied the day before. *And he has gone and you will never see him again.*

Her treacherous imagination took her back to the bed in the Lamb and Flag. What would have happened if she had not opened her eyes, but had let herself fall into his embrace, let that brief kiss linger, allowed his arms to hold her, his legs to tangle with hers, his body to roll her into the deep feather mattress and his weight to cover her?

He would have made love to her, that was what would have happened, and she would have discovered what it is like when a man treats a woman not as a child bride, not as a fragile piece of porcelain, but as a flesh-and-blood creature capable of as much passion and pleasure as he was. And now she would never experience that.

The sound of the household waking up and going about its business finally roused her from her thoughts. Today was Sunday and somehow or another she was going to get up, put on her Sunday clothes and her Sunday face and struggle to school her thoughts into calmness and reverence.

Once she and Jane were walking at the head of the little procession of servants wending their way to church, prayer books in gloved hands, best hats and bonnets firmly on heads, she began to feel more in control. It was amazing what the discipline of routine and the need to behave properly in front of the servants could do for a breaking heart.

Jane was inclined to fuss over her at first, but Amanda's apparent serenity, her lack of a fever and her determination to attend Matins soon set Miss Porter's mind at rest. Several friends and neighbours greeted them as they met and mingled at the north porch. The servants, whispers hushed, made their way to their pews in the rear of the church, the bell ringers shuffled in from the tower arch and Amanda and Jane made their way down the aisle to where their high box-pew sat just across from that belonging to Glaven Hall.

Amanda knew very well the comforts hidden behind the high panelled door. Charles had had the velvet cushions replaced, she had embroidered the kneelers herself over several long winter months and there were even velvet curtains on brass rods to draw to keep the draughts from penetrating where the oak panelling met the grey stone of the pillars.

Her own pew now was less imposing, as befitted one of the lesser households in the valley. The verger was opening the door for her with a bow when Cousin Humphrey stood up in his pew, making Jane jump. 'Will you not join me, Cousin?' he enquired. The verger hurried to open that door in turn, almost tripping over his long verge as he did so. Amanda had no wish to join her cousin, but she had even less desire make an exhibition of herself arguing about it in front of a full congregation.

'Thank you, Cousin, thank you, Mr Berry, come,

Jane,' and she stepped into the box, blithely ignoring the look of chagrin on Humphrey's face. He had had no intention of inviting the companion, now he had to shuffle along the bench to make room as the two ladies bowed to Mrs Clare senior and took their places.

If Amanda had wanted to find a counter-irritant to her thoughts, she could not have done better than to sit with Mr Clare. Her attempts at quiet reflection were broken into by him officiously finding her place for the next reading or hymn; he dropped his hat, enquired in a loud whisper if she felt at all cold as he had a rug under the seat for such an eventuality and instead of being able to listen closely to Mr Maddison's sermon, she was mortified by him nodding vigorously and exclaiming 'Quite right, sir!' all too audibly at intervals.

His mother merely sat bolt upright, fixing Amanda, whenever she caught her eye, with a fishy stare that appeared to blame her for Humphrey's excesses. Finally the Rector began to read the banns. When he reached the announcement for Kate and Tom Green, Mrs Clare's expression became even chillier and her mouth set into a thin line of disapproval. Amanda knew she was imagining the worst and wondered just how, short of an untruth, she was going to protect Kate's good name when the village tabbies began to gossip.

As the service ended she was careful to stand well clear of the pew door to make it very obvious that she expected Humphrey to give his mother his arm and allow her to take precedence as he was showing alarming signs of ushering Amanda out first.

Her good manners did not save her from a vigorous interrogation as soon as she had shaken hands with the Rector and was outside the church, waiting for her little household to reassemble.

'This is very sudden, the marriage of that maid of yours, is it not?' Mrs Clare demanded. 'A scrambling way of doing things, I declare, one could almost imagine she has need for haste.'

'Surely not,' Amanda replied calmly. 'If that had been the case, why, they could have married by licence. Jane, where can the boot boy have gone to, can you see him anywhere?'

'A licence!' Mrs Clare was aghast, the black beads in her bonnet flashing with her vehemence. 'Aping her betters!'

'No doubt, ma'am,' Amanda responded, apparently giving it little importance. 'Where has that boy got to! I have no intention of leaving without him and having him arrive back at goodness knows what hour, covered with mud. Not upon a Sunday, in any case.' She saw Jane hurrying the miscreant back from a hiding place amongst the tombstones and turned her attention back to Mrs Clare. 'It is a very long-standing attachment, ma'am, so I am not at all surprised, although sorry to be losing such a good servant, of course. May I walk with you to your carriage?'

Mollified, if still inclined to speculate, Mrs Clare allowed herself to be guided firmly down the churchyard path. Amanda was relaxing when her next sharp question made her jump.

'What do you know of this man Jay that Humphrey has taken up with? A Captain Sharp, is he?'

'I know very little of his circumstances,' Amanda replied truthfully, trusting that the warmth of the sun would explain any colour in her cheeks.

'You have had him in the house, for that is where Humphrey came upon him.'

'Oh, yes, but one is duty bound to entertain and assist

visiting gentlepeople. Although who am I to remind such a notable hostess as yourself of the fact? Mr Jay was brought to my attention as a gentleman enquiring about agricultural matters and I was happy to give him what information I have. Naturally, he found his meeting with Mr Clare of inestimable interest.'

The combination of Amanda's disinterested tone and her flattering remark about Humphrey did much to lull Mrs Clare's suspicions. 'I am sure he did,' she retorted sharply, but with a pleased glint in her eye. 'I am glad of your opinion of the man—not that your experience is wide, but I have no reason to believe you do not recognise a gentleman when you see one.'

'Thank you, ma'am, praise indeed,' Amanda murmured. 'Here is your carriage, I will bid you good morning.' They exchanged bows and Amanda walked briskly away, cutting the corner to avoid meeting Humphrey as he bustled after his mama.

Jane occupied the walk back to the house with a discussion of the best way to discipline the boot boy—'An incorrigible child!'—appreciation of the Rector's sermon—'Always so much matter for contemplation afterwards in Mr Maddison's addresses, do you not think, dear?'—and very mild praise for the floral arrangement at the altar—'Such a lack of imagination when one thinks what a wealth of bloom is available just now.'

It was not until the ladies were ensconced in the parlour with a half-embroidered kneeler apiece for the Lady Chapel on their laps that she spoke of what had obviously been filling her mind. 'I was so taken aback by Mr Clare's actions this morning! He has never done such a thing before.'

'I know.' Amanda sighed, reaching for her embroidery scissors. 'I felt so conspicuous. Why, he could hardly have made his intentions clearer if he had posted a notice in the porch!'

'How did his mama react?' Miss Porter enquired. 'I could not see her face without bending forward, and naturally I could not do that.'

'She was not pleased, although she was distracted by the news about Kate's marriage. If she does make her feelings plain to Cousin Humphrey, do you think that will be enough to discourage him?'

Miss Porter set a few stitches thoughtfully. 'If it were just a passing fancy, it might, but reflect, dear, we have decided that not only does he covet your lands and appreciate your skills as a housewife, we had long recognised that he was attracted to you…that is he found you attractive—' She broke off blushing.

'I suppose it is too much to hope that his relationship to Charles puts him within the prohibited degrees of marriage for me?' Amanda exclaimed, suddenly hopeful. 'They are listed in the prayer book.' She picked up the book from the table beside her and riffled through the pages. 'Here we are…parents, brothers, uncles… No, if he had been Charles's uncle, then it would be forbidden, but there is nothing at all about cousins.'

'You will just have to tell him the truth, that is all,' said Miss Porter firmly. 'His mind is not elastic, and it may take several repetitions before he gives up, but surely that is the only way.'

'Tell him that I do not think we should suit, you mean?' Amanda asked, resuming her stitching.

'Of course, if that is the only reason,' her companion answered calmly, apparently not noticing the hectic blush which rose in Amanda's cheeks. 'Do you think this dull gold is better for the lettering here, or should I use the brighter yellow?'

The night brought no better rest for Amanda. The feverish dreams persisted and by the morning she felt so tired and out of sorts that her normal sense of humour had quite deserted her. Despite the fact that Jay had remained true to his word and had not contacted her since Friday, she found herself blaming him for the nature of her dreams, just as though he had been indulging in the most persistent attentions to her.

How dare he intrude into the calm, happy, orderly world she had built for herself? How could he flirt with her so carelessly, charm her with that lazy smile, those deep green eyes? Why could he not be a gentleman and endure a little cold while she took the air on the beach?

The entire household felt the change in Amanda as she swept down to breakfast. Not that she exhibited the slightest ill temper to anyone, for she would have been ashamed to do so, but the string of orders she delivered left no one in any doubt as to her mood.

'Kate, it is about time that all the clothes presses were emptied and aired and fresh wormwood hung up for the moth. And when you have done that, please reline all the drawers. Mrs Howlett will give you fresh lavender to refill the lavender bags. Jane dear, shall we turn out the linen cupboards as we have been promising Mrs Howlett we would do this month past? A complete new inventory is needed, she tells me.' She paused for breath and surveyed her staff, apprehensively assembled in the hall.

'Howlett, I cannot think why, but all the windows look smeary in this sunshine. Please set the footmen to work on the inside and the grooms can get out the ladders and do the outsides. And do you not feel it is about time the cellar was reviewed and we decided what new order to send off to Grimble and Hodgkiss in Norwich? I do not want to risk having inadequate wines when we have company.'

She spotted the boot boy trying to vanish under the stairs. 'And you, Jeremy, can blacklead every grate in the house until Mrs Howlett is satisfied.'

Leaving them breathless behind her, Amanda picked up the sheets of paper that contained the linen inventory and swept upstairs. 'Come along, Jane, let us start with the cupboard on the top landing.'

By mid-afternoon the staff were hot, bothered and dusty, but the windows sparkled, the grates gleamed and a substantial order was sealed, waiting to be dispatched to the wine merchant.

Jane, who after one intent look at her employer's expression had shaken out sheets, tugged at hems and condemned worn pillow cases for dusters without complaint all day, finally sat back on her heels and announced. 'I think that is the very last sheet in the house, leaving aside what is on the beds, of course.'

Amanda wrote the last correction on the inventory and conned it critically. 'I do not know what the servants do to their sheets! I could swear that we ordered twelve new pairs last year at this time and there is hardly an undarned one in the house. But beside that, and an order for some new pillow cases, I do not think things are too bad.'

She put down her pen, untied her apron and tossed it on to the table, noticing her companion's weary stance for the first time. 'Oh, Jane, I am sorry! Are you very tired? I should have noticed, and we hardly stopped to eat.'

'It is quite all right, my dear.' Miss Porter got to her feet and folded her apron. 'It is no bad thing to do such a task all at once, and I am sure we will suffer no harm for having had a light luncheon. After all, we are dining out this evening.'

'Oh my goodness, I had quite forgotten.' Amanda brushed her hair off her forehead and regarded the smudge on the end of Miss Porter's nose. 'A hot bath for both of us, I think. What shall we wear?'

'You said that Mr and Mrs Maddison have been invited, which probably means that several other couples have as well. Mrs Clare would regard that as an economy to return all her outstanding invitations at one time. Therefore we had better look our best, do you not think so? It will hardly be a family dinner.'

'Yes,' Amanda agreed. The anger with Jay was still running hot in her veins and the thought of dressing up, of putting on her jewels, of making an impression, was very tempting. Perhaps some single gentlemen had been invited. In that case, she would flirt—very discreetly, of course. That would show him, she thought, although how he would be expected to know about it, she had no idea. 'Yes,' she repeated. 'Let us dress up, Jane, I am sure Mrs Clare would appreciate it.'

Chapter Ten

Amanda stepped down from the carriage outside Glaven Hall in the full knowledge that she was looking magnificent. She was not vain about her looks, nor was she given to dressing to make an impression, although Charles had liked it when she had appeared on his arm in striking gowns and wearing the jewels he had bought her.

But she did enjoy beautiful clothes. In recent times the opportunities to dress her hair, take the diamonds out of their box and show off her latest gown had been few and far apart, so she intended to make the most of this one.

The gown she had decided on for this evening was one of her purchases in Norwich, an over-dress of the palest sea-green gauze draped elegantly over the under-tunic of a deeper shade of the same colour in a fluid silk with a deeply beaded hem. The neckline was almost plain, with just a thin line of the same beading, but it skimmed low to show off her bosom and shoulders, which were lightly veiled in a gauze scarf that the vendeuse had assured her was, 'Just the colour of the seafoam, madame.'

Diamond-drop earrings trembled against her neck, the matching necklace was simple enough not to distract from her pale skin, yet flashed with the true depth of stones of the first water. She hesitated over her hair, which was piled high with one curl tumbling artlessly down, then fastened the two diamond pins just where the curl twisted free of the coiffure.

A touch of rice powder where a critical eye might discern the faded bruise, a final touch of jasmine water behind the ears and on her lace handkerchief and she was ready.

Jane was full of admiration at the effect, and more than happy to receive compliments in return for her neat but elegant gown of bronze silk with a braided hem. 'We are very fine,' she commented as the carriage turned into the long drive up to the Hall.

'Indeed we are,' Amanda agreed, her eyes sparkling, her smile rather more brittle than her companion was wont to see it. All that was wrong with her, she had decided, was a lack of society. If she mixed more, met more men at dinner parties or on the dance floor, then she would not be so ridiculously affected when one of them paid her some attention. The disturbing impact of a pair of green eyes, or a length of well-muscled leg, would soon be put in proportion.

In this combative mood Amanda swept up the front steps and smiled brilliantly upon her startled host, who suddenly felt as though a biddable and pretty kitten had turned into a veritable tigress. She shook hands with Mrs Clare and allowed herself to be shown into the long drawing room where she had entertained on many occasions herself.

As she and Jane had speculated, it was indeed full with perhaps twenty couples and she was glad she had dressed for the occasion. One or two of the faces were unfamiliar, although she guessed that no one was there from very far afield from the fact that everyone she could see was engaged in very easy conversation. And there were certainly at least half a dozen men in their twenties and thirties, ideal to begin her resolution to put the memory of Mr Jay firmly into proportion.

A small knot of guests who were partly obstructing the doorway broke up to allow her through and she was immediately greeted by Mrs Maddison. 'Good evening, Mrs Clare. What a very enjoyable gathering, to be sure. May I make my nephew Mr James Williams known to you?'

Mr Williams proved to be amiable, admiring and eager to make conversation. 'Allow me to find you a chair, Mrs Clare. Here, perhaps, away from the crush by the door?'

Amanda let him guide her into the room, refused the chair and set herself to make small talk. The young man soon found himself joined by several others: two were the sons of local landowners, another the junior partner of the leading Holt firm of attorneys.

Somehow Amanda became aware that she was becoming the centre of attention. Why, she did not quite know. Several of the ladies were at least as well gowned as she and there were also a number of handsome women in the room against whom she knew herself to be quite eclipsed in looks. Nor was she talking loudly or making any attempt to draw attention to herself. And yet her mood seemed to communicate itself to those around her, spreading a dangerous edge of excitement.

Then the pattern of groups at the far end of the room shifted and reformed and she found herself looking down the expanse of floor to one man who was standing alone in front of the wide marble fireplace. It seemed to Amanda that the voices in the room fell silent, then the swell of conversation filled her ears again as Jay walked towards her, his eyes fixed on her face.

He paused as a footman passed him with a tray of glasses, lifted two of them and walked on. As he reached her he nodded pleasantly to the young men surrounding her, said, 'Gentlemen,' and they seemed to melt away. Amanda found herself standing alone with him, perforce having to accept the champagne flute he was holding out to her.

'Good evening, Mrs Clare. You are in great beauty tonight.' His eyes lingered like a caress over the smooth curves revealed by the low-cut dress and came to rest on her face.

'Good evening, Mr Jay.' She managed to smile as she said it, but her voice was hard.

Jay's eyebrow lifted and the green eyes lost their habitual look of sleepy amusement. 'You are not pleased to see me? Have I done something to offend you?'

'You can ask me that?' she hissed, then turned and smiled at a passing matron. 'Good evening, Mrs Wilmott, yes indeed, the flower arrangements are quite lovely.'

Jay continued to look politely baffled. 'I really do apologise, Mrs Clare, but you have me at a loss.'

'Saturday!' Amanda snapped. 'Need you ask?'

'Ah!' Oh, provoking man! As if he had not known all along what she was talking about! 'You are angry with me for not stopping to greet you? But I thought we had agreed it would be better if we did not meet.'

'Greet me?' Amanda's voice rose to an unflattering squeak and she hastily lowered it. 'How could you sug-

gest such a thing when you were…you had no…your clothes…'

'Well, naturally, I mean after I had resumed my clothing—' He broke off to move aside for a couple making their way down the room. 'But as you seemed unwilling to acknowledge me, I did wonder if you had failed to recognise me, so I thought it better to leave.'

'Recognise you!' Amanda gasped at the effrontery of the man. 'Of course I recognised you!'

Jay said nothing, but his expression was so wicked that Amanda wanted to slap him. 'I mean…that is, of course I did not recognise you immediately with no clothes…'

He was obviously struggling now with a strong urge to laugh, but Amanda was saved from blundering any further into the morass by the arrival of Mr Bateson, an elderly farmer who took an avuncular interest in his young neighbour and who had apparently caught the tail end of what she had said.

'Mrs Clare, how very lovely you look this evening my dear. And you have found a gentleman willing to discuss clothes with you, have you? Keep a firm hold of him, not many gentlemen will do more than worry about the *bills* for the clothes, now will they, sir? Ha!' He ambled off in search of the footman with the tray, leaving a fulminating Amanda behind him.

'And where did you get that suit of evening clothes, might I ask? Or have you found someone from whom you *are* prepared to borrow money?' The suit was of good quality, but the jacket stretched taut across Jay's shoulders in a way that even the most extreme dandy might consider too tight.

'They were left by a gentleman who did a midnight flit from his accommodation at the Half Moon without paying his shot. He overlooked one portmanteau and Bream has been keeping hold of it to see if the money turns up. The housekeeper took in the trousers, but could do nothing about the shoulders—it would appear that the owner was a portly man of unimpressive physique.'

'You really have no need to angle for compliments about your figure, sir,' Amanda said icily.

'Amanda.' He took her gently by the elbow and steered her closer to the first of the pairs of long windows overlooking the terrace. Without making a scene she could hardly resist, but her arm was stiffly unresponsive under his fingers. 'Amanda, what exactly are you so angry about? I am sorry I gave you a shock on the beach, but although I am more than willing to lay down my life in defence of your safety or your honour, I am damned if I am going to freeze to death to preserve you from a few blushes!'

'Freeze to death?'

'Have you ever swum in that sea at this time of year?'

'No, of course not, this is hardly Brighton!'

'Well, it is damnably cold, I can tell you. I had gone with Bream down to the harbour in Blakeney while he was about some business and on impulse got one of the fisherman to row me over to the Point. I thought a brisk walk would do me good, but I got more than I bargained with on that shingle. It wasn't long before my ankle was hurting like the devil again. I decided a quick plunge would reduce the swelling. I had swum for about five minutes and decided I had better get out again before my blood turned to ice when you appeared.'

'Well, what do you expect?' Amanda demanded, suppressing her anxiety that he had damaged his ankle. 'It is a public beach, after all.'

'As you yourself said, it is hardly Brighton. I think I can be excused for not expecting young ladies to be wandering down it. I thought I could stay where I was until you turned round or passed by, but no, what must you do but sit down virtually on top of my clothes.'

'I wanted to think,' she said indignantly.

'Well, you certainly gave me furiously to think. I could die of cold—and I assure you I was rapidly losing all feeling in my legs—or I could get out, expecting you to modestly avert your gaze while I did so.'

Amanda blushed. 'I was shocked, and then, of course, alarmed.'

'Alarmed? What by? I can assure you, you have nothing to fear in the way of amorous attentions from a man who has been immersed in freezing water for ten minutes!' He was sounding every bit as angry as she was now, and the effort of having to conduct this argument in whispers while maintaining the appearance of normality was helping neither of them stay calm.

'Sir!'

'Oh, really, Amanda! If you had been an innocent débutante I might have been a gentlemanly fool and let myself sink without trace. But you have been a married woman, for goodness' sake! Please do not try and tell me you have never seen a naked man before.'

'I…' Amanda felt the tide of crimson rise up her throat and suffuse her face. 'How dare you?' She looked frantically around, but there was nowhere to hide her blushes without everyone noticing. 'Oh, go *away!*'

With an abrupt bow Jay turned on his heel and took a hasty stride away from her, then, obviously recollecting where he was, began to stroll slowly across the room. She watched just long enough to see him caught up in a conversation with a group of men around Humphrey before turning her burning face towards the windows.

Had anyone noticed? She struggled to take deep, slow breaths, willing the blood to leave her face. After what seemed an age she felt the heat subside, but did not turn when Mr Williams joined her. She could see his reflection in the glass and pretended to be admiring the darkening garden beyond the terrace.

'A very fine view in daylight, I recall,' he remarked. 'May I fetch you another glass of wine, ma'am? Oh, I see you have not finished that one. Would something else be to your taste?'

She could hardly spend the rest of the evening with her back to the room. Taking a deep breath, Amanda turned and smiled at the young man. 'No, but thank you. I shall finish this. It is indeed a fine view. From the terrace you can see down over the lake, which is not large, but does sit very prettily in the landscape.'

The champagne was crisp on her tongue and she sipped it gratefully. Whether it was the effect of undemanding conversation with a pleasant young man, or the wine that calmed her, she did not know, but by the time dinner was announced Amanda was feeling able to face the rest of the evening. Unless, of course, that involved any further contact with Jay.

Unfortunately, he was placed on the opposite side of the long table to herself, although not directly in front of her. With the first remove of dishes she spoke to her right-hand neighbour, a local landowner whom she suspected Humphrey had invited to meet Jay. There were rumours that he might have to sell land to meet the debts of his sons. However, he seemed in a good mood for someone on the verge of bankruptcy, so Amanda put the rumours down to mere speculation and had a pleasant discussion about the success of a locally bred racehorse, the very fine memorial glass window that had been erected in a nearby church and the shocking rise in poaching nationally.

With the second remove she turned, obedient to etiquette, to converse with her left-hand neighbour. This brought her diagonally in line with Jay, who had similarly turned. Conversation was more difficult with this gentleman, a somewhat studious young man who obviously found making small talk with ladies a strain. The effort not to raise her head and meet Jay's eyes was enormous.

Eventually she gave in and flashed a quick glance across the table, but he was apparently engrossed in what his neighbour, a very pretty relative of Mr Bateson, was telling him. She gave a little trill of laughter and he smiled, then looked up so quickly that Amanda was unable to glance away in time.

Their eyes held, but this time the smile stayed in his, not mocking her, but gentle. Amanda managed a small, answering smile and turned back to the young man, her heart beating oddly.

All the ridiculous anger had gone, drained away as suddenly as it had possessed her. Of course it was not Jay's fault that she had come across him on the beach, and he had been perfectly reasonable to expect her to turn away at once, and, in any case, not to be too shocked. How was he to know what a strangely sheltered marriage she had had? She ought to apologise to him, but that would not be easy without telling him more than she felt able to about very private memories.

She glanced across once or twice more during the course of the meal, but did not catch his eye again. Whether he looked at her she did not know, although she felt his presence as strongly as though he were sitting next to her. Finally Mrs Clare got to her feet, gathered the ladies with a glance and led them from the room. Behind them the sound of scraping chairs as the men resumed their seats was cut off by the closing doors.

Several ladies slipped away at once to the bedrooms set aside as retiring rooms and Amanda followed them. She peered anxiously into a mirror and placed a dab or two of rice powder on her cheeks, but the hectic blushes of the evening did not appear to have inflamed her injured face and there was nothing in her appearance to cause comment.

How was it possible to be so filled with churning emotion and yet show nothing of it on the outside? she wondered. Are we all hypocrites, hiding our innermost thoughts, showing only a social mask to the world?

'You are thoughtful, Mrs Clare,' one of the ladies observed.

Amanda forced a light laugh. 'I was just thinking how easily we hide our innermost thoughts behind our social faces. We are all so accomplished at it, are we not?'

'Indeed, yes.' It was the young lady who had sat next to Jay at dinner, engaged now in teasing out the curls which clustered on either side of her face. 'Take Mr Jay, for example. Why, he chatted to me so very pleasantly all through the second remove at dinner and I am sure his mind was quite elsewhere.' She pouted slightly, for she was not a girl used to taking second place in a man's thoughts. 'He is very good looking, is he not, Mrs Clare?'

'I suppose so, I am not really acquainted with him.'

'Are you not?' the older woman enquired, a slight

smile on her lips. 'You found plenty to talk about before dinner.'

Inwardly Amanda winced. So they had been noticed after all. 'We found we did not agree on everything we discussed,' she said with a careless laugh. 'There is nothing like a disagreement to prolong a conversation, is there?'

Conversation amongst the ladies was general and Amanda found relief in sitting quietly and allowing her seniors to carry the weight of it. Jane made her way over and sat beside her.

'Mrs Clare was remarking upon your gown very favourably to me. I think she is beginning to approve of you.'

'Oh, never say so!' Amanda whispered back. 'Her disapproval and opposition are my chief weapons against Humphrey!'

'Have you seen that Mr Jay is here?' Jane enquired with a sideways glance.

'Indeed I have.' Amanda hesitated, but the need to confess her bad behaviour was too strong. 'I have had a quarrel with him,' she admitted.

'A quarrel? Here? What about?'

'Yes, here. And it was really about nothing at all. It was my fault, I behaved very badly.'

'Well, you must find the opportunity to apologise,' Jane said robustly, inwardly smiling to herself. In her experience—admittedly as an onlooker—it was a sure sign of building attraction when a man and a woman quarrelled over nothing. Just so long as she was right about Jay…

The evening was becoming sultry and Mrs Clare senior suggested that the ladies might like to return to the long reception room and have the doors on to the terrace thrown open. 'I believe there are enough married ladies here to chaperon the débutantes if anyone wishes to take a turn outside,' she announced with surprising benevolence.

The reason for this soon became apparent when the gentlemen joined them. Amanda saw Humphrey exchange a pleased smile and nod with his mama when he saw the open windows and he turned from her to scan the room.

Before Amanda could avoid him he was at her side, one slightly damp palm under her elbow. 'Do come out on to the terrace, Cousin,' he urged.

'Of course, how delightful. But only if the others join us,' Amanda responded with a merry laugh. 'I cannot risk my reputation by being seen alone with you!'

Apparently taking this as flirtation, Humphrey preened himself and was soon urging other couples outside.

It was a lovely night. The moon was almost full, the sky spangled with stars and the air still warm enough to be comfortable. But it was not a night to find oneself being steered inexorably towards the steps to the lawn by a persistent and unwelcome suitor. 'You are lovely, you know.' Humphrey was breathing hotly close to her ear. 'Come down here where we can be alone and let me show you how I feel.'

Amanda gave a squeal and pulled her arm free. 'Oh, a bat! A bat! It will get in my hair!' Unbalanced by her movement, Humphrey grasped the balustrade for support, missed and sat down hard, and painfully, on the top step. Amanda slipped silently away and took refuge in the bushes that fringed the terrace, safely out of sight.

But her escape had not gone unnoticed. A dark figure appeared before her, its sleeve brushing the branch, and a wave of scent from the tumbled blossoms washed over her. 'Amanda?'

'Jay!'

They stood for a moment, neither able to see the other's face in the dark, then both spoke at once.

'Jay, I am so sorry, I was completely unreasonable—'

'Amanda, I should never have teased you. And I made assumptions—'

'Go on,' she urged as he broke off.

'Not here, come down these steps, I think your cousin has retired inside to nurse his dignity.'

Amanda allowed herself to be steered down the shallow flight of steps, across the grass and into the little stone temple, which commanded a charming view of the lake. Now the moonlight bathed its columns in light and tipped the little wavelets on the water with sparks of brightness. The scent of jasmine followed them, lingering on the sleeve of Jay's coat as he raised one hand to rest it against the column behind her head.

'Beautiful,' he said. His voice deepened slightly, and he quoted, 'The moon shines bright; in such a night as this, when the sweet wind did gently kiss the trees and they made no noise, in such a night—' He broke off. 'No, I cannot recall the rest.'

Amanda sighed. 'Is it Shakespeare? "Did gently kiss the trees''... That is lovely.'

Jay did not pursue the elusive quotation. After a moment he said, 'Amanda, I am sorry. I teased you when you were upset, which was unforgivable, and I had no intention of shocking you so.'

'No, it was my fault. I reacted—overreacted—so foolishly. I was...upset that we had parted with so much unresolved. I had no right to lose my temper like that, and, I must admit it, I do not know why I did so.'

There was silence. She was very conscious of his arm so close to her bare shoulder, of his warmth, of the scent of his citrus cologne underlying the jasmine. She had only to lean back a little and her skin would touch his sleeve. What would he do if she did that? She made no move except to turn her head a very little, but it was enough.

His voice was husky as he said, 'I am not made of stone, Amanda.'

She was aware suddenly that she was shivering; a fine vibration seemed to posses her body, centring on a deep, swirling ache inside her. Something caressed her shoulder, then she realised it was her own curl, moving as she shivered, disturbing the jasmine scent on her own body, sending it warm and sweet to his nostrils.

Then he moved.

Chapter Eleven

Startled by the swiftness of Jay's movement, Amanda was momentarily confused, then saw that his long stride had taken him across the full width of the little temple to stand facing her across the marble floor.

'I am not made of stone,' he repeated. 'We agreed it would be better not to be together.'

'Yes,' she agreed, uncaring that her voice shook.

'Do you know what I want to do at this moment?' His voice sounded curiously angry.

She shook her head.

'I want to take you in my arms and kiss you until you beg me never to stop. I want to pull that lovely gown from your shoulders and kiss your naked body in the moonlight and then I want to make love to you, here on this marble floor.'

There was silence as he finished speaking. Amanda found she was gripping the column behind her with both hands. The swirling tension inside her made it difficult to hold on to any sense of reality. 'Yes,' she faltered, unsure whether it was a question, a plea or simple agreement.

Jay moved again sharply to turn his back on her. She

saw the ring on his hand flash in the moonlight, transformed from gold to silver by the light, as he hit his clenched fist against the column next to him. 'And I am going to do none of those things because I do not know who I am and I suspect I have hurt you quite enough already—' He broke off, then added, 'I have been dreaming.'

'What do you dream about?' she asked, knowing she dare not do what her senses were screaming at her to do and cross the distance between them.

'I dream the same dream every night,' he said bleakly. 'I dream that I will never discover who I am.'

'I cannot believe that,' she protested. 'You will find out, I promise we will find out.'

'And if we discover I have the wife and children you are in the habit of warning me about?' Something of the old humour was back in his voice, but there was bitterness behind it.

'Then you will be happy to have rediscovered them,' Amanda promised, trying to make herself believe it. 'You will go home and this will be the dream that will fade away like mist in the morning, or the characters at the end of a play.'

'And you?'

'I will be glad for you. Not every play can have a happy ending,' she added, almost to herself. She could not stay there, it was unbearable for her, utterly unfair on him. 'Wait for five minutes, I will go back to the house. Good night, Jay.'

Somehow Amanda found herself back in the reception room, her absence apparently unmarked. Guests were beginning to make their farewells and she cast around for Jane, who suddenly appeared at her side.

'There you are, dear. My goodness, Amanda, you are as white as a sheet!'

'Humphrey attempted to lure me down to the lawns.'

'Then the sooner we leave the better! What an unfortunate experience.' They found themselves almost at the door. 'Oh, goodnight, Mrs Clare, what a delightful evening. Thank you so much for the invitation.'

By the time they had retrieved their wraps, the coach had been called and they were seated, Jane's head was nodding and she soon dropped off to sleep. Amanda was alone with her thoughts for the short distance between the Hall and her home.

The intensity in Jay's voice as he had made that declaration! She felt the shivering begin again at the memory of it. That had been desire: pure, unalloyed, intense physical desire, and she had felt it too. No wonder it could bring down nations, wreck alliances, ruin lives: she had no idea it could be so all consuming.

But it was not love. He had never spoken that word. And without love she could never give way to desire, and, unless he was free, she could not allow the word to be spoken.

That she loved him she was certain now. But who was this man she loved? Someone with no name, no past, no present. And if his dreams told the truth, he was also a man with no future. The carriage pulled up with a jerk as the sleepy driver misjudged the position of the front door, and Jane woke.

'Are we home? We must go straight to bed! What an eventful evening this has been.'

The next morning brought an unexpected note for Amanda, just as she was sitting at her little writing desk penning a few words of thanks to Mrs Clare for the previous evening.

It was from Humphrey's mother herself. 'Look at this, Jane.' Amanda handed her companion the note. 'It has just arrived.'

'How strange. She says there is a matter of some urgency upon which she wishes to consult with you and urges you to call this morning. I would have thought she would be resting after her exertions last night, not sending out notes to solicit calls.'

'I suppose I had better do as she asks,' Amanda said, still puzzling over the note.

'Can you not put it off until tomorrow? You are looking sadly pale, my dear. Did you not sleep well last night?' Jane enquired solicitously.

'Oh, as well as can be expected after last night's excitements,' Amanda said lightly. And as well as one might expect after receiving a passionate declaration from a man who wishes to make violent love to you in the moonlight, she could have added with some justification. 'I will walk over, the fresh air will do me good.'

'Would you like me to come with you?'

'No, please do not disturb yourself, Jane dear. I can tell you are tired too, and I fail to see why both of us should dance to Mrs Clare's bidding. She probably wants to tell me that the recipe I sent by Kate for pickling walnuts is quite incorrect, and she wonders at it that I have been using such an inferior receipt for so long.'

Jane laughed at this and returned to the long letter she was sending to an elderly relative who would enjoy every detail of a party such as the one last night. Amanda changed her slippers for a pair of boots, swung a pelisse around her shoulders and set out briskly for the Hall.

Using the shortcut across the park it did not take her long, and she was soon knocking on the wide front door through which she had once walked in and out by right. It was a strange sensation, which she found took several minutes to subdue on every occasion when she called.

The butler ushered her through to the library, which surprised her, for she had expected Mrs Clare to be receiving in the morning parlour. All was explained, however, when Humphrey got to his feet from the depths of one of the leather wing-chairs.

'My dear Amanda—' he began.

'I do beg your pardon,' Amanda cut in. 'I must have failed to make myself clear to Peters. I have called to see Mrs Clare, she sent me a note this morning.'

'No, there has been no mistake.' Humphrey was looking inordinately pleased with himself. 'Mama wrote the note, but at my request. I knew you might feel a slight reserve at calling on a gentleman, yet I felt we could be uninterrupted here.'

'Indeed, I do feel such a reserve,' Amanda said firmly. 'I have no chaperon with me.'

'Mama and the housekeeper are both about somewhere,' Humphrey assured her.

'Then let us call one of them.'

'No, no!' Humphrey had moved surprisingly quickly and before she knew what he was about he was beside her, one arm hovering at her back, urging her towards a chair. 'After all, what need of a chaperon do you have in your own cousin's house?'

Common civility prevented her from making the honest answer and Amanda allowed herself to be seated. 'In what way can I assist you, Cousin?' she enquired coolly. 'Miss Porter is not feeling quite well this morning, and I really do not want to leave her too long.'

'Too much champagne, eh?' Humphrey chortled. 'You indulge a paid dependent too much, my dear.'

'Miss Porter is a dear and loyal friend,' Amanda replied repressively. She did wish he would sit down and not lurk about just behind her chair. The high back and enveloping wings restricted her view and made her feel quite trapped.

Suddenly he was beside her, clumsily falling to one knee and catching her right hand in both of his. 'Amanda! My darling!'

'Mr Clare!'

'Call me Humphrey, I beseech you.' His plump cheeks were shiny with emotion. Amanda wriggled back into the chair, but it only made her feel more confined.

'Please, sir, this excessive display of feeling…'

'It comes from my heart, beloved!' What on earth had he been reading? Ignoring her shocked expression and efforts to free her hand, Humphrey ploughed on with what was obviously a prepared speech. 'For many months my admiration for your many fine characteristics has been growing to the point where I cannot hide from you any longer my ardent desire to make you my wife.'

'But, Mr Clare, I know you have often disapproved of my actions and beliefs. How can you think that I would make a conformable wife to you?' Amanda had a sinking feeling that appealing to reason was not going to work, but she had to try.

'Once we are married, I know that these odd starts, these little acts of feminine rebellion, will cease. You need firm guidance, the protection of a virile and energetic husband. You nobly supported my ailing and elderly cousin, now take your reward for faithful duty!'

'Charles was not elderly and I did my best to be a good wife to him because I most truly loved and valued him!' Amanda flashed back. 'My reward, if indeed I deserved one, was in his love and companionship.'

Humphrey gave a little shudder of what appeared to be excitement. 'Oh, your spirit! How I long to subdue that, teach you to love and obey me!'

Amanda felt queasy. Her hand was beginning to hurt in his grip. Against her instincts she tried wheedling. 'Please, Humphrey,' she whispered, 'you are hurting my wrist.'

'Fragile flower!' He released her wrist only to grip her hand and begin to shower kisses upon it. His mouth was wet and the touch of it on her shrinking skin disgusting. Her struggles only seemed to inflame him more and before she knew what was happening he had pressed her back in the chair and was trying to kiss her mouth.

Once, early on in their courtship, Charles had rescued her from the amorous advances of some buck who had caught her alone in a theatre box while the rest of the company was temporarily absent. Having hit the gentleman neatly on the point of the chin, he had shut the door of the box and proceeded to show Amanda exactly how to best apply her knee should she ever find herself in such a fix again.

She had never required the lesson before, but now, with a mental whisper of thanks to Charles, Amanda used her knee as he had told her. The effect was miraculous. Humphrey went red, staggered back clutching his groin and began whooping for breath.

Amanda did not stop to see how much damage she

had done. She was out of the chair, through the door
and into the hall in a moment, considerably startling the
butler. She paused in front of the cheval glass and adjusted her bonnet. 'Good day, Peters, thank you.' She
hesitated on the threshold. 'I do not think Mr Clare
wishes to be disturbed for a while. He is thinking something over.'

The butler bowed and shut the door. Amanda suppressed a desire to sit down on the front step and give
way to strong hysterics, but instead walked across the
gravel sweep, down the sloping lawn and towards the
point where the river opened into the lake. She could
follow the path to the weir, cross on the footbridge and
cut back to Upper Glaven House from there. It would
give her a chance to compose herself before recounting
the experience to Jane. Just at the moment she doubted
if she could articulate a single coherent word.

Two declarations in the space of a few hours. But
what a difference in them. One of passion and desire,
the other soliciting marriage. But it was the latter that
filled her with disgust. Her hand felt damp from Humphrey's grasp and his kisses. Her wrist hurt too, perhaps
enough for there to be a bruise tomorrow. She would
bathe it in the river where it pooled at the weir.

The tranquil river began to gurgle and eddy as she
walked upstream towards the weir. Just before it there
was a crescent cut in the bank where the grass sloped
to a little beach. She crouched there and rinsed her hand
in the cool water, dipped her handkerchief and wrapped
it around her wrist. That was not a bruise she wished
to explain to anyone.

Amanda walked on, around the bend to the weir, and
realised she was not alone. It was a good fishing spot,
Charles had told her, and guests at the Hall often took

a rod and line there. The man sitting with his back against the bank, legs stretched out, and the rod propped on a rest beside him, did not appear to be a keen angler, however, more someone enjoying a sleep in the sunshine.

He was not asleep. As she stopped he opened his eyes and regarded her steadily. 'Hello, Amanda.'

'Hello, Jay. I did not look to see you here. No, please do not get up.'

He sank back on to the turf. 'Your cousin pressed me to try my luck with his fish. It seemed a relaxing thing to do.'

'Have you caught anything?' She sat down too, perhaps four feet away from him.

'No, I have not even baited the hook.' His eyes scanned her face. 'Amanda, last night…'

'Last night the moon was full and the air was full of dreams. I am sure that whatever happened and whatever was said were simply part of those dreams.'

'Do you believe dreams come true?'

'Some of them. Others do not. We must wait and see, and perhaps not stand in the moonlight exchanging dreams. Sometimes the morning brings too much reality.' Her voice must have shaken, for Jay twisted to look sharply at her.

'What has happened? You are too pale—and your wrist…have you hurt it?'

She had thought that she was coping quite well with the shock of Humphrey's proposal, but the warmth in Jay's voice quite overset her and she gave an abrupt sob, stifling it with her hand.

'Amanda!' He was on his knees beside her, reaching for her, but she held him off with her bandaged hand. 'What has happened? Let me look.'

He unwrapped the wet handkerchief with gentle fingers, peeling it back to reveal the reddening marks of a male grip imprinted around the narrow wrist, overlaying the fragile bones.

'Who did this to you?' His voice was coldly angry.

'Humphrey. Just now, he was proposing.'

'Proposing! By breaking your wrist?' Jay got to his feet. 'Wait here, I will not be long.'

'Where are you going?'

Jay looked down at her. 'To find Humphrey Clare and break his jaw for him. That should prevent him making any further proposals—of any kind.'

'No! Please, Jay, please do not.'

'He has insulted you, he has hurt you. Someone must call him to account for it.'

'Jay, I do not want you to do this. He will not try again, believe me. I cannot afford a scandal and if you and he fight there will be certain to be talk.'

'I have no intention of fighting with him. I have every intention of beating him within an inch of his life.'

'If you go, I will cry,' Amanda stated flatly.

'Do you expect that to stop me?' There was a faint edge of amusement in his voice.

'No,' she admitted honestly. 'But I thought it worth a try. Please, Jay, I promise he has not got away scot free.'

He dropped back to the grass beside her. 'What did you do to him?'

'Charles showed me how to deal with that sort of advance. By using my knee.'

Jay gave a shout of laughter. 'You kneed him in the groin?'

'Yes. It worked very well. He went red and whooped. A bit like a turkey.'

Jay was almost helpless with laughter now. 'I wish I had seen it,' he managed to gasp.

'Would it have hurt a lot?' Amanda was ashamed to find she hoped very much that it would.

'I think you may be certain you could have done nothing more painful to him,' Jay said, dragging a pocket handkerchief out and mopping his eyes with it. 'A man is very vulnerable in the, er…groin area.'

'Good.'

'Can you bear to tell me what happened? It might help.'

Amanda found it did indeed help to recount the entire episode, from the letter from Mrs Clare to the butler's impassive expression as he had let her out.

'The man's a fool,' Jay observed dispassionately. 'Of all the insane ways to propose, pinning you in a chair and slobbering all over you.'

'He did slobber too,' Amanda recalled with a shudder. 'All up my arm.'

Jay gently took her bruised hand in his. 'Now that was very ill advised of him. When kissing a lady's hand, the last thing one wants to do is to kiss it.'

'What do you mean? That does not make sense.'

'Like this.' Jay lifted her hand to his lips and gave it the merest touch with his lips. The sensation was intense, delicate, yet sent shivers up her arm. 'But one does not want to let go at that point: the fingers can achieve so much more than the lips in this situation.'

Mesmerised, Amanda felt his fingertips gently caressing the inside of her wrist, so lightly that the bruises did not hurt, so sensitively that she felt as though every nerve was exposed to his touch. 'And then, of course, there is the thumb.' The ball of his thumb began to move insidiously against the swell at the base of hers. Amanda felt a little moan escape her lips.

'You see, there is absolutely no need to slobber all over a lady at all.' He leaned down the bank and rinsed out her handkerchief, wrung it out and bound it gently around her wrist again. 'There.'

'Thank you,' Amanda said shakily, clasping both hands firmly in her lap. 'You promise you will not do anything to Humphrey?'

'I promise.' He leaned back, his eyes on the stream as it chuckled and swirled its way towards the lake. 'Tell me something.'

'Yes?'

'What is Coke's Clippings?'

Of all the questions Amanda might have expected, this was the last. 'Coke's Clippings? Why on earth do you want to know about that?'

'Someone mentioned it last night and it was suddenly very familiar—and important. I could hardly expose my ignorance by asking anyone there.'

'It is the name given to the gatherings that Mr Coke holds every year at Holkham during the shearing. You know he inherited the estate from a relative when he was a young man? No? Well, he knew nothing about agriculture, but he saw that so much needed to be done, if only he knew how to go about it. So he began asking knowledgeable men to visit him at the shearings, and gradually it grew and grew into one of the great events in the countryside.' Amanda's admiration for her famous neighbour showed in the pride in her voice.

'People come from all over the world—America, Russia even. He holds open house for many guests and feeds all who come. From being a young, ignorant man he has become the expert and people come to sit at his feet and learn. It is a social event as well, with country people, yeomen, tradesmen as well as the aristocrats and landowners all meeting and exchanging ideas. Mr Coke is a very great man.'

'Indeed, he sounds it. Do you attend?'

'Yes, every year. At first I went with Charles and we used to stay at Holkham Hall. Now I go for one day only, but I would not miss it for the world. It is next week: will you come with me?'

Jay looked thoughtful. 'Yes, I will. I have no idea why it should stir the slightest memory for me, but something tells me that the answer to this puzzle of my presence here lies at Holkham.'

Chapter Twelve

'The first day of the gathering is Wednesday next week,' Amanda said, reluctantly standing up and brushing off her skirts. 'Just look at the state of this dress!'

Jay, who had got easily to his feet and was holding out a hand in case she still felt shaky, laughed. 'Hardly surprising! First crushed by Humphrey's not inconsiderable weight and then sat on amongst the damp grass of the river bank. No,' he reassured her as she twisted round to look at the back of her skirts, 'no grass stains. Would you like me to drive you to Holkham on Wednesday?'

'Thank you, but no, I will drive Jane and myself in the phaeton with a groom up behind. It is what I normally do and any change from that might cause comment. But I would be very glad of your escort if you can prevail upon Will Bream to lend you something better than that slug he has been mounting you on. I know he has a very nice young hunter in his stables that he refuses to let me ride.'

Jay grinned at her. 'And why not, might I ask?'

'He says it is too big, too strong and not a lady's

mount. He is hoping to bring it on this year and sell it next hunting season for a good profit.'

'And if I borrow it you hope to wheedle me into letting you ride it at some point in the journey?'

'Certainly not! The thought had not crossed my mind,' Amanda said indignantly. 'I just thought it would suit you very well. It is a thought, though... I am sure my saddle would fit in the phaeton—'

'No! If Will Bream says it is too strong for you, that is the end of the matter. That man's judgement is uncommonly sound.'

Amanda wrinkled her nose. 'He is too protective of me. He was devoted to Charles, you see.'

'From what I can see, you need all the protection you can get,' Jay said grimly.

'Surrounded with rakes as I am?' Amanda teased, skipping neatly onto the plank bridge across the weir. 'We will meet you at the crossroads at eight of the clock on Wednesday morning. Will will show you where.'

'Until Wednesday, then,' Jay raised a hand in farewell. 'Unless you need me. Send at once if Mr Clare gives you the slightest annoyance; you have no idea how I long to have an excuse to break my promise to you and hit him from here to perdition.'

Amanda's sunny mood lasted just as far as the garden gate, then reaction set in. She had enjoyed telling Jay how she had bested Humphrey, had loved being there on the riverbank with him. The memory of his caress still tingled in her palm.

Now the nausea that Humphrey had evoked returned, along with the nagging worry of how she was to maintain some sort of relationship with the Hall when she no longer trusted him to be in the same room with her.

To make a break with the Clares would cause a scandal all around the district.

And Jay's conviction that the Clippings held a clue had sounded so optimistic that she had not thought through what it might mean. On dragging feet she wandered round, through the shrubbery and sat in the summerhouse, one hand cupping her chin.

Jay could be wrong and they would find no help there. Or he would discover who he was and what he was doing in Norfolk—and find that he was married or affianced. Or, having recovered the knowledge of his true identity, he might not be the same person as he appeared now and his feelings for her would be different too.

Whatever those feelings were. He desired her, that was very apparent. But did he love her? Was he simply not saying those words in case he proved not to be free—or because that was not what he felt?

From being full of optimism, Amanda gloomily concluded that the odds against this whole adventure having a happy ending were stacked high against her. She tried telling herself firmly that if Jay was restored to his rightful place, whether or not that included a wife, that must be a happy ending, but this very proper reflection did not provide the comfort it should do.

'Amanda! Mrs Clare!' It was Jane calling. Amanda called back and after a moment Miss Porter peeped around the side of the tree. 'Did you want to be alone, dear? Only I saw you come in the gate and you looked so serious I was quite worried. Is anything amiss at the Hall?'

'Come and sit down, Jane.' Amanda patted the bench beside her. 'I need to tell you what has occurred and it is better out here: I would not have the servants hear for anything.'

Jane listened wide-eyed to the tale of Humphrey's declaration, the tip of her nose growing pinker and pinker as her indignation rose. 'And your wrist!' She unwrapped the handkerchief and tutted in dismay at the sight of the marks on Amanda's arm. 'The brute! Oh, for a man to call him to account!'

'I have just spent some time making Jay promise he would do no such thing,' Amanda admitted. 'I came across him fishing down at the weir, and he could see I was upset. Foolishly I blurted it out.'

'And you managed to stop him taking any action?' Miss Porter sounded sceptical. 'Mark my words, he will have gone up there the moment your back was turned.'

'He promised me,' Amanda assured her. 'I told him what a scandal it would cause. Oh, Jane, what are we to do if Humphrey calls? Or Mrs Clare invites me to the Hall? It would cause such talk if I stop going there or receiving them. And we meet so often—in church every week, in other people's houses...' Her voice trailed off.

Miss Porter looked thoughtful. 'You go nowhere you might meet him alone. Kate or I will always go with you. If he calls, I will sit with you. When we meet them, we will speak with perfect cordiality, but without the slightest note of encouragement.'

'It sounds very unpleasant,' Amanda said drearily. 'I have never liked them, but I do so hate being on cool terms with anyone.'

'It may not be for long,' said Miss Porter, then looked extremely confused.

'Whatever can you mean, Jane?'

'Oh…er…they may go up to town, or visit relatives. Or you may go to town.'

Amanda regarded her quizzically. What on earth was causing poor Jane such embarrassment? Possibly she had been too frank in describing Humphrey's assault. She changed the subject.

'Jay heard someone talking of the Clippings last night and has a strong conviction that if he goes there he may solve this puzzle of who he is and what he is doing adrift in the countryside.'

'How strange. Is he certain?'

'How can he be? But it seems so improbable that it may be true—it is not the sort of thing you imagine. Anyway, I have suggested he escort us on Wednesday and we will see what results.'

The rest of the week passed uneventfully. There was an ominous silence from the Hall and silence also from Jay, although one of Amanda's grooms reported seeing 'that fine new hunter of Will Bream's' being exercised on the heath by the mysterious gentleman from the Half Moon. 'He can't half ride, ma'am,' the man added. 'That's a fierce strong beast, but he don't mess about with that gentleman up.'

By Sunday Amanda was able to remove the broad velvet band she had been wearing around her bruised wrist and the ladies set off for church in a spirit of considerable apprehension.

Miss Porter was filled with a mixture of nervous indignation, a fear of there being a scene on sacred ground on the Sabbath and a fixed resolve to preserve Amanda from the disgusting clutches of Mr Clare at whatever cost to herself.

Amanda, while sharing her concerns about encountering Humphrey in full view of the local congregation, was finding that with every day that passed the cold, tight knot of uncertainty in her stomach got worse and worse. She went over and over in her mind the various outcomes from their visit to the Clippings and the more she thought, the more fearful she became. If only she knew the worst, somehow that would be better than this awful uncertainty.

They arrived before the party from the Hall and reached the safety of their high-walled pew with relief. Amanda sank to her knees and tried to compose her mind but she found all that filled her thoughts was the image of Jay. She was so shocked and horrified at herself that she pushed the hassock aside, and knelt on the cold, hard stone until she could achieve a coherent frame of mind and offer up penitent and reverent prayers. Still shaken, she sat and read some of the more severe Old Testament prophets until the wheezing of the organ bellows and the first notes brought the congregation to their feet.

The Clares had entered and taken their places unseen by her, which was a blessing, but in her present frame of mind she found herself wondering if she should not approach Humphrey afterwards and make some offer of reconciliation.

Further reflection decided her that to risk a scene in the churchyard would defeat the whole purpose of such an approach. Instead she must act as if nothing had happened and receive what friendly overtures might be offered.

It was a subdued Amanda who emerged into the sunshine after service and although her heart sank at the sight of Mrs Clare senior beckoning her towards where

she sat in her barouche, she obediently walked over. Of
Humphrey there was no sign.

'Good morning, ma'am.'

'Good morning, Amanda. Please be so good as to
step into the carriage. Wilkins! Get down from the box
and go to their heads, I wish to speak to Mrs Clare.'
She waited while Amanda sat opposite, then fixed her
with a quelling stare. 'I suppose you think you know
what you are about, trifling with my son's affections in
this callous manner?'

'Trifling, ma'am? I protest, I have done no such
thing. I found myself unable to return Cousin Humphrey's sentiments and told him so. To have led him to
believe I felt anything else would indeed have been trifling.'

'And all the encouragement you have been giving
him these last months?'

'Encouragement?' Amanda's voice rose and she hastily lowered it. 'I have done no more than act in a neigh-
bourly way and as I hope I should to my late husband's
kinsman.'

'So you say now.' Mrs Clare regarded her through
narrowed eyes. 'Something has occurred. You have decided you have fatter fish to land and have cast aside
my worthy son in the process. Well, at least he has had
his eyes opened. I can only trust for the sake of this
family's reputation that whatever you are about now
will not cause a scandal. Good day, Amanda.'

Amanda was so angry she could not reply, simply
bowing abruptly to the older woman and jumping down
from the barouche without waiting for the groom to
hurry to the door. Would that spiteful creature start
spreading gossip about her? Had she realised the attachment she felt towards Jay, or observed them at her

party? Would she find herself stigmatised as the sort of fast young widow she had teased Jay about and be cut by those worthy neighbours whose good opinion mattered to her?

All the way up the hill Amanda struggled with her anger. If she could forgive Mrs Clare, would that not go some way to mitigating her wandering thoughts in church? It would at least be good discipline. By the time she reached home and Jane asked her what had transpired, she was able to reply moderately.

'She reproached me for refusing Cousin Humphrey. She feels I have given him unwarranted encouragement. I can understand her anger: she is ambitious for him and my land would be a considerable benefit to him.'

Monday brought a note from Jay. *I have identified our meeting place and will be there at 8. Do* not *bring a saddle—under no circumstances are you riding this horse. J.*

That produced the first gurgle of laughter from Amanda that Jane had heard for almost a week and she nodded to herself with a little smile, which soon vanished when she thought of all the things which could go wrong with the plans she fondly imagined for her friend.

The house was all of a bustle from early on Wednesday morning. The phaeton was loaded with rugs and a picnic hamper in case of a change in the weather or a delay on the road. Indoor shoes were slipped in bags under the seats in case Mr Coke should come across them and invite them into the house to eat, Amanda brought her most frivolous new parasol and Miss Porter her largest umbrella.

At last Ned swung up on to his perch at the back, Miss Porter settled her rug around her knees, Amanda took up the whip in one hand and gathered the reins into her hand, tightly gloved in York tan leather. 'Let go their heads,' she called and the pair, tossing their manes, trotted smartly out of the yard.

'They are very fresh this morning,' Miss Porter commented, holding rather more tightly onto the edge of her seat than usual.

'I have had them inside for three days on double rations of oats,' Amanda admitted as the horses shied skittishly at a milestone.

'Why ever did you do that?' her companion demanded. 'You will be exhausted at the end of the journey if they continue to behave like this.'

'Jay does not believe I can handle a difficult horse. I intend to show him I can manage two. I only wish this were a high-perch phaeton.'

Jane cast up her eyes, but refrained from comment. After a brisk mile during which the pair fought every inch of the way to get the bit between their teeth and Amanda fought just as determinedly to get them to keep to a trot, the crossroads came in sight with a lone rider waiting beside the milepost.

Jay rode forwards, touching his whip to his hat brim. He looked the pair over as Amanda brought them to a halt and remarked, 'Good morning, Miss Porter. Have you been feeding these beasts double oats, Mrs Clare?'

Amanda chose to ignore the question. 'Good morning, Mr Jay. I hope you have not been kept waiting?'

'Indeed, no, you are commendably prompt.' He wheeled the big bay horse and fell in beside the carriage, his eyes on Amanda's hands on the reins. After ⌐ few minutes he let his attention relax, but she was very much aware of the scrutiny. It appeared she had passed muster.

In her turn she glanced at his mount. 'That is a well set-up animal of Will's.'

'Yes,' Jay agreed. 'It is up to my weight and more. I may well make him an offer.' He saw the question in Amanda's eyes and added, 'If things work out.'

There was not much she could add, with a groom standing behind and well within earshot. Amanda let the greys lengthen their stride a little and once she was confident they had steadied, cast a surreptitious glance at Jay riding alongside the phaeton.

He seemed in his element astride the big bay. Amanda was conscious of long legs gripping the saddle above boots polished to a high gloss. His riding coat sat well on broad shoulders and the laundry maid at the Half Moon had produced linen that shone in the sunshine. He was riding one-handed, the other, holding the crop, resting lightly on his thigh. The horse moved beautifully, with a long, even gait, but Amanda was not deceived by its apparent docility: its ears flicked continuously and the one eye she could see rolled back and forth as it assessed its chances of getting away from the man who was mastering it with such confidence.

They rode on in silence for a while, passing through the little coastal villages and skirting the coastal marshes that ran between each settlement. At last the road opened out with not so much as a packhorse in sight and Amanda called challengingly, 'Would you care for a race?'

Jay did not hesitate, but drew the bay onto the wide grass verge and said, 'To that bend? Very well, at your mark, Miss Porter!'

'Oh, dear!' Miss Porter gripped the seat with one hand and her hat with the other. 'Very well... Go!'

Amanda sprang the pair, who gathered their hind legs under them and took off at a gallop. There was a whoop of exhilaration from the groom, clinging on for dear life behind, and the sound of hooves on grass as the hunter got into its stride.

Not daring to turn her head and see where Jay was, Amanda gasped, 'Do we have a lead, Jane?'

'Yes... No!'

The bay swept up level with them, then gradually lengthened its stride until it was neck and neck with the pair. Jay glanced round: his teeth white, then he leaned over the horse's neck and urged it forward. But the pair were into their stride now, full of fidgets and over-excited by the presence of the big horse. They re-sponded to Amanda's voice and she found she was laughing out loud with the excitement as they gained ground.

The bend was nearing. Jay was going to win, as she expected, the pair with a full carriage behind them were no match for the hunter, but she had acquitted herself well, she felt. At that moment a farm cart began to back out from a concealed gateway in front of Jay. He shouted, but the carter was apparently oblivious.

Amanda tried to judge the distance. Could she pull up in time?

Even as she thought it, Jay yelled, 'Whip them up!'

Jane gave a little shriek, the groom could be heard uttering a string of blasphemies, but Amanda under-stood him at once. For the first time she laid the whip across the horses' backs and they hurtled towards the gap. Then they were past in a swirl of dust and

at the edge of her vision she saw the hunter leap the
cart in a powerful arc, Jay poised low over its neck.

Amanda pulled up, the horses coming to a stand in a
snorting, head-tossing slide. Jay reined in beside her as
behind them the cart rumbled out on to the road.

'You win, Mrs Clare,' he said, one hand gentling the
sidling horse. 'That was fine driving.'

Jane glanced from one to the other of them and saw
the look that passed between them. She let her breath
out in a gasp, then hastily straightened her bonnet. Miss
Porter considered herself immune from the tenderer passions, but that shared, intimate glance made her feel
both hot and cold all at once.

Amanda simply smiled, shaking her head. 'No, you
would have won easily if it were not for that prodigious
jump.' She twisted in the seat, 'Are you all right Ned?'

'Bloody h— I mean, yes, thank you, ma'am.' The
groom gingerly unclenched his hands from the rail. Jay
turned the hunter and walked it back towards the carter
who was standing, cart and horse still across the road,
regarding them with some astonishment. Amanda saw
a coin change hands. 'Cor, ma'am,' the groom continued, 'that Mr Jay can't half ride. The width of that cart
in one jump, didn't even bank it! Must have thigh muscles like iron.'

'Er, yes.' Amanda, trying not to think about that,
turned back and patted her hair into place.

The rest of the journey proved uneventful, although
the closer they got to Holkham, the denser the traffic of
carriages and riders became. Amanda broke off several
times to wave to acquaintances and was aware of Jay,
eyes shaded under the brim of his hat, scanning faces
as they passed.

Amanda, knowing the routine of old, joined the

queue of carriages approaching the stables and pad-
docks where the visiting horses would be accommo-
dated for the duration of their owners' visits. Once they
were fairly close to the Hall she reined in and called to
the groom, 'Can you take them now please, Ned?'

Jay swung down out the saddle and handed down first
Miss Porter and then Amanda. The groom hesitated.
'Shall I take your horse in, sir?'

'No, better not, he is more than inclined to take liberties in strange hands, I will walk him up. Where may
I meet you, Mrs Clare?'

Amanda handed her whip up to Ned, then turned to
scan the parkland, which stretched before them from the
Hall down to the lake. 'I want to start at the shearing
pens, if that is agreeable to you. Miss Porter and I will
go into the Hall to sign our names in the book—you
had better not add a forgery! Shall we meet at that grove
of oaks just there?' She pointed to a knot of evergreen
holm oaks halfway between the house and the shearing
pens. 'It would be easy to miss each other if we go
separately into that crowd.'

Jay agreed, and strode off after the phaeton, the
hunter following behind and shying at every passing
creature. Amanda heard Jay's voice. 'Come on, you
fool. Have you never seen a sheep before?'

'Well!' Miss Porter commented as they walked up to
the Hall. 'That was a very exciting race. How very well
Mr Jay rides: one would go so far as to say he looks
magnificent on a horse.'

'Indeed.' For once the image of Jay thus conjured up
did not hold Amanda's attention. 'Jane, do you feel we
re being watched? I have the nastiest prickling between
shoulder blades.'

course we are being watched! Well, at least you

are because you look so fine, my dear, and we have many acquaintances who will be looking at us, I am sure.' They reached the doors and were ushered in to sign the visitors' book and to seek out the retiring rooms set aside for the ladies.

Jane was just brushing out the dust from her hem when a tall woman came up and greeted her warmly. 'Miss Porter! How glad I am to have come upon you. Mr Coke has been making some improvements to the garden and has invited some interested ladies to walk round with the head gardener. Will you not join us?'

'Lady Grahame.' Miss Porter and Amanda curtsied slightly.

'Good morning, Mrs Clare, I did not see you there. Will you join us?'

'I thank you, Lady Grahame, but I must decline: I am expected at the shearing pens directly. No, Jane,' she added as she saw Miss Porter was about to make her own excuses and insist on escorting her. 'You go with Lady Grahame, it sounds too interesting an invitation to resist. I shall be quite all right—as always, Mr Coke's outdoor staff will be all over the grounds to keep an eye open for undesirables.'

Emerging into the sunshine at the top of the steps, Amanda unfurled her new parasol and scanned the scene before her. The greatest activity at the moment was at the shearing pens, but groups of men were gathered around various wagons, temporary pens set up all over the grass or pieces of agricultural machinery, which were drawn up in lines.

Ladies strolled amongst them and the occasional knot of children, laughing in excitement, tumbled past. Over to one side a piece of turf had been roped off and

Amanda guessed that Mr Coke's Eleven would be challenging a scratch team of farmers that afternoon.

There was no sign of Jay, so she walked down the steps and began to make her way towards the grove of trees. It looked pleasantly shady, but so far the day had not become so hot that anyone was seeking out its cover and it was slightly set aside from the main route down to the pens. Amanda stopped once or twice to shake hands with old friends and to be introduced to new acquaintances. It was comfortable, happy throng and she could find no reason for the sense of unease that gripped her again. She gave herself a determined little shake: of course no one was following her, it was just the apprehension she had been feeling all week about the outcome of this day.

The grove when she reached it was empty: the queue at the stableyard must be worse than usual, she decided, strolling across the grassy area ringed by the trees and the scrubby underbrush, which often concealed deer. Now it was uncannily silent and deserted. As she thought it a pigeon erupted in panic from the boughs above her, making her jump and a twig snapped on the grass behind.

'Jay!' Amanda turned thankfully, then froze, for the man making his way across the clearing towards her was not Jay.

Chapter Thirteen

'Cousin Humphrey! What are you doing here?' So that was why she had been experiencing such an unpleasant sensation of being spied upon ever since she had arrived. More annoyed than alarmed, for, after all, they were surrounded by people, even if they were out of sight, Amanda allowed him to walk up to her. It was better that they had this confrontation here—she had no desire, if she had to speak to him at all, to risk a scene where everyone could see them.

'I have as much right to be here as you,' Humphrey observed in a knowing tone, which set her teeth on edge. 'There is no need for me to enquire what you are doing, is there? And it isn't taking an interest in agriculture. I saw you arrive with that Jay fellow.'

'I thought you admired Mr Jay,' Amanda observed coldly.

'Nothing wrong with him, whatever his real name is, but I know a rake when I see one, and I can guess what you are about with him, madam! And it isn't selling him land,' he added with a coarse chuckle.

'How dare you—' Amanda began, but Humphrey was ploughing on.

'You turn down an honourable proposal from a respectable man to go flaunting yourself about with a London buck…'

'Honourable proposal! It was no such thing. You tricked me into calling, you mauled me, insulted me, insulted Charles's memory…'

'And it isn't an insult to his memory for you to be carrying on with that man when you are hardly out of mourning?' Humphrey's face was red with fury and through her own gathering anger Amanda realised that the wound to his pride of her refusal was made even more painful by his suspicion that she preferred the superior attractions of the mysterious stranger.

'I am not "hardly out of mourning",' she protested, 'and I am not "carrying on".' At this point her own innate honesty made her realise that in the eyes of most members of polite society that was exactly what she was doing, and she blushed scarlet.

Humphrey saw the betraying colour and closed in. 'You see! You cannot deny your shameful conduct. Well, madam, if you can give it to him, you can damn well give it to me too,' and with that he seized her in a bear hug and pushed her back against the nearest tree.

Amanda was momentarily made breathless by both the crudity of his words and the violence of the attack. Then she tried to push him off while simultaneously straining to raise her knee or kick him. But Humphrey had learned from their previous encounter and he was giving her no room to hit back.

With space, and the advantage of surprise, she had 'ended herself easily; now Amanda found herself 'ed by his weight and was utterly powerless. At Hall she had never feared more than embarand his unpleasant kisses, but now she was becoming seriously frightened that he meant far, far, worse. All fear of attracting attention was long gone: the appearance on the scene of a dozen sturdy yeoman was what she prayed for and she opened her mouth to scream, only to have it closed by Humphrey with his own.

It was the most disgusting experience she had ever had. His mouth was wet and loose and he was trying to force her lips open with his tongue while one hand pushed off her bonnet and the other groped at her clothing. Amanda shut her lips tightly and tried to twist her head away, but to no avail and she was becoming terrifying aware than he was bearing her downwards towards the grass.

Then suddenly he was gone from her. Amanda staggered back and clutched the tree behind her for support. By the time her head had cleared, Humphrey was flat on his back two yards away, his hands to his face and blood trickling from between his fingers.

'Jay! Oh, Jay!' Amanda hurled herself into the arms of her rescuer and clung to him. It felt so good to be held like this. The smell of clean linen, the scent of him, the heat of anger that was rising from his body all made her feel utterly safe. He held her tightly to him, his face buried in her hair until at last she relaxed enough to loosen her grip.

He tipped up her face gently. 'Amanda, darling, what did he do to you? Are you hurt?'

She shook her head, bending it to avoid looking into his eyes, so dark with anger that they looked more black than green. 'No... He grabbed me and pushed me against the tree and he kissed me.'

'I told you I should have dealt with him on the last

occasion. When you feel a little better I will take you up to the house and then I will come back here and—'

'No, Jay.' Amanda clung to his arm, still too shamed by the recollection of Humphrey's words to look up at him. 'He was angry because he said I was flaunting myself with you. He accused us of...of...' The crude words failed her. The sound of a faint snarl was all the response she got, so she faltered, 'If you fight him he will spread it all over the neighbourhood. Oh, Jay, I know I have behaved imprudently, but I could not bear it if I lost my reputation.'

There was a silence, then Jay said, 'I see. What do you want me to do with him?'

'No...nothing. He has been humiliated, surely he will do nothing—oh, Jay, look out!'

Over his shoulder she saw Humphrey, blood-streaked face contorted into rage, stumbling towards them a broken branch in his hand.

Jay swung round, pushing Amanda behind him as he did so and flinging up one hand to catch at the branch. But he was off-balance, hampered by the woman so close behind him and he missed, only succeeding in deflecting it from hitting him in the face. Instead, it caught him a glancing blow on the side of the head, which sent him reeling.

Amanda could not see his face, but Humphrey could and whatever he saw there turned his own frustrated anger into quivering terror. He turned to run, was caught by one shoulder, spun around and hit squarely on the jaw with the full force of Jay's right fist. Amanda would not have believed that a man of his weight could be sent flying through the air if she had not just seen it. Humphrey landed with a thud on the turf, lay motionless, then with a whimper began to scrabble feebly away on hands and knees.

But he was safe from pursuit. Jay staggered, clutched his head in both hands and sank to his knees. Amanda knelt beside him, one arm around his shoulders, trying to search through the thick hair on the side of his head for a wound.

'Jay! Jay, speak to me! Where are you hurt?'

He shook his head, winced, then sat back on his heels staring at her. She saw his eyes were open, the pupils wide and black and his expression unfocused as it had been when he had lost his temper over Charles's portrait.

Terrified that Humphrey's blow had done real damage, Amanda did not know whether to stay with him or run for help. Then the unfocussed gaze sharpened and he said, 'Amanda?'

'Yes, yes. Keep still. Can you sit back against this tree while I go for some help?'

'Amanda.' It was a statement. His hand closed around her wrist, preventing her from getting to her feet. He paused, then said, 'And we are at Holkham? At the Clippings?'

'Yes, but do not try and think! You need to rest.'

'It is all right. The bast—sorry, the wretch, must have caught me in the same place as the blow during the coach accident. Where is he?'

'Trying to hide under a bush,' Amanda said witheringly. 'Never mind him now… Jay, stop it, you should not be getting up!'

Doggedly he hauled himself to his feet and stood staring at Humphrey who stared back, transfixed, from his position on the ground. Slowly Jay walked across the space between them until he reached Humphrey's sprawled figure.

'You have hurt and insulted this lady who should expect nothing but support and protection from you. You deserve that I should call you out for that.' His voice was frigid with anger and contempt. 'You have attacked an unarmed man with his back to you. Again, for that I should call you out. But Mrs Clare is too sensitive of any scandal attaching itself to the name of her husband's family, however richly its present head may deserve it, and I shall therefore let you go.'

The expression of relief on Humphrey Clare's face was pathetic to behold and Amanda looked away from him to Jay, too worried about the effect of the blow to concern herself with the figure quailing on the ground. But Jay's next words riveted her attention as nothing else could.

'Before you crawl away, remember this. If one word of this gets out, if I hear a single whisper of speculation or one slighting word about Mrs Clare, I will seek you out and force a quarrel on you in the most public place I can contrive. And just in case you are in any doubt about who you are dealing with, my name is Jared Mansell, Earl of Severn.'

He had remembered who he was! Amanda gave a gasp and took a step towards the two men, then stayed back: she could not risk Humphrey realising there was any mystery here. The Earl of Severn? The name meant little to Amanda, who had never mixed in such circles, but it appeared to mean something to Humphrey, who went even paler as he got unsteadily to his feet and stumbled out of the grove.

'Jay, oh, Jay!' Amanda ran across and caught his arm. 'You have remembered who you are!'

'Do you mind if I sit down?' Jay took at few steps to a fallen tree and collapsed on to it, pulling her gently down beside her. He twisted to look at her and smiled wryly at the expression on her face. 'It is all right, Amanda, truly. I just felt a little dazed, and I expect I will have the devil's own headache in a while.'

'And you remember everything, Jay—?' She broke off. 'I am sorry, my lord, I mean.'

'Jay will do very well.' He touched her face gently. 'I have grown accustomed to it on your lips.' He paused as she looked anxiously into his eyes, worried that she could still see some trace of that unfocussed look. 'And yes, I remember most things. Some are still a jumble, but I expect they will all come back in time. Did you recognise my name?'

'Not really,' she admitted. 'I was aware of it, of course, but I have hardly been in the position to mix with the peerage, and I rarely go to town. Humphrey appeared to know it.'

Jay smiled. 'I have a certain reputation.'

'As a duellist?'

'Amongst other things.' His smile deepened as he saw the apprehension in her eyes. 'There is nothing to worry about, Amanda, I am not in the habit of strewing the countryside with corpses. I prefer to fight with the rapier: one has more chance of ending things with a minor wound and honour satisfied on all sides.'

'But you fight many duels?' she persisted.

'I have to admit, Amanda, that my suspicion that I was a rake was quite correct. And as I am sure you will know from the cautionary warnings of your respectable relatives, rakes gamble, associate with ladies of, shall we say, flamboyant natures, and engage in gambling and sporting pursuits. And all of those things tend towards the occasional dispute and the need to defend one's honour.'

'Oh.' Amanda digested this. 'And the ladies to whom you refer?'

'I will not lie to you. There is one, very expensive, barque of frailty, who is unaware of the fact that she will shortly be leaving my protection.'

'Too expensive?' Amanda queried wickedly, suddenly aware of a great bubble of rising happiness inside her.

'No,' he said, his eyes reflecting back the mischief in hers. 'But inappropriate to my newly reformed lifestyle.' What did he mean by that? Her heart gave a little leap. 'And while we are on the subject, Amanda, I am not married, I have no fiancée and definitely no children.'

'I am glad to hear it, my lord,' she said primly.

'Why, Amanda?' He had captured her hand and his thumb was working its insidious magic on the inside of her wrist.

'I have been very concerned about the anxiety your unexplained absence would be causing them. And, given what you have just told me about the, er…barque of frailty, one can only be happy that they have not been deceived in you. If they existed, that is,' she finished, confused. If he did not stop what he was doing with her hand, she did not know what she would do. Thought was becoming very difficult.

'What else would you like to know at the moment?' he asked, watching the play of emotion on her face.

'Everything…no, nothing. You should not be forcing your memory. You will end up with brain fever.' Amanda reclaimed her hand with an effort of will and stood up abruptly. 'We will go back to the house. If we go in through one of the side entrances we should escape notice and comment and then I will find the housekeeper and request the use of a bedchamber for you. We can tell her you were struck by a falling branch, which is nothing less than the truth.'

Jay pulled her back down on to the tree trunk. 'There is no need. Unless things have gone very much awry, I only need to announce myself to be shown to my duly allotted chamber.'

'Your allotted chamber? You mean you are a *guest* here?' Amanda realised that her mouth was unbecomingly open and shut it hastily. 'So that was why you found the Clippings familiar! But what on earth has an, excuse me, rake got to do with agrarian reform?'

'Absolutely nothing,' he admitted. 'But as I told you just now, I am reforming my style of life. I have become aware that I have responsibilities to my estates and their people and, enjoyable as a life of pleasure is, there are other ways of finding it than in the clubs and haunts of fashionable London. It was becoming a bore.'

So, this 'reform' predated their meeting. It had nothing to do with her after all. Amanda lowered her lashes to hide the sudden hurt and said, 'Go on.'

'I was staying with my friend Oughton near Norwich. He is of a like mind, and had already done some reading and was in touch with Mr Coke. He has taken his estates in a firm hand and has thoroughly surprised himself by enjoying the experience.'

Jay leaned back against the tree stump and stretched his legs out in front of him. 'His friends were sceptical about this transformation and convinced there was some other reason for his absence from town, so he invited us down to demonstrate his new interests. I gather he mentioned to Mr Coke that he was being visited by several reactionary landowners who needed a good example and the result was an invitation to all six of us to come to the Clippings and stay at the Hall.'

Amanda was transfixed with curiosity. 'But how did you get on the stagecoach with no cards and hardly any money?'

'We were playing cards,' he began.

'Yes, you remembered that when Miss Porter spoke about gambling.'

'Indeed. Well, we had been playing cards into the small hours, and drinking too. Young Eden—do you know him? Lands near Hunstanton, but a complete rip, never there, always in town—was bemoaning the fact that he was in debt again and his trustees were being damnably unsympathetic. I am afraid I was equally so and told him he would not be in such straits if he was more moderate in his expenditure. As I had just won two hundred guineas off him, he could hardly be expected to take the lecture in good grace.'

'I should think not,' Amanda said. 'There is nothing more aggravating than being lectured by someone who has all the faults you have.' She paused, thoughtfully. 'Unless it is being told off by one's man of business for outrunning the bailiff and spending too much on gowns, I suppose.'

Jay grinned. 'Yes, I am afraid I know all about the cost of fashionable gowns—you see how honest I am being with you, Mrs Clare? Anyway, Eden said that it was all very well of me to lecture but he had never seen any signs of my applying the slightest self-restraint or economy and I would fail miserably if I did.'

'So you had a bet on it.' By this time Amanda had curled up at the other end of the tree trunk, utterly engrossed in the unfolding tale. 'Go on!'

'We—or rather my loving friends—agreed that I should be cast out into the world with a change of linen, my razors and a few guineas in my pocket to survive until we met today at Holkham. I had every confidence that a fortnight of simple living would be no problem at all; they were all convinced I would be starving within the day.'

'You did look as though you were enjoying yourself when you boarded the coach,' Amanda remarked. 'Where were you bound for?'

'Wells. I thought as a small port it would have cheap lodgings in plenty which would allow me to live on as little as possible. And it is only a few miles from Holkham, so if I was penniless by this morning I could always walk here.'

'And what were you going to live on?' Amanda demanded. She could recall what had been in Jay's purse in the inn and even the cheapest lodgings would swallow that up in two weeks.

'Samphire off the marshes, crabs caught off the harbour wall, gulls' eggs from the dunes, and if all else failed, I would take to poaching and placate my landlady with a rabbit or two.'

Amanda laughed. 'Can you snare a rabbit?'

'Of course. Like all well brought-up young gentlemen, I ran away from my tutor at regular intervals and mixed with the riff and raff of the neighbourhood. I will have you know I can snare rabbits, tickle for trout, net pheasants and make a rook stew if I have to, all thanks to old Jensen, a smelly old man and a complete rogue.'

'Well, do not let the Holkham keepers hear you, that is all I can say!' The bubble of happiness inside her was rising and rising and any moment it would burst like champagne in a glass. Amanda looked at him, unaware of the feeling in her eyes, the tenderness of her slightly parted lips.

'Amanda, come here,' Jay said abruptly, holding out one arm to beckon her along the log.

Obediently she did as he asked, trustingly settling back into the curve of his arm against his chest. She could not see his face, but she could feel the rise and fall of his breathing and his breath disturbed the fine hairs on the back of her neck. She was conscious that she had lost her bonnet and that her hair was seriously disarrayed, but none of that mattered. The world might be going past just the other side of the protective wall of greenery, but she hardly gave them a thought. She was here in Jay's arms.

'Do you miss your husband?' he asked abruptly.

She did not pretend to misunderstand him. It was not Charles's conversation he was referring to. She thought for a moment, then answered him honestly. 'I was very young when Charles married me, and very innocent. I did not, from what Mama had told me, expect to find… some…parts of marriage enjoyable. I think he was very conscious that would be the case, and I sometimes wonder if his first wife was, perhaps, a somewhat nervous woman.' Jay sat very still, just the even rise and fall of his chest and the faint caress of his breath reminding her she was not simply recalling the past aloud to herself.

'He did everything to avoid alarming me. You said that surely I had seen a naked man before. Well, I never had, for we always…went to bed in the dark.'

Jay stirred at this, and murmured, 'I am sorry, I should have known better than to make assumptions.'

Amanda shook her head, dismissing the incident. 'He treated me as though I was made of glass. After the first time, it was no longer painful, and I gradually overcame the embarrassment, but I cannot say that I ever *enjoyed* it. But then, you see, I never expected to.

'But, I did enjoy the mornings.' Her voice brightened. 'He would come in in his long Indian-silk dressing gown and we would sit up in bed and drink our chocolate and plan the day, tell each other things. I learned so much from him, and he made me very happy.'

'But you are a very passionate woman,' Jay said, his arms finally closing around her waist.

'I do not know if I am. I did not know how I was meant to feel. You see, there was never another woman I could confide in about these things. I do not know now...'

'How do you feel in my arms?' Jay asked, his voice husky. 'How do you feel when I kiss you?' He turned her in his embrace until she was cradled on his knee, supported by one arm while the other caressed her face, trailed down the curve of her neck, caught her close to him.

'I feel—'

He kissed her, his lips covering hers gently. It was unthreatening, so very soft and undemanding, yet Amanda felt as though her entire body was on fire, that she would burn up if he did not stop, would fall to pieces in his hands if he did. Her body stirred against his and his lips hardened against hers until her mouth opened and she felt the startling intrusion of his tongue.

Greatly daring, she let her own flutter against the invading tip and was stunned by the heat of his mouth, by the sensation that lanced through her body. Her breasts suddenly seemed be too sensitive to touch even the fine lawn of her chemise, and as if he knew his hand caressed downwards to stroke over the curve as she arched instinctively against his palm.

Jay groaned deep in his throat and Amanda let the tide of heat wash over her. This was what passion was, this was what her body had been telling her she would experience with Jay if only she knew he was free and could surrender to him. And at that moment she had no doubt at all that love went hand in hand with passion.

Chapter Fourteen

What would have happened if things had continued uninterrupted Amanda had no idea. She was beyond thought, caught up in a torrent of physical sensation that drowned all of her thoughts except one great, overarching, feeling of happiness.

'Coom up, boy! In here, John, good deep shade by the looks of it.' The shout was echoed by another cry of 'Get on there!' and the barking of a dog, intermingling with the unmistakable sound of a flock of sheep approaching.

Amanda found herself swung neatly on to her feet with Jay's tall figure between her and the approaching shepherds. She scooped up her bonnet and attempted to cram her tumbled hair under it. Jay swung her round, put her hand on his arm and walked slowly, but directly, out of the other side of the grove as the hot sheep entered.

Amanda knew she was pink with embarrassment and the aftermath of his kisses, and try as she might she could not tie her bonnet strings without getting strands of loose hair caught in the knot.

'Jay,' she hissed. 'I cannot be seen like this.'

He cast her a concerned glance, which rapidly turned to one of amusement. 'Once again in our short acquaintance, Mrs Clare, you appear to have been dragged through a hedge backwards. Quickly, in here.' He side-stepped behind a tall bush, untied the much-abused ribbons, pulled off her hat and thrust it into her hands. 'Hold this, please.' Then with remarkable dexterity he smoothed back her hair, gathered up the loose weight of it and, using what few pins remained in the coiffure, secured it into a pleat. He whipped the hat out of her hands and placed it on her head before the hair could even think about escape again and ran the ribbons between his fingers to flatten them. With narrowed eyes he tied a neat bow to one side of her chin and stepped back to admire the effect. 'Perfect.'

'How on earth—?' Amanda caught the wicked twinkle and sighed. 'Practice, I suppose.'

'I am afraid so. I do not think there is much we can do about the marks on your skirt, which I think come from the tree your cousin pressed you against, but the housekeeper will doubtless be sorry to hear of your fall and will be able to brush away the worst.'

'She will think us a somewhat accident-prone couple, will she not?'

'It is not her place to speculate,' Jay remarked severely. 'Now, let us skirt our grove and its new occupants again and make our way back as quickly as possible.' He glanced down at her after they had covered some distance in silence. 'How do you feel now?'

'How do you think?' Amanda demanded. The few moments of walking, and the sensation of being surrounded by half the county, brought her back to reality with a jolt. 'I am delighted that you know who you are and that your friends will be here, but I have been assaulted by my cousin, watched a fist fight, confessed some of my most intimate secrets and been passionately kissed!'

She broke off as she realised an elderly gentleman had stopped and was bowing to her. 'Good day, Lord Matcham, yes, indeed, what lovely weather, but Mr Coke is always so fortunate in that respect, is he not. Oh, excuse me,' she added as the two gentlemen nodded at each other, 'Do you know Lord Severn?'

They assured her they had met, exchanged bows and Lord Matcham, after a few jovial remarks about the fame of their Norfolk event being able to attract the Pink of the *ton*, strolled off.

'Pompous old boy, but kindly,' Jay observed. 'Belonged to my father's clubs, I rarely come across him. Now, where were we? You were berating me for kissing you—was it for being too passionate or not passionate enough?'

'Oh, shh! I was not berating you. It was as much my fault as yours and I do not know what has come over me! Oh goodness, there is Mrs Ambrose, quickly, turn behind this wagon, she will prose on for hours.'

Jay obediently swerved to put the wagon between themselves and the overbearing matron and then resumed his path towards the house. 'Well, I know exactly what has come over me, but this is hardly the time and the place to tell you about it.'

Amanda glanced up at him, but his attention had been distracted by the group of young men walking across the grass towards them.

'Severn!' the one in the lead hailed him. 'Look, Eden, here he is, just as I said he would be. No signs of starvation and he hasn't even had to pawn his boots!'

'Your friends, I collect?' Amanda whispered.

'Indeed. Now, keep smiling and I'll introduce them.'

'But we have not even agreed a story—!' Amanda broke off and smiled as the gentlemen came to a halt in front of them, doffing their hats at the sight of a lady. They were obviously all agog to question Jay, but their good manners restrained them. Taking pity, she said, 'If you will excuse me, my lord, I will go and meet Miss Porter.'

'Not at all, Mrs Clare, I rely on you to uphold my account of my adventures, which these gentlemen will doubtless disbelieve without collaboration.' Jay held up a hand to silence their immediate protest and began to introduce them. 'Mrs Clare, may I present Lord Oughton, Mr Eden, Major Greene and Lord Witherington. Where is Hampton?'

The gentlemen bowed to Amanda in turn, then Lord Oughton remarked, 'Gone off to guess the weight of a pig, or some such frippery. Our friend Mr Hampton was convinced he had the eye for it, ma'am, so we left him to it.'

Amanda laughed. 'You do realise, gentlemen, that if he is the winner he will receive the pig itself as a prize?'

'My word! Well, let us go at once and bribe the good stallholder to amend our friend's guess. I cannot conceive what Hampton would do with a pig in his chambers in Albany!' Lord Oughton fell in beside Amanda and Jay and continued to chat as they made their way towards the cluster of sideshows, one of which was topped by a crude painting of an enormous pig. 'And you can vouch for Lord Severn's having abided by the terms of our challenge, can you, ma'am?'

'Yes indeed.' Jay said nothing to help, so she assumed he was happy for her to tell as much of the tale as she could. 'You should know that his lordship was involved in an accident to the stagecoach from Norwich and sustained a dislocated shoulder and a twisted ankle.'

She broke off while the news was absorbed and commented upon, then continued. 'I happened to be in a position to take up his lordship in my carriage and convey him to Holt where I recommended the Half Moon inn to him. Lord Severn—using an alias, of course— has remained at the inn for the past fortnight.'

'Living off what, might I ask?' Mr Eden demanded. 'If Mrs Clare has been kind enough to lend you your shot, or fed you every evening, then I call that cheating!'

Jay smiled at the indignant younger man. 'I have been earning my keep overhauling the landlord's chaotic books, and believe me, that was no easy task!'

Lord Oughton raised his eyebrow as he caught Amanda's eye. 'I cannot believe Lord Severn did not cause some speculation in the neighbourhood.'

'Indeed, yes, my lord. The general opinion, which I have to say he made no attempt to deny, is that he is indeed using an alias in order to view estates before making a large purchase at a keen price.'

This was greeted with some amusement, the view being expressed by his friends that the Earl of Severn had more land than was good for him already. Amanda watched Jay covertly from under her lashes. He was taking the teasing in good part, but she was conscious of a tension about him. She suspected that he could not remember everything yet and was treading carefully so as not to betray himself. If only they had not been together! She realised now that to tell the truth about his loss of memory would lay her open to speculation about exactly why she rescued this accident victim.

She decided she liked his friends. Lord Oughton was

amiable with charming manners and, she felt, a good mind behind a light-hearted manner. The Major was taciturn, somewhat correct, but obviously willing to take an interest in all around him and to be pleased with his company. Lord Witherington had the slight air of a dandy and made no secret of his alarm at finding himself in close contact with herds of beasts and their attendants. He was bewailing the coming together of one of his exquisite boots and the results of a herd of cattle being kept standing in one place, but Amanda guessed that this was more a pose than genuine disdain for his friends' interests. Mr Eden was much the junior of the group and they treated him like a younger brother: she suspected that he hero-worshipped Jay but would have died rather than admit it.

It appeared from their conversation that the missing Mr Hampton was the comedian of the party, apt to sudden enthusiasms and stumbling from one near-disaster to another, from which his long-suffering friends retrieved him. When they came upon him, leaning on the hurdle surrounding the pig pen holding the prize beast, he proved to be only a little older than Mr Eden, chubby-faced and very friendly.

The stall holder recognised her at once and hurried forward, doffing his hat and urging her to take a seat on a straw bale, the better to admire the animal. 'Mrs Clare, ma'am! What a pleasure to see you. And will you be investing your shilling on your estimation of this fine beast of mine?'

Amanda shook her head, laughing, but duly admired the enormous porker. Lord Oughton came and told her what his friend had guessed and she shook her head reassuringly. The gentlemen were in no danger of having to find a home for a pig that night.

She felt curiously light-headed to be sitting here, admiring a pig, in the middle of an agricultural gathering and surrounded by a cheerful group of town bucks she had only just met. She knew she should be feeling shocked by Humphrey's assault, ashamed of her own passionate response to Jay, but all she was feeling was anxiety over how rapidly he was recovering his memory and increasing apprehension about what would happen to them now. All her happiness seemed to have vanished and the cold, small knot of fear was back in her stomach.

Young Mr Eden's question shook her out of her reverie. 'And when do you expect to claim your winnings, Mansell?'

All eyes turned to Jay and Amanda could see from the faces of the men that this was the source of some amusement. And from the sudden blank look in Jay's eyes, that he had not the slightest recollection of what it was.

'Oh, do tell me what the wager was for!' she exclaimed brightly, looking directly at Lord Oughton.

He fell neatly into her trap and answered her at once. 'Well, ma'am, it is a horse of young Eden's. One that he bought last month.'

She saw Jay's eyes narrow in a secret smile directed just at her and felt encouraged to continue. 'But you gentlemen appear to find that amusing. Is a horse not something worth winning? I should think that Mr Eden is regretting his gesture.'

'Not if you saw the horse,' the Major remarked with a sudden grin. 'Eden here is possibly the worst judge of horseflesh you will ever have the misfortune to meet.' He ignored the indignant protest of his victim and explained. 'He was gulled into buying this beast by a Captain Sharp who knew a flat with a few guineas to waste when he saw one. It has the manners of a mule and the conformation of a coal heaver's cart horse.'

'Then why did Lord Severn accept such a wager?' Amanda demanded.

Jay smiled ruefully. 'I regret to say, ma'am, that I was drunk at the time.'

'Shocking,' she said, with a shudder which produced an answering twinkle from the Earl.

'I know, I am a sad rake, ma'am.'

There was no possible response to that and Amanda, feeling the conversation was slipping on to dangerous ground, stood up and dusted the hay off her skirts. 'It has been delightful meeting you gentlemen, and I thank you for your escort, but I really must go and find my companion before luncheon.' The parkland was dotted with stalls selling everything from fresh bread to flagons of ale and Amanda and Jane had intended to make some purchases and have an impromptu picnic.

Lord Oughton was gallantly stooping to remove a thistle that had caught in the hem of her walking dress when she heard the Major say to Jay, 'I knew there was a piece of news to tell you. The latest *on-dit* is that Lord Langham has offered for Diana Poste. Turn up for the book is it not, a man of that stamp offering for a girl hardly out of the schoolroom?'

'*What?*' Jay's voice was so sharp that Amanda jumped.

'Thought you would be surprised,' the Major continued. 'Some sort of cousin of yours, isn't she?'

'Distant,' was all that Jay said, but Amanda could see from the look in his eyes and the set of his jaw, that here was another area of his memory which had been lost until this moment.

'I have heard of Lord Langham,' Amanda said, low voiced, to Lord Oughton. 'He does not have a good reputation from what I can recall.'

'Dreadful,' his lordship agreed, one wary eye on Jay, who was looking more serious than Amanda had ever seen him. 'In his mid-forties now, but maturity has not put a stop to his, er…pleasures; in fact, they have become more scandalous.' He shot a quick glance at her face and added, 'Not the sort of thing I should be talking about to a lady. All you need to know about Langham, ma'am, is never to be alone in a room with him.'

'If you will not tell me about him, then tell me who this Diana Poste is.'

'Her mother was a cousin of Severn's—second cousin once removed or some such thing. Never met her, she died in childbirth, I believe. Miss Poste is scarce out of the schoolroom—not out until this coming Season, I imagine, although one has seen her at the occasional small party in town—' He broke off, a faint smile on his lips.

'And?' Amanda prompted with a growing sense that she did not want to hear his answer.

'Well, when she does come out there is going to be an uproar on the Marriage Mart—or at least, there would be if she wasn't already promised to Langham.'

'But why?' Amanda was watching Jay, who was in earnest conversation with the Major and Lord Witherington.

'Most beautiful female I have ever set eyes on,' Lord Oughton said simply. 'Absolute and utter perfection.'

Amanda felt a cold wave of apprehension come over her. Despite the sunshine she shivered. Knowing in her heart what the answer was going to be, she said, 'Indeed? Do describe her to me, my lord.'

He needed little persuasion. 'Blue eyes—that deep cornflower blue, and dark, curling lashes. Blonde hair, very long and absolutely straight. Thoroughly unfashionable, of course, but she makes no attempt to curl it and it is so fair, and so heavy and long, that one simply accepts it as beautiful. And the most lovely gentle smile: she smiles at you and you just want to—' He broke off in confusion. 'As I said, very, very lovely and with that wonderful fresh innocence one misses in so many débutantes who all think they must appear world-weary.'

Amanda blinked hard to keep back the tears that she felt gathering. It was the woman Jay had described when he had experienced that incredible flash of memory and emotion. But it did not all fit: he had known then that she was marrying an older man, and he described his own feelings of powerlessness to stop it. Perhaps it had been a premonition.

'The Earl appears to be highly concerned at this news,' she remarked. The entire party had begun to walk back to the Hall, Jay still apparently planning something with the Major. 'Was he not aware of Lord Langham's pretensions to his cousin's hand?'

'I am sure he was, there have been rumours. In fact, I believe he went to remonstrate with Sir James Poste about it, point out what an eminently unsuitable husband Langham would be. But, of course, he has no rights in the matter—it is not as though he were a trustee. I rather think Sir James told him to mind his own business in forthright terms.'

'If he has done his best, why should he feel the necessity to take some action now?' she pressed, for it was obvious that Jay was asking the Major to do several things for him: the military man was scribbling rapidly on a piece of paper as they walked and breaking off to fire questions.

'Oh, the general opinion is that Severn has been waiting for her to leave the schoolroom before he proposed marriage to her himself. Once we had seen her, none of us doubted that.'

Amanda had the sensation of a heavy door slamming shut. It was impossible to speak and so she walked beside Lord Oughton, pretending to be engrossed in avoiding thistles and ruts.

Jay half-turned and caught her eye, a rather abstracted expression on his face. 'Mrs Clare, I wonder if I could presume upon your good nature to have your groom take a message to Will Bream at the Half Moon?'

'Yes, of course,' she said as prosaically as she could. 'I assumed that would be necessary if you are to remain here with your friends tonight. Will you be riding back in a day or two?'

'No, I find I must go into Leicestershire urgently. I intend offering to buy the horse, at whatever price Mr Bream names, so I hope he will see no objection to that. As for my few possessions there, and my portmanteau, I will write again with instructions and money to have it sent on.'

So he had no intention of returning. He was not even going to leave via Holt and call to see her. 'Very well,' she agreed. How could he make plans to walk away from her so calmly after what had passed between them? Was he going to make no effort to speak to her alone? Or had it all been a rake's flirtation and, now he recalled the beautiful girl he had decided to make his wife, he would forget this Norfolk interval without a qualm?

They had reached the foot of the sweep of steps up

to the front door. As they climbed Amanda heard the
Major saying, 'Yes, your curricle, horses and groom are
all safely established round at the stables. We came over
yesterday at an easy pace, so they will be quite fresh
for you tomorrow. If you are sure I've got a list of all
your obligations in town, I will cancel them for you as
soon as I get back. And I will drop this list in at the
house in Grosvenor Square and have your valet pack
for you and travel up.'

'Are you staying with friends, my lord?' Amanda enquired, desperately trying to keep up an appearance of
mild interest in front of these men.

'I have a hunting box there,' Jay answered. 'It is convenient for the call I have to make.'

He did not appear to wish to confide anything further,
but Lord Oughton hissed in her ear, 'Sir James Poste
lives about ten miles from the hunting box.'

At the top of the steps the party came face to face
with Miss Porter, Lady Grahame and half a dozen other
ladies, all apparently scanning the parkland. 'I cannot
think where she is,' Miss Porter was saying, then, 'Mrs
Clare! There you are, we were just hoping to see you.'

'Well, here I am indeed!' Amanda exchanged bows
with the other ladies and turned with a sense of mixed
misery and relief to the men. 'My lords, Major, gentlemen. As you see, I am claimed by my friends. Thank
you for your escort. Lord Severn, I trust you have a safe
journey into Leicestershire. If you ask a servant to take
your letter for Will Bream to my groom round at the
stables, I will make sure it is delivered.'

She kept her countenance friendly as she nodded politely to each man. Jay held her gaze with his for a long
moment, but she could not read his expression and he
said merely, 'Goodbye, Mrs Clare. I must thank you for

your unfailing kindness. Miss Porter, I hope your garden flourishes.'

The two parties separated. Amanda could see the intense speculation in Jane's eyes, but she whispered, 'I will tell you later.'

Lady Grahame smiled at her. She rather approved of the young widow. 'A dashing collection of blades you had collected as escorts, Mrs Clare, and the Earl of Severn too—a real feather in your cap!' She was not displeased by Amanda's blush, seeing it as charming modesty, and continued, 'I have a picnic all set out on the lower terrace where Mr Coke has kindly allowed us to establish ourselves and admire the grounds. Will you not join us?'

'Thank you, ma'am, I would be delighted.' Amanda fell in with the other ladies and followed Lady Grahame through the house and on to the terrace where a pair of footmen were setting up what appeared to be a full-scale luncheon party rather than a light alfresco meal.

Amanda swallowed hard. Just how long was she going to have to maintain a brave company face before they could go? To say nothing of the fact that leaving immediately after luncheon would cause comment from those who expected to speak to her during the course of the day. And even then, she would not be able to speak to Jane of anything but trivialities all the way home because of the groom perched up behind.

Jane caught her arm during a moment's disarray while the seating was sorted out. 'Is everything all right, dear?'

'Oh, yes,' Amanda said, managing to keep a bright smile on her face. 'Jay has recovered his memory, discovered that he is an Earl and is reunited with his friends. He is single, and not yet affianced.'

'But?' Jane could read Amanda's eyes despite what her lips seemed to be saying.

'But he is about to leave for Leicestershire where the lady he wishes to marry is about to be forced into marriage with an unsuitable man.'

'Oh, my goodness,' Jane whispered, appalled. 'Which means…' Her voice trailed away.

'Which means,' Amanda supplied, her voice hard with the effort not to cry, 'either he will return with a fiancée, or having been disappointed in his courtship of a girl I am informed is the most beautiful ever seen in Society. In either case, I imagine a flirtation with a Norfolk widow is unlikely to trouble his thoughts much.'

Chapter Fifteen

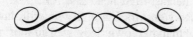

The picnic was long, lavish and extremely lively. The group of ladies who had gathered around Lady Grahame were all confident matrons from local society with much in common and plenty to talk about. Amanda knew many of them, if only slightly. At first she felt too bruised and shaken by her abrupt parting from Jay to do more than respond mechanically to any questions or observations directed at her, but after a while she found herself drawn into the wide-ranging discussions of everything from the use of laurels in shrubberies to the problems of keeping reliable servants.

The necessity to shield her feelings and to maintain a bright social front was surprisingly helpful, she realised. After a while it was as though what had happened was distanced, not quite real, and she could manage to exist on this level quite easily. She was aware of Jane's anxious glances, but smiled reassuringly. It would not do to worry Jane, and her own pride would not let her admit to anyone else that her heart was broken—if that indeed was what this incredible empty feeling was in her chest.

'Indeed, I do sympathise with you, Mrs Agnew,' she

responded to a worried young mother on her right who was bemoaning the loss of her children's excellent nurse to a position in a London household. 'I am about to lose my lady's maid, who is getting married. I am delighted for her, of course, but she will be hard to replace.'

Lady Grahame, who appeared capable of keeping an ear tuned to half a dozen conversations at once, inclined her elaborately coiffed head and remarked, 'I may be able to assist you, Mrs Clare. My sister-in-law writes to me to say that her own lady's maid—of whom she cannot speak too highly—has a younger sister who is wishful to follow in the same path. My sister-in-law knows the family and can recommend the girl for honesty, intelligence and good character. Would you wish me to say that you may be interested in seeing her?'

'Why, yes, that would be most welcome,' Amanda said gratefully. 'The thought of finding someone has been worrying me, I must confess. Where does the young woman live?'

'In London, I understand. I believe she is presently employed at home where her mother has been unwell, but she is now fully recovered so the daughter is released.' Lady Grahame reached into her reticule and scribbled on one of her tablets, which she passed to Amanda. 'There is my sister-in-law's direction, Mrs Clare. Please feel free to write.'

Amanda glanced at the note—a Mrs Thornton, in a most select part of town—and tucked it away with a word of thanks.

The party eventually broke up at three o'clock. Normally Amanda would have continued to stroll around the gathering for at least another two hours, meeting people and collecting information, but now she felt as though she had been up all night, or was about to come down with a cold. The thought of the drive home was tiring even to contemplate.

She turned to Jane, who was making her thanks to their hostess and when she was free said, 'I will walk around to the stables and find Ned. I hope you do not mind, but I am feeling quite worn out and would prefer to start home now. Will you wait for me at the front of the house?'

'Of course I do not mind,' Miss Porter assured her, with a covert glance of concern. 'I have had a delightful day. I will wait for you at the front of the house—the view of the entire scene is so stimulating from there. Would you like me to drive?'

'No...yes, please. I think I would, Jane,' Amanda agreed gratefully. Her companion was an excellent whip and the greys would be considerably subdued after their brisk drive in that morning.

Amanda walked round the side of the house, through a gate in the wall and made her way through a shrubbery towards the stableyard. As she rounded a corner she found herself face to face with Lord Severn. Jay was half-sitting on the balustrade, looking out over the plantings with a look on his face that suggested his thoughts were not pleasant.

His expression did not lighten noticeably at her approach, but he stood up and removed his hat. 'Amanda. I am sorry that we have had to part so suddenly.'

'I quite understand.' Her heart was beating so erratically that she wondered it was not visible through the thin lawn of her bodice, but by some miracle she found she could keep her voice light and cool and her face free of her betraying thoughts. 'Some family matter of urgency I understand from Lord Oughton.'

'Yes…of sorts,' he agreed. 'I have just given a message for Will Bream to your man. I regret having to leave without thanking him in person. He is a fine man, and deserves to do well at his new career.'

'Indeed, he is,' Amanda agreed. 'You set out tomorrow?' Sheer pride was keeping her here, calmly talking to him like this. The thought that he might suspect how she felt was appallingly humiliating.

'Yes—' He broke off, a sharp line furrowing his brow. 'Amanda, I cannot thank you enough for what you have done…'

'Oh, nonsense!' She was proud of the light laugh. 'Why, I told you I was incurably curious and managing. A mystery such as the one you presented does not come one's way every day!'

'It meant nothing more?'

What did he want from her? she thought, suddenly angry. He goes off to another woman and he seems to expect that I will humiliate myself by admitting to an attachment!

'Of course, I am greatly in your debt for dealing with Cousin Humphrey so effectively. I am sure I will have no further trouble with him. And I do not forget that if it had not been for you, I would have been far more seriously hurt in that accident.'

Jay moved closer and looked down into her eyes. His own were dark, but she kept her gaze steady. 'Earlier today you were in my arms, Amanda. The other night—'

'Was a dream,' she finished for him. 'And this morning…I am sorry I burdened you with my memories. I will not deny that you have…awakened part of me that was perhaps hidden. But one must be realistic about these things, my lord. Summer idylls come and go.'

'*My lord?* It was Jay this morning.'

'I did not know then who you were. But Jay does not exist, does he? And the Earl of Severn, who comes from a very different world, does.'

He moved away abruptly and she added, 'I told you I was a practical woman, my lord. And one with a life to be living, not spent on wakening dreams. This past fortnight has been an amusing interlude—if sometimes a worrying one on your behalf—but it is over and things move on.' She held out her hand to him. 'I will bid you goodbye, my lord, and good fortune.'

He took her proffered hand and held it while he looked at her. After a moment his thumb began to run gently over the swelling base of hers. Amanda snatched back her hand as though stung. 'Good day, my lord!' She swept round and stalked off towards the high wall that hid the stable yard. There was a crunch of gravel behind her, then it stopped as she vanished through the wicket gate and into the bustle and smells of the yard.

'...now pronounce you man and wife.' The Rector stopped speaking as Tom Green, blushing hotly, kissed an equally flushed Kate. An appreciative murmur of congratulation rose from the congregation and Miss Porter disappeared into a large lawn handkerchief, from which the occasional sentimental sniffle could be heard.

Amanda remained resolutely dry eyed, despite the swelling feeling of happiness for Kate and Tom that rose inside her. She had been telling herself 'You will not cry, you *will not* cry,' over and over again in the five days since she had parted from Jay at Holkham and it appeared to be working.

Not a drop had brightened her eye to betray her to her household or to Jane. Jane had been bitterly disappointed to hear that Jay had gone, and that he had another attachment, and was extremely anxious about the effect on Amanda. She had had no hesitation in saying so.

'I had so hoped that the two of you would make a match,' she said, when they were finally alone the next day. 'My dear, this must make you very unhappy, I so wish there was something I could do.'

'Nonsense,' Amanda had retorted briskly. 'I liked him very much, and I will not deny I enjoyed flirting with him, but that was all it was. And a good thing too,' she added. 'An Earl is not the match for me!'

Jane had not looked in the least convinced, and had said no more, but Amanda knew that she was watching her closely. At first she resented it, then was grateful that there was something else to bolster her pride and stop her breaking down and giving in to grief. If Jane guessed how she was feeling she would be even more sorry for her, and Amanda hated the thought of being pitied.

This frozen state was not comfortable, however. With one part of her mind and heart rigidly disciplined not to think of Jay, not to feel for him, the rest of her found it hard to cope with the preparations for Kate's wedding on the Monday following the third reading of the banns.

Thankfully Kate appeared to notice no restraint; if the other servants thought their mistress more than usually subdued, she assumed they put it down to her sorrow at losing such a close attendant.

If she had heard the conversation in the servants' hall after dinner every night, she would have been horrified. 'What does a town buck like that think he's about, coming down here and trifling with our lady?' Mrs Howlett would demand indignantly, provoking a tumult of remarks from all around the long table.

'Pity she's no father to look after her', 'Needs a shot gun taking to him!', 'That Humphrey Clare should be doing something.' 'What, him? Useless slab of lard!' 'Poor lady, so white and all, he's broken her heart, that's what he's done.'

Mr Howlett would wave a magisterial hand and quieten the protests. 'All we can do is pretend we haven't noticed. And if he does come back, he'll find the door shut in his face,' he added viciously.

The congregation stood as the bride and groom passed down the aisle together and out into the sunshine. Amanda and Jane followed them out to join the rest of the guests throwing rice.

'Throw your flowers, throw your flowers!' the group of single girls who gathered on the path in front of Amanda called to Kate. She laughed and turned her back on them, all the better to throw blind for the lucky girl to catch.

'I do wonder where that superstition comes from,' Jane remarked as the little flock of maidens jostled and giggled.

'That the one who catches it will be the next bride? I do not know either, but possibly the Rector does,' Amanda suggested, twisting round to look for him. 'He has a great interest in that sort of folklore.'

At that moment something struck her on the brim of her bonnet. She put up her hands instinctively to find them full of the posy of rosebuds and asparagus fern which Miss Porter had so prettily assembled for Kate.

The guests turned to look at her, some of them calling congratulations, some obviously wondering what to say. Amanda flushed. 'I am sure that was an accident and not what the Fates intended at all,' she said, trying to laugh it off. 'Will the charm work if Kate throws it again?'

But the wide-eyed girls all shook their heads and said, no, it must be true that Mrs Clare would be the next married. None of them dared tease her for the name of the lucky man. Flushed, Amanda returned the flowers to Kate, who took them without comment, knowing only too well that the mysterious Mr Jay had gone and her mistress had been sad ever since.

The big barn was hung with cloths and decorated with flowers for the wedding breakfast, with food spread out on big trestle tables and bales of straw set around for the guests to sit on. The sun shone, the ale flowed and soon a fiddler struck up and the dancing began.

Amanda danced with the bridegroom, the Rector, her butler, several local farmers and then found herself claimed for the next set by Will Bream, resplendent in his best waistcoat. By this time she was thoroughly enjoying herself and was surprised, when the music came to a halt, to find Will firmly steering her around the side of the barn away from prying eyes.

'What is the matter, Will?'

'That's what I was going to ask you, Mrs Clare, ma'am. I had a very civil letter from Mr Jay—his lordship, I should say—with more than enough to cover his expenses with me and a very fair price indeed for that hunter. Very civil indeed it was, but no word about coming back here and it seems like you aren't expecting to hear from him again, ma'am.'

'There is no reason why I should, Will,' Amanda said, shifting uneasily under his penetrating gaze. Will, fiercely protective of his late master's widow, took liberties with his plain speaking that none of her servants—or even Miss Porter—would dream of. 'We move in different worlds.'

'You don't fool me, Mrs Clare,' he stated, ignoring her protest. 'He's been flirting with you, hasn't he, and him going away has hurt you, hasn't it?'

'Oh dear, Will, I really don't want to talk about this.' He regarded her stolidly until she admitted, 'Yes, we flirted, and yes, I wish he had not gone away.'

'Was flirting all he did?' Will demanded.

'*Will!* You shouldn't be asking me something like that!'

'You haven't got a brother or a father to ask it, and that Mr Humphrey Clare is neither use nor ornament, so it's up to someone like me who cares about you to ask it,' he said.

Amanda knew she was blushing a deep, betraying red. 'He kissed me, Will, but that is all, truly.'

'Humph. Well, if you say so, ma'am, then of course it is so.' He looked slightly mollified, like a large dog that has finally lowered its hackles after another dog has walked past its gate.

'Will, what would you have done if I said he had…if things had been…?'

'Made him do the right thing, of course,' Bream looked astonished that she had needed to ask.

'My goodness.' Amanda regarded him wide-eyed, the vision of the inn landlord marching up to the Earl of Severn's front door armed with a shotgun rising in her imagination. 'I do believe you would. I thank you, Will, I could not hope for a stauncher defender, but believe me, I do not need such extreme measures.'

It was his turn to look bashful. 'Promised Mr Charles

I'd look after you, best I could, and I will. But I can't stop you falling in love with a rake, can I?'

'No, Will, you cannot.' Amanda bent forward and kissed him on the cheek, causing him to blush hectically. 'I am afraid no one could have stopped that. Now come along, all the girls will be wondering where such an eligible partner has gone.'

That night Amanda dreamed that she was walking up the aisle towards the Rector, Kate's bouquet of flowers in her hands. The pews were packed with friends and neighbours, the church bells were ringing, but where the bridegroom should be standing there was simply a swirl of mist.

Then she was aware that she was escorted by Will Bream, his shotgun held in his other hand. As they reached the altar rail and the Rector the mist vanished, leaving nothing in its place and Will said, 'Now don't you fret, Mrs Clare, I'll fetch him back for you.'

Amanda sat bolt upright in bed, still shaking with reaction. It was as though everyone she knew had been in that congregation and now they were aware of her feelings for Jay and knew that he had left her—and were either pitying her or gloating, depending their point of view.

Of course, it was not true, she told herself fiercely, then started to think about it. Jane knew, Will knew, Kate doubtless guessed and Humphrey, once he stopped feeling sorry for himself, would also suspect. If he did, he would tell his mama, and she, no doubt, would thoroughly enjoy spreading the news of the young widow's humiliation around the district.

'But I cannot run away!' she whispered to herself, then, after a moment's reflection, 'Yes, of course I can—and I will.'

Next morning at breakfast she waited until Jane was sipping her second cup of coffee and enquired, almost casually, 'Would you find it very irksome if we were to go up to town for a few days?'

'London?' Jane put down her cup with a rattle and looked at Amanda in surprise. 'Is he...?' Then she caught herself up and said, 'I mean, whatever do you want to do in London at this time of year? The Season is over and it will be half-empty of society.'

'I want to take up the introduction Lady Grahame has given me to her sister-in-law. Do you recall she said she was able to recommend a new lady's maid? And I really must see about a new riding habit, my old one is quite beyond the pale. Have a fashionable new crop, perhaps.' She watched Jane's face. 'Would you be un-utterably bored?'

'Why, no, of course not. A change of scene would be delightful. When would you like to set out?'

'By the end of the week, I think. I will write to an hotel and bespeak two rooms and a parlour. We had better take a maid with us: who do you think? Maria, perhaps? She will not be able to dress our hair, but we can do each other's, I am sure. So that is the two of us and Maria. I must make sure the travelling carriage is cleaned and the traces checked over.' She reached for her tablets and jotted down *Hotel, carriage*. 'Is there anything else we need to do?'

'Which hotel?' Jane asked. 'Grillon's?'

'No, the Clarendon, the food is better.'

'How do you know that?' Jane looked puzzled. 'Have

you ever stayed there? I thought you always used Grillon's.'

'I have no idea…oh, yes, I do, someone recommended it to me.' And the sound of Jay's voice in the
inn parlour in Saxthorpe came back to her. For a moment it was as though he was in the room with them.
'We will travel by easy stages, I think,' she said hastily.
'There is no need to rush.'

It was consequently a whole week later before the
two ladies, and a maid rendered completely speechless
by excitement, drew up in front of the Clarendon Hotel
on the corner of Albermarle and Bond Street. Porters
hurried out for their luggage and the doors were flung
open wide to usher them in. At such an unfashionable
time of year Amanda had had no trouble securing a fine
suite of rooms and the sight of the two well-dressed
ladies with their large train of luggage galvanised the
hotel manager into obsequious welcome.

When they were finally settled in their rooms, Jane
remarked, 'They certainly appeared impressed by our
luggage. Are you sure you needed to bring so much,
Amanda dear? I thought we were only going to stay for
a week.'

Amanda stopped flitting about the private sitting
room examining it. 'Oh, well, I am not sure. If we
wanted to stay longer it seemed foolish not to have everything. Although I am sure we will want to make
many purchases.'

Miss Porter grimaced. Shopping was not her favourite
occupation. Still, if it took Amanda's mind off the Earl
of Severn, she would gladly submit to an entire month
of it.

She spied a London directory on the shelf. 'Do you

have the name and direction of Lady Grahame's sister-in-law to hand? It might be as well to call as soon as possible, for if the girl is already suited, or you do not like her, that will give you more time to try the domestic agencies.'

Amanda agreed and found the slip of paper. 'Here we are, Mrs Thornton, Upper Brook Street. Can you find it?'

Jane flicked through the pages. 'Yes, Number Four, almost on the corner with Grosvenor Square. Her eyes ran idly over the list of residents as she had the book open in her hands. A very distinguished company, and... Oh, my goodness!'

'What is the matter, Jane?' Amanda looked back from the window from where she had been surveying the street below.

'No...nothing, my dear,' Miss Porter said, hastily shutting the directory. After all, Lord Severn was safely about his courtship in Leicestershire, there was no risk of him being at home in his town house in Grosvenor Square. No, better not to mention it to Amanda at all.

Chapter Sixteen

Two days later Amanda set out for Mrs Thornton's house in Upper Brook Street, accompanied by Maria. She had received a most encouraging note in response to her own, assuring her that the young woman in question was indeed still free and about to seek employment, and inviting Mrs Clare to visit to interview her.

Susan Wilkes proved to be a neat little person with immaculate hair and well-kept hands and a great deal of shy reserve. Yes, she very much wanted to be a lady's maid. Yes, her sister had explained all the duties and had taught her how to mend and press and how to dress hair. Yes, she knew she had a lot to learn about caring for jewels and that sort of thing, but she was very willing to learn if only Mrs Clare would give her an opportunity.

Mrs Thornton, who had remained in the room during this conversation, suggested kindly, 'Why do you not retire to one of the bedrooms, Mrs Clare, and allow Susan to dress your hair? I always think there is no better way to judge if someone is careful and has potential.'

Nervously Susan followed the ladies to a small blue

bedchamber and hurried to pull out the chair before the dressing table. She took Amanda's hat and laid it carefully on the bed, smoothing the ribbons as she did so, then waited to be told what to do.

'Just unpin it, brush it through and put it up again, only this time, let a ringlet show on either side under the hat brim,' Amanda suggested.

Susan's hands shook, but she was confident with the brush and pins and soon had Amanda's hair just as she had requested. Amanda approved her clean, neat dress and apron, her short nails and the slight scent of lavender water.

'That is very good,' she remarked. 'Thank you.'

'Thank you, ma'am.' Susan bobbed a curtsy and waited, eyes downcast.

She was certainly a contrast to bubbly, noisy Kate, but perhaps she would come out of her shell with confidence and familiarity. Amanda asked her if she still wished to be considered for the position and mentioned the wage she had in mind.

'Oh, yes, ma'am!'

'And you realise it will be in the country? We are only a small household and although I entertain quite frequently, it will not be the same as being with a town household.'

Yes, Susan realised all that and confided that she would be frightened to start in a big town house. 'I'm used to the country, ma'am.'

She happily agreed to a month's trial, starting when Amanda returned to Norfolk, which would give her time to tell her family and collect up her belongings. Amanda took her direction and explained how she would be in touch.

As she went downstairs again to report success to her

hostess she heard the patter of feet as Susan ran along the landing, obviously seeking out her sister to tell her the good news.

Amanda felt happier than she had for days as she emerged on to the steps of Mrs Thornton's house a while after, Maria at her side. She had been dreading replacing Kate, for in their little household it was important to find someone who would fit in and contribute to the friendly atmosphere that Amanda found essential to her own contentment. Quiet Susan might be, and she would need training in many things, but Amanda felt confident that she was the right choice.

She was hesitating on the bottom step, wondering which way to take to Piccadilly and Hatchard's bookshop, when a figure, familiar from Holkham, approached from the direction of Grosvenor Square. Jay's friend Lord Oughton was strolling along, apparently in no hurry, and his face lit up when he saw her before him.

'Mrs Clare, ma'am! What an unexpected pleasure.'

'Lord Oughton, good afternoon. I am in London to engage a new lady's maid and for some shopping. I had not looked to find anyone I knew here at such a season.'

'I am waiting on my mama,' he explained, replacing his hat. 'May I escort you anywhere, ma'am?'

'I was just wondering which way to take to Hatchards, my lord, but I have no wish to turn you from your path.'

'It would be a pleasure, and you put me in mind that my sister wanted some novel or another collecting. I can combine duty with pleasure,' he added gallantly, offering her his arm.

'Thank you, my lord, in that case, I would be delighted.' Amanda took his arm and they strolled along,

Maria behind them, trying not to get lost or tread on their heels yet take in all the sights of the busy streets as she went.

Hatchard's proved a treasure trove and Amanda had soon found two new novels and an account of travels to the East, which Jane had thought sounded interesting. Lord Oughton, who had collected his sister's package, proved more than willing to browse amongst the shelves and tables loaded with new publications and to tempt her with more suggestions.

Amanda found him very good company, and was soon laughing with him over his teasing suggestions of which frivolous novels might appeal to a lady with time on her hands.

'With London so thin of company,' he was saying as they walked out on to the pavement again, 'you will need at least one book a day to keep you entertained. Will you not allow me to take you driving to fill some of these long hours while your tailor stitches your new habit?'

'That would be delightful, thank you, my lord. But will Lady Oughton be able to spare you?'

'Mama is happily occupied with her plans to move to Brighton for the summer. She has been much put out because not all of them are falling into place... My goodness, see who is there, ma'am, the young lady in the barouche.'

Obediently Amanda looked at the vehicle, which was pulled up a little further along Piccadilly. It was facing towards them, its occupant leaning out to speak to someone who appeared to have walked across the street to speak to her, for he was standing on the road side of the vehicle, obscured from their view and all Amanda could see was the lower part of a pair of boots.

'Is it someone you know, my lord?'

'That is Miss Poste, the young lady I was telling you about at Holkham.' Lord Oughton tucked Amanda's hand under the crook of his elbow and began to stroll along the street towards the carriage.

'Oh!' was all Amanda could manage. She had no wish to meet the youthful object of Jay's affections, yet she felt extremely curious to see her. She rallied slightly. 'Are you acquainted with the lady, or do you simply know her by sight?' That was as near as she could venture to demanding whether she was about to be introduced to Miss Poste, and she soon received her answer.

As they came up to the barouche its occupant looked across and saw them. 'Lord Oughton, good morning.'

His lordship stopped and doffed his hat. 'Miss Poste, how do you do. I believe you will not have met Mrs Clare.'

He moved forward and Miss Poste moved to lean out and shake hands. Amanda, who was taking in the fact that Lord Oughton had not exaggerated one whit in describing Miss Poste's extraordinary beauty, was conscious of a hastily suppressed exclamation from the other side of the carriage. Good breeding stopped her glancing in that direction while she shook hands in turn with Miss Poste and with the thin lady introduced as 'Miss Woodley, my companion', who occupied the forward seat.

Only then did she turn her head to look at the gentleman standing on the far side of the barouche, and, with a sinking sense of inevitability, saw it was Lord Severn.

'Mrs Clare,' he said formally, raising his hat and making her a slight bow.

'Lord Severn,' she acknowledged him coolly. Her heart seemed to be in her mouth and she wondered if she had gone as white as she felt. She was conscious of Miss Poste's gaze on her as Jay made his way around the carriage to join her and Lord Oughton on the pavement and schooled her expression to one of polite indifference. Those huge blue eyes had sharpened at the greeting and Amanda was careful to maintain a light flow of chit-chat with the ladies in the carriage while Jay greeted Lord Oughton.

'I had no idea you were in town,' she heard Jay remark to his friend. She longed to look at him, but did not dare risk her face betraying her. All she wanted was to be close to him, to look into his eyes and read how he felt, how he was. In that first glimpse he had seemed thinner, as though his features had sharpened, but perhaps that was just her imagination.

'Summoned by my mother,' Lord Oughton replied. 'Heard that you were here, though—in fact, I was just returning from a fruitless visit to you in Grosvenor Square when I was fortunate enough to meet Mrs Clare.'

This was enough to focus attention on Amanda and she said, smiling, 'And poor Lord Oughton has paid for his kind offer of escort by being dragged into Hatchard's and then burdened with books for his pains.'

There was general laughter at his lordship's gallant attempts to protest that it was no burden at all and Jay enquired, 'Do you make a long stay in town, Mrs Clare?'

'I have not yet decided,' she said calmly. How could she stand there like this, in the middle of bustling Piccadilly, when she wanted to run to his side, trace the lines of his face with her fingers, reassure herself that he was well? 'Possibly.' She had no intention of explaining herself or her presence.

Was it her imagination or was the atmosphere prickling as though at the onset of a thunderstorm? She glanced around the group: the chaperon was sitting poker-faced and silent. She did not appear either welcoming or disapproving of the group gathered around her charge, but it was not she who was contributing to Amanda's feeling of discomfort.

Being close to Jay was, of course, very uncomfortable. She felt embarrassed, which was hardly surprising, but she also sensed that he was angry about something. Nothing showed on his face and his eyes were unreadable. In any case, she mused as she chatted lightly about the prospects for the weather, what on earth could he feel angry *about*?

The she saw his glance flicker towards Lord Oughton, who was certainly taking his role squiring her seriously, As well as patiently carrying her books, he had twice moved to protect her from any risk of jostling from passers-by on the bustling pavement and was standing very close, one hand at her elbow. Surely Jay could not be feeling jealous of his old friend? Could he be such a dog in the manger when the very lovely object of his own attentions was sitting so close?

She had tried hard not to appear to stare at Miss Poste, who might well be thoroughly weary of people gawping at her quite astonishing looks. Now, she caught her eye and, under cover of discussing the theatrical entertainments that would be available at that season, took the opportunity of studying her more closely.

Diana was patently very young—just seventeen, if Amanda was any judge—and her skin had the bloom of a fresh apricot, completely without blemish. Her eyes

were as Lord Oughton had described them: huge, cornflower blue and expressively fringed with long dark
lashes, which caressed her high cheekbones as she modestly lowered them. Her nose was small and straight,
her mouth sweetly curved and her chin had a little dim-
ple. Despite her youth, her figure was well formed and
her simple muslin gown modestly displayed a curva-
ceous form.

The wave of dislike that swept over Amanda was so
violent that she almost gasped. How could she react like
that to a young woman she had scarcely met? *And I was
thinking Jay was jealous*, she chastised herself furiously, forcing a smile. The poor child cannot help being
born so lovely, nor could she help the attentions of men
who found her so. Diana tossed her head slightly and
the heavy mass of straight hair, which hung so gracefully down her back, rippled slightly. Amanda found
herself looking for the men's reactions.

Jay's mouth tightened and she caught just the flash
of appreciation in Lord Oughton's eyes, then both men
were speaking of something together and the moment
passed. But she also caught the look in Miss Poste's
eyes and realised that the girl was not as unaware of
the effect she was having as she first appeared. As soon
as the men's attention was turned from her Amanda
caught her glancing from one to the other with an as-
sessing look. *She knows what effect she has*, Amanda
thought. *She knows and she is toying with them, seeing
how well she scores in gaining their attention and playing one off against the other.*

Well, could she blame the girl? It was not her fault
if her perfection of looks led others to expect her character to be as perfect. In a young woman with less an-

gelic features, perhaps, one would not think twice about
that look of calculation.

Then, out of the corner of her eye, she saw the glance
Diana was directing at her. That, too, was calculating,
and it was exactly the look that she had last seen on the
face of a society lady about to unsheathe her talons and
set about dealing with a rival. *She suspects something
between Jay and I*, Amanda thought, and ridiculously
felt a tiny twist of fear. What was there to fear from
this child? She was just rather spoilt.

'Are you out yet, Miss Poste?' she enquired, knowing
the answer, but thinking it a question she might be expected to ask.

'No, not until next Season,' the girl replied. 'Although Papa allows me to attend country dances and
the theatre and so on. In fact...' and her glance slid
sidelong to see the effect of her words on Jay '...in fact,
I may be married before next Season.'

'I must felicitate you,' Amanda said, with all the
warmth she could muster. 'I had not seen the announcement.'

'No, nothing has yet been announced.' Diana said
this with a strange smile, as though at a secret she was
not going to share.

Amanda was aware of Jay's back stiffening, and
could feel, as strongly as though he had spoken the
words, that he was willing her to drop the subject. She
ignored the sensation and said, knowing she sounded
patronising, but almost hoping to goad the girl, 'Perhaps
your papa might wish you to wait a little. After all, you
are *very* young and it would be a pity not to enjoy your
first Season as a débutante.'

There was a flash of anger in the blue eyes. Obviously Miss Poste did not relish advice from older ladies.

'Oh,' she said sweetly, 'do you recall your first Season so clearly after so long?'

Why, you little cat! Amanda thought. 'I recall it vividly,' she replied, maintaining her smile. 'I met my husband then, so it has happy memories for me.'

'And is he in town?' Diana enquired.

'I am a widow,' Amanda told her and watched the calculation in the cornflower gaze. *I am obviously past my first youth, and of no more than passable looks compared to her, so can be discounted on those grounds,* she thought, interpreting the look. *But as a widow I have more freedom than most married ladies, and certainly more than a single girl. And 'widow' has certain connotations if combined with an independence and passable looks. Oh, yes, she has seen me as a rival.*

The atmosphere had lost none of its charge, despite the polite interchanges between all those gathered around the carriage. Amanda felt that Jay's hackles were rising, that Lord Oughton was uneasy and that Miss Poste was definitely hostile. She felt ashamed of herself for goading Diana into exposing herself, although she very much doubted if either man had noticed anything amiss with the exchanges between the two ladies.

'I really must be going, it was delightful to meet you, Miss Poste, Miss Woodley. Good day, Lord Severn. No, no, Lord Oughton, I have presumed on your time far too long and those books are hardly any weight at all.'

His lordship, however, was not to be deprived of his burden and, promising to call on Jay later, he raised his hat to the ladies and steered Amanda back along Piccadilly, Maria following at a discreet distance.

Despite her feelings, Amanda was conscious of a little amusement. He was obviously dying to comment on the encounter, but was in difficulties, for his good manners forbade him to enthuse about the beauty of one woman to another. Kindly, Amanda put him out of his misery.

'What a very lovely young lady,' she commented. 'You did not exaggerate in the slightest. No wonder Lord Severn is enamoured.'

She was so convinced that she had read Lord Oughton's mood accurately that his answer took her aback. 'I cannot say I approve.'

'Really? It is not a brilliant match, I will grant you, but respectable.'

'She is too young.' He broke off to guide Amanda round a barrow, which had become wedged against the kerb, then appeared to be unable to continue.

'Well, I expect her father will postpone the actual wedding until later.'

They turned into the comparative quiet of Albermarle Street and he finally said, 'It makes me uneasy. Miss Poste is almost exactly the same age as my sister Lizzie and yet she seems ten years older in many ways. I know how I would feel if men admired Lizzie the same way as they do Miss Poste—and I would not feel happy if she received their attentions with so much—' He broke off, obviously lost for the right word.

'Aplomb?' Amanda suggested. 'She does seem very mature for her age, I will grant you. But girls all mature differently. Your sister will amaze you by growing up all of a sudden.' She fell silent, working out her own impressions. 'I may be wrong, but I am not sure she knows her own mind about either man: doubtless she is flattered by being the focus of admiration.'

'Yes.' He seemed happier for a few minutes, then said, 'Forgive me for being so frank, ma'am, but I feel

I can confide in you. I am just uneasy that my friend Severn should show such attention to her. It is unlike him.'

'Surely you do not doubt his good intentions towards her?' Amanda asked, shocked, but was reassured by Lord Oughton's expression of horror. 'No, I can see that you do not. It is unusual in him to pay court to débutantes? He normally prefers more…mature ladies?'

Lulled by the calm way she expressed this outrageous question, Lord Oughton agreed that that was exactly the case, then blushed scarlet at what he had implied.

Amanda took pity on him. 'Then perhaps he has decided it is time to settle down and he feels that a very young bride will suit him better.' They had arrived at the steps of the hotel at this point and Lord Oughton was saved from considering this tricky question further. He handed her parcel of books to the doorman and asked, 'At what time may I collect you tomorrow for our drive? Will two-thirty suit?'

The time agreed, he took himself off, leaving Amanda to climb the stairs slowly, her mind a whirl of jostling emotions. She had seen Jay and had managed to behave with calm dignity, despite how she had felt inside, but now reaction was setting in and she realised that her feelings for him had not abated one jot for all the days they had been apart. But then, how could she expect them to? Surely love did not change like that. If he was besotted by Diana Poste, then her opinion of his judgement had undergone a change, that was all.

'Love is not love which alters when it alteration finds,' she was saying to herself as she opened the door of their sitting room.

'What did you say, dear?' Miss Porter glanced up from her sewing. 'Is that Shakespeare you are quoting?

How very literary of you!' She saw the pile of books in Amanda's hands and exclaimed, 'Ah! That explains it, you have been browsing in a bookshop.'

Amanda was tempted to let it go at that, but she felt the need to confide. 'Yes, I have been in Hatchard's, Jane. But that is not why I am quoting Shakespearian sonnets, I am afraid. Lord Severn is in town.'

'Lord Severn! Oh, my goodness! Did you meet him in Grosvenor Square?'

'No.' Amanda looked puzzled, not knowing of Jane's unsettling discovery of his address. 'No, I was fortunate enough to secure Lord Oughton's escort to the book-seller's and we met with Jay and his cousin Miss Poste and her companion. The ladies were in their barouche and he was on foot.'

Miss Porter blinked as she tried to assimilate so much information. 'Lord Oughton? Oh, yes, you spoke of him. How very kind of him. And this Miss Poste, is she as beautiful as you were led to believe?'

'Even more so,' Amanda admitted.

'And Mr Jay…Lord Severn, I should say?'

'Very attentive to Miss Poste and not best pleased to see me, I suspect.' Amanda cast off her bonnet and began to unbutton her pelisse.

'Oh, dear.' Jane sighed. 'And I suppose a cool reception has done nothing to change your feelings for him, hence your quotation?'

'I am afraid not.' Amanda sank down in the window seat.

'Do you…do you *love* him, dear?'

'Yes.'

'Oh.' The ladies sat in silence for a while, then Miss Porter said, with the air of someone who knew they should not ask, but could not restrain themselves. 'And what did you think of Miss Poste? Will she make him a suitable wife, do you think?'

Amanda took a long, considering breath. 'Miss Poste is beautiful, spoilt and I think will prove to be a complete little madam. I pity any man who takes her to wife.'

'Oh, my! I do not recall you saying that Lord Oughton made any such judgement on her character, although I suppose he hardly would.'

'I do not think that gentlemen perceive her real nature: she is too stunning, and so very young. And she takes more care about how she presents herself to men than to women. But, interestingly, Lord Oughton did express doubts about the wisdom of the match to me. She makes him feel uneasy, I think, and not just because he finds her so beautiful.'

Jane cheered up slightly. 'Lord Oughton appears to be taking an interest in you: first he escorts you, then he shows a flattering degree of confidence in confiding in you. What do you know of him? I do wish I had met him.'

'Well, you will tomorrow afternoon, for he is engaged to take me driving. All I know is that he is in London waiting on his mama's pleasure while she makes plans to go to Brighton for the summer, and he has a young sister of about seventeen called Lizzie.'

Miss Porter had jumped to her feet and was thumbing through a rather worn *Peerage* which was on the shelf. 'Here we are. James Henry, third Baron Oughton. Hmm, twenty-eight, single, son of…sister Elizabeth Georgina…principal seat…' She put the book down. 'Do you like him? He seems extremely eligible.'

'Well, yes, I like him very well, Jane. But however eligible he is, he is not courting me—why, we have only met twice, and in any case, I am not looking for another suitor. He is simply a very friendly, personable man who enjoys company.'

'What a pity,' replied Miss Porter with a sigh. 'Well, tell me about your visit to Mrs Thornton. Is the young woman she recommends a suitable lady's maid?'

Chapter Seventeen

Amanda enjoyed driving in Hyde Park with James Oughton and had no hesitation in accepting a second invitation for the following day, once she was sure Miss Porter would not be neglected by her absence.

Over the tea that she was pouring for Lord Oughton and Amanda on their return from the park, she assured them that she was more than occupied. 'Providing Mrs Clare does not require me.' She had a wide circle of friends in town and had also promised herself visits to a number of libraries, so was perfectly happy to be left to her own devices, especially—although naturally she did not express the thought—if it allowed Amanda more time to spend with her pleasant new friend.

She was convinced, whatever Amanda might say, that Lord Oughton was courting her, and thoroughly approved. She admitted to herself that she had quite lost her own heart to Jay's dangerous charm, and knew it would take Amanda a long time to recover, but Lord Oughton struck her as a decent and a patient man and not someone who would be rebuffed by a first refusal.

Amanda therefore found herself collected at half past two the next afternoon. James Oughton helped her up into his curricle and began to guide his team of striking Welsh bays through the narrow streets towards the park. 'Will you forgive Hyde Park for a second time, Mrs Clare? I had promised my mother that I would pass on her invitation to take tea with her this afternoon, and if we go any further afield that would cut down on our time driving.'

'How kind of Lady Oughton, I would be delighted to take tea with her, and of course I do not mind Hyde Park. It is very lovely at this time of year, is it not?' Whatever Jane said, Amanda had no stirring of doubt over whether Lord Oughton was courting her. There was nothing in the slightest bit lover-like in his demeanour, he simply appeared to enjoy her company. Or perhaps he was simply taking the opportunity to introduce a new face to his mother, at a time when London was thin of society. She resolved to stay alert, though, for she had no wish to trifle with his affections.

Once within the park boundaries, he offered her the reins. 'I gather you had driven yourself to Holkham in very dashing style, Mrs Clare. Would you care to try my bays?'

'I would be delighted!' she replied with real pleasure. 'I have been admiring them almost to the point of jealousy. But are you sure? You have no idea of my skill and I might jab their mouths for all you know.'

'I have every confidence,' he said with a smile, handing her the reins, and then, once she had arranged them in her gloved hands, the whip. He sat back as she gathered the team confidently, letting them feel the bits and then giving them enough rein to trot out along the tan carriageway. 'Severn told me you were a notable whip and I see he was correct.'

Her start of surprise must have communicated itself to the horses, for the leaders tossed their heads and she had to give them all her attention. 'Really?' she asked with a light laugh after a moment. 'Do tell me what he said.'

'He said that he had never seen such a combination of courage and light hands, and he wished he might see you with a team instead of just a pair.' Amanda blinked back a tear of sheer pleasure. That was a compliment indeed, and she could just hear the warmth in Jay's voice as he said it. Lord Oughton added, 'He is about to have his wish fulfilled.'

It was all Amanda could do to keep her hands steady on the reins, for Jay was indeed riding towards them at a controlled canter, the hunter he had bought from Will Bream showing every sign of disapproving of this restraint.

He reined in by the side of the track and Amanda felt she could do nothing else but pull up as well as the team came alongside. The day before yesterday she had been too conscious of Miss Poste's sharp eyes to do more than throw the most indifferent and fleeting of glances towards Jay. Now, with every excuse to keep a sharp eye on the horse and rider so closely to her team, she reflected once again what a very striking figure he cut on horseback. His riding attire showed no exaggeration of cut; in fact, it was elegantly simple, but it showed off his long, well-muscled legs and the width of his shoulders to perfection and Amanda had to take herself severely to task for the sudden stab of desire that shot through her. Fine behaviour for a respectable drive in the park!

'Good afternoon, Mrs Clare.' He removed his hat. 'Oughton.'

'Is that the beast you bought in Norfolk, Mansell?' Lord Oughton regarded it with some doubt. 'Very big, isn't it?'

'Too big for the Shires, possibly,' Jay admitted, cursing the animal softly under his breath as it sidled and fretted at having to stand. 'But it can jump a hedge bank from a standing start and will go all day. No manners yet, but that will come with work.'

'You observe that Lord Oughton has kindly allowed me to drive his team?' Amanda asked, for Jay appeared set on exchanging the merest commonplaces with her, if that, and she wanted so much to provoke him. 'I understand I owe this honour to you.'

'To me?' His eyes narrowed and he looked from one to the other.

'Well, Lord Oughton tells me you remarked kindly upon my driving skill, so he feels able to risk his team with me.'

'No risk at all,' retorted his lordship cheerfully. 'I have never seen a lady better able to balance a team— and not many men either, come to that. You were quite right in your praise, Mansell.'

Amanda shot him a glance of glowing appreciation at the generous tribute, then caught Jay's eye. He looked furious. Suddenly she felt angry: what did he think she should do with herself? Take her bruised feelings and stay modestly in her Norfolk backwater, being grateful that she had attracted the attention of such a well-known rake? Or, having ventured out, go scuttling back again once she realised he was in town, just in case she embarrassed him by her presence?

'Are you jealous, my lord?' she enquired sweetly.

'Jealous?' The reaction was all she could have hoped for. His brows drew together sharply and the look he gave her would have sparked tinder. She felt her heart beat faster and a warm glow spread through her. This was a foolish and dangerous game, but to know she had the power to force a reaction from him still, even one of anger, was balm to her wounded feelings.

'Why, yes. Jealous that Lord Oughton should have the confidence to allow me to drive, when you did not have the courage to let me ride your new hunter.'

Unfortunately, for it seemed that she had finally provoked him to the point of incandescence, Lord Oughton broke in. 'Ride that animal? Why, I should think not, Mrs Clare! You might be a notable horsewoman, but that beast would be too much for you.'

'If you say so, my lord,' she responded meekly, then hated herself. She had no right to involve James Oughton in her conflict with Jay: why, she was behaving no better than Miss Poste. 'You are quite right,' she said with a laugh, 'and I am very wrong to tease both of you. That horse would cart me from one end of the park to the other—if it did not have me off its back in three seconds—and I know it quite well.'

This frank admission, however, did nothing but bring a glow of admiration to Lord Oughton's grey eyes, which caused her to blush, more at her own foolishness, than for any fluttering the look produced in her heart.

'When do you return to Norfolk?' Jay asked her abruptly.

'As I believe I said before, my lord, I am not certain.' There was no doubt about it, he wanted her gone, and she was not going to give him the satisfaction of meekly telling him her plans.

'Do you stay long in town?' Lord Oughton asked Jay. 'I wonder if there are enough of us to make up a party one evening.'

Jay was as curt as she had been. 'I expect to leave within the next few days.'

'And Miss Poste?' Amanda could not resist it, then was so flustered at having asked such a stupid question that she dropped the long whip, making the bays snort and back nervously.

'Are you all right, Mrs Clare?' Lord Oughton asked anxiously, earning her abiding gratitude for not taking the reins from her. 'Can you hold them while I jump down and get it?'

'Yes, of course, I am sorry to have been so clumsy.' She steadied the animals, but they had already moved on several paces and Lord Oughton had to walk back to pick up the whip.

Jay edged the big hunter closer to the box and said, low voiced, 'I suggest, Mrs Clare, that you stay away from Miss Poste.'

Amanda stared at him, too taken aback for a moment to reply. His eyes were hard and his mouth a thin line. Whatever had prompted such a remark? 'You *suggest* I stay away from her?' she asked in a puzzled voice, unable to quite comprehend such an abrupt order.

'Very well, ma'am, if that is not clear enough, I *insist* that you stay away from her.'

Then, as she was gathering breath to retort, he raised his voice and said, 'Good day to you. Good day, Oughton.' And was gone, turning the hunter off the track and cantering away into the trees.

Lord Oughton climbed back to his seat and handed her the whip. 'Where on earth has Lord Severn gone to in such a hurry?' he enquired. It was obvious that the hissed exchange had gone unheard.

'Insufferable man!' Amanda exclaimed, suddenly too angry to watch her tongue. She caught a glimpse of

Lord Oughton's face and hastily added, 'Lord Severn, I mean.'

'Well, it did seem an abrupt departure,' James Oughton began, then, seeing Amanda's stormy expression, added, 'But I can see it is more than that! Tell me, Mrs Clare, has Lord Severn done anything to distress you? I would not have it for the world, and you have only to say for me to take him to account.'

'Oh, my goodness, no! The merest irritation of the nerves on my part…you must excuse such an intemperate remark.' It seemed that she was doing nothing but stopping men stalking off to challenge others on her behalf—first Jay with Humphrey, now James Oughton looking darkly serious about how Jay had upset her. She could hardly tell him what had annoyed her so much, especially as it was quite inexplicable why Jay had spoken as he had.

Lord Oughton still looked concerned, so she added, 'It is merely something we cannot agree about and Lord Severn lays down the law about it somewhat.' She made herself laugh lightly. 'I cannot imagine why he takes such a dogmatic line over nothing.'

Even as the words left her lips, she realised exactly why Jay had wanted to stop her speaking to Diana Poste: he thought she would be indiscreet enough to let slip something which might disclose their…flirtation. She felt injured that he would so misjudge her tact. Surely he knew her better? Then she realised the full explanation, and a shock of hot embarrassment seemed to surge right through her. He thought she would *deliberately* say something! He thought that because he had left her so abruptly and with hardly any explanation she would behave like a scorned woman and spitefully meddle to turn the girl he wanted to marry away from him!

The thought was so embarrassing that she almost let go of the reins and had to exercise every bit of self-control to continue driving steadily. Surely she must be blushing scarlet? She felt as though she had been dipped in hot water from head to toe. The thought that anyone at all, let alone Jay, should glimpse her broken heart and could think that she would behave in such a way as a result was deeply shaming.

Amanda doubted she would feel worse if she was driving along with a placard on the carriage telling the world that she had been foolish enough to fall for a rake, to almost succumb to his lovemaking—and was now behaving like an embittered gossip as a result.

The carriage reached the end of the driveway and she asked, 'Which way, my lord? Or would you like to take the reins again? The traffic is rather heavy here.' It was incredible how calm her voice sounded, how steady her hands were, as she handed the reins and whip to him and sat back while he turned the team neatly out of the gate by the Tyburn turnpike and began to drive down Oxford Street.

'Is Lady Oughton accompanied by any of your family?' she asked. It would not do to sit like a dummy beside him.

'My sister Elizabeth—Lizzie to the family—is with her. She is just seventeen and Mama intends for her to make her come-out next Season. She is taking her about a good deal to give her a little confidence before she is officially out.'

'How very wise,' Amanda remarked. 'I wish I had had the opportunity to find my feet a little before my first Season! One feels such a green goose: one minute half in the schoolroom, the next with one's hair up and skirts down, expected to behave like a young lady of fashion.'

'And all the gentlemen surveying this year's débutantes through their quizzing glasses?' James Oughton said teasingly.

'Oh, the gentlemen were no problem at all,' Amanda smiled, thinking back. 'It was all the mamas, and the dowagers and the matchmakers. They look and criticise and demolish any poor girl they take a dislike to: one can be quite crushed by their unkindness. In fact, I had nothing to compare it to until I began to go to market and watched the farmers leaning on the sale ring fence, criticising the unfortunate beasts up for auction.'

This made Lord Oughton laugh so much he was still chuckling when they turned into Holles Street and then into Cavendish Square. They drew up in front of one of the impressive corner houses and the door opened even before he could jump down.

Amanda, ushered in by an imposing butler and two footmen, reflected that, despite his easy-going demeanour, Lord Oughton kept a very fine establishment indeed. 'Mama insists on bringing Hodgkins and a good two-thirds of the country staff up to town with her. It sets up the back of the steward here, and half the footmen have nothing to do, but there's no arguing with her.'

This disclosure did nothing to make Amanda feel any easier: by the sound of it, the Dowager Lady Oughton was going to prove every bit as formidable as the matrons who had turned her knees to jelly at her come-out.

Lord Oughton ushered her up the stairs and threw open the door into what was obviously the principle salon to be greeted with a shriek, a cry of pain and a fleeting glimpse of what appeared to Amanda's startled gaze to be a large, highly coloured feather duster.

'Peters, for heavens sake stop leaping around like the village idiot and seize the thing!' an imperious feminine voice demanded.

'It's bitten me, my lady!' The anguished cry came from a very young footman who was shaking his bleeding right hand and ducking as a large blue and scarlet parrot flapped around the room.

Lord Oughton hastily shut the door behind them and the scene of chaos resolved into two footmen, a young lady helpless with laughter on a sofa and a small, but elegant, grey-headed lady who was attempting to organise her deeply reluctant staff into catching the bird.

Amanda instinctively put out a hand to catch James's arm and the parrot landed on her forearm with a painful thump. There was silence and a sudden stillness as everyone observed the bird. It sidled up Amanda's arm, not hesitating to dig in its claws at every step, eyeing her sideways with an expression of sly calculation as it went.

'Pretty Polly,' she ventured, receiving a black look of contempt for her pains.

'Be damned to the French!' it announced loudly and settled on her shoulder. Amanda felt a twinge of alarm for both her ear and her bonnet trimmings.

'I am so sorry, my dear,' the lady declared. 'You must be Mrs Clare—what an introduction to our house! Lizzie, get up off the sofa and see if you can persuade Nelson to come down off Mrs Clare's shoulder before he eats her ribbons. Peters, wrap my handkerchief around your finger and go straight down to Mrs Doughty and have it bandaged. Watkins, if you will pick up the perch…'

Lizzie coaxed, Amanda stood very still, the second footman advanced stealthily with the perch and, with the air of a bird who had no intention of doing anything but behave in the most obliging manner, Nelson sidled on to it and permitted a chain to be clipped to his leg ring. 'Keelhaul the bastards!' it announced, causing the younger ladies to cover their ears and Lady Oughton to declare.

'Take him straight down to the scullery, Watkins, with my apologies to Mrs Doughty. The Admiral will just have to take him back, I do not care what he says about the inconvenience.' She turned to Amanda with an impish smile, which took thirty years off her age. 'He belongs to my brother, Admiral Fitch, who begged me to take him while he is in the West Indies. He is home now, and the wretched bird can go back to him directly.' She gestured towards the girl who had conquered her giggles and was now waiting to be introduced. 'My daughter Elizabeth. Do, please, sit down, Mrs Clare. I will ring for tea and we can all relax after that imbroglio.'

Amanda liked the Oughton ladies at once. They were charmingly informal, made her instantly at home, and managed to make her feel as though she had known them for years. The ludicrous incident with the parrot quite banished the encounter with Jay in the park from her mind and, with the ice broken so thoroughly, Amanda was relaxed and, had she known it, at her most endearing.

Lady Oughton shot a grateful glance at her son. He had suggested that she might like to meet Mrs Clare, knowing that she was finding London short of company and that she was disappointed with part of her plans for their stay in Brighton. She had discriminating tastes in her confidantes, but if she was going to take a liking to someone it was almost always at first sight.

With the apparent impetuosity that characterised her, she asked, 'Do you intend to remove to Brighton this summer, Mrs Clare?'

'Why, no, ma'am, I had not thought of it. In fact,' Amanda confessed, 'I have never been. Living beside the sea as I do, I suppose it does not occur to me to travel to another coast for relaxation.'

Lady Oughton laughed. 'But, my dear, delightful as I am sure it is, the north Norfolk coast is hardly Brighton!'

The words chimed strangely in Amanda's head and she seemed to hear an echo of her own voice saying, 'This is hardly Brighton!' *Déjà vu*, it had to be. 'Why, no, ma'am, I am sure it is not. I had merely planned to come up to town to engage a new lady's maid, which I have done, and to have a new habit tailored. When that is ready, in a day or so, I suppose I will return to Norfolk.'

'But you have no pressing commitments at home?' her ladyship persisted.

The vision of Cousin Humphrey filled her mind unpleasantly. 'No, I confess I have not.'

'Then why not remove to Brighton? It is charming at this time of year.'

'Yes, do come,' Elizabeth chimed in eagerly. 'We are going at the end of the week, Mama has secured such a charming villa.'

'It is very tempting,' Amanda agreed. 'But I am sure that such accommodation must be engaged well in advance of the summer and I would not care to stay in an hotel.'

'Indeed, normally all the best places have long been

booked, but by a happy chance I have the option upon two properties. I thought my sister and her younger children were going to join us and I took a smaller villa next to ours for them. The children have now got measles, of all the maddening things—'

'Chicken pox, Mama,' Lizzie corrected.

'Maddening,' Lady Oughton persisted, 'and I was about to write to the agent to cancel it. But you can take it instead.' She smiled round the room triumphantly. 'There, is that not a good idea?'

'Splendid, Mama,' her son agreed, looking enquiringly at Amanda. 'But Mrs Clare must be feeling quite breathless at such a sudden suggestion. And perhaps we have put her off with our lunatic parrot!'

'Why…' Amanda looked at the three friendly, pleasant faces and thought of parties and dances and a fashionable promenade. 'Why, I would be delighted! So long, that is, as my companion Miss Porter does not object.'

'Then that is settled.' Lady Oughton clapped her hands in delight. 'Lizzie dear, ring the bell and have the particulars fetched, for Mrs Clare must approve them before she commits herself.'

'Oh, I am sure that if they were your selection they will delightful,' Amanda demurred. Yes, she and Jane would have a holiday, far from Norfolk, far from London. And if Jared Mansell, Lord Severn, thought that he could send her packing off home with one arrogant word, then he had better think again. She looked around the room again, her eyes sparkling with a delight tinged with anger. 'I am sure I must replenish my wardrobe. I do hope you can advise me on what will be suitable, Lady Oughton.'

'We will go shopping!' Lizzie crowed, her delight overriding her brother's faint protest and earned a smile from her new friend.

Chapter Eighteen

The ladies did indeed go shopping. Even Miss Porter, intrigued by the novelty of a seaside holiday, purchased three new gowns and a smart new parasol. Her luggage was also weighed down by the addition of the latest guidebook to the resort, which she had been persuaded to pack rather than to put in her reticule to con upon the journey.

'I am afraid we will seem very provincial, never having been to Brighton before,' she confessed, as their carriage rattled over the cobbles, heading south. 'I should be reading the guide in advance.'

'Nonsense,' said Amanda bracingly. 'Lady Oughton will tell us how to go on, never fear.'

Jane cheered up at this. She thoroughly approved of Amanda's new acquaintances, although at first she had been amazed at the speed with which they had taken up the young widow. But having met them, and seen Lady Oughton for herself and even heard the story of the parrot, her mind was set at rest. She was still curious about Lord Oughton: Amanda was adamant that he was not courting her, and there was nothing of the lover in his open, friendly manner, but Jane tried a little fishing as the hired chaise left the outskirts of town.

'I must say I like the Oughtons very much,' she remarked. 'Lady Oughton is quite an original, is she not? Few ladies would take such an instant liking as she did to you, and then manage to whisk their new friend off on a holiday at such speed.'

'Yes, as you say, an original,' Amanda agreed, laughing. 'And Miss Elizabeth is a charming girl.' Her face clouded slightly. 'Very unlike the beautiful Miss Poste I told you about. Lizzie is so unaffected and enthusiastic.'

'And Lord Oughton,' Miss Porter persisted. 'Very attentive, is he not?'

'I agree, a very good son, and yet not at all tied to his mama's apron strings,' was all Amanda could be led to remark upon.

Oh, well, Miss Porter thought, as the chaise rattled over the cobbles. *Time will tell. She fell for Lord Severn too hard and too fast, perhaps if this young man is interested he will have the sense to court her more steadily.*

The journey down passed uneventfully, although the impressive train of vehicles, consisting of Lady Oughton's travelling coach, Amanda's chaise, the two carriages with luggage and servants, Lord Oughton's curricle, the groom driving his phaeton and the second groom leading two riding horses, caused not a little comment in the villages they passed through.

'I feel as if we are a travelling circus,' Amanda giggled at one point as they descended at an inn to change horses and take refreshments. The ostlers were too busy to stare, but several yokels paused to gawp and the maids hung out of the upper windows to assess the arrivals' fashions and carriages.

'Well, we are not the only cavalcade of such a size,' Jane pointed out as another party clattered past, obviously heading for a change at an inn further along the street. 'They should be used to it on this road.'

'What…?' Amanda shook her head. No, the glimpse through the inn yard arch of carriages and horses in a cloud of dust was too indistinct. There must be any number of large, raw-boned bay hunters on the roads. She was imagining things again. Ever since that encounter in Hyde Park she had been seeing Jay wherever she went—and always finding her eyes, or imagination, were playing her false. She firmly stamped down the humiliating memories of that brief exchange and concentrated on what Lady Oughton was calling as she descended from her carriage.

'My dear, I swear I have been jolted half out of my senses! Never mind, let us see what refreshment we can find within.'

The two villas on Marine Street were every bit as delightful as Lady Oughton's agent had promised. Amanda and Jane, accompanied by both Maria and Susan Wilkes, could find nothing at all to criticise in a pretty house of three stories with a parlour overlooking the bustling street and with tantalising glimpses of the sea, four small but elegant bedrooms to choose from and a resident cook-housekeeper whose first dinner boded well for the remainder of their stay.

The only fly in the ointment of their holiday was Susan. Almost vibrating with nerves, she was trying too hard to be the perfect lady's maid and Amanda found herself spending more time reassuring her than she had expected to spend instructing her.

The next morning Susan became hopelessly muddled and laid out a combination of riding habit, half-boots and a straw bonnet when requested to get ready Amanda's new promenade dress. When the mistakes were gently pointed out, she burst into tears and sobbed inconsolably, convinced she was about to be sent back to London in disgrace.

Amanda was consequently somewhat late in setting out for her walk, perforce accompanied by Maria. Miss Porter had pushed her firmly out of the house saying, 'Get out in the sunshine, dearest, I will calm Susan down.'

Calling first next door to enquire if either of the Oughton ladies wished to accompany her, or had any commissions for her, Amanda was amused to discover that her idea of a late start to the day did not agree with theirs, especially on the morning after a long journey.

So she and Maria went off alone to explore. 'Where shall we go first?' she asked the maid.

'The Pavilion, please, ma'am,' Maria announced, eyes shining at the treat. 'They were telling me all about it last night in the servants' hall, like a fairy tale it is, they say.'

'Then that is where we will go. It will be as well to find it early on so we can take our bearings from it.'

Progress proved slow for there were many things to distract them, from a glimpse of bathing machines—'Ooh, ma'am, you wouldn't, would you? Doesn't seem decent somehow'—to the shop windows, including Donaldson's book shop, which seemed certain to meet with Miss Porter's approval.

Amanda was quietly pleased to see that her own new promenade gown of fawn twill with a trimming of ribbed silk ribbon in a darker shade, a bonnet to match with one small ostrich feather curling under the brim and a particularly frivolous parasol in deep pink were every bit as fashionable as any she saw on her walk. It was doubtless a lowering thought that one's spirits could be so much elevated by a new gown, but she refused to feel guilty about it.

The Pavilion took their breath away, although Amanda suspected that her feelings were not quite those of her maid. After standing speechless for a full minute Maria announced, 'It's even better than the circus!'

Amanda could admire the sheer enormity of the confection, the wild imagination behind it and even some of the details, but the entire building seemed so bizarre, sitting here in an English seaside resort, she could not take it seriously.

'It looks as though a magic carpet has set it down here, all the way from India,' she said at last, still not quite able to make up her mind about it.

'Look, ma'am,' Maria pointed. 'There is a gate and we could walk in the gardens.' Indeed, it did appear that the public might approach right up to the walls of the Pavilion, and there was nothing to prevent the vulgarly curious from peering in at the windows.

Amanda opened the gate and they began to stroll through the gardens, stopping every so often to marvel at some conceit of plasterwork, filigree or gilding. The plantings were quite thick in places and Amanda was walking around one large shrub, craning to make out the detail on a minaret, when she walked into a gentleman striding briskly in the opposite direction.

'I beg your pardon, ma'am.' Jay had lifted his hat

from his head before he recognised her, then the expression of concerned apology on his face turned to anger. 'Amanda! What the devil are you doing here?'

'Will you kindly mind your language, my lord?' she snapped in return, glancing round for Maria. The wretched girl was nowhere to be seen.

Jay made no attempt to acknowledge her reproof. 'Are you following me?'

'Following you?' Amanda gasped. Of all the arrogant, impertinent... She searched frantically for an adequate response. 'I would not follow you, my lord, if you had the last loaf of bread on this earth!'

Jay flushed angrily. He was rather too close for comfort and Amanda stepped back, away from the cold green eyes, to find she had backed herself into a holly bush. 'Ouch!' An equally hasty step forward and she was close enough, should she be so foolish, to touch him.

'Then what are you doing in Brighton, might I ask?' He sounded not just irritated with her, but downright furious, and Amanda could only assume that finding her here had only added to his assumption that she was an angry, jealous woman pursuing her former lover, intent in placing a spoke in the wheel of his new courtship.

'I can see no reason why I need explain myself to you, Lord Severn, but as *I* have no need for secrecy, I am doing what hundreds of other people are doing and spending a few days at the seaside.' She was pleased with the cool indifference of her tone .

'Are you telling me that you secured lodgings at this short notice? You had no intention of coming here a few days ago.' He had been holding his tan gloves in one hand and Amanda was pleased to see that he was now wringing them tight in both fists. She was certainly succeeding in provoking him, and for some reason that was producing a fizzing feeling of exhilaration in her.

'I can see no reason why I should have shared my plans with you,' she observed, twirling her parasol nonchalantly. 'However, although at first I had no intention of coming down here, Lady Oughton suggested it and was able to put me in the way of a very eligible lodging next to hers.'

'Lady Oughton?' His brows drew together darkly. 'She is very busy about her son's affairs.'

'I have no notion what you mean by that remark, but it would become you to speak with more respect of the mother of a close friend.' Amanda had a sinking feeling she knew exactly what Jay meant and that he had concluded that James Oughton was paying court to her. She did not want to be the source of friction between the two men, even less did she want to give Lord Oughton the wrong impression of her feelings, but the discovery that Jay was jealous was intoxicating.

That feeling lasted for only a few seconds. Jay ignored her last remark and said, 'I trust you remember what I said to you on the subject of Miss Poste?'

Of course: Diana Poste. He might indeed be jealous, but only because he expected her to be pining for him, not because he wanted her rather than Miss Poste. Insufferable, arrogant man! Amanda regarded him with lips compressed, searching for something sufficiently cutting to say. Insufferable, arrogant…exciting…The man who had saved her on the stagecoach, rescued her from Cousin Humphrey, the man who could ride like the devil and make love like…

'I remember your impertinent orders, my lord. I assume from you having the ill grace to repeat them that Miss Poste is in Brighton. Let me make myself clear: I had no intention of obeying you then, and I have none now.' With her chin up, she confronted him. 'Now, if you will kindly step out of my way...'

He did not move. He stared down into her defiant eyes and said slowly, 'You are the most infuriating, aggravating, provoking, troublesome woman I have ever encountered, and if you were not such a little innocent...'

'I am not a little innocent!' Amanda protested, ridiculously affronted.

'No?' His voice was suddenly soft, but under it she could read a throb of anger, and something else.

'No!'

He took her in his arms with such suddenness that Amanda dropped her parasol, stepped back into the prickly shrub and then recoiled, only to find herself locked in the embrace. Jay's hands were hard on her arms and his mouth, when it captured hers, was equally unyielding. He had kissed her before with passion, he had kissed her teasingly, sleepily and formally, but he had never kissed her like this, in anger.

His mouth plundered hers despite her reaction, despite her attempts to bite and kick. She had never been so aware of his size and his strength and the sheer power of him. Unbidden, the memory of him walking naked out of the sea came into her mind and a wave of sheer desire came over her. It made her angrier, both at him and at herself, more determined to break free before she made any more shaming discoveries about her responses to him.

Jay let her go as abruptly as he had taken her. Amanda took a long, shuddering breath, raised her right hand and hit out. He parried the blow with insulting ease on the flat of his palm and they stood for a moment, frozen in a pose of arrested violence. Then Lord Severn turned on his heel and walked back the way he had come.

Amanda stood staring at the point where he disappeared from view, then shakily looked around. No one, thank goodness, was in sight although she could hear Maria calling, 'Mrs Clare, ma'am!'

What on earth did she look like? Amanda straightened her bonnet and dabbed her flushed face with her pocket handkerchief. Her mouth felt tender, swollen, and she pressed the back of her hand against it, shutting her eyes as she struggled with the memory of that furious kiss. Her feelings were too confused to allow her to think straight, and as to what had prompted Jay, she did not like to contemplate.

'Maria!' she called at last and was rewarded by the sight of her errant handmaiden, running around the side of the shrubbery.

'Oh, ma'am, I am that sorry…'

'Where have you been?' Amanda demanded angrily. 'All I ask is that you stay with me, and you vanish into the gardens—whatever might have happened to you, wandering about on your own?'

That was the pot calling the kettle black with a vengeance. Amanda felt a twinge of guilt, but the girl had been at fault and her mistress's irritation did at least provide an excuse for Amanda's flushed face and agitation.

'I'm sorry, ma'am, I only looked in a window for a moment, and you were gone.'

'Looked in a window! I am ashamed of you, Maria! This is a private house and regard for other people's privacy, let alone your respect for his Royal Highness, should have told you better.'

'Yes, ma'am.' She hung her head. 'Oh, your parasol, Mrs Clare!'

The beautiful pink parasol was indeed on the ground and covered in dust. It also, Amanda realised, snatching it up, bore the imprint of a large, masculine boot. Amanda flapped at it with her handkerchief and turned on her heel. 'We are going home directly,' she announced. 'Now, this time, do try to pay attention and stay close!'

To walk through the streets, thronged with fashionable visitors, with a flushed face, disarranged hair and a crushed and dirty parasol was salt in the wounds Amanda felt she had just received. She took a chance on remembering the map in Jane's guidebook and took Edward Street rather than hazard the crowds on Marine Parade. After one or two false turns they found themselves back at Marine Street and Amanda sent a chastened Maria off to the kitchens.

She walked slowly upstairs, untying her bonnet strings and trying to sort out just how she felt. It was surprisingly difficult to formulate a coherent thought. She met Jane on the landing and saw in her face confirmation of her dishevelled looks.

'My dear Amanda! Whatever is the matter?' Miss Porter hustled Amanda through her bedchamber door, took her bonnet and gloves and pressed her down into a chair. 'My love, you look positively distracted.'

Amanda looked back into her kind, anxious eyes and all her confusion and desire welled up inside her. 'I met Jay at the Pavilion, and he kissed me, and I hate him!'

And she burst into a storm of angry tears.

Miss Porter patted and clucked and produced clean handkerchiefs, *sal volatile* and sympathy until Amanda calmed down. She emerged from the depths of a handkerchief and remarked, with a brave attempt at a watery smile, 'I'm as bad as Kate.'

'What!' Miss Porter dropped the bottle of smelling salts. 'You are not—'

'No, no! Good heavens, Jane, of course I am not, er…with child.' She blew her nose firmly. 'All I meant was that I have just made as much of a noisy exhibition of myself as Kate did. I am amazed it has not fetched the servants up from the kitchens!'

'Shall I ring for a cup of tea?' Jane enquired anxiously. Taking Amanda's rather distracted nod for assent, she did so, intercepting Susan on the landing and telling her that Mrs Clare had a severe headache and she was to leave the tea tray on the landing table and not disturb her by knocking.

'You told her no untruth,' Amanda admitted ten minutes later as she wanly sipped at the tea. 'I feel as though my head is in a vice. What a perfectly horrible morning.'

'Can you tell me about it yet, dear?'

'Maria and I managed to become separated in the Pavilion gardens and I bumped—quite literally—into Lord Severn. He and Miss Poste must be staying here too. He was furious that I was here, angry to discover that Lord Oughton had had a hand in it and ordered me not to have anything to do with Miss Poste.'

Jane, who had been listening with rapt attention, had no difficulty in reaching the same conclusion that Amanda had. 'Why, that is outrageous!' she exclaimed. 'Does he think you would deliberately say something to that child out of spite?'

'I can think of no other explanation. Humiliating, is it not, to be thought of by the man you love as a jealous, spiteful woman?'

'You still love him? You said you hated him.'

'Love him…hate him…I do not know, Jane.' Amanda looked down at her clasped hands. 'He kissed me, Jane. He was so angry…it was a horrible experience, and yet…oh, Jane, I *wanted* him so much!'

Miss Porter turned a rosy shade of pink. 'Oh.' She thought a moment, then bravely asked, 'I do not know about this sort of thing, of course, but do you think it is because it is rather a long time since your poor husband died and you…that is…?'

'No, I do not.' Amanda considered her feelings as objectively as she could. 'I think I desire him because I love him. And I am well aware that no well-bred lady would express such a sentiment, but I am not going to start lying to myself, or to you. And, yes, I know what you are going to ask: why do I still love him when he is being so horrible?'

Miss Porter agreed that, yes, that was exactly what she was wondering.

'I have no idea Jane, unless that is how I know it truly *is* love.'

'And what will you do if you meet Miss Poste?'

'Be as pleasant as I can be to her. She might be a spoiled young beauty, but she is very young and it sounds as though she is in the middle of a tug of war between her father, Lord Severn and this man with the horrible reputation.'

'Lord Langham?'

'Yes. It must be a horrible position to be in, especially if her father really does favour Lord Langham's suit. The poor child needs all the friends she can muster.'

'But if by befriending her you assist her in marrying Lord Severn?' Jane ventured. 'What then?'

Amanda bit her lip. 'He is not going to marry me, that is for certain, so it will be better all round if he marries the girl he loves.'

Miss Porter reached over and took her hand. 'That is very noble, dear, but is it really what you want?'

Amanda gave a dry sob. 'No, of course it is not what I want, but I think it is what is right.'

Chapter Nineteen

After luncheon Amanda did her best to put on a brave face, but Lady Oughton, calling round to thank her for her earlier offer, took one look at her and declared that she should rest.

'You look worn to the bone, my dear Mrs Clare. The journey must have taken more out of you than you thought and going out so early this morning did not allow you the rest you needed. Lizzie is just the same—she bounced out of bed at seven of the clock and now is yawning her head off.'

Amanda agreed that, yes, she did not feel quite herself.

'I find the sea air often has that effect on new arrivals. After a day you will feel thoroughly invigorated, I promise. Now, I intend going and writing our names in the book at the Pavilion—not that I expect any receptions there just at the moment, but we must not neglect any attention due to his Royal Highness—and also at the Assembly Rooms. The Master of Ceremonies will then be certain to inform us of all the dances and card parties at the Old Ship and the Castle inns...'

'Is there much regular entertainment, then?' Amanda

asked. She had never felt less like dancing, but this might be the place to begin her campaign to propel Miss Poste into Jay's arms.

'Indeed, yes. Nothing to compare with Almack's, as you would expect,' Lady Oughton said somewhat dismissively. 'But the refreshments are infinitely more acceptable—not that that would be difficult! The society varies a great deal, depending on who is in town, of course. One has to resign oneself to a more limited circle of acquaintance, but one doesn't regard that too much when one is away for a relatively short time.'

The next day the ladies spent in strolling around Brighton and window shopping. Lady Oughton dealt firmly with Miss Elizabeth's pleas to try sea bathing, but encouraged Amanda to try it. Amanda was equally firm in denying all desire to venture out into the waves, even from the sanctuary of a bathing machine under the supervision of one of the formidable bathing women.

'Look how public it is,' she protested, waving a hand towards the young gentlemen who were casually strolling along, pretending not to ogle the distant bathers.

'They cannot see anything.' Lizzie laughed, then stopped abruptly as her attention was drawn to a telescope, which could be seen protruding from an upper window on Marine Parade. 'Men are *beasts*!' she announced, just as her brother joined them.

'In that case, I shall turn on my heel and go straight back to our lodgings,' he said in a wounded tone. 'I had only sought you out in case I could assist with any parcels, but if my entire sex is repugnant to you…'

'Not you, James!' Lizzie lowered her voice. 'But all these men positively ogling the bathers. Is it not deplorable?'

'Deplorable,' he agreed solemnly, catching Amanda's eye. 'There is no justification for it, however attractive the ankle glimpsed might be.'

Amanda repressed a giggle and accepted his proffered arm, his mama and sister having announced that they wanted to sit upon one of the benches and admire the prospect for a while.

'Dear Lizzie,' he chuckled. 'She is very young, and still not at all up to snuff. I am afraid the wicked flirtations of the gentlemen she will soon be encountering will be a shock to her.'

'She is very charming, and I do not think she will have trouble dealing with rakes. One scandalised look from those innocent big eyes and they will retreat in disorder.'

'Speaking of rakes—' Lord Oughton waved a hand in greeting. '—here comes Severn.' He felt the involuntary stiffening of Amanda's arm and glanced down. 'Are you and he still at odds?'

'No, not in the slightest,' she managed to say.

Jay crossed the road in response to his friend's signal. Amanda scanned his face anxiously as he approached them. What would his mood be? She struggled to compose her face into an expression of amiable disinterest, which she felt was the most socially acceptable response in the situation, and was amazed to see that he appeared not only friendly, but positively pleased to see her. She felt her eyes narrow suspiciously and forced a smile.

'My lord.'

'A happy coincidence,' he remarked after greeting Lord Oughton. 'I was coming to call upon you, Mrs Clare.'

'Indeed?'

'I was going to invite you to drive with me on the Downs.'

'I am afraid I am engaged.'

'Not every day, surely, Mrs Clare?'

She kept her gaze firmly to the front as she walked slowly between James Oughton on one side and Jay on the other. All she could see of him was the flash of polished leather and the swing of the tassels on his Hessian boots at each step, but the warmth of his shoulder and arm, so close to hers, seemed to burn in a way that the touch of Lord Oughton's forearm under her hand did not.

'I thank you, my lord, but I do expect to be engaged every day.'

She expected him to show some anger at this snub, especially after his reaction to her defiance the day before, but when he replied she could hear the smile in his voice. 'And will you be attending dances while you are here?'

'I will be guided by Lady Oughton,' Amanda replied. 'I have no plans of my own.'

'Running scared, Amanda?' Jay enquired wickedly.

Her frosty, 'I *beg* your pardon?' coincided with Lord Oughton's 'What do you mean, Severn?'

'Merely that I wished to tease Mrs Clare for pretending to be a country mouse and not daring to venture out except under the guidance of Lady Oughton,' Jay answered placidly.

Wretched man! He appeared to have smoothed down his friend's hackles, for James Oughton laughed and enquired, 'Is your cousin Miss Poste in Brighton?'

'Yes, her father has taken a house along the Old Steyne. I believe they intend to make a long stay.' Jay's voice was perfectly indifferent and Amanda risked a glance at him. He was looking relaxed, tanned and fit and perfectly at harmony with all around him. Amanda longed to puncture what she was certain was a front.

'And is Lord Langham also in Brighton?' she asked. 'Miss Poste is engaged to be married to him, is she not? I have heard so much about him that I long to see this notorious rake for myself.'

'He has no need to take lodgings,' Jay said, with, she was interested to note, the first hint of reticence in his voice. 'His country seat is not far out of Brighton. I believe he stays at the Castle inn on occasion.' He met Amanda's gaze and there was a hint of a challenge in his. She smiled into his eyes, then swallowed at the sudden flash of fire in their green depths.

Being with him was painfully pleasurable, like eating a delicious sweetmeat when one had a bad tooth and having the pain lance through the delight when one least expected it.

'If you will not drive with me and cannot tell me where you may be found in the evening, I am at a loss, Mrs Clare.'

'Why is that, my lord? Oh, look, Lord Oughton, there is Lady Oughton and Miss Elizabeth, we should rejoin them.'

'Excuse me one moment, Mrs Clare.' Lord Oughton freed her arm and strode across the road to join his family. Amanda could see an earnest discussion was starting, with each of them apparently having a different view on where to go next.

Jay paused for a moment, then answered her question. 'I need to speak to you.'

'Is that necessary? A note of apology for your behaviour yesterday would be acceptable—in fact, more so than your presence.'

'You made me very angry, Amanda.' He took her arm and steered her slightly away from the passing pedestrians.

'And that is your excuse for…for *assaulting* me?'

'No, not an excuse.' He hesitated and for the first time Amanda guessed that he was genuinely uncertain how to proceed. No doubt it was difficult to tell a lady just how poorly you feared she would behave towards the new object of your affections, but she was certainly going to give him no help. 'I need to explain something to you.'

Amanda regarded him with eyes that sparkled with angry, unshed tears. If the Earl of Severn thought she was going accept his explanation, he was seriously mistaken. She had a sinking feeling that if she stayed close to him a moment longer she was going to cry, and that if he touched her she would humiliate herself by throwing herself into his arms and telling him she loved him whatever he did.

Help was at hand. Lady Oughton, her children behind her, swept out into the road with a sublime disregard for the traffic and bore down upon them. 'Lord Severn! How well you look. Is Brighton not charming at this time of year?'

The five of them lingered for a few moments together exchanging pleasantries. Amanda, distracted though she was, had a feeling that the dowager was well aware of the tension between herself and Jay.

Her parting shot filled Amanda with dread. 'It is Thursday today, is it not? Ah, yes, then tonight is the dance at the Ship. Will we see you there, Lord Severn?'

'I hope so,' he responded with a polite bow. 'Does all your party attend?'

'If Mrs Clare and Miss Porter are willing, then certainly we will all be there.'

In the face of this Amanda could do no more than reply that she would be delighted and had no doubt that dear Jane would be too.

Indeed Miss Porter was only too happy to display her new gown and indulge, as she put it, in a little 'raking'. 'We do not have many opportunities to dance at more than small gatherings,' she explained to Lady Oughton. 'Why, I cannot recall the last one. It is several weeks even since the dinner at the Hall, is it not, Mrs Clare?'

Amanda hoped that no one had noticed the blush that rose to her cheeks at the reminder. She had no idea how she would react if Jay asked her to dance this evening: her only consolation was that there was no moonlit garden, no classical temple, to be alone with him in. There would be no opportunity for either lovemaking or quarrelling in such a public place.

Almost defiantly she dressed in exactly the gown and jewels she had worn for the dinner at Glaven Hall. She did not know whether it was because she wished to rekindle the memory of that night in Jay's heart or because she wished to demonstrate to him that she did not care whether he remembered or not.

Lord Oughton collected the ladies and had secured chairs for them for the comparatively short distance to the Ship inn. 'Mama felt it would be better than all of you risking crushing your skirts in the carriage,' he explained as he marshalled his little flotilla of chairs and their bearers.

When he helped them out, he remarked to Amanda, 'I think you will be impressed by the ballroom here,' and indeed she was startled into admiration by the great classical chamber with its rows of columns and painted freeze.

'It is not at all what I expected in an inn,' she admitted. A rapid glance around had revealed some faces that were familiar to her, but there was no sign of Jay or of Diana Poste.

'Eighty feet long, I believe.' James Oughton sounded somewhat distracted. Amanda realised that the Oughton ladies had disappeared into the throng. 'Mrs Clare, could I beg the indulgence of a few words alone?'

'Why, yes,' Amanda agreed, her heart sinking. Had she been wrong and Jane right and he was about to make her a declaration?

He drew her aside into a curtained alcove and said, 'I hope you will forgive me if this is an impertinent question, but I feel you are under my protection at the moment.'

Not a proposal of marriage, she thought with relief. But what on earth was he about to ask? 'Please, ask whatever you wish my lord.'

'It is simply that I fear there is something very amiss between you and Lord Severn, and if he is causing you any distress, you have only to say the word and I will speak to him.'

Amanda stared at him, too taken aback by this very frank query to produce an instant, light response to dismiss it.

'I see there is something,' he said slowly, a frown marring his normally amiable expression.

'Yes…but there is nothing you can do or say. And please do not think that Jay…that Lord Severn is in any way making, er…unwelcome advances or anything of that sort. We have disagreed about something and I am too stubborn, and he is too autocratic, to settle our quarrel easily.'

If Lord Oughton picked up her slip over Jay's name, he said nothing of it. 'Very well, but do tell me if there is any way in which I can assist you.'

'I will, and thank you,' Amanda replied with genuine warmth. 'I think I had better return to the ballroom or Lady Oughton will be wondering what has become of me.'

'Yes, I will follow in a moment.' Lord Oughton took her hand and kissed her fingertips. Amanda could not help remembering Jay's lips on her hand, his thumb tracing erotic havoc in her palm.

She parted the curtains and left him, stepping rather blindly out into the bright lights of ballroom. The place was becoming thronged and it took her a few moments to make her way more than a few steps forward. Glancing around, her eyes met Jay's across the dance floor and she saw his eyes narrow suddenly. His gaze was focused over her shoulder and she realised that Lord Oughton had emerged from the curtains behind her.

Unable to cope with facing either of them, Amanda began to weave her way through the throng. At length she emerged towards the back of the ballroom into a slightly quieter area and saw Miss Poste standing with her companion Miss Woodley and chatting to two other young ladies. She saw Amanda and her remarkable blue eyes widened, but she did not seem unfriendly and Amanda walked towards her, a smile firmly on her lips.

The other girls faded away at the sight of an unknown matron and Miss Woodley effaced herself, leaving Amanda and Diana Poste effectively alone amid the crowded room.

'Good evening, Mrs Clare.' As befitted a much younger woman she curtsied neatly.

'You remembered me, then,' Amanda said pleasantly. 'I was not sure that you would.'

There was none of the sharp, watchful expression on the girl's face this time and she murmured. 'You were very kind when we met, ma'am. I am afraid I was not polite.'

'It is not always easy when one is just out to always strike the right tone,' Amanda said conciliatingly, wondering if she had misjudged the child. It had been a frank apology. She tried to respond in kind. 'And perhaps one's elders can seem just a little patronising?'

Diana flashed her a grateful look, then bit her lip. 'Might I...might I confide in you, Mrs Clare?'

'Why, of course, anything which it is proper for you to discuss with a stranger.' Amanda was taken quite aback by this sudden question. It was what she had been hoping for, but the speed of the girl's approach startled her. 'After all, you have your companion...'

'She has not been married.' Diana cast down her eyes and blushed, managing to look, if anything, even prettier.

'Oh.' Amanda stepped back into a embrasure with an unoccupied sofa. 'Well, you may ask me what you wish, but I cannot promise that I will answer everything!'

'Thank you, ma'am.' Diana clasped her hands in her lap and burst out, 'Should I be guided absolutely by what Papa wishes?'

'You mean in marriage? Well, you should listen most carefully to his advice; after all, he will be trying to do his best for your future.'

'He wants me to marry Lord Langham,' Diana whispered. 'He is much older than I am.'

'I do not know his lordship,' Amanda temporised, wondering if she really should pursue this conversation.

'He is over there. See.' Diana made a little gesture. 'The tall, slender man talking to the lady in the puce toque.'

One look at Lord Langham and Amanda felt she could not, under any circumstances, do anything but oppose such a match. His lordship was certainly an elegant figure, but his face was alive with a hard, wicked, satirical intelligence and a lifetime of experience and dissipation seemed to speak from every feature.

'He is much older than you,' Amanda said, shaken. *I would not like to find myself alone with him*, she thought and an involuntary shiver ran through her.

'He is forty-five, I think,' Diana confessed. 'I am a little afraid of him.' She flushed delicately.

'I am not surprised,' said Amanda, nailing her colours to the mast. 'I do not think you should marry him at all!'

'Oh.' Diana gave a little breathy sob. 'You see, there is someone else.' She was obviously overwrought, for her voice quivered with what Amanda could have sworn, under other circumstances, was laughter.

'Who?' she prompted gently, patting the girl's hand. It tensed under hers, curling into a little claw, then relaxed. Poor child, she thought, forgetting her own pain, she is a mass of nerves.

'The Earl of Severn,' Diana whispered. 'You know him, of course. He is a distant cousin of mine.'

'You love him?' *You see*, her inner voice told Amanda, *it is perfectly possible to do the right thing.*

She loves him, he loves her. What does your breaking heart matter?

'Yes.' Diana buried her face in a lace handkerchief, her shoulders shaking.

'Try not to cry, dear, you might be observed,' Amanda said gently, wishing she could burst into sobs herself.

'Of course.' The perfect little face emerged from the lace, not a tear in sight. 'I must control myself, I know. Do you think there is any hope for me?'

'You must explain to your papa, Miss Poste. Surely he would consider a match with an Earl more than eligible?'

'Under normal circumstances, yes.' Miss Poste lowered her voice and added, 'But I think Lord Langham has a *hold* on Papa. And darling Jared has done something to annoy him, so Papa will not listen to him. They had the most awful row only the other week.'

Darling Jared… 'You must be strong,' Amanda counselled, wishing she could follow her own advice. 'Explain to your papa respectfully, but firmly. He can hardly force you to the altar.'

'If only I knew where my duty lay.'

Really, Amanda thought, *she has been reading too many novels!*

'I cannot believe that any young lady's duty lies in sacrificing herself to a hardened rake,' she was saying tartly when Miss Poste's lips parted in a little sigh, showing two rows of perfect white teeth.

'Oh, here he is!'

Amanda looked up, bracing herself for a confrontation with the sinister Lord Langham, only to find Jay approaching them, an expression of considerable displeasure on his face.

'Cousin Jared!'

The name rang uncomfortably in Amanda's ears. *He's not your Jared*, she longed to protest, *he is* my *Jay!*

'Diana, my dear, surely you should be with your companion and not talking to strangers? Mrs Clare, may I have the pleasure of this dance?'

Amanda swallowed. Beside her she could feel Diana, almost vibrating with emotion at this comprehensive snub. She wanted to say, *He is angry with me, not with you*, but that was impossible, so she stood up and said, 'Good evening, Miss Poste, it was delightful to meet you again. I am sorry, my lord, I do not dance this evening.'

She began to walk past him, but somehow Jay was standing in her way, quite uncaring that Diana was right beside them.

'Oh, I think that you do ma'am,' he said with a chilly calm and with a quick movement had encircled her waist, taken her right hand and whirled her into the waltz, which was just striking up.

Chapter Twenty

Amanda was forced by Jay's peremptory move to take several rapid steps to keep her balance and to scoop up her trailing skirts with her free hand. By that time they were on the floor and, short of wrenching herself free and storming off, she had no option but to dance with him.

'How dare you!' she hissed while keeping a fixed smile on her lips. Her fingers quivered against his palm, his other hand seemed to burn through the thin fabric at her waist.

'I told you, Amanda, do not talk to Diana Poste.' He was smiling too, a smile that did not reach his eyes.

'You have certainly snubbed the poor child comprehensively.'

'She needs to learn discretion,' Jay replied coldly. 'If it is not too late.'

'She may well attend to your instructions, but how do you intend to enforce your demands on me in the middle of the dance floor?' Amanda enquired sarcastically. 'You can hardly kiss me into silence here, can you?'

'Believe me, the temptation is considerable.' His

smile this time was genuine, but the quality of it made her shiver. 'On this occasion, my intention is simply to remove you from that end of the ballroom and to deliver you to your suitor and his family at the other.'

'He is…' Amanda choked back the words. She had no intention of telling Jay that she and James Oughton were friends and no more. He had forfeited all rights to ask her about anything in her private life. If he wanted to raise it with Lord Oughton, then let him see where that got him!

'So you do not deny it, then. You have done well to secure his regard, Amanda, he is a good man.'

'I am well aware of that,' she snapped, then hastily refixed her social smile.

'So we are in agreement on something,' Jay said, almost pacifically. 'Then why do you not relax and enjoy this dance?'

Everything she could think of to say was either spiteful, petty or exposed her broken heart. Amanda shut her lips and tried to do as Jay told her. They danced in rigid silence for a long minute, then the music claimed her and she let herself go with it, go with his lead. It was as though they had been made to dance together, she realised hazily. His long, fit body guided her without effort, without any compulsion. He appeared to have an innate sense of rhythm and balance, weaving her between the other dancers until she felt they were in a world of their own.

She was not aware that her eyes were closed, that her lips were parted in a tender, sensual smile. Across the dance floor James Oughton swore softly under his breath and his mother said, 'I thought that was how the land lay.' She shot her son a sharp glance. 'Had you any thought of…?'

'No. I think that if I allowed myself to, I would be very attached to Amanda Clare. But almost from the start I have sensed something between them.' He frowned, watching the circling couple. 'I wonder if I said something tactless at Holkham. I mentioned an attachment I thought Mansell had made, but I think now I was wrong.' He thought for a while longer. 'No, I could only make things worse if I try and interfere now. Those two have got their problems to resolve and I do not think that my well-intentioned meddling is going to help!'

'No,' Lady Oughton agreed thoughtfully. 'Best to leave well alone. They are two grown people, after all.'

The music ended with a flourish, depositing Amanda and Jay neatly in front of the Oughtons. Amanda reluctantly opened her eyes and met the somewhat quizzical gaze of Lady Oughton. She blushed and curtsied to Jay. 'Thank you, my lord.'

He bowed to her and the dowager and directed a somewhat ironical smile towards Lord Oughton, then walked away around the edge of the ballroom.

Amanda looked round to find that James had vanished and that the dowager was regarding her with a raised brow.

'Ma'am—' she began.

'What a good dancer the Earl is,' Lady Oughton remarked blandly. 'I understand you have known him for rather longer than you have been acquainted with James?'

She began to stroll along the room, exchanging nods and greetings with other matrons, and Amanda could do nothing but follow.

'Yes, ma'am. Lord Severn introduced us at Holkham.'

'Hmm. About time that young man settled down.'

'Er...which one, Lady Oughton?'

The dowager laughed. 'Why, both of them, my dear! Now, where has Lizzie got to? I am being a very lax chaperon.'

Amanda scanned the room, looking for the errant debutante. James she could see on the other side of the floor, dancing a country measure with an attractive redhead. She looked further along and saw a very dark head close to a striking blonde one and realised that Jay had made his way back to Diana Poste. Amanda knew she should not stare, but she could not help herself. They seemed deep in serious conversation: she could not see Jay's face, but Diana's was turned up to his, a look of earnest attention on her features. As Amanda watched she nodded and Jay took her arm and steered her back towards the chaperons.

Some instinct made Amanda look in the other direction and there was Lord Langham watching them, his face very still. As if he felt her gaze on him, his eyes turned and met Amanda's. Even across the room she could see them widen in a look of blatant appraisal. She felt as though he had stripped off her dress and she hastily turned her head and hurried after Lady Oughton. Ugh! Awful man! The thought of him touching that pretty child...

Lady Oughton had found her daughter, who was sitting on a sofa beside Miss Porter, sniffing miserably at a vinaigrette.

'Oh, Lady Oughton!' Jane got to her feet and drew the dowager and Amanda closer to the seat. 'Poor Miss Oughton has the most afflicting migraine. I was about to seek you out: I really feel she should go home at once and rest.'

'Indeed she must! I must thank you for looking after her, Miss Porter. Excitement sometimes has this effect. There, there, Lizzie dear, we will soon be home.'

With a word, Amanda slipped away to find James Oughton. Luckily his dance partner's red head was visible amidst the throng and Amanda caught him as he escorted her off the dance floor. 'My lord, please excuse me, but your sister is feeling unwell and your mama thinks she should be taken home at once.'

Lord Oughton soon returned with the news that chairs had been called. As his mother and Miss Porter shepherded the wan figure of Lizzie towards the door, he stopped and took Amanda's hand. 'There is no need for you and Miss Porter to spoil your evening. Why do you not remain and I will return to escort you home later?'

'I would not dream of it,' Amanda protested. 'To stay here while poor Miss Elizabeth is feeling so unwell! No, we will return with you in case there is anything we can do to assist your mother.'

'You are very good,' he said warmly, raising her hand to his lips.

'Nonsense.' Amanda smiled back, then saw Jay watching her over James's shoulder. It seemed he had been walking towards them; now he turned on his heel and vanished into the card room.

Amanda left the Castle inn in a state of inner turmoil which she congratulated herself was not visible to her friends. However, she had underestimated Jane's powers of observation, although, as so often, Miss Porter favoured the oblique approach.

Back in their little villa she perched on the edge of Amanda's bed and remarked, 'I saw Lord Severn there this evening.'

'Really? So did I. In fact, we had one dance together.' Amanda unclasped her necklace and handed it to Susan. 'That is right, the blue box, with the earrings.'

'He was entering the card room,' Jane continued. 'Something had obviously annoyed him: his face was like thunder.'

'Indeed? Thank you, Susan, if you will just help me out of this gown and into my robe, you may go to bed. I will manage my own hair.'

She waited while Susan shut the door behind her and then began to sweep the brush through her loosened hair. 'I spoke for some time to Miss Poste and he was annoyed by that.'

Miss Porter got up and came to take the hair brush, smoothing the tangles at the back of Amanda's head. 'And what was your opinion of Miss Poste on closer acquaintance? Do you still think her spoilt?'

Amanda wrinkled her nose thoughtfully. 'I am not sure. She is very young, and at times her conversation was positively banal—almost too predictable. Which is odd, because I do not think her unintelligent. But she showed none of that sharp, unbecoming, edge I noticed in London. I think it may have been nerves and gaucheness.'

'And did she speak about Lord Severn?' Jane prompted.

'Oh, yes,' Amanda said with a short laugh. 'She informed me that she loved him, but that she thought she should do what her father wanted and marry Lord Langham.'

'That seems very strange,' Jane mused. 'Why should anyone prefer a middle-aged rake of the lesser nobility to an Earl for their daughter?'

'Diana maintains that Langham has a hold of some

kind on her father. I thought it melodramatic, but having seen the man I can believe he might well stoop to blackmail to get what he wants.'

'What is he like?' Jane put down the brush and sat down on the bed again. 'Come, get into bed and tell me all about it.'

'There is not much to tell,' Amanda admitted, snuffing out the dressing table candles and climbing into bed. She plumped up the pillows behind her and settled back. 'Are you warm enough, Jane? There is a rug on the chair. Diana tells me he is forty-five, and he certainly looks every one of his years. I did not speak to him, I am glad to say, but he struck me as…oh, reptilian.'

'It is you who are being melodramatic now, surely!' Jane hooked the rug off the chair, wrapped it around her shoulders and settled back against the post at the foot of the bed.

'Indeed I am not! The man gave me the shivers, even across the width of the dance floor. He caught my eye, Jane, and the look he gave me! Why, I felt besmirched.'

'Then it is easy to understand why Miss Poste prefers her cousin Severn. Surely she only has to tell her father so?'

'She appears to be torn between her duty to her papa, fear that he will make her marry Langham whatever she says, and adoration for Jay.'

'Have you seen them together?'

'Yes.' Amanda cocked her head on one side in thought. 'He snubbed her thoroughly for talking to me, but a while later I saw them together and he appears deeply concerned for her. I think the way he spoke to her was simply over-protectiveness and he does indeed care for her.'

'Then you are determined on this course of bringing them together?'

'I could not, in all conscience, do anything to obstruct it, that is for sure.' Amanda sighed. 'It is every bit as difficult as I thought it would be. It would be even worse if Lord Langham was not so dreadful: how can I not make a push to at least try and help her avoid his clutches?'

Miss Porter looked worried. 'You know, my dear, you have often owned to me that you are constitutionally inquisitive, managing and—'

'Interfering?' Amanda finished for her. 'Well, and so I am!'

'Yes, dear, and that is all very well about your own affairs and with our own people in Norfolk. But here you are meddling with the affairs of two prominent men. And one of them, by all accounts, is a very unsavoury character.'

'And the other is autocratic, insufferable, arrogant and determined to get his own way,' Amanda finished for her. 'I know that, and I have no hope at all that I am going to emerge from this without suffering, at the very least, some knocks to my self-esteem.'

Shaking her head at this obstinacy Jane folded the rug and made her way to her own bedchamber. Amanda, left alone in the darkness, drifted off to sleep, a sleep filled with the whirling images of the dance floor as she spun round and round in Jay's arms.

'I love you,' she murmured against the pillow and in her sleep tears rolled gently down her cheeks and soaked into the linen.

The next morning dawned bright and warm. Lady Oughton sent round a message asking if Jane and

Amanda would care to join her and Lizzie in a carriage expedition along the coast road.

It will blow away the remains of her migraine, she wrote, *and a change of pace from the hustle of the town will calm her. I am sure you will enjoy the scenery and I know of a charming inn where we may take luncheon in a private parlour. Dear James has to go back to town on a matter of business for two days, but we will take a footman with us.*

'That does sound tempting,' Jane remarked when Amanda passed her the note over breakfast. 'The scenery is so different from what we are used to, I would enjoy seeing more of it. What do you think, my love?'

'You go, Jane. I have so many letters I must write, and there is a very complicated one from my steward that I have been putting off wrestling with for three days! It seems hard to think about a dispute over drainage rights here, but I cannot leave it any longer.'

'You will not be writing letters all day, surely,' Jane protested. 'To miss out on such a lovely day as this seems a shame.'

'I will take a walk later,' Amanda promised. 'You go, or I will feel guilty.'

It was almost eleven when she sealed the letter to Mr Pococke and her head was spinning from studying his minute drawings of ditches and boundaries. In the end she had to agree with his proposed course of action and she was rather mutinously thinking that she need not have expended so much effort at all when a guilty pang reminded her that she had never spent so much time away from the estate before. There was something to be said about a subject as prosaic as drains, she mused, ringing for Susan, it most certainly took one's mind off other troubles.

'Susan, these letters are to go in the hall to be collected for the next post to London. Now, if you will fetch our bonnets and my parasol, we will go for a walk.'

The new maid hurried off, leaving Amanda reflecting how much she had improved with the short time they had spent in Brighton. She was still not exactly chatty, but she had calmed down and proved herself a very competent young woman once her nerves were under control.

They set off along Marine Parade, stopping at Royal Crescent to admire the fine new houses with their facing of black mathematical tiles, and the rather less impressive statue of the Prince Regent, which was already crumbling badly under the force of the sea winds and spray.

They had turned back and began to retrace their steps when Amanda saw a smart carriage with a crest on the door forced to halt on the other side of the road by a child chasing its hoop into the roadway. There was a flurry of activity with the panicking nursemaid, the crying child and the coachman expressing his views on 'Wimmin wot can't look after so much as one brat!'

The hubbub was cut short by a cold voice from the carriage enquiring whether the coachman intended to sit there all day?

Amanda, who had been watching the child with some concern, looked at the carriage properly for the first time. The speaker, a man, had obviously let down the window on the far side from her and was leaning out, but looking out of the near side window was Diana Poste.

She met Amanda's eyes and immediately her face became twisted into an expression of imploring despair. Her lips moved, soundless, but Amanda thought she had mouthed, 'Help me!'

The man sat back next to her and Amanda realised that the profile, sharp against the blue sky, was Lord Langham's. With the light bright on the carriage it was quite plain that there was no one else in it—no companion, no chaperon. The child and its hoop were removed from the road to the accompaniment of loud wails and the carriage moved off. Behind it, strapped on, was a pile of expensive luggage.

'Mrs Clare, ma'am?' Susan was at her side, obviously wondering why her mistress was standing stock still, staring at the vanishing carriage.

'One moment, Susan, I must think.' What could this mean? There was no respectable reason Amanda could imagine why a young lady should be alone, unchaperoned, in a closed carriage with a man who was not her father or her brother. Yet there was Miss Poste, obviously in distress, with the notorious libertine her father was attempting to force on her. And the pile of luggage gave the impression that this was not simply an imprudent drive, but a journey with a destination other than Brighton.

Try as she might, Amanda could come to no conclusion other than that Lord Langham, wearied by Diana's prevarication and Jay's interference, had simply snatched the girl, knowing that her father was likely to turn a blind eye and countenance a marriage after, rather than before, its consummation.

Blindly she began to walk again. Who could she ask for advice? Jane and Lady Oughton were gone for the day, James Oughton was away for two days. That only left Jay and she had no idea of his direction. She stopped again, making Susan hop sideways to avoid running into her.

'Who would know?' she said out loud.

'Ma'am?'

Of course! The Master of Ceremonies would have every visitor of the *ton* in his famous Book. She would have thought of it earlier if Lady Oughton had not undertaken the task of inscribing the names of her entire party herself. 'Come along, Susan, we must go to the Assembly Rooms at once!'

If the Master of Ceremonies, a portly and stately functionary, was surprised to be summoned from his offices to attend a breathless lady enquiring about one of the most eligible bachelors in town, he did not allow it to shown on his face.

'Please take a seat, Mrs Clare, ma'am, may I offer you refreshments?' Mr Yardley said, pulling out a chair. 'I do hope you are having a pleasant stay in Brighton. If there is anything, anything at all—'

'Indeed there is,' Amanda interrupted, as calmly as she could. 'I require Lord Severn's direction as I find I have something of his that he dropped when we were speaking yesterday and I have no idea how to return it.'

'Of course, ma'am. Or I can have a porter take it round for you now?'

'No, I thank you, I would welcome the walk. If you would just...'

With a maddeningly stately bow the Master of Ceremonies dipped his quill in the standish and wrote an address. 'There you are, ma'am. And I wish you good day.'

This was said to the tail of Amanda's skirts as she whisked out of the door and away. Mr Yardley raised an eyebrow. Over the years in his exalted position he had seen many a scandal, all of which were locked discreetly in his breast, not even to be shared with Mrs Yardley. This appeared to be yet another developing. How very interesting.

Susan, hurrying in the wake of her mistress, was equally intrigued. She had heard from her sister that the Quality were given to queer starts, and also that she must expect to observe many a flirtation and even illicit goings-on. Still, Mrs Clare had not seemed that sort of lady at all. It just went to show! Calling at a gentleman's lodgings, even with a maid in attendance, was fast indeed.

Amanda, with a hasty glance at the paper in her hand, was conning the numbers of the houses along St James Street, just off the Steyne. She found the one she wanted and hurried up the steps to rap the knocker.

The door was answered by a smartly liveried footman who managed to restrain his surprise at the sight of a lady on the doorstep. 'Madam?'

'Is Lord Severn in?' Amanda demanded.

'His lordship is not at home, ma'am.'

'Do you mean he is in but not receiving, or out?' Amanda demanded. 'This is a family matter of the utmost urgency.'

The footman bowed. 'I regret that his lordship is away, I believe for the rest of the day, ma'am. Would you care to leave a message?'

'Yes…no.' What on earth could she write? She needed to speak to Jay, and in any case, every minute's delay could be fatal to Diana's reputation and well-being. 'Do you know where his lordship has gone?'

'His lordship has not confided that, ma'am.' The man

was obviously becoming embarrassed by her persistence.

'Thank you.' Defeated, Amanda turned and walked down the steps. What now? She had counted on finding Jay at home, which was foolishly optimistic, she now realised. She had felt absolute trust that he would cope with the situation, now she was on her own again.

Well, Amanda Clare, she chided herself, beginning to walk back to Marine Street. *You pride yourself on your common sense and practicality. Now deal with this yourself.*

Lord Langham had a house near Brighton, Jay had told her that, she recalled. That must be where he was taking Diana: surely any further with a reluctant girl would be out of the question.

She hurried through the door, calling for the landlady. 'Mrs Charles! Mrs Charles, are you at home?'

The landlady was and able at Amanda's request to name a convenient and reliable livery stables. She was also happy to send off her maid to engage a gig for Amanda's immediate use.

With a breathless Susan on her heels, Amanda swept into her bedchamber. 'My riding habit and gloves,' she ordered. 'Oh, and Susan, find me the *Peerage*.'

She opened the book on the dressing table and flicked through it. Here it was: Langham...principal seat Downsmore House near Steyning.

Susan helped her out of her promenade dress and into her habit. Amanda sat down while the maid unpinned her hair and dressed it more simply to go under her riding hat and veil. Suddenly she pulled open a drawer and fetched out notepaper and a quill. The standish was to hand as well and she began to write, her hand shaking slightly as she attempted to put the facts into the briefest and most coherent form.

But halfway down the note she stopped and read it through again. No, it was hopeless. What was the point of sending this to Jay's lodgings? By the time he returned it would be too late in any case. Amanda screwed up the note and tossed it aside.

'I can hear the gig, I think,' Susan announced, running to peer out of the window. 'Yes, here it is, ma'am. I will fetch my bonnet.'

Amanda nodded, then called, 'No, I will go alone, Susan.'

'But, ma'am, will you not then take a groom?'

'No…no. Susan, this is a matter of some delicacy. It may be that I will be returning with a young lady and in that case there will be no room for three of us. And I do not want a groom standing up behind—it is not as though we have any of our own people here who I can rely on absolutely. No, I will go alone, but I will be back before dinner time, never fear.'

The clock struck twelve. 'Ma'am, will you not take luncheon first?' Susan did not have the confidence, as Kate would have done, to argue further.

'No, no time.' Amanda ran down the steps and was helped up into the gig by the groom from the stables. The horse, she was relieved to see, looked a quality animal, fit to go to Steyning and back without any problem. She adjusted her veil, took the whip with a word of thanks and, urging the animal to a trot, took the road out of town.

Chapter Twenty-One

Amanda had conned the guidebooks often enough during her short stay in Brighton to know which road to take for Steyning and she made good time. Once closer to the town, however, she found she had to stop several times to ask the way to Downsmore House.

She received several knowing looks and one landlord, when she stopped at his inn to enquire the way, was almost insolent. The flash of angry eyes behind the veil made him alter his tone, but Amanda was heartily glad she would have no cause to revisit the area. Lord Langham's reputation was obviously widespread.

It was three o'clock, she estimated, by the time she turned the now somewhat weary horse into the carriageway leading to Downsmore House. The gatekeeper agreed that yes, his lordship had arrived back that day, although whether he was receiving, he could not say.

Amanda, who had no intention of asking for his lordship, thanked the man and drove on, feeling uncomfortable. The unwisdom of calling alone on such a man was beginning to oppress her. Still, she was not going to turn back now.

A groom came out to hold her horse as she pulled

up by the front door, and led the gig away before she could protest that this was just a short visit. However, the butler who opened the door to her was an eminently respectable-looking upper servant and her confidence rose again.

'I understand that Miss Poste is staying here? I would appreciate the favour of a few words with her on a matter of urgency. Here is my card. There is no need to disturb his lordship.'

To her surprise the man opened the door wide without further ado and ushered her in. 'If you would wait here, ma'am.' He showed her into a small retiring room and closed the door. He was back in a few minutes. 'Miss Poste asks if you would attend her in her chamber, madam.'

Amanda followed him up the long sweep of double staircase, which rose on either side of the hallway. The whole house seemed dark and hushed as though holding its breath. She shook herself for being so fanciful and was led down a corridor to a panelled door. The butler knocked, opened it, announced 'Mrs Clare, Miss Poste,' and went out, leaving her in a big, shadowy room.

The furniture seemed to loom over the figure of Diana Poste who stood up as Amanda came in. She was smiling, but Amanda stopped dead as she registered the expression. This was not a smile of relief, but one of malicious triumph.

'Why, this is famous!' The girl laughed, clapping her hands. 'I was sure you would fall for it, although Robert said no one would take meddling so far as to *follow* us.'

'Miss Poste, Diana…I gather that you are not here against your will and that you are congratulating yourself on having played a trick on me, which I must tell you is both cruel and foolish.' Diana merely pouted at the reproof. Amanda choked down her rising anger and persisted. 'But however ill judged your sense of humour, I beg you to consider your position. You told me you were in love with Lord Severn…'

'Well, I am not, although it was fun to tease you. He only cares because of my mother. I am tired of his lectures. I want to marry Robert.'

'Are you certain?' Amanda demanded anxiously. 'There is still time to go back, you know, you can come with me. Do consider, leaving aside his reputation, you are so very young to be thinking of marriage to a man of his age.' Getting no response, she struggled to find other arguments.

'You cannot have considered. He may be very indulgent now, but there are other things in marriage, things you are too innocent to know about yet. You will find that intimacy with someone of his sophistication, his age—'

She broke off in confusion at Diana's peal of laughter. 'But I know all about that,' she scoffed. 'Robert is a wonderful lover.' The knowing caress in her voice left Amanda in absolutely no doubt that the girl was not referring to flirtation.

'You mean that you and he…that already…'

'Oh, yes.' Diana's smile made Amanda go cold all over. 'A *wonderful* lover,' she repeated.

Amanda tried one last desperate throw. 'But in a few years,' she stammered, 'he is so much older than you…'

'He does not mind sharing me with his friends,' Diana said, running the tip of her tongue around her lips. 'Some of them are quite young enough. And so many of them…' She broke off, laughing at the sight of Amanda's horrified face. 'Oh, yes, Mrs Prim and Proper. *Orgies.* Just like all the tittle-tattle says.'

There was the sound of carriage wheels on the drive below. Diana flitted across to look out of the window. 'The first guests are arriving now. Soon the house will be full. We will be having such a wonderful party tomorrow night.'

Amanda felt frozen as though her feet had taken root to the floor. She could not believe that this beautiful girl had been so corrupted, so debased. Surely she was parroting the words of Lord Langham, making up these shocking things to hurt the woman she saw as interfering in her life.

Then a smooth, silky voice behind her spoke and Amanda knew it was all true. 'Yes, a wonderful party tomorrow night, and you, Mrs Clare, appear to have invited yourself.'

She spun round. Lord Langham lounged elegantly in the doorway, his smile saturnine as he watched her face. 'Come here, my love.' Diana ran to his side and he put an arm around her, caressingly. 'Such a clever girl. Such a fast learner, Mrs Clare.'

'Stand aside, my lord,' Amanda said, trying to keep her voice steady and confident.

'But no, you are our guest. I insist,' he said with an emphasis on the last word. 'You invited yourself here, you will participate—fully—in our revels tomorrow night.'

'You mean...' Amanda could hardly believe the nightmare she had stumbled into.

'Exactly. There are never enough young ladies to go around for try as one might, one simply cannot get the quality one's friends require.' He smiled at her as though asking her to share in his difficulty over recruiting domestic staff.

'That would be rape!'

'That all depends on you my dear.'

'I will have the law on you! You cannot abduct respectable women off the streets!'

'Abduct? But my dear—Amanda, is it not? You came here of your own free will. I have no doubt you enquired the way along your route, and enquired it of people of the first respectability who will all testify that you were alone and under no duress. You asked for me at the gate house, and you walked in here quite willingly, as my butler will testify. Where is the abduction? And before you advance any other arguments, I think a married lady is going to have a problem proving rape, is she not? Always assuming you have the courage to expose yourself to the resulting notoriety attendant on making a fuss about this.'

'I would rather die!' Amanda spat at him.

'They all say that,' he remarked languidly. 'They never mean it, you know. Now, I have guests to receive. Food and hot water will be brought up to you. Until tomorrow night, I bid you farewell.'

The door shut and the key turned. Through the heavy panels Amanda could hear the faint sounds of Diana's laughter. She stood in the middle of the room, fighting down her fear and nausea, until things stopped spinning around her and her breathing calmed.

'I must not panic!' Amanda said out loud and the sound of her own voice in the stillness steadied her. She had walked into this nightmare and it was up to her to get herself out. She had told no one where she was going or why, so there could be no hope of rescue. She almost gave way to self-recrimination, then shook herself out of it. How could any sane person have imagined such a situation or have guarded against it?

The door was indeed locked and none of the other

doors in the room led to anything but the most shallow closets. The chimney was wide, but as she peered up she saw there was a heavy iron smoke baffle across it: doubtless it could be removed to admit a chimney boy, but it was too heavy for her to shift.

That left the window. It was locked shut and the panes were firmly bedded in their leading. It might be possible to smash it open, but only by creating the most incredible amount of noise, and once open there would be no escape. The brickwork seemed to fall straight to the ground with nothing, not even ivy, to offer a hand-hold.

It did, however, offer a fine viewpoint, for it appeared to be the window over the front door. Amanda observed a number of carriages pull up, exclusively with male occupants, and shuddered. If she could not get out, was there any weapon to be had? A search of every drawer and closet produced only a long silver skewer, possibly pressed into service at some time as a letter opener. It was not very sharp, but Amanda did not want to kill anyone, simply make her escape, and it made her feel a little more secure.

With the skewer clasped in her hand, she resumed her post at the window and tried to see who was arriv-ing. Perhaps six carriages came, and then there was a lull. Despite her fear and horror, Amanda realised she was very hungry and thirsty. When would a servant come with the promised food and water? Would there be any chance of making her escape then?

Someone on foot appeared from the direction of the stables. Amanda frowned, she did not think she had missed anyone arriving. Then she saw it was Jay, stroll-ing up to the front door in his riding dress.

'Oh, thank God!' Amanda pressed her face to the

glass, terrified that this was simply a vision brought on by her mental state. Then, as he vanished under the door canopy, she realised that he could not be here for her, for he did not know where she was.

'No!' The single despairing whisper seemed to fill the room. If he was not here for her, then he was a guest… The implications were so awful that all her courage, all her self-control, ebbed away, leaving her huddled on the window seat, too devastated even to cry.

There was a noise at the door. Amanda lifted her head and listened. Yes, unmistakably the key was being turned. Suddenly she did not care what she had to do to get out of this place. With the skewer held like a dagger in her fist, she flew across the room and stood behind the door as it swung open.

A man walked in and shut the door behind him and with a sob of determination she lunged at the unprotected back. The little noise gave her away. He spun round, catching her upraised hand, then pulling her to him in a smothering embrace. His fingers round her wrist were so tight she dropped the skewer with a cry of pain, then she realised who was holding her.

'You!'

Jay held on to her out of sheer self-defence, for her eyes were spitting fury, her teeth were bared and her fingers curled into talons. 'Amanda, stop it! You are safe now!'

'Safe! What are you doing here?'

'Looking for you.' Then her meaning must have sunk in and he stared down into her anguished face. 'Looking for you, Amanda,' he repeated.

'How did you know I was here?' she demanded. 'You are a guest here, are you not? Tell me the truth, I am sick of these hideous games.'

'No! My footman described you. He said a lady had called and was anxious and distressed. I went to your lodgings and your maid—Susan, is it?—told me you had gone out in the gig and that you were upset. She let me into your room when I asked her what you had been doing. I found the *Peerage* open as you had left it and your note, screwed up on the dressing table.'

'Oh! Oh, Jay, I am so sorry.' Amanda collapsed shaking against his chest. 'I saw you walk in here so calmly and openly, and everything else had turned into such a nightmare, I—'

'You did not know who to trust,' he finished for her. 'The easiest way to get into somewhere where you should not be is to act as though you had every right to be there. My face is not unfamiliar to Langham's servants: I just walked in and airily announced that I had ridden on ahead and my carriage was half an hour behind me. They were in such a flurry that I was able to slip upstairs. Luckily your door was the only one I could see with the key on the outside.'

Amanda clung to him, hardly understanding the words, just drawing comfort and strength from the feel of him, the warm, familiar scent of him. Jay pressed her down into a chair.

'Now tell me, has he touched you?'

'No! No…just words. Just the promise that I would be forced to join his…party tomorrow night.'

'My God!' Jay spun away from her and took two rapid paces across the room. He took his hand from his pocket and Amanda saw he was holding a slender, long-barrelled pistol. 'I am going to kill him,' he said, quite calmly.

'No!' Amanda got to her feet and clung to his arm.

'Please, Jay, the scandal! Too many people know I am here. And then there is Diana.'

She saw his lips tighten. 'Oh, Jay, I am so sorry to have to tell you this, but she is already his mistress.' He said nothing. 'And not only that. Jay, I cannot repeat what she said, but I am afraid he has utterly corrupted her.'

'Her upbringing had already done that,' he said at last. 'Langham has merely finished the process.'

'You knew, then?'

'Oh, yes, for many months now. But because of her mother, I felt I had to keep trying.'

'Her mother?' Amanda was completely confused. 'Lord Oughton told me at Holkham that you intended to marry Diana. What has her mother got to do with it?'

'Oughton!' Jay looked at her, then slowly shook his head. 'So that was why you were suddenly so cool towards me!'

'But of course.' She walked away from him and took the chair again. Her legs were too shaky to stand.

'I will have words to say with James Oughton when I can find him,' Jay said grimly. 'I had not expected an old friend to play me such a trick for his own ends.'

'Oh, no.' Amanda could almost see the humour in the situation. 'He is not courting me, we are only friends. And he honestly believes you to be in love with Diana—he is quite worried about it.'

Jay shook his head, his face suddenly alight with laughter. 'What a tangle! Now, we must get out of here.'

'Not before you promise me that you will not call out Lord Langham,' Amanda said fiercely. 'It will compromise me, and whatever Diana is, you could be ruining any chance of her at least marrying the man.' And you could get killed, she thought, but did not say it. Jay was too angry to be prudent on his own behalf, she could only hope he would be careful on hers.

'If you can swear to me he has not laid a finger on you.' She nodded and Jay shrugged. 'Very well, Miss Prudence, if that is your wish.' He looked out of the window. 'Damn it, there are more guests. We had better stay here until they have been received.'

'Tell me about Diana's mother,' Amanda prompted. 'Is she anything to do with that strange flash of memory you had? Do you recall when you were so angry to discover that I had married an older man?'

'Yes, how could I forget it?' There was no other chair in the room, so he came and sat on the floor beside hers, his back against it, his eyes on the door, the elegantly lethal pistol in one hand. 'Clarissa was my second cousin, and four years older than me. She was the happiest, sweetest person you could ever meet. She was a cross between an angel and an older sister, and as I grew older she became, I suppose, my first glimpse of what else a woman could be. Not that I understood that, I was only thirteen when she married: all I knew was that I worshipped her.

'Her father fell into debt and, quite literally, sold her off to Poste who was a libertine even then. His first wife was dead, no one quite seemed to know how, and within a year, so was Clarissa, giving birth to Diana.'

He fell silent. His dark head was resting against the arm of the chair, his hair just out of touch of Amanda's fingertips. She longed to touch it, caress it, but she did not dare break the mood. 'Poor lady. And poor Diana,' she said after a moment. 'No mother and a father like that.'

Jay got to his feet, his eyes shadowed. 'Enough ancient history,' he said briskly. 'Time to get out of here.'

'We are surely not going to walk out of the front door?'

'No, not this time. Come, and stay behind me.' Jay checked the corridor and gestured for her to come out, turning the key in the lock and leaving it there. 'They will give themselves a headache wondering how you escaped,' he whispered as they trod softly to the head of the stairs.

There was noise from the rooms at the rear of the hall, but no servants in sight. Jay hissed, 'Follow me,' and they descended the stairs to the point where a tapestry cloaked the wall. 'Wait,' and he was across the hall and trying the door opposite. After a moment he gestured to her and she ran, whisking in after him as another door opened and the sound of voices swelled.

Then it was the work of a moment to open a window, climb out and run across the grass to the concealing shrubs. 'My gig,' she whispered.

'Is it hired?' She nodded. 'I'll compensate the stables, forget it now. I have a chaise on the other side of the park. Can you manage?'

'Yes, of course,' said Amanda stoutly, and promptly fainted.

Chapter Twenty-Two

Amanda came round to find herself being handed up into the grasp of a burly stranger and tried to struggle.

'It is all right, Amanda, this is my groom, John,' said a voice in her ear and she realised that Jay was holding her. She stopped fighting and was soon seated in the curricle with Jay beside her and the groom tucking a rug around her knees.

'She looks in a poor way, Mr Jared,' he observed gruffly.

'Mrs Clare has had an unpleasant experience, John, and the sooner we can get her away safe the better.' He saw Amanda's expression at the free use of her name and added, as the man swung up behind them, 'John has been my groom since I was a boy—as you can tell by the disrespectful way he addresses me. You may trust him as you would trust me.'

There was a chuckle from behind. 'Can't be doing with all this "me lording."'

'He is fierce enough of my dignity in front of others, though,' Jay remarked, giving his team their head now they were out onto the road.

'Yes, well, I'm an Earl's head groom, and they had better not forget it,' John muttered.

Amanda managed a small smile. 'It is his dignity he is defending, my lord, not your own.'

'I fear so. Amanda, you need to sleep, but I do not think it is safe for you to do so while we are driving at this pace. Can you hold on for a few miles? I know of a respectable inn, off this road a way. I cannot believe Langham will attempt to follow you, and he has no way of knowing you can get far away: I think we can be assured of some peace and rest there.'

Amanda murmured that she was quite all right, and set herself to prove it. It was no easy task, although the fresh air and the swaying of the curricle provided some counter to the wave of exhausted lethargy that was sweeping over her.

She was safe. Jay did not love Diana Poste. Those two facts kept whirling in her brain until she was dizzy. But did he still have any feelings for her? He had said nothing of love: she could place no reliance on his desire to challenge Lord Langham. Any gentleman confronted with that libertine's actions towards a lady would have done just the same. And she had—if only for a moment—believed he was part of Langham's infamous circle. Could he forgive her that?

Jay was setting a killing pace and the curricle swayed and lurched along the post road. John's muttered commentary from behind her provided a bizarre chorus to the entire ghastly experience. 'You'll break our necks, that's what you'll do, Mr Jared...watch that leader... there now, look at the way you caught that whip point, taught you well, I did... Damn it, sir, you'll have the wheel off!'

Jay appeared to ignore him completely until after one

particularly vehement protest he said, 'Be quiet, do, John. Mrs Clare does not need to hear you complaining about your rheumatism!' This effectively silenced the groom, who subsided muttering.

At last Jay slowed and turned the team into a side road. A mile further on at a crossroads he pulled up in front of a substantial and well-kept inn. 'It looks as though the recommendation for this place was correct, John,' he remarked as the groom jumped down to fetch the landlord.

'Lord Witherington is rarely out when it comes to good food,' the groom agreed. 'House, there!'

The landlord hurried out and Amanda noticed the inn sign. 'Two Magpies,' she murmured. 'Two for joy...' Everything was slipping away again, but she was just conscious of Jay's voice as he lifted her down into John's arms.

'We have had an accident on the road, landlord. My wife is very shaken up and all our luggage lost. Do you have a room and a private parlour where we can rest while my man goes...?' His voice faded away and Amanda circled down into darkness.

She came to herself to find she was sitting in a comfortable wing chair in a cosy parlour, her feet on a stool and a rug over her knees. A respectable-looking woman in a vast white apron was setting a tray down on the table and exclaimed, 'There now, sir, she is opening her eyes, poor lady!'

Amanda blinked, tried to focus and realised Jay was at her side. 'What you need, my dear, is a glass of wine and some food. Mrs Brownsmith has not eaten since this morning,' he added to the landlady, who went out clucking and saying that if they wanted anything at all, he only had to ring, otherwise she'd leave the poor lady to rest and not disturb them until the morning.

'Mrs Brownsmith?' Her mouth seemed to be full of flannel and it was an effort to speak.

'Convenient, is it not, that we have an alias ready to hand?' Jay was pouring wine, ruby red, into a glass and holding it for her. 'Here, try this. Although I seem to recall being mortified by you telling Mrs Clay at the Lamb and Flag that my given name was Augustus. I think I will stick with Jared—or Jay, it is your choice.' He pushed the glass back towards her lips when she tried to reject it after only one sip. 'No, you are as weak as a kitten with shock and exhaustion. Another sip and I will give you some of our hostess's vegetable broth.'

He patiently spoon-fed her the warm, savoury soup and gradually the mists seemed to clear and some strength come back into her limbs. It had seemed that they were back in the inn after the stagecoach accident and that everything in between was simply a nightmare, but now reality came back.

'Thank you,' she said. 'I feel much better now.'

'The wine is by your side, try and drink a little more.' Jay looked at her closely, seemed satisfied with what he saw, and took a chair at the table. He began to eat soup, bread and cheese, washed down with a tankard of ale and let her sit quietly, nodding approvingly when she sipped a little of the claret.

'What has happened?' she asked at length.

'Since we arrived here? John has borrowed a hack and has ridden into Brighton with a note from me to Miss Porter, assuring her of your safety and promising you will be returned to her tomorrow. Meanwhile the Brownsmiths, who you must agree are a well-travelled, if adventure-prone, couple, are settled here for the night.

Mrs Whiteleaf the landlady has assured me that she has set out for you a nightgown, a brush, a comb and you have only to ring for whatever else you might require.'

Amanda felt the strength gradually flowing back into her body. Her mind, too, seemed much clearer and she was no longer getting flashes of Lord Langham's face or memories of the absolute despair she had fallen into.

'And where are we sleeping?' she asked. She saw Jay's eyes narrow in amusement at the sharp edge to her voice.

'There are two bedchambers,' he said equably. 'You have only to choose.'

'Oh.' She had expected to have to be firm with him, to insist on a separate bedchamber, to explain that whatever the situation in the past, she could not carry on with the dangerously passionate relationship they had had. Yet, even though the ambiguities and mysteries were all swept away, he had said nothing of his feelings for her, which meant, as one realised if one was sensible about it, that he had none deeper than attraction and friendship.

'Unless,' his voice said softly in her ear, 'unless of course you wish to economise on our shot and share a room, my darling.'

Amanda twisted round in her chair, her heart leaping. He had moved so silently she had not realised he was there.

'Ja...Jared...what did you call me?'

'My darling. Do you dislike it? I must say that I like the sound of my real name on your lips. I had grown used to Jay, but the way you say Jared...say it again.'

'Jared,' she said and his lips covered hers.

She found herself lifted and carried across the room, through a door and into a bedchamber. Jay...Jared laid her down on it and stepped back. 'You are tired, I should not have said anything.'

'No!' Amanda struggled to sit up in the enveloping feather bed and held out her arms. 'Jared, I am feeling much better, I promise you. You called me your darling.'

He sat on the edge of the bed, just out of her reach, looking at her. His mouth twisted wryly. 'I dare not touch you. You look so white, so fragile. My God, Amanda, when I think of you in that house, in Langham's power...'

'It is over,' she said gently. 'A bad dream.'

'I wanted to tell you I loved you, but to even speak of it in that place, let alone kiss you, that would make everything I felt seem smirched. And you thought that I was part of that group—' He broke off.

'No, stop! I am so sorry,' she cried. 'I knew almost at once it couldn't be so, my heart could not believe what my eyes were telling me. Jared, please forgive me!'

'I would forgive you anything Amanda,' Jared said simply. 'Anything. The question is, can you forgive me for my arrogance?'

'Which particular incidence of arrogance?' Amanda enquired wickedly, suddenly realising that against all the odds, the dream was coming true, that surely everything was going to be all right.

Jared shot her a gleaming look. 'Minx,' he said appreciatively. 'I should have told you about Diana, told you what I was about. But it was going to be a squalid affair, however things came out. I had no confidence that I could extricate her—at that point, remember I had no notion of just how mired in this she had become. I feared I would end up calling out Langham and that alone would have created a mighty scandal. I thought I could go and deal with it as best I could, make one last throw to help Clarissa's daughter, then come back to you.'

'And at Holkham I was cold?'

'And I was too worried to realise what you might be thinking. And of course, I had no knowledge that my helpful friend was convincing you that I had fallen for a beautiful schoolroom miss!'

'And in London?' Amanda prompted.

'By then I had a good idea of exactly what that young woman was about. The last thing I wanted was you going anywhere near her poisonous tongue, her evil little manipulative schemes.'

'But why did you not tell me?' Amanda demanded. 'Have you any idea what I thought you were so anxious about?'

'No, I just thought you were angry with me and that you had found a much more satisfactory admirer in Oughton!'

'I thought you were afraid that I would behave like a spiteful, rejected woman and poison Diana against you. I did not relish being portrayed as the cast-off, bitter lover, believe me.'

Jared looked at her aghast. 'I would never…no wonder you were so angry with me. But why on earth were you so anxious to try and save Diana from Langham? You did not know the girl, you did not know her story, you had no reason to help any connection of mine.'

'I thought you were in love with her,' Amanda said simply. 'She told me she was in love with you, but had to obey her father. Besides trying to help any girl in such a position, I thought it would be best for you.'

He looked down at his clasped hands for a long moment, then looked up and met her eyes. 'I thought…I hoped that you were in love with me. Was I wrong?'

'No, Jared.'

'But you were prepared to do that because you thought I loved her?'

'Yes.'

'My God, Amanda!' He was on his feet, one fist thudding into the bedpost, his face dark with an emotion she had never seen before.

'I am sorry if my feelings embarrass you, I do not have any claim on you, I am going away…' she began to stammer, appalled at what she had unleashed, her happiness replaced by an aching void of hurt.

'Embarrass me!' He swung round to face her, green eyes gleaming, face alive with a sort of astounded wonder. 'I am just wondering what I have done to deserve you, how I can ever be worthy of you.' He came to her side and fell on one knee, catching up her hands in his. 'Amanda, I love you to distraction. I've loved you since that moment in the field just outside Holt when you looked up at me and said that one should make every effort to help one's friends. Do you remember? You said it with such a mischievous twinkle in your eye, and off you went to do battle on my behalf, risking reputation and peace of mind without a qualm.'

'I had qualms,' Amanda admitted. 'I was finding you dangerously attractive even then and repeated daily the reminder that you probably had a wife and four children!'

'Those children!' He was laughing now. 'How I came to dread the look that came over your face. I knew I was about to be reminded of them yet again, poor little devils.'

'Why poor little devils?'

'Because I assumed I was a dreadful father—you were making me certain I was a dreadful husband.'

'I am sure you would make an excellent father and husband,' Amanda said, keeping her voice absolutely neutral.

'Really?' He carried her hands to his lips. 'Do you think four is a good number of children, my love? Perhaps three, or six?'

'Is that a proposal, my lord?' It was curiously hard to speak.

'It is, madam. Will you do me the honour of becoming my wife?'

'Oh, yes, Jared! With all my heart.' And then she was in his arms and he did not seem worried any longer that she was too fragile to touch. His mouth roved from her lips to her throat, to the swell of her breast then back to her mouth until she was whimpering with desire, her fingers moving from his hair to the fastenings of his shirt, never still.

Somehow all her clothes were gone and he was looking down at her stretched beneath him on the big soft bed. She had expected to feel shy, but all she could do was glory in the look in his eyes.

'Jared!'

He smiled at her and began to pull off his own clothes and she could, at last, run her hands down the hard muscles of his back, flatten her palm against the smooth planes of chest and thigh, find her eyes widening at the aroused strength of him.

She had been so used to the gentle, almost apologetic lovemaking that was all she had experienced before. Jared's strength, his certainty that she could feel as powerfully as he, was utterly intoxicating. Each touch was a new sensation as his hands roved where they wanted, making her gasp and arch against him. His mouth lingered on the apex of each breast in turn, sending slivers of delight from each taut nipple and the stubble on his unshaven chin sent a delicious *frisson* through her as it touched her sensitised skin.

When she thought she could bear no more, that she was going to shatter into a thousand pieces of sensation, he paused, looking down into her wide gaze with eyes dark with passion. 'Yes, Amanda?'

'Oh, yes, Jared.' Then agreement turned to exultant delight. 'Oh, yes, oh, Jared, oh, yes…'

'I love you, I love you…'

Mrs Clare floated gently up into a delicious state of half-sleep, half-waking and hovered there for a few moments, lulled by the reassuring sound of deep, regular, male breathing from the other side of the bed.

Her hand touched a warm, naked flank and her body sank into the central dip of the bed, to touch his lightly.

Amanda Clare moaned gently, wriggling closer to the long form beside her, then sighed as a strong arm gathered her close in a comforting, sleepy embrace. She began to wake again, to become conscious of his nearness and her own pleasurable anticipation.

Very cautiously Amanda opened her eyes and found herself looking into the sleepy green gaze of her bedmate. He was so close that their noses were almost touching. Amanda realised that she was holding her breath and that her heart was banging so hard against her ribs that they felt bruised.

The man's eyes widened slightly, then crinkled into a smile as he leaned forward and kissed her firmly on the lips. 'Good morning, my love.'

'This time you remember where you are?' she teased.

'Oh, yes,' replied Jared Mansell, Earl of Severn. 'I recall exactly where I am, who I am and most definitely who you are, my love. But should you have any difficulty recalling it, I intend to remind you all over again.'

And he did, to such effect that Mrs Whiteleaf, knocking on the door with the breakfast tray, gave up and went away again. 'Poor things,' she muttered as she went down the stairs. 'I do hope they slept well.'

* * * * *

The Dutiful Rake
by
Elizabeth Rolls

Award-winning author **Elizabeth Rolls** lives in the Adelaide Hills of South Australia in an old stone farmhouse surrounded by apple, pear and cherry orchards, with her husband, two smallish sons, three dogs and two cats. She also has four alpacas and three incredibly fat sheep, all gainfully employed as environmentally sustainable lawn-mowers. The kids are convinced that writing is a perfectly normal profession and she's working on her husband. Elizabeth has what most people would consider far too many books, and her tea and coffee habit is legendary. She enjoys reading, walking, cooking, and her husband's gardening.

Elizabeth loves to hear from readers and you can contact her at: books@elizabethrolls.com or via her website at www.elizabethrolls.com

Chapter One

Beguiling green eyes glimmered up into cold light grey as Lady Hartleigh circled the crowded floor in the powerful arms of Marcus Langley, Earl of Rutherford. That tall, lithe figure seemed perfectly indifferent to the sylph-like form in its sheath of gold silk. Not the most censorious of Almack's patronesses could have found anything to cavil at in the way they danced. His lordship kept a proper distance at all times, his thighs did not brush against her ladyship's skirts, his hand remained just above her waist as was considered decent and they chatted unconcernedly without gazing passionately into each other's eyes.

For all that, several haughty dames cast outraged glances in their direction, albeit surreptitiously. After all, if the rumours were true and Marcus really was considering marriage at long last, then the last thing anyone wanted to do was offend him. He was one of the richest prizes on the Marriage Mart and it was not only his positively indecent fortune that made him so eligible.

There was the title as well—one of the oldest and most illustrious in the realm. Add to that his lordship's undeniable good looks, prowess as a sportsman and his elegance of dress and it was no wonder that so many lures should have been thrown out to him over the years since he'd returned from serving with Wellington's forces. Lures which had been totally ignored. Until now.

At five and thirty the Earl was marked as a confirmed bachelor. No one could ever remember him showing the slightest interest in any marriageable female. He preferred to live a life of hedonistic pleasure when in the capital, which was only during the spring anyway. The rest of the year he seemed quite happy to spend largely on one or another of his estates, which were scattered around the country.

Tales had drifted back to town about house parties held at those mansions. House parties at which no respectable female was to be seen. For it was not to be thought that his lordship had no interest in women. Quite the opposite. He was a most dangerous and accomplished rake. Husbands might well look to their errant wives when he was around, although, to his credit, it was said that he had no interest in seducing the young and innocent, nor would he pursue any lady whose husband was likely to take a dim view of the matter. Widows, of course, were considered fair game.

Those more cynical, or better acquainted with his lordship, averred that his avoidance of innocent young things sprang not from motives of chivalry, but from a complete lack of interest coupled with a well-developed instinct for self-preservation. He had absolutely no desire to find himself trapped into marriage with one of the fashionable society virgins launched on the Polite World each spring.

Nevertheless, despite his appalling reputation, his title, looks, charm and above all fortune rendered him an eminently acceptable suitor to the highest of sticklers. So to see him dancing with Lady Hartleigh, a widow of somewhat dubious reputation and scanty jointure but unbounded ambition, was enough to send ripples of conjecture eddying around the assembly rooms.

Lord Rutherford's elder sister, Lady Diana Carlton, viewed her brother's interest in the lovely widow with extreme disapprobation.

'Oh, for heaven's sake!' she said in tones of vexation to Jack Hamilton, who was sitting out the dance with her. 'What next will he do? Surely he doesn't intend to marry *her*!'

Hamilton held his tongue but Lady Diana knew her brother's best friend too well to be deflected by his silence.

'Jack, you must know what he intends!' said Lady Diana. 'You even have some influence with him. Which is more than anyone else can boast. Say something!'

Jack Hamilton looked down at her in some amusement and said, 'Oh, I wouldn't say that, Di. After all, you and Lady Grafton managed to get him as far as thinking of marriage. Quite an achievement, that.'

The grey eyes, so like her brother's, snapped fire at this innocent-seeming disclaimer. 'You know perfectly well that Aunt Regina and I never meant him to consider Althea Hartleigh as his *wife*.'

'Precisely,' said Hamilton drily. 'Which is why I have every intention of keeping my mouth shut. Unless, of course, Marc happens to raise the subject with me. If he asks me what I think, then I'll tell him. Otherwise I shall mind my own business.'

There were very few people from whom Lady Diana would have taken that. Fortunately for himself, Jack Hamilton was one of the privileged few.

She sighed. 'I suppose you mean that he is doing this just to vex us. Do you happen to know how far he means to go?' A delicate hand was laid on Hamilton's sleeve. 'You know, Jack, the title must not be allowed to pass to our cousin Aubrey. He is a dear, but quite unsuited to the responsibility. And he doesn't even desire it. Marc must marry! You know he must.'

Hamilton nodded. 'He knows it too. But he has no desire to wed for any other reason than to beget an heir. I fancy he hoped Aubrey might prove a suitable heir. Lord knows the lad's steady enough, but all he wants to do is remain in Oxford with his books and fellowship. Frankly, if I were you, Di, I should leave well alone.' He hesitated and then went on. 'The reason I have some influence with Marc is because I...er...don't beat him over the head with it.'

Lady Diana stared up at him. 'But...'

He nodded. 'Leave it alone, Di. He knows he has to marry. He knew that without you and Lady Grafton descending upon him to demand he secure the succession!'

She grimaced. 'That was Aunt Regina's notion. She favours the direct method.'

'Mmm. Rather like a brace of nine-pounders,' agreed Hamilton.

The grey eyes glared at him unsuccessfully and then twinkled ruefully. 'Thank you, Jack. Your compliments have always the charm of originality.'

He grinned and said comfortably, 'Naturally. That's why I'm still a bachelor.' He turned his head as a tall, exquisitely garbed gentleman joined them. 'Hullo, Toby! What the devil are you doing here? Dancing's a little energetic for you, isn't it?'

Sir Toby Carlton, Lady Diana's husband, shuddered

artistically. 'Perish the thought! Really, Jack—it's exhausting enough just watching Marc whirling Lady Hartleigh around. Let alone hearing Di cursing about it.' He cast his wife an affectionate grin. His lazy, effete pose was just that—a pose. One that amused everyone, himself included.

He viewed his brother-in-law and his fair partner critically. 'Shouldn't have thought he was any more interested in her than any other female he's bedded over the years. Less, possibly.'

'True,' said Jack thoughtfully. 'But if I'm not much mistaken, that is precisely the danger. He doesn't want to care—doesn't want anyone that close.'

His gaze went to the tawny head that towered over nearly every other man in the room. The waltz had just ended and Marc was escorting his lovely partner to the refreshment rooms. He frowned slightly. As little as Lady Diana did he wish to see his best friend throw himself away on Althea Hartleigh.

It was not the fact that he knew her to be Marc's mistress already. If he thought that she and Marc were in love, he would not have given a damn. And he did Lady Diana the credit to know she would have accepted it as well. It was just that he wished Marc could find someone to care for. Someone who could break through that impenetrable wall of reserve with which his lordship held most of the world at bay.

Marriage with a woman who would betray him at the first opportunity was not likely to achieve that. Quite the reverse!

His thoughts were interrupted by Lady Diana. 'Oh, curse it! Here comes Sally Jersey. No doubt she will have something to say.'

The Countess of Jersey sailed up to them. 'How

charming! Old friends having a comfortable cose! Good
evening, Di. And Toby! How tiring for you! Dear Jack!
To what do we owe the pleasure? Are you on the catch
as well as Marc? I vow that would be too good to be
true…'

Jack Hamilton eyed her thoughtfully and said simply,
'Sally, bite your tongue.' Again his position as the head
of an old, if untitled, and horrendously wealthy family
saved him from annihilation.

Lady Jersey pouted and shrugged her shoulders. 'Oh,
very well! I dare say the last thing needed is for anyone
to tell Marc his business!' She added shrewdly, 'No
doubt it would only encourage him!'

She rustled away and Sir Toby heaved a sigh of relief. 'Thank God! She's even more tiring than a waltz!'

Diana giggled and said, 'Darling, you really are
dreadful. What if she'd heard you?'

Sir Toby grinned. 'My dear, I'd simply tell her that
I'm saving my energies. For later.'

Lord Rutherford, having procured a glass of orgeat
for Lady Hartleigh, was idly surveying the assembled
throng and wondering how soon he could politely take
his leave. Having done what he came to do—namely
stir up all the tabbies and give his sister a nasty shock—
he could see little reason for remaining.

He slanted a considering glance down at Lady
Hartleigh who was sipping her orgeat unconcernedly.
No, he could hardly escort her home. That would be
going too far, even for him.

'Shall I see anything of you in the next week,
Marcus?' Her soft, caressing voice held only idle curiosity, but the green eyes betrayed a whole world of
meaning.

He knew perfectly well what she wished to know. When did he mean to take his pleasure with her again? Thoughtfully he gave the question at least half of his attention.

Then, with a shrug of his broad shoulders, he said, 'I have to go out of town tomorrow, Althea. Estate business in Yorkshire. It will take me about three weeks, I should think. Sorry.'

'Three weeks?' She pouted. 'An eternity! Cannot your agent deal with it? I am sure Hartleigh never concerned himself as you do.' Her discontent with his conviction that he must take a personal hand in any and every matter pertaining to his large and scattered properties was obvious.

'Very likely not,' replied Rutherford coldly. He did not consider the way in which the late Lord Hartleigh had run his property to be an example for his emulation. 'And in this case I have to see the property. I have only just inherited it and I understand it to be in a disgraceful state.'

'Then why bother?' Her ivory brow puckered in genuine puzzlement. 'Surely you can just sell it and pocket the proceeds.'

'No, I can't.'

His chiselled lips closed firmly, and Lady Hartleigh recognised at once that he was decided. No amount of cajolery or teasing on her part would change his mind. She might as well accept the inevitable. Besides, he would come back positively eager for her favours and there was no saying what he might not be inveigled into after three weeks of celibacy.

She did not delude herself that he was attached enough to her personally to eschew other women, but she was tolerably certain that if he were engaged on business he would have little time to pursue any passing fancy. If, indeed, there were anything to tempt him up in the wilds of Yorkshire. She could imagine nothing more unlikely than Marcus showing any interest in a rustic.

His lordship looked down at her with a faint smile. 'Just so, my dear. And when I return I think we must have a little discussion about the future.'

'The future?' Lady Hartleigh tried to keep the eagerness out of her voice. Could he possibly mean…? Despite her hopes she had not seriously believed he could really be considering marriage. Cold triumph blazed in her lowered eyes. This would be an achievement indeed.

'The future,' he repeated blandly. Then a steely note crept into his voice. 'So do…er…look after yourself, my dear.'

Her eyes flashed up at that and encountered steely cynicism. So he had noticed! She would have to take steps to discourage Sir Blaise Winterbourne! If Marcus were considering marriage, then Sir Blaise would cast out lures in vain. She was not fool enough to play that dangerously. She might have known that Marcus would notice Blaise. After all, the man was reputed to make a habit of bedding all Rutherford's mistresses. He could wait. Althea Hartleigh was not going to risk a possible marriage for the sake of an illicit tumble. No doubt Blaise Winterbourne would be just as happy, if not more so, to bed the new Countess of Rutherford.

The following morning saw Lord Rutherford leave his mansion in Mount Street at the shockingly early hour of nine o'clock. He was clad in immaculate inexpressibles of palest fawn, which clung to his long legs in a way which displayed their muscles to admiration. His coat of dark blue superfine was similarly moulded to his broad shoulders. His only jewellery was the heavy gold signet ring which never left his finger and a pearl pin which nestled chastely within the snowy folds of his cravat.

He mused on his situation as he strolled around to Brook Street to call on Jack Hamilton. There was little doubt that word of his intentions had leaked out. He had been positively besieged the previous night. Matrons who had never before bothered to accord him more than a passing interest had been assiduous in presenting their virtuous treasures for his inspection.

A cynical smile curved his lips. Usually they were only too careful to warn those same virtuous fillies against the predatory Earl of Rutherford. Quite apart from his physical inclinations, he had encouraged his reputation to a great extent as protection against that sort of thing. He had no taste for simpering, virginal débutantes without two thoughts to rub together in their heads and no idea of how to please a man.

In that regard Lady Hartleigh would suit him very well as a wife. He had ascertained beyond all possible doubt that her ladyship knew to a nicety how best to satisfy his desires.

He was still meditating on Lady Hartleigh's voluptuous charms as Hamilton's elderly valet Fincham ushered him into the snug and extremely untidy chamber that served Hamilton as a dining parlour.

'Lord Rutherford, Mr Jack,' said Fincham and closed the door.

Hamilton waved Marcus to a chair and finished his mouthful of sirloin. He washed it down with a draught of ale before saying. 'Morning, Marc. What brings you here so early? Can't that enormous staff of yours manage a decent breakfast?' His eyes twinkled as he carved a plateful of ham for his lordship and poured him a cup of coffee.

Marcus disposed himself in the chair, stretching out his long legs, and sipped his coffee as he regarded his friend who was calmly continuing with his own breakfast. 'Come on, Jack. Tell me the worst. What are they all saying?'

Playing for time, Jack looked at him inquiringly. 'Saying? About what?' Then encountering an amused lift of one eyebrow, 'Oh, your matrimonial plans! Well, the general consensus is that it's about time you realised your bookish young cousin is neither suited to the position nor even desires it.'

'And Lady Hartleigh?' The grey eyes were suddenly intent. 'What did my dear sister have to say on that head?'

Jack's eyes were sober as he said, 'Not exactly taken with the idea.'

Marcus snorted. 'Perhaps it will teach her not to be such an incorrigible busy head. Not to mention my Aunt Regina!'

'Mmm. It's possible,' said Jack, with a complete lack of expression that suggested that Marcus was indulging his optimism too far.

Marcus sighed and said, 'Say it, then. Come on, don't spare me!'

'You really want to know what I think?' Jack asked seriously. 'You'll think I've run mad.'

'Nothing new in that,' said Marcus grinning at him.

'Very well then.' Jack took a deep breath and embarked upon a forlorn hope. 'I think Althea Hartleigh would be the worst possible choice for you.' He hesitated and then went on. 'Wouldn't say this if you hadn't asked. But since you do... Tell me, Marc...do you really want a wife who can be counted on to entertain herself with half the men in London if she gets a chance?'

Marcus shrugged. 'Who am I to be hypocritical about such matters? After all, I have been amusing myself with such women for years. As long as she has enough sense to provide an heir or two, or at least be breeding before she seeks other amusements, I cannot see that it is any of my concern. After all, most of the women of my acquaintance conduct themselves like that and very convenient I have found it too. And I am hardly going live like a monk just because I've taken a wife. It seems a trifle churlish not to extend my wife the same courtesy.'

Jack grunted. 'No doubt. For God's sake, Marc! Think to the future. Do you really want to be tied to Althea Hartleigh for the rest of your life? Don't you think, if you looked about you, that you might find a girl or woman to care for?' He saw the amazement in his friend's eyes and grinned reluctantly. 'Aye, I knew you'd think I'd run mad.'

'You must have completely slipped your moorings!' Marcus agreed with alacrity. 'Why should I find someone to care for when all *she* will care for is my wealth and my title?' There was a bitter twist to his lips.

As bad as that, thought Jack, observing this. All he said was, 'I think you do yourself an injustice there. Why should some female not value you for yourself?' He paused briefly and added deliberately, 'As your mother valued your father.'

The bitterness around the mouth became even more pronounced. 'Because I seriously doubt the existence of such a paragon, Jack! Every female I have ever had anything to do with has been first and foremost concerned with my purse strings.' He ignored the last part of Jack's comment.

Jack was silenced. It was true enough. Mainly because Marc never allowed a woman sufficiently close to see beyond them to anything else. They saw nothing but Marcus, Earl of Rutherford—gazetted rake and confirmed cynic. Very few people ever saw Marc Langley—certainly none of his mistresses did.

So he shrugged and said, 'I admit you have a point, but even if you feel a marriage founded on love or at least affection to be unlikely, might I suggest that one founded on mutual respect rather than lust is more likely to be convenient and bearable?' He looked at Marcus ruefully. 'Sorry, I didn't mean to preach. Have some more ham.'

Marcus helped himself. Jack's last point had hit home. Maybe he was right. And anyway, marrying in a fit of pique to annoy Di would be positively corkbrained. Another thought suddenly presented itself as he sliced ham. Althea had been married to Hartleigh for at least six years and in all that time there had been no children to bless the union. It would be the height of lunacy to marry for the sake of an heir if there were the slightest indication his countess might not be able to oblige.

'I'm going out of town,' he said abruptly. 'Di knows all about it. Our Great-uncle Samuel has cocked up his toes. Since the old miser had no children and was too clutch-fisted to pay a lawyer to draw up a will, the estate comes back to me. And from all I hear it is in an appalling state. I'll have to be gone for several weeks.'

Jack nodded. 'Your father's uncle, wasn't he? The one in Yorkshire?'

'That's him,' said Marcus. 'Apparently he had some connection of Great-aunt Euphemia's to housekeep for him and she's left totally destitute, according to the lawyers, so I'll have to settle some money on her. Uncle Samuel had plenty, so why he didn't deal with the matter himself is beyond me.' He finished his coffee and stood up. 'I just came around to tell you I'd be away. In fact, I'm leaving this morning.'

A friendly grin lightened Hamilton's sombre countenance. 'I'm honoured, my lord, that you deigned to grace my poor table.'

'Oh, go to the devil!' recommended his lordship. He paused. 'Jack, I will give what you said some thought. Oh, not that rubbish about caring for a girl.' The finely moulded mouth tightened slightly, as though in pain. 'Even if it were possible…it's not…not what I want. But I dare say you may be right about the rest of the business. Thanks. And I don't know that you need to tell Di about this conversation.'

'Of course, I always pass on the confidences of my closest friends to their sisters!' said Jack sardonically.

Marcus grinned. 'Sorry. I didn't mean to be offensive.'

He took his departure, leaving Jack Hamilton in a state compounded of concern and relief in equal parts. At least Marc was thinking twice about Althea Hartleigh, but the utter cynicism and contempt for the opposite sex betrayed by his comments did not bode well for a happy union with any woman. Ten to one, even if some female did discover and succumb to his lordship's personal charm, he would find some way to hurt her and ensure that she regretted ever doing so.

Ruefully he wondered if, after all, Althea Hartleigh would be the best choice. At least Marc would know what to expect and there was not the slightest chance of the lady being hurt by his cold humours and likely strayings. There was more to it than straight-out cynicism over the dubious motives which spurred some women to marriage. Still, after nearly twenty years, Marc could not bear to speak of his adored mother. Jack shook his head sadly, remembering the outrageous and delightful woman she had been.

He sighed. No doubt Marc would go his own way to the devil and if it gave him the illusion of happiness then there was not a thing anyone could do for him! Unless, of course, Blaise Winterbourne seduced Althea Hartleigh before she became Countess of Rutherford.

Very few people realised just how deeply Marc disliked Winterbourne. Certainly no one but Jack knew why he did so…and the reason why Winterbourne took such pleasure in seducing Marc's mistresses.

Chapter Two

Three days later Marcus sat in the library of Fenby Hall, wondering if the rest of the house could possibly be in as shabby a state as this room. The wainscoting all looked as though it might as well be torn down; the hangings had obviously not been attended to for years. They hung tattered and faded over windows for which cleaning was a distant memory. When he had taken a volume from the shelves in curiosity, a cloud of dust and several moths had attended it.

The only positive aspect of the room was the fact that it had not succumbed to the atmosphere of damp prevailing in the rest of the house. A phenomenon which Marcus had no hesitation in ascribing to the circumstance of his uncle having used only this room and forbidding fires in any other.

The rest of the house was cold, damp and unspeakably dreary. Rugs were badly worn, although he could see where tears had been carefully mended. Curtains were faded and in many cases ragged. The furniture, he noted, was well dusted except for this room. It was even waxed in the parlour. But everywhere there was evidence of decay.

Certainly the linen was in an appalling condition. He had put his foot through both sheets last night and a brief inspection that morning had revealed that, despite frequent mending and being turned sides to middle, they had long ago reached the point where they would have disgraced a rag-bag.

He sat at the large mahogany desk and perused the estate books. Obviously his great-uncle had taken no interest in his patrimony for years. There was no record of any improvements being made; the wages remained what they had been twenty years ago. Samuel had apparently been content to live on his considerable investments and permit his home and dependents to decay around him.

He had arrived too late yesterday to see anything of the estate, but he'd wager that the workers were housed in cottages he'd be ashamed to see on his land. What the devil had the old man been about to let things come to such a pass? And what was the housekeeper, Miss Fellowes, doing to let the house fall into such a state?

He had not yet had the felicity of meeting Miss Fellowes. When Marcus had inquired for her the previous evening, the old retainer, Barlow, had said apologetically that Miss was laid up with the influenza, having taken a nasty chill at the master's funeral.

'She did tell me to assure your lordship that she would be gone as soon as may be,' explained Barlow nervously. 'Going to Mrs Garsby over at Burvale House as nursery governess she is, but the truth is she ain't too steady on her pins at all. Mrs Barlow did persuade her to stay, feeling sure your lordship would understand.'

Marcus thought sardonically that, from the look of things, Miss Fellowes had been suffering from influenza

for the last five years if the state of the house was anything to go by. He hoped his uncle had not paid her a
large wage because she certainly hadn't earned it.

Keeping this thought to himself, he nodded and said
coldly, 'Inform Miss Fellowes that she is welcome to
stay until she is fully recovered. Has a message been
sent to Mrs Garsby to inform her of this illness?'

'No, my lord.'

'See to it at once. And where will I find the household accounts?' He would have a look and see just what
Miss Fellowes had been doing with herself.

'Miss Meg will have them, me lord.'

'Then ask one of the maids to fetch them, please,'
said his lordship firmly.

Barlow opened his mouth, shut it again and left the
room.

Some half-hour later a stout, elderly woman wearing
an apron entered the library, bearing a large ledger.
Marcus looked up frowning from his desk and stared.
This was no maidservant!

'Mrs Barlow, your lordship,' she said in answer to
his querying gaze. 'Here be the accounts.'

Marcus stared at her and said, 'You're the cook, dammit! Why are you running errands beyond your kitchen?
Why did not one of the maids—?'

'Because there ain't none,' was the startling reply.

The hard grey eyes widened in disbelief. 'None? You
can't be serious!' A look around the room and the memory of his bed linen served to convince him that she
could be serious.

'Then who…?'

Mrs Barlow said, 'Well, Miss Meg does her best, me
lord, but since she also gives me a bit of a hand, being
as how the master wouldn't hire no help, it don't leave

her a lot of time an' it's a big house.' She dumped the book on the desk with scant ceremony and stalked out.

Marcus was horrified at these revelations and mentally made the afflicted Miss Fellowes his apologies. Obviously Great-uncle Samuel had been an even bigger lickpenny than he had thought. A glance at the household accounts confirmed what Mrs Barlow had said. No domestic staff was employed beyond the Barlows. One groom kept the two horses and a couple of carriages in some sort of order.

By the time he had ascertained from the painstaking accounts that the house was run on a budget that would have been laughably inadequate were it quadrupled, he was wondering just why Miss Fellowes had not removed herself years ago. The previous housekeeper had been dismissed four years earlier according to these records, resulting in a saving of twenty pounds a year.

Marcus very much doubted that his economically minded relative had bothered to pay Miss Fellowes a penny. There was certainly no record of it here. Which suggested that she was not, after all, a servant, but rather a dependent that the old devil had used shamefully. And then to leave her destitute! It passed all bounds! He would have to settle some money on the old lady. Marcus began to have a very definite picture of Miss…what was her name? Meg? Margaret, no doubt…Fellowes. Small, in her sixties at least, white hair, an air of nervousness. Probably she had nowhere else to go and no one to turn to and Samuel Langley had treated her like a dog! Damn the old skinflint! How difficult would it have been to leave the poor woman a respectable sum of money? Now he would have to do it as tactfully as possible and try to atone for Samuel's lack of responsibility. Perhaps she would enjoy a stay in London with Di?

Irritably, he dismissed this very minor matter from his mind and turned his attention back to the books. Tomorrow he would have to look over the estate and see what needed doing. Doubtless it was in as bad heart as the house.

A day spent riding around the estate with the bailiff, an individual clearly hired because he fell in with all Samuel Langley's notions of economy, confirmed Marcus in his worst fears. The estate was in ruins, its fields unproductive for much of the year and its tenants housed in conditions that would have shamed their new landlord had they been discovered on any of his other lands.

His face became grimmer and grimmer the more he saw, and Mr Padbury, misunderstanding his new master's cold anger, sought heartily to assure him that there were many more economies that could be made.

Ten minutes later, his face white with shock at the explosion his reassurances had engendered, Mr Padbury was in no doubt that things were about to change rapidly at Fenby. His lordship had informed him that, if he wished to keep his position, he would at once set in train arrangements for the relief of the cottagers and, furthermore, reduce the rents to a more reasonable figure.

Sitting in the library before dinner, contemplating the amount of work needed to bring the estate into order, Marcus wondered if his great-uncle had been merely eccentric or if there had been a hitherto-unrealised streak of insanity in the old man. It was going to cost a fortune to restore the estate. He sincerely hoped the old curmudgeon would spin dizzily in his grave at all the money that would have to be spent.

His cogitations were interrupted by Barlow, who came in and coughed apologetically.

'Yes, Barlow? Is dinner ready?' His annoyance over the ruination around him made his voice rather sharp.

Barlow looked awkward. 'Well, it is, me lord, but that ain't what I came to tell…ask you.'

He hesitated and Marcus, seeing that the old man was actually scared, said more gently, 'Go on, then.'

''Tis Miss Meg, me lord. Just took her dinner up on a tray I have, an' I reckon she's pretty bad. Agnes— Mrs Barlow, that is—saw her this mornin' an' thought the doctor did ought to be called but—'

'Have you done so?' interrupted Marcus, frowning.

'Oh, no, me lord!' Barlow said in soothing accents. 'Not without your permission! An' you was out all day so…'

Sheer disbelief robbed Marcus of speech momentarily. What the hell was going on here? He stared at Barlow for a moment and then said carefully, 'What the devil have I to say to anything? If Miss Fellowes requires or desires the attendance of a doctor, then she is perfectly at liberty to summon one!'

Barlow looked scared and confused and then, his face working, he burst out, 'We told Miss Meg days ago she did ought to have the doctor, but she won't acos she can't pay him. Master wouldn't never let her call the doctor, not even when she broke her arm! Doctor came anyway that time, acos Agnes got a message to him an' the master refused to pay the bill! So Miss Meg won't call him—'

'Enough!' Marcus was horrified. His mental query

about his uncle's sanity was patently answered. The old man must have been next door to a Bedlamite!

He saw Barlow flinch and said, 'Send a message for the doctor at once and assure him that his bills, including the one for Miss Fellowes's broken arm, will be met! I will come and see your mistress at once to reassure her that she need have no fears for the future!'

It was the least he could do. It was not right to leave the poor old lady worrying about her prospects. He had every intention of settling a large enough sum on her to enable her to hire lodgings and live in decent comfort. The idea of her having to go out and earn her living after a Langley had treated her so shabbily was utterly repugnant. Clearly Samuel Langley had not possessed the least idea of what his position entailed.

Barlow stared and said, 'I dunno as it'll do much good, me lord. Right feverish she is. I don't think she even knew I was in the room just then.'

It was Marcus's turn to stare. He said slowly, 'How sick is she?'

Barlow flushed. 'Mortal bad, me lord. I...I haven't been up today on account of Agnes bein' took ill. I been tryin' to help her as well an' now she've took to her bed.' He misinterpreted the look of consternation on his lordship's face and hastened to set his mind at rest. 'Dinner's all ready, me lord,' he said soothingly. 'An' we got Farmer Bates's second girl to come in to help during the day, bein' as how you said this mornin' extra help could be hired.'

'Damn and blast my dinner!' exploded Marcus. 'Conduct me to Miss Fellowes's chamber at once!'

Five minutes later he stood staring down at the feverish occupant of a very large and old-fashioned tester bed, festooned with moth-eaten velvet hangings. Her face was ashen grey in its pallor and sheened with sweat in the flickering light cast by a branch of tallow candles. Thin hands shifted restlessly on the counterpane and her breath rasped harshly. Every few moments the slight frame was racked by paroxysms of coughing.

'Hell!' said Marcus in shock. 'Barlow, get down to the stables on the double. Tell Burnet to harness my bays to the curricle. You are to go with him to fetch the doctor. I don't want him getting lost. Stop! Where will I find firewood?'

The room was pervaded with a chilly damp that seeped into the bones. No wonder she was so ill, thought Marcus. She should have had the doctor days ago. It might have started out as a touch of influenza, but he was willing to bet it was a fully fledged inflammation of the lungs now!

Barlow said, 'I'll send young Judd up with firewood, me lord.'

He was gone, leaving Marcus staring down at Miss Fellowes. He could have kicked himself for not checking on her two days ago. To his admittedly inexperienced eye, she was seriously ill and he felt appallingly responsible. And there was another thing apart from her health to bother him about her.

Miss Fellowes, far from being elderly, was not even middle-aged. He would be very much surprised if she could boast more than twenty summers to her credit. And it was entirely possible, he thought in sinking fear, that she might not live long enough to see this one.

By the time the doctor arrived, Marcus had done a fair bit to make Miss Fellowes more comfortable. A crackling fire was rapidly dispelling the chill of the room. He had bathed her brow and wrists repeatedly with cool water. He had even lifted her slight frame from the pillows when she roused and held a cup of water to her lips, compelling her to swallow some.

She had choked and protested, opening her eyes briefly to gaze at him in mild confusion. Then she had apparently decided he was harmless and said, 'Thank you,' in a faint whisper, before closing her eyes again. Marcus took some encouragement from this. A concern with her manners argued that perhaps she was not quite as ill as he had thought.

Doctor Ellerbeck, a bluff-looking man of about fifty, took one look at Miss Fellowes and said, 'My God! Why the devil didn't you call me sooner?'

Feeling absurdly guilty, Marcus explained. Ellerbeck listened and then turned to examine his patient.

Which presented Marcus with another problem. He definitely ought not to be in the room while the doctor examined Miss Fellowes. It was most improper. On the other hand, it would be even more improper to leave her alone with the doctor. He swore and turned his back. In the absence of Mrs Barlow, that would have to do.

At last Ellerbeck stepped back from the bed and asked, 'Where is Agnes?' And swore when he was told. 'This child needs someone with her constantly. I may be able to find someone tomorrow; but who is to sit with her tonight? I have a woman in labour to attend.'

'I'll sit with her,' said Marcus, feeling that his life had just spun totally out of his control.

Ellerbeck frowned slightly. 'It will be no sinecure, my lord. She'll need the medicine I'll leave with you and a saline draft. That fever is likely to rise before morning and she'll be very difficult to handle.'

Marcus shrugged and said resignedly, 'There's no one else, Doctor. And it's partially my fault. I should have checked on her two days ago. You can't blame the Barlows. They weren't to know I wouldn't behave like my uncle.' He felt sick to his stomach at the thought of the girl lying there, too proud to call the doctor because she couldn't pay him, and too scared to let anyone know how ill she was. To be that alone in the world, to have no one to care for you! An icy band contracted around his heart at the thought. He looked down at Miss Fellowes's ashen face. At least for the next few days she had someone to take care of her.

Ellerbeck regarded him intently and then said slowly, 'I do not mean to offend you, my lord, but it is the sort of thing that will be frowned upon, and while I do not listen to gossip—'

Marcus cut him short, saying ruefully, 'My reputation is disgraceful. You will have to take my word for it, Ellerbeck, that even were I in the habit of seducing the innocent, a girl as sick as this...'

'I was not concerned for Miss Fellowes's safety at your hands, my lord!' said Ellerbeck caustically. 'Rather I was concerned at what the reaction of the local gabsters may be.'

'And do you think I care more for their tattle than for my own opinion if I leave her unattended?' asked Marcus quietly. 'As I said, there is no one else. Frankly, I should not even have been in the house with her; but I was under the mistaken impression that she was an elderly woman. And now, if I put up in the village to save her reputation, she may well lose her life.'

A brief silence ensued as Ellerbeck considered his options. At last he said, 'Very well,' and proceeded to give Marcus his instructions. These were issued with all the authority of a general who expected to be obeyed in every particular. Marcus, who had received orders directly from Wellington himself, was impressed as well as amused. He listened closely, asking questions occasionally.

Finally Ellerbeck was finished. 'I'll send my man back with the medicine and a saline draught. Give her plenty of fluids. It will help to keep the fever down. Oh, try to keep her propped up against the pillows. It will be easier on her breathing.'

'I sponged her face and wrists...' Marcus's tone was questioning. He was starting to feel extremely nervous. The girl looked so ill and she was muttering to herself and moving restlessly.

Ellerbeck followed his gaze and frowned slightly. 'Just the thing,' he said. 'I'll come back in the morning. You can send for me sooner if necessary. My man will know where I am.' He sat down on the bed and took one of those restless hands. 'Miss Meg...Meg. Open your eyes.' His voice was gentle but commanding.

To Marcus's immense surprise the heavy lids fluttered open. Eyes of a deep blue-grey focused confusedly on the doctor, who said kindly, 'Good girl. Miss Meg, you are very ill with this wretched influenza. You need not worry, this gentleman is a friend of mine. His name is...' He looked questioningly up at Marcus.

'Marcus...Marc,' he responded automatically, and then wondered what had possessed him to use the name only his family and closest friends knew him by.

'Marcus. He is going to look after you. I have to look in on Agnes and then help Mrs Watkins with her baby tonight. I have told Marcus just what to do for you. He will give you your medicine and anything else you need. You may trust him as you would myself.' Ellerbeck gave the hand a reassuring pat.

Gradually some of the confusion cleared in the hazy regard and it shifted slightly to include Marcus. A faint smile touched the pallid lips and a weak voice said, 'You were here...before. Gave me a drink...a flannel.'

Surprised that she remembered, Marcus smiled down at her and nodded. She smiled back and shut her eyes wearily. As sick as she was, the smile held a great deal of sweetness.

Ellerbeck stood up to leave and said quietly to Marcus, 'No need for her to know who you are yet. Only worry her.' Shrewdly he looked at Marcus and said, 'Don't you worry too much, either. She'll do well enough now we've caught it. Believe me, little Miss Meg has the constitution of a horse.' Seeing the doubt in the taut face and frowning grey eyes, he said, 'I mean it, my lord. She's a very sick lassie but I'll warrant she'll be up in a few days.'

Left alone with his charge, Marcus wondered what to do. Miss Meg...no, dammit! Meg! If he were going to be her nurse, then there was little point in adhering to the usual rules governing polite intercourse. He'd already broken most of them anyway and was about to break a fair few more.

Meg seemed inclined to sleep peacefully for the time being. Reflecting that this was likely to be of short duration, he pulled a large and battered leather armchair up to the bed and settled down to wait.

A soft knock at the door announced the return of Barlow. 'Brought some dinner up, my lord, and broth for Miss Meg. It ain't just what you'll be used to, but it's better than nowt. Would there be aught else?'

Marcus shook his head. 'Not at the moment, Barlow. But stay...how is your wife?'

Barlow smiled. 'Doctor says she's not too bad. Not

like Miss Meg. He told her to remain in bed for two or three days.'

'Good.' Genuine pleasure warmed his tones. 'Go and look after her, Barlow. I can manage Miss Meg.'

When Barlow had gone he turned his attention to the laden tray. It held a roast chicken, very cold, and dumplings along with fresh bread and a pat of butter. He grinned. There had been times during the war in Spain and Portugal when this would have been considered an extravagant meal for several famished officers in Wellington's army.

Also on the tray was a *veilleuse*, a combination night lamp and food warmer. He could remember his mother using one years ago when she had been ill. Barlow had already lit the oil lamp in the bottom section, its cheerful glow shone through the apertures in the porcelain. On top was the lidded bowl, doubtless containing Meg's broth.

What to do first? Meg was asleep and the heat from the lamp would keep the broth warm. After some thought he decided to let her sleep while he had something to eat. Accordingly he set the *veilleuse* on the nightstand, and addressed his own dinner. He was hungry after a long day in the saddle and made short work of the meal.

Now, he thought, Meg. He had noticed a small curved porcelain sickroom-syphon on the tray, its lower end pierced. Barlow, he realised, was an unexpected treasure. He'd thought of everything. No doubt it would be a great deal easier to let Meg use this, rather than trying to spoon broth into her—a procedure that he suspected might have been more than a trifle messy.

After putting the bowl of broth and syphon on the small bedside table, he followed the doctor's example and sat down beside her on the bed to pick up a small hand. Chafing it gently between his large ones, he spoke her name quietly.

'Meg…Meg, wake up.'

At first there was no response, but then a sigh was heard and the eyes opened. They were very cloudy and wandered around the room before settling on Marcus with a puzzled frown. Gradually recognition dawned and she smiled. 'Marc.'

'That's right. You remembered.' He felt absurdly pleased that she remembered his name and her smile for some unknown reason warmed him. No doubt it was relief to think that Ellerbeck was right, and she was not so ill as he had first thought.

'Oh, yes.' The expression hazed over slightly. 'I don't know anyone else so handsome…nice.' She closed her eyes, patently unaware of having said anything untoward.

Somewhat startled, Marcus tried again. 'Meg…it is time for you to have some dinner. Come.'

Again the eyes opened.

'That's the way,' said Marcus encouragingly. He slipped an arm around her and helped her to sit up. She was pitifully weak and leaned against him, shaking. He could feel her trembling, feel the heat of her fevered body clear through her nightgown as he held her against him. With his free hand he picked up the syphon and presented it to her.

A feeble yet outraged protest greeted this. 'I don't need that blasted thing!'

'Rubbish!' he responded succinctly, firmly suppressing a delighted smile at her intransigence. 'Do as you are bid.'

Rather to his surprise she obeyed without further argument and took it. He reached out for the bowl and held it so that the pierced end of the syphon rested in the broth.

'There you are, my dear, drink it up.' He was conscious of a swell of satisfaction as the level in the bowl dropped. Half the broth was gone before she shook her head. Marcus did not insist. She could have some more later. Thanks to Barlow's forethought, the broth could be kept warm for hours.

'A drink?'

She nodded against his shoulder. He brought the glass to her lips and held it for her to take several swallows. When she had finished, he held her steady while with his free hand he rearranged the pillows. Carefully he sat her back against them and drew the blankets up around her.

Her eyes were shut again, but he did not think she was asleep. Sure enough, a moment later her eyes opened and she surveyed him with mild curiosity.

'Who are you?' Her voice was weak and cracked slightly as though her throat were sore.

'Marc. I'm a friend.'

That seemed to puzzle her. 'Oh. I didn't know. You're a very nice one. Sorry I was rude.' Then the eyes fluttered shut again.

As the night wore on she became more confused and restless. Marcus was kept extremely busy in his efforts to help her be quiet and comfortable. Once when he was building up the fire he heard a noise and turned around to find her getting out of bed. Horrified, he strode across and lifted her effortlessly in his arms to put her back. She struggled at first, but submitted when he spoke.

'Meg, sweetheart—' the endearment slipped out unconsciously '—you must stay in bed.'

'Am I sick?' She clung to him as he attempted to tuck her in. 'Oh, that's right. Ellerbeck was here!' Suddenly she panicked. 'I can't pay him! There's no money for me, Cousin Samuel says.'

It was like a blow over the heart to hear the fear in her voice. What would it be like to face destitution as this girl did? To face your entire life knowing that there was not a soul in the world to care what became of you and to have to go out into that world to earn your living. It must be a nightmare for anyone at the best of times, and must be so for her if it could even penetrate the feverish fog clouding her mind.

Still holding her in his arms, he tried gently to reassure her. 'Don't worry, Meg. The bills are all paid and there is plenty of money. You are quite safe with me. Go to sleep.' His hands automatically stroked the thick dark curls, which felt lank and lifeless to his touch.

Much to his surprise she seemed to accept this and settled down. He found though that when he left her she became upset and scared. Ironically he thought that, although he had spent countless nights with a woman clasped in his arms, this one would stand out in his memory as the most novel of his entire misspent career. Resignedly he climbed back on to the bed beside her and pulled her to him, nestling her into the curve of his arm to rest against his side. He firmly repressed the thought that she felt rather nice snuggled against him.

With a contented little sigh her head drooped on to his shoulder and she slept.

Oddly enough, Marcus found that he got a great deal more rest this way. When she stirred he could recall her wandering mind simply by speaking to her gently. She seemed to remember him and trust him quite happily. Occasionally she even spoke his name in her mutterings.

His heart twisted as she murmured, 'Marc is here…a friend…' What had her life been that she should find the thought of an unknown friend so sustaining? He wondered if there were anyone else she could turn to. Surely she didn't have to hire herself out as a nursery governess! She was obviously gently born and Samuel Langley had behaved in a totally inappropriate way, turning her into a servant. There must be some relative he could find to take her in. Unconsciously he held her closer, leaning to rest his cheek on the limp, dark curls.

For two nights and a day between Marcus was in constant attendance on Miss Fellowes. He found that he was required to do everything for her. Most of the time she lay in a semi-conscious daze, rarely stirring except when he fed her or gave her a drink. He even had to hold her steady while she perched on the spittoon he found under the bed. Marcus thought ruefully that if she remembered any of this, Meg was going to be extremely embarrassed. Not many husbands would have had to do as much for their wives as he had done for this unknown, helpless waif.

He found that he thought of her as a child, although he had ascertained from Barlow that she was nearly twenty. Her form was so thin, not at all like the rounded, voluptuous curves he was used to in a woman. Just as well, he thought, given that he had ended up spending most of the night with her in his arms.

She would be quite tall though, he surmised as he watched her that afternoon. He liked taller women. Not too tall, but enough so that he didn't get a crick in his neck stooping to kiss them. And he supposed that if she were not so ill and had some flesh on her bones, that she might fill out quite nicely. Her eyes were certainly lovely, deep blue-grey, fringed with curling dark lashes and with strongly marked brows above them. He complexion, despite the ashen hue, was definitely good.

The fever seemed to abate during the day but rose again towards the evening, although Marcus thought she was not so ill as when he had first seen her. He found her eyes open several times, staring at him with a puzzled frown, but she asked no questions beyond the time and what day it was. He suspected that she was too tired and weak to indulge in curiosity.

Ellerbeck called again in the evening and pronounced her much improved. 'Much better, my lord. And Agnes Barlow will be up tomorrow. She should stay in bed longer, but she is in a terrible state about Miss Meg and insists that she must get up. So you will be relieved.'

Marcus nodded. 'Good. I cannot think that Miss Meg will feel at all comfortable with me once she is well enough to realise who I am. If Mrs Barlow takes over tomorrow that can be avoided.'

'Aye, that will be best,' agreed the doctor. 'I'll tell you to your head, my lord, she's a great deal better. And that can go down to your credit. I'll warrant you didn't have an easy time with her. If ever you need a reference as a nurse, my lord, drop me a line.'

Marcus shrugged to hide his pleasure and said off-handedly, 'The job had to be done, sir. No one could have let the girl take her chances.'

A sceptical snort from the doctor made him look inquiringly. 'Old Samuel wouldn't have seen it like that. Nor, I might add, did any of the so-called ladies in the district. Told you I'd try to get a woman, didn't I? Well, I did try, and not one of them was willing to come or even send a maid to help the girl!'

'What?' Marcus was aghast. 'Why not?'

Ellerbeck looked self-conscious. 'Er…they seemed to feel that your reputation…'

White hot fury seared through Marcus. His usually cold eyes were blazing with rage and his big frame was absolutely rigid. If this were the case, it made his plans for Meg's future very dangerous. If he settled money on her, then it would be whispered that she had been his mistress. She would be a social pariah. In his estimation she had suffered enough through Samuel Langley's irresponsibility without another member of the family completing the job. He would have to think of something else.

All he said was, 'Charming that they would then leave a sick girl to my care.'

It was not the first time he had been confronted with the hypocrisy of society in general and women in particular. He did not doubt that if he appeared socially and showed the slightest interest in any of the eligible females, that he would be courted and toadied to glory. None of them would have cared a rap for his reputation did they but think his fortune and title were going to embellish one of their daughters.

They would not care if he had ruined Meg Fellowes in fact or merely compromised her technically. Meg's reputation would be mud while he was still a matrimonial prize.

He was still seething on and off and wondering exactly what he should do about it when Agnes Barlow appeared the following morning to remove him from his position as nurse. Although she looked far from well, she ejected him from the room unceremoniously, muttering that things were come to a pretty pass if a young lady was expected to have a gentleman to nurse her.

'Not but what the doctor was sayin' you was very good to Miss Meg an' she ought to be grateful you was here! But what I say is, the less she knows about it the better. Now get along with you, lad...me lord...an' have your breakfast. Farmer Bates's girl Nellie ain't much, but she can cook ham an' eggs!'

From which Marcus gathered that, despite her disapproval of the necessity that had put him in charge of the sickroom, Mrs Barlow was far from disapproving of him personally. He definitely hoped the Barlows were going to agree to stay on under his management. Naturally if they wanted to be pensioned off, he would do so, but he rather thought that it would be preferable to have two such loyal and intelligent servants remain here.

Chapter Three

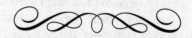

Miss Marguerite Fellowes was very puzzled when she awoke later that morning. Not only was the room warm, but she felt very much better. She felt so much better that she was ready to be curious about the tall and handsome stranger who had been in attendance while she was so sick. A very elegant stranger at that. And so kind.

Except for the Barlows and, of course, the Vicar and Dr Ellerbeck, Miss Fellowes couldn't think of anyone who was kind to her. And that reminded her…had someone called Dr Ellerbeck? She hoped it was just a dream that he had been to see her, because she couldn't imagine how she was going to pay him. Frowning, she tried to remember properly. She was sure he had been…yes…she recalled him introducing Marc to her, saying he was a friend.

Expectantly she looked around for Marc. And found Agnes sitting in the armchair, turning the heel of a sock. Conscious of a feeling of crushing disappointment, Meg realised that Marc must have just been a dream, a fever-induced vision compounded of her deepest romantic fancies. And she had certainly had some peculiar fancies while she was ill. But to think a gentleman had nursed her! She might have known it was a dream. As if any gentleman, let alone one as handsome as that, would ever be so kind to Meg Fellowes. No, only an imaginary man could possibly have held her so safely and soothed her so tenderly.

He had fed her too, she suddenly remembered. Out of that revolting syphon of Cousin Samuel's. And hadn't he helped her when she had to...surely she would not have imagined those sort of things! Not being able to pay the doctor's bill would be a small embarrassment compared to this.

'Hullo, Agnes.' She smiled as Mrs Barlow looked up. 'Have you been there long?'

Caught off-guard, Mrs Barlow replied, 'An hour or so, dearie. How do you feel? Doctor said as how you'd pull up quick once you turned the corner.'

Meg thought that she still felt fairly gruesome, weak and achey. But at least her wits were her own again. And her head didn't feel as though a blacksmith had set up business in it. Nor was her throat still sore. That was something. No doubt she could get up later and do her packing. It would not do to keep Mrs Garsby waiting too long for her nursery governess or she might decide to offer someone else the position.

Then her gaze lit on that beastly syphon, lying beside the bottom half of the *veilleuse* on the nightstand. Her eyes widened. Oh, dear! Maybe she hadn't been dreaming after all! But who...?

Nervously she cleared her throat and asked, 'Agnes, who looked after me while I was sick? Was it you?'

Agnes Barlow shook her head reluctantly and Meg realised from her demeanour that something odd was going on. A deep and mortified blush swept over the pale face and throat.

'Agnes! Who was it?' Meg's voice came out as a startled squeak.

'His lordship,' said Agnes. 'I'm that sorry, Miss Meg, but I was sick too. Not like you was, but I wouldn't have been much good to you. Barlow looked after me and I'll tell you one thing.' She lowered her voice. 'It may not have been what you call proper, but Barlow told me his lordship was that careful with you. And he insisted on paying for the doctor to come out. Cross as anything he was that we hadn't told him sooner.'

'His lordship?' echoed Meg. 'I don't know any lord-ships!' Let alone one she called Marc and who claimed to be a friend.

Agnes elaborated. 'Lord Rutherford, dearie. Turned up t'other night. Right put about he was when Barlow told him about you…'

Meg stared in horror. She had fully intended to be out of the house before Cousin Samuel's horrid heir arrived! And she would have been if the Barlows hadn't practically forced her into bed and told her to stay there. She had heard *all* about the Earl of Rutherford and he hadn't sounded at all the sort of person she wanted to know…or, for that matter, the sort of person to nurse a stranger through an attack of influenza. Especially a girl with her history.

All she could find to say was, 'Did someone send over to Mrs Garsby? She…she was expecting me.'

Agnes pursed her lips in evident disapproval. She had voiced her opinion of Miss Meg's proposed employment at Burvale House often enough for Meg to have it by heart. Despite all the gossip and nastiness of some people who called themselves ladies, Miss Meg was a young lady and ought not to be cast out on the world like an unwanted kitten, and so on, and so on.

She opened her mouth, clearly intending to say it all again, but Meg said, 'Oh, Agnes, please don't! I have to live after all. What else can I do? I can't remain here any longer. Was a message sent?' There was real fear in her voice.

Agnes nodded with obvious disapproval. 'Aye. Barlow sent a message, sayin' you was took sick.'

Relief flooded through Meg. It would never do to lose her situation before she had even started. She was determined never to ask for charity or assistance again in her life. She would starve rather than ever be someone's poor relation again. She reflected that, after Cousin Samuel's pointed lessons in economy, she would be able to save a great deal for her old age out of the twenty pounds per annum that her prospective employer had offered.

To Meg, who had never had any money of her own, it seemed a fortune, but she was wise enough to realise that her wages must be husbanded carefully against times when she might be without a job and particularly against the time when she was too old to work.

A knock at the door presaged the entrance of Nellie Bates with a tray.

'Nellie! What are you doing here?'

'Temp'rary 'elp, Miss Meg,' said Nellie proudly. 'To 'elp Mrs Barlow. Just days, mind. Me mam won't let me stay o' nights. On account of 'is lordship's reputation. Real wicked, they say 'e is!'

A snort from Mrs Barlow as Nellie left the room suggested that her help was not entirely appreciated. She softened it by saying, 'She means well, I'll say that for her. Not but what some folks 'ud do a sight better to worry 'bout their own beams afore they goes looking for motes in other folks' eyes.'

Meg thought things were definitely taking a turn for the better. If Marc...Lord Rutherford was hiring help, then perhaps he was not such a shocking lickpenny as Cousin Samuel, who had given new layers of meaning to the term, 'of a saving disposition'. That would mean better times for everyone on the estate.

Agnes bustled over with the tray, placing it on her lap. It held a plate of bread and butter and the bowl from the top of the *veilleuse*. Suspiciously Meg raised the lid. Ugh! More broth! Well, at least this time she had been provided with a spoon rather than that horrid syphon. She could not recall how many times she had carried the thing to Cousin Samuel after he had bought it. He had agonised over the purchase price and consequently had been determined to get his money's worth out of it, so he had used it every time he had so much as a head cold.

Meg remembered the time she had suggested that, at four pence, he could afford to keep it for special occasions. The old man had practically had a seizure, moaning that she was a wanton, extravagant hussy, just like her mother, and would bring him to ruin with her spendthrift ways!

And now she had used it! She had a very clear memory of Marc...his lordship, giving it to her...she was very much afraid that she had sworn at him. Blushing once more as she spooned up the broth, Meg realised that she would have to see his lordship again, if only to thank him for his care of her and to apologise for trespassing on his hospitality. She hoped he would not think she was angling for a handout.

* * *

In the event, Meg did not see his lordship for several days. Her voiced intent of getting up to pack and remove herself to Burvale House to take up her duties there, was dealt with summarily, if vicariously, by Marcus. Having been informed by Mrs Barlow of the patient's plan, he had charged her with the message that if Miss Fellowes was such a pea goose, he would personally strip her, put her back to bed and tie her to it if necessary, until the doctor gave her permission to get up.

While deprecating the blunt nature of Lord Ruthford's graphic threat, Mrs Barlow relayed it faithfully and was bound to acknowledge that it had its effect. Nothing more was heard from Miss Fellowes about getting up for another five days, by which time the doctor was perfectly satisfied with her progress.

Inwardly fuming over his lordship's high-handed attitude, Meg had to admit that she didn't really want to get up all that much. Certainly not enough to risk calling his lordship's bluff. If indeed he was bluffing, which she thought extremely doubtful. So she remained in bed, happily reading, for five days.

Having been informed by Ellerbeck that in his opinion the patient was recovered enough to leave her bed, Marcus sat waiting at the desk in the library to inform Miss Fellowes of her future. He had it all sorted out. She was most definitely not going to take up that position at Burvale House. It would be quite ineligible for a young lady, which she undoubtedly was.

First off, she could go to stay with Diana. He would send her to London post. That would get her out of this neighbourhood, where there might be some spiteful whispers about her sojourn under his roof. After a decent interval he would settle some of Samuel Langley's money on her, which was what the scaly old nipcheese ought to have done in the first place. He would tell her that Samuel had desired him to do so when the extent of his obligations and debts should be known. No need for her to think she was being handed charity. He would write to Diana tonight and send a note over to Mrs Garsby in a day or so, informing her that she would need to find another nursery governess.

He smiled to himself in anticipation. He simply couldn't wait to see her face. She would be disbelieving at first, would probably demur. Then she would be excited, happy. Her face would be flushed with pleasure, anticipation.

A tap at the door informed him that Miss Fellowes had arrived to be told of the change in her fortunes.

'Come in.'

Meg heard the deep rumble and trembled slightly. His voice was just as she remembered it, dark and velvety...it was the sort of voice that made you want to stroke it...like a big cat. Nervously she opened the door and went in, wondering if her eyes had remembered as well as her ears.

They hadn't. She really must have been quite out of her wits with that influenza. Marc—faced with him she had trouble reminding herself to think of him as Lord Rutherford—sat there at Cousin Samuel's old desk, looking even more lethally handsome than she recalled. His frame looked impossibly large and powerful, the shoulders too broad to be contained in any coat made for a normal human being. His hair was, as she remembered, a rich tawny brown. The eyes puzzled her. She had thought them warm and kind. Now they were cold

and impassive, the sort of eyes that held their own counsel and gave nothing away.

Perhaps if she concentrated on those chilly eyes she
might be able to remember that this was Lord
Rutherford—that Marc was a dream.

Marcus was delighted to see that Miss Fellowes—he
must remember to call her that—looked so much better.
She was still far too pale, in stark contrast to the shadows under her eyes, but she looked as though she had
put on a little weight in the last few days since he had
seen her. There was actually some colour in her lips,
which were, he noticed, quite beautifully cut, soft and
full. Just the sort of mouth, he caught himself thinking,
which begged to be kissed. Frowning, he reminded himself that kissing was not on his agenda for Meg...
dammit! Miss Fellowes!

Seeing the frown, Meg quailed inwardly and flushed;
no doubt he thought her dress shabby, not at all the
thing to wear for meeting an earl. Well, it was the best
she had and if he didn't like it then that was too bad.
She didn't like it either, being tolerably certain that dull
black was not calculated to make her look her best. And
it must look so dowdy to one used to women in the
highest kick of fashion. She knew the crossover bodice
was years out of date. So she held her head high, determined not to be flustered. From all Agnes had said,
he did not have the slightest idea who she was.
Fellowes, after all, was a common enough name.

'Good morning Miss Fellowes,' said Marcus politely.
'I trust you are recovered.' He noted the slight flush.
Better not to say she looks much improved. No need to
rub her face in the fact that I nursed her.

But Meg was made of sterner stuff. 'I am very much
better, my lord. For which I am given to understand I

must thank you.' Not for worlds would she have admitted that she could remember in detail all that he had done for her, including holding her in his arms for the whole of one night.

Very embarrassed, he waved her thanks aside. 'It was nothing, Miss Fellowes. A trifling service. I could wish Barlow had informed me earlier of the severity of your illness. You might then have been spared my very inexpert assistance.' He thought he had never heard himself sound like such a pompous jackass, so cold and uncaring. Yet this was the face he always presented to the world.

Meg thought he sounded bored, as though she had been a complete and utter nuisance. Which, she admitted, she probably had. Still...perhaps she ought to hold on to her memory of Marc...so kind and tender...yes, that would be a better memory to cherish in the lonely years ahead. Even if it had been a dream, it was better than the icy reality before her.

Marcus cleared his throat. What on earth had brought that odd smile to her face? It was perhaps the loveliest smile he had ever seen, shy and considering, as though she smiled at something inexpressibly dear and private.

With a mental snort for this whimsical flight, he said, 'I am informed that you had the intention of taking up a post as a nursery governess in this neighbourhood.'

Acutely Meg picked up his use of the past tense and replied firmly, 'Yes, my lord, the Vicar arranged it for me. That *is* my intention.'

Just as acute, Marcus heard the slight stress on the tense. Flatly he said, 'It will not do. You are unsuited for such a position and I will not countenance it.' As soon as the words had left his mouth he wondered if he had made a serious tactical error.

Meg's eyes widened and she could practically feel her hackles rise. Having just buried one loathsome guardian, she was not about to submit to another. Especially not one who had not the slightest right to wield authority over her. She opened her mouth to administer a blistering snub and reconsidered. Had he, after all, found out who she was? Was that why he considered her unfit to have charge of children? Better to find out what he meant without losing her temper. If she riled him, he could make it impossible for her to find employment.

'What then, my lord, do you recommend for me?' Her voice was sweet and reasonable, her eyes modestly downcast. Meg had learned long ago that it was generally best to find out the lie of the land without giving the least hint of her own thoughts, leave alone her feelings.

It took Marcus in completely. Phew! He had thought she was about to rip up at him. Doubtless she was just surprised. Relieved, he outlined his plans for her, dwelling on the pleasure it would give his sister to entertain her indefinitely, pointing out that, with a respectable sum settled on her, she might even make a creditable marriage.

She listened, unbearably tempted. To visit London, be able to buy a pretty dress, perhaps marry and have her own babies rather than easing her longing in caring for another woman's children. But it was not possible. Despite his lordship's kindly untruth—yes, he was kind after all under the icy exterior: in telling her Cousin Samuel had asked him to settle money on her, he had tried to spare her pride—she knew it for a lie.

And she seriously doubted that his lordship's sister would wish to have a stranger foisted on to her.

Certainly not one with no pretensions to fashion, wealth or even beauty. Certainly not once she knew just who Miss Marguerite Fellowes was. Obviously his lordship could not possibly know or he would never have suggested such a thing. And once he knew then she would be out on her ear. Even her own family had kicked her out. No, Miss Fellowes preferred to remove herself voluntarily.

For a moment the thought occurred to her that she could take the money and run before he found out the truth, but she instantly dismissed that as dishonourable. She could not take advantage of his kindness and ignorance so shamefully.

Resolutely she stifled her longings and said very calmly, 'No.' Then, as an afterthought, 'No, thank you.'

Had she protested angrily Marcus would have believed she was merely making a token resistance, trying to make him think she couldn't possibly accept such generosity, when all the time she intended to capitulate at the right moment. The quiet, unemotional voice in which she had uttered her carefully polite refusal told him at once that she was deadly serious.

Throttling the urge to issue a series of autocratic decrees and carry her position by storm, Marcus asked equally quietly, 'Will you tell me why not?'

Meg thought about that, frowning slightly. It was none of his business, after all, what she chose to do with her life and the habit of keeping her own counsel was strong. But perhaps, having made such a kind offer, he deserved better than to have it flung back in his face without any explanation. She owed him part of the truth.

Drawing a deep breath, she said, 'To start with, I cannot possibly accept money from you. People would think—'

'Rubbish!' said Marcus. 'I told you—'

He was interrupted in his turn. 'My lord, Samuel Langley didn't give a damn for me! He made no pretence of that, to me or to anyone else. He died intestate because he was too miserly to pay a lawyer to draw up his will and the only reason he permitted Cousin Euphemia to take me in was because he saw in me a potential housekeeper he wouldn't have to pay!' She hadn't meant to say that, but once she had started it seemed some of the anger she had kept leashed for years had come spilling out. Gritting her teeth, she forced herself to take a deep breath, reaching for self-control. He must not know the truth…Marc she might have been able to tell…but not this cold, dictatorial earl.

Seeing that she had silenced his lordship's charitable lies, she went on more temperately. 'So you see, I cannot take your money. And I most certainly will not impose upon your sister. I have not the least claim on her and, to be frank, sir, I do not wish to continue as a poor relation, dependent on another's charity. I thank you for your kindness, but I will do as I had planned.'

Silence hung between them for a moment. Marcus could definitely see her point. Obviously her position had chafed her, but he failed to see how it could possibly be better as a governess. Indeed it might, depending upon her mistress, be even worse. He knew of many fashionable women who treated their children's preceptresses with undisguised scorn and the contempt of the strong for the weak, using them as underpaid drudges, blaming them for every piece of misbehaviour and overturning any attempt made to discipline their high spirited darlings.

He couldn't permit it. It was unthinkable. Something icy seemed to contract around his heart at the idea of

Meg at the mercy of one of those women. He didn't say what was going through his mind. His emotions were far too confusing. Which was in itself confusing. Lord Rutherford always kept his emotions under strict control!

So he fell back on issuing commands, using storm tactics. 'Very well. You have made your point. Now that is said, I will send a message over to Mrs Garsby in the morning informing her of my decision. We will remain here for another week to allow you to recuperate, then I will take you to my sister. That is all. There is no more to be said on the subject.' The firm lips clipped together and his eyes were as cold and impersonal as his voice had been

'Oh. Very well, then.' Again her eyes were downcast, her voice unassuming.

He eyed her narrowly, suddenly suspicious of her meek demeanour. All at once her submissiveness seemed out of character. And he couldn't put his finger on why.

'You have nothing more to say, Meg?'

Her Christian name slipped out unconsciously. He clenched his fist slightly. The name brought back all the intimacy of her illness. His body tingled at the memory of how she had snuggled up to him so trustingly. At the time he had not felt any physical interest. But now he was burningly aware of it. His estimation that she would be attractive when restored to health had not been wrong. Even now, when she was still out of sorts, her slender, lissom grace could not be obliviated by the shapeless excuse for a dress which hung on her.

'No, my lord. Good morning.' She dropped him a small curtsy and left the room.

She went back to her room with her head held high.

So his lordship thought that she would dance to his bidding, did he? Well, if he thought that yet another Langley was going to ride over Marguerite Fellowes roughshod, then he had another think coming. There might be nothing more to be said on the matter, but there was certainly something to be done!

Heavy grey clouds were pressing in ominously from the west at four-thirty as Meg jumped down from the gig at the front door of Burvale House and held her hand up to young Tom Judd who had driven her over.

'Thank you Tom. Goodbye. And please ask Barlow to give this to his lordship.' She handed him a sealed letter with a hand that trembled slightly. His lordship was going to be furious, but she couldn't help that. She couldn't accept his offer and he had to know why, but she couldn't bear to see him turn away and withdraw his offer, or worse, swallow his disgust and renew it.

Tom touched his cap and said cheerfully. 'Aye, Miss Meg. Good luck to ye.' He turned the cob and shook up the reins. 'Walk on there!'

Meg watched the gig bowl away down the avenue. It seemed to go very quickly, leaving her cut off from the past to face the future alone. She lifted her chin in an oddly gallant gesture and clutched her scarlet woollen cloak more closely around her. Nothing had changed really, she had always been alone. It was just that now that fact seemed harder to face, doubtless because for one blinding moment she had thought that it might be different.

Blinking to clear her eyes, she told herself angrily that the best thing to do now was to banish all thoughts of what could never be and concentrate on what must be. Especially she must banish all thoughts of her friend

Marc. He was a creature of her fevered imagination. The reality was Lord Rutherford, a kind enough gentleman to be concerned at the fate of an orphan, but proud and aloof. He would not have been so concerned had he known who she was, why none of the neighbouring ladies had felt it necessary to assist her.

Bravely she picked up the shabby portmanteau which held her belongings and trod up the steps, telling herself that at least she would be with children and would actually have some money of her own. It might even turn out that Mrs Garsby's unnerving resemblance to a basilisk was merely due to Meg's own state of mind during the interview. Perhaps she was kind and considerate and would raise Meg's wage very soon when she realised how devoted Meg was to her children. Clutching at this unlikely notion along with her courage, Meg tugged at the bell chain just as the first heavy drops of rain fell.

Twenty minutes later, Mrs Garsby had largely confirmed Meg in her original impression. No one had answered the door for several minutes and, by the time a supercilious manservant appeared, Miss Fellowes was drenched to the skin in the downpour.

The servant seemed unwilling to admit her, but she insisted that Mrs Garsby was expecting her and put her foot in the door. At last, with a faint sneer, he permitted her to, 'Step into the hall while I see if the mistress is at home…'

'It doesn't matter if she is at home or not,' explained Meg wearily. 'I keep telling you, I am the new governess!'

She wondered if she dared to sit down as he stalked off to find Mrs Garsby. On the whole she thought not. Her clothes were dripping all over the flags as it was

and her cloak, once so warm and comforting, was a
sodden weight on her slim shoulders. If she sat down
on any of the beautifully upholstered chairs in the hall
she would soak them. To take her mind off how numb-
ingly tired she was she began to imagine just what
Cousin Samuel would have had to say to all the luxurious ostentation displayed in this entrance hall to impress visitors. She was tolerably certain it would not
extend to the room assigned to the nursery governess!

A cold voice interrupted her. 'Might I know what you
are doing here, forcing your way into my house?'

A sick, clammy fear twisted itself around Meg's suddenly pounding heart as she looked up at the stony face
of her prospective employer. An icy, high-nosed stare
was directed upon her as Mrs Garsby sailed down the
stairs.

'I...I am here to take up my position, ma'am,' said
Meg. 'You...you asked me to come as soon as I
could...I meant to come straight after the funeral but
I...I contracted the influenza. I did not think you would
want the children exposed to it...and then I was too
ill... If there has been any inconvenience...I do apologise...'

Her voice trailed off under that chilly regard. Fear
solidified in a hard, suffocating knot in her breast at the
look of amazement on Mrs Garsby's arid countenance.

When she finally spoke it was in tones of lofty moral
condescension. 'Out! Your family history I was prepared to overlook at the Vicar's request, but to come
here expecting employment in a respectable household
now! Influenza, indeed! Could his lordship not suggest
a better tale to cover up your *liaison*?'

Meg's jaw dropped. This aspect of her situation had
not previously occurred to her.

'But I *was* ill!' she protested. 'You may ask Dr Ellerbeck!'

Mrs Garsby snorted her disbelief. 'Even so, to remain in the house once his lordship had arrived! No doubt you thought to entangle him, you presumptuous little slut! Take yourself off at once! No doubt his lordship can find a more suitable position for you. One in keeping with the colour of your cloak. I should be failing in my duty as a Mother were I to permit your contaminating influence anywhere near my family!'

Ten years ago Meg had heard similar words. Then she had not known what they meant, only the tones had struck home into the heart of a confused, grieving little girl. Then she had turned away in mortified hurt, but now she was no longer that defenceless, ignorant child. Now she understood what was being said to her, and the injustice of it enraged her. Despite years of hiding her feelings under a meek façade, Meg's temper began to rise and Mrs Garsby's next words were all that was needed to fan it into fiery utterance.

'My sister said I would regret my generous impulse to accede to the Vicar's suggestion that you would suit. What is bred in the bone will come out in the flesh!'

'Will it, Mrs Garsby? Will it indeed?' Meg's voice was low and bitter. 'Then I thank God that I am not to have the charge of your children!' Her voice rose in passionate fury. 'For I have not the slightest doubt that they would be just as unchristian and mean-spirited as their mother! I hope that you are proud of casting the first stone. Good day, Mrs Garsby!'

With that she picked up her portmanteau and walked proudly to the front door. Opening it, she stepped out into the now-blinding rain and slammed the door as hard as she possibly could. Behind her she could hear the crash echoing through the hall with a most satisfying resonance.

The crash was promptly followed by another as a peal of thunder rolled overhead. Meg raised her dripping face and realised that there was not the slightest prospect of the rain clearing. She might as well start walking.

Buoyed up by her fury and satisfaction at having finally told at least one of the local matrons exactly what she thought of her, Meg did not at first realise just what was before her. By the time she had traversed the avenue and had reached the road again, reality had broken around her ears with greater force than the thunder and bucketing rain. Grimly she faced her situation. She would have to go and see the Vicar. Perhaps he could help. Even if it was only entry into the nearest Magdalen. Miserably she thought that indeed that might be her best course. At least they would provide her with some training and she would be placed with charitable people who would not throw her past up in her face too much.

She would go straight to the Vicarage...no, it was fifteen miles. Fenby Hall was only ten. Even if she got a lift part of the way, she couldn't possibly go to the Vicarage tonight. She would go home and slip into the house for the night. No one need know that she was there. She could go to the Vicar tomorrow.

Plodding on down the increasingly muddy road between the dry stone walls, she gradually became aware that she was crying, her tears mingling with the rain on her cheeks. Never in a life of loneliness had she ever felt quite so abandoned. At least this morning she had had the prospect of employment in a respectable household. Now she was literally out on her own.

Briefly she considered going to Lord Rutherford, only to reject the idea. No, she had refused his offer of assistance. She could not now go back and beg. Besides, in the past ten years she had not confided in anyone. She wouldn't even know where to start. A sensible little voice suggested that she was being rather silly. After all, she liked Marc…he was kind…gentle…he would look after her… Perhaps he wouldn't care about her history…her parents…?

She thrust the thought away. How could he not care? Besides, Marc was really Lord Rutherford. He did not exist beyond her feverish imaginings. She plodded on, pretending that the salt mingling with the rain was seawater. She had never seen the sea…but she had heard it was salty.

A yell from behind her broke in on her gloomy reflections. She swung around hopefully and saw a farm cart with a familiar field hand driving it. At least she wouldn't have to walk the whole way home.

Marcus came in late from his day's business, his heavy frieze cloak dripping. It had kept out the rain, but he was definitely chilly. He went to the parlour and rang the bell for Barlow, thinking that he would have a bath and then see Meg. Try and talk some sense into her. He'd been too abrupt with her earlier, too dictatorial.

A fire had been lit and he stood in front of it, warming his hands. Meg's determination to make her own way impressed him as much as it surprised him. Not many girls in her situation, he thought, would have refused what he had offered. Cousin Samuel must have really rubbed in her status. Parsimonious old curmudgeon!

Barlow appeared and started talking immediately. 'Thank God you're back, me lord! It's Miss Meg!'

A chill stole through Marcus's heart. What the hell was wrong with Meg? Was she ill again?

'She's gone.'

'Gone!' Marcus exploded. 'What the devil do you mean? Where has she gone?' Then he realised. He'd thought she was just a bit too meek this morning. Obviously she had decided to act before he could inform her employer of any change in her plans. She had thought thereby to forestall him, putting herself beyond his reach. Well, she would learn her mistake! And then, stealing through his anger, came a surge of admiration for the little vixen. She'd hoaxed him completely with her agreement that there was nothing more to be said on the matter of her future. Little devil, he thought ruefully.

Barlow watched him in some trepidation. 'Aye. Gone to Mrs Garsby. Agnes and I knew nowt. She slipped out and got young Judd to drive her over in the gig. I'm that sorry, me lord! She sent this back for you.' He held out the letter.

Marcus took it. 'Thank you, Barlow. Is the water ready for my bath?'

'Aye, me lord. Shall I draw it?'

Marcus had already opened the letter and simply nodded, beginning to read as Barlow withdrew.

Dear Lord Rutherford,

I hope when you read this letter you will understand why I did not feel capable of fully explaining myself this morning and the reason why I must decline your generous offer of assistance. When I tell you that I am the daughter of Sir Robert

Fellowes and his wife Lady Caroline, I think you must realise why. You are old enough to recall the scandal of my parents' deaths. My mother was a connection of Cousin Samuel's wife, which was why he took me in afterwards. My father, in the light of my mother's behaviour, had completely disinherited me in favour of my cousin Delian. I believe, had he lived long enough, he would have disavowed me. My cousin Delian and his wife refused to house me in case I should pollute their children.

I should have told you this, but I was too cowardly to do so. Thank you again for your care of me while I was ill. I shall never forget it.

Sincerely, Marguerite Fellowes

Marcus stared at the letter, his emotions in turmoil. Robert and Caroline Fellowes's daughter! Good God! No wonder none of the good ladies would have anything to do with the chit! He remembered the scandal quite well. Sir Robert's suicide after catching his wife and a lover *in flagrante delicto* and murdering the pair of them had been the talk of the town for months ten years ago. He had never heard there had been a child, though. Certainly Sir Delian and Lady Fellowes had never mentioned it. And she had been here with Samuel the whole time.

He shook his head, dazed. What to do now? He considered his options. He would have to go after Meg, of course; but should he leave it until morning or go at once? Little fool! Why the hell hadn't she told him? Surely she hadn't thought he would turn his back on her! He grimaced. Perhaps she had. He'd purposely been cold with her as he was with most people. And no doubt plenty of people did shun her. Indeed, her own cousin had refused to assist the orphaned child. This must be the reason that no one had come to help her.

Blast old Samuel! If he had done the right thing by the girl, then her story need not have been such a liability. As it was, it had been allowed to take hold in the popular imagination until it had assumed ridiculous proportions.

He read the letter again. Too cowardly? He shook his head. That was the last thing Marguerite…no… Meg…Fellowes had to reproach herself with. Too proud was more like it. Too proud to accept his offer made in ignorance of the truth and too proud to tell him and perhaps have to see him turn away in disgust, or worse, pity her. And the letter itself! A more unemotional, *uninvolved*, explanation of a tragic situation, he never wished to see. The most personal part of the letter was her brief acknowledgment of his care of her!

He thrust away the thought that this was his own usual way of dealing with the world. That he had, in fact, tried to deal with Meg in that way—with disastrous results.

Now what to do? Go after Meg in the morning or have his bath and go tonight? He thought hard. He hated the idea of leaving her until morning, but the weather would make going at once impossible. Besides, she was probably exhausted and would be the better for a night's sleep. If he fetched her tonight, she would not be in bed before midnight. No, he'd go and fetch her in the morning.

Well, now that all that was taken care of, he could go up to his room and enjoy a nice luxurious soak. After dinner he would write to Di, warning her to expect an indefinite houseguest. Surely between the pair of them they could launch Meg and get her safely established. What the girl needed was a husband. Someone who didn't give a damn what people thought. Someone who would treat her kindly and make sure others did so. Someone she could trust.

As he went up the stairs, Marcus vowed that he would take a close look at anyone who wanted to marry Meg. He was damned if he'd have her used as a drudge again! He was running over possible *partis* in his mind, and dismissing them all out of hand, when his attention was caught by a sudden rustle.

He stopped just at the head of the stairs and looked around but could see no one. Yet he was sure someone was there. All his senses were on the alert, screaming that he was being watched. Had someone slipped into a room? He didn't think so. All the doors squeaked and creaked atrociously. The curtains over the window at the far end of the hall caught his eye. There was an embrasure behind them, deep enough to hold someone. Determinedly he walked towards it.

Terrified, Meg stood as still as possible, watching through a small rent in the curtain as that tall, leonine figure stalked towards her hiding place. He mustn't find her now! He had her letter in his hand! He would think it was all a take in! That she was trying to engage his sympathy! Worse, he might think, given her parentage, that she would welcome another sort of offer. The sort to which Mrs Garsby had referred.

He was coming closer. His powerful frame loomed nearer. She couldn't think straight, she was so bitterly tired and cold and her cloak was so horribly heavy. All she could think was that Marc might hold her again, comfort her, perhaps let her cry on his shoulder. In her exhaustion, she could not imagine what else such broad shoulders could possibly be for. But no, it was Lord Rutherford, not Marc. He would be disgusted, would inquire coldly just what Miss Fellowes thought she was doing in his house.

She would not be found cowering like a frightened cur! She wouldn't! With her head held high, she stepped out from behind the curtains, clutching her sodden portmanteau, to meet his startled gaze.

'Meg!? What on earth are you doing here?' He strode forward and caught her in his arms. 'My God, you're soaking! You silly child! They told me you had gone, gave me your letter.' His keen eyes took in her exhaustion, her muddied cloak and the even muddier hem of her dress showing beneath it. 'You did go! Meg, what happened?'

It was Marc! Not Lord Rutherford. It was Marc who had found her. Marc, whose worried eyes held that look of tender concern. She could tell Marc what had happened. At least…no, she couldn't! Not all of it. If he found out what had been said, then he would feel obliged to offer for her—at least Marc would…she wasn't so sure about Lord Rutherford. Confusion fogged her mind.

'She had already…filled the position. She couldn't wait…' It was probably true; Meg consoled herself with the thought that it wasn't an outright lie. And he was holding her again, enfolding her against his big frame, warming her, his arms a barrier against the world and its bitter chill. She leaned against him, barely conscious.

'And you walked home? Ten miles!' Horror stabbed through him at the thought. Ten miles in the pouring rain! She had only got out of bed for the first time that morning. What sort of woman would kick a girl out like that? Mrs Garsby was going to be the recipient of a very nasty letter on the morrow. And if she ever showed her face in London, he would have very great pleasure in letting her know exactly what the Earl of Rutherford could do to anyone who crossed him!

In the meantime he yelled loudly for assistance. None was forthcoming. The Barlows were well out of earshot. Increasingly worried, he scanned Meg's face. Her teeth were chattering and there was a blue tinge about her mouth. Her slight frame sagged against him helplessly and her flesh felt stone cold through the soaking garments. Damn it! She shouldn't even be out of bed! She was still sick and if he didn't get her warmed up quickly, she was going to suffer a relapse! Swearing under his breath, he swung her up into his arms. Desperate straits called for desperate remedies.

Meg's brain began to function again as he lifted her. She must be soaking him. And it was Lord Rutherford, after all. His eyes had gone icy again. She must not call him *Marc* in that familiar way.

'Please, my lord, I must change.' She would feel better once she was dry. Warm would be nice too but she'd settle for dry. She did not think that she would ever be warm again. Unless, of course, Marc continued to carry her down the hall like this. That might warm her up... Carry her? What on earth was he doing? And this was his room! Why was he carrying her into it?

Suddenly frightened, she began to struggle. And discovered that Marc's powerful arms were more than sufficient to subdue her efforts to escape. They were like iron bands clamping her to his chest. She heard the door bang shut behind them and panicked. It must be Lord Rutherford after all! He had a dreadful reputation... Where was Marc?

'Take your clothes off.' She was standing on her own two feet again.

'N...no!'

'Meg...' Lord Rutherford was beginning to sound like Marc. Or was Marc sounding like Lord Rutherford? Whichever it was, he sounded exasperated. 'Meg...take your clothes off and get into that bath at once! Before you catch your death of cold!'

Stupidly she stared at him. She couldn't undress in front of him! She might be ruined in an academic sense, but she wasn't *that* dead to shame.

With a muttered curse Marcus caught her to him and began to undress her. Shocked, she tried to push him away, but she was feeling far too weak and confused. One large hand caught both her wrists and held them imprisoned behind her back while his free hand continued to make short work of the buttons of her high-necked spencer and then the ties of her gown.

Despite his efforts not to touch her as he stripped her, his fingers inevitably grazed across her soft skin, searing into her and circumventing her struggles more surely than his grip on her hands. Bemused, she stood helpless as his light, accidental caresses burnt into her trembling body. Indeed, she was no longer sure whether she was shaking with cold—or pleasure at the tantalising touch of his long fingers.

In no time the gown was off, landing on the floor with an audible splat, and she stood shivering in her chemise and petticoat. Marcus found to his horror that his body was showing definite signs of interest in the procedure. And in her undoubted response to his unintentional advances. She was staring up at him with a completely bemused expression, her delicate lips slightly parted, presenting him with an appalling temptation. In addition, the soaking undergarments revealed what he had suspected, and steadfastly managed to ignore, for two long nights. Namely, the manifold charms of Miss Marguerite Fellowes.

Stifling a groan and shackling his sudden desire, he shut his eyes momentarily to block out the sight. And then opened them again. Good God, the girl was literally soaked to the skin, her cotton chemise and petticoat clinging to her slim body; every curve, every nuance was laid bare to his heated gaze. He swallowed hard. Two creamy, rounded breasts, their peaks puckered with cold, thrust from under the thin material. A sinuous waist and the long lovely line of her thighs! God, she was beautiful! What would she be like to lie with? To taste? To love? He could imagine it…soft… yielding…utterly entrancing…

What the hell was he thinking of? He was supposed to be giving her a bath to warm her! Not thinking about taking her to bed! Although the way he was feeling, that would certainly warm her… Swearing audibly now, he picked her up again and strode towards the bath.

'Marc? What are you doing?' She was terrified, not least by the fact that she couldn't force her body to struggle any more. If Marc were about to ravish her, then she… Her fears were put abruptly to rest as he dumped her with an unceremonious splash in the hip bath.

'Oh! Oooooh…' Her gasp of shock was transmut_d_ to a sigh of pleasure as warmth began to steal back her body. Beyond caring about the impropriet situation, she closed her eyes in utter bliss a back against the bath. A moment later sh being tipped over her and opened her e kneeling beside her, soaking up water in a sponge and squeezing it over her shoulders and breasts.

It felt simply marvellous. Not only was she actually getting warm, but Lord Rutherford seemed to have disappeared completely, leaving Marc in his place. She smiled at him, the horrors of her afternoon receding into the haze of steam rising from the water. Later on she would have to face the ghastly reality with Lord Rutherford, but just at the moment she had Marc to care for her and she might as well sit back and enjoy it. Blissfully she allowed her mind to drift away with the clouds of steam.

Marcus shut his eyes to block out the sight of that trusting, endearing smile. Not to mention the sight of her body with the soaking, transparent cotton clinging to every contour, except for her legs. The petticoat floated around them, revealing the long slender limbs in a teasing, shadowy way. Grimly he thought that if Mrs Garsby ever heard about this, then the only place for Meg would be the nearest Magdalen. Despite Meg's gallant lie, he had absolutely no doubts as to why she had been turned away.

He cleared his throat. 'Are you warmer now, Meg?'

'Oh, yes!' Her response came on a sigh of sheer sensual delight which seemed to ripple through her entire body. Marcus didn't like to think about the devastating effect such a sigh would have on his already beleaguered senses in other circumstances. His own body was already rebelling furiously against his brain which was keeping the reins tight. *For God's sake, she's little more than a child! She's still sick and she's in quite enough trouble without you getting her into more!*

Abruptly he stood up. He couldn't trust himself to Long strides took him to the bellpull. He would send for Mrs Barlow, as in fact he should have done ten minutes ago. He couldn't imagine what had come over him not to do so. He had just been conscious of an overwhelming tenderness and desire to look after her himself. It had not even occurred to him to summon other assistance. It had seemed perfectly natural and right to do it himself.

Now, as he stood shaking with his back to her, he realised his mistake. Lord! And he'd thought that youth and innocence held no allure for him. He couldn't have been more wrong. A knock at the door interrupted his churning thoughts. Barlow. He went to the door and opened it a fraction.

'You rang, me lord?' Barlow looked very puzzled to see that Marcus had not yet availed himself of the bath. 'Is something wrong?'

'Yes,' said Marcus baldly. He hesitated and then said, 'Miss Meg has returned. I've dumped her in my bath. Mrs Garsby refused to take her in and she walked home in that storm. Could you please ask your wife to come up and dry her and help her get into some dry clothes?'

Barlow's jaw dropped and his lined old face worked for a minute. All he could say was, 'That *bitch*!'

'Quite,' said Marcus in savage agreement. 'In fact that…' He added a number of colourful epithets to describe Mrs Garsby which left Barlow in no doubt that his lordship was quite as angry as he himself was.

'I'll fetch Agnes right away, me lord. An' she walked home? In that storm? Poor little lass.'

Barlow was gone and Marcus turned back into the room. Meg's portmanteau caught his eye and he opened it. And swore violently. It was soaked through and everything in it. She didn't have a stitch to wear thanks to Mrs Garsby's callous disregard for common human decency.

Cursing under his breath, he went to his chest of drawers and found a nightshirt. It would swamp Meg's slight frame, but at least it would be warm. His dressing gown of heavy red silk lay across a chair. That would help too…and… He cast his eyes about the room…ah, yes! His driving coat…and a couple of blankets, and she could sit up and have something to eat in reasonable modesty. From his point of view, the more clothes she had on, the better! He studiously avoided looking too closely at Meg as he went back and forth.

Agnes Barlow entered the room without even bothering to knock. 'My lord! Just what—?' She broke off as she caught sight of Meg dozing in the bath. Her gentle old eyes seemed to blaze. For a moment Marcus thought she was going to say something, but she just went and dropped to her knees beside the bath and shook Meg's shoulder. 'Come along, dearie. 'Tis time to get you dry, afore you gets all wrinkly!'

Marcus felt his heart turn over at the gruff tenderness in her voice. Was this the only kindness Meg had known in the last ten years? And she had been lucky. He shuddered to think what might have been her fate in a more fashionable household where the servants took their tone from their employers. At least here she had been in the care of the Barlows, dour, independent country folk who thought for themselves and formed their own opinions on the evidence before them.

Agnes turned to him. 'I'll get her out now, me lord. If so be you'll remove yourself! Which I'll take leave to say you should have done in the first place! A bath might be just what Miss Meg needed, but you had no call to strip her!' Her voice echoed with indignation at his lack of propriety.

'Her...her things are all wet,' said Marcus awkwardly. It was a measure of his embarrassment that he felt no annoyance at having his actions called to account by one of his servants. 'You can put these on her.' He held out his peculiar collection. 'If her bed is still made up, put her in there. Otherwise she can have my bed and another bed can be made up for me.'

He paused at the door. 'Tell Miss Meg that I will see her in the morning to discuss her situation. I will tell Barlow to send up some dinner.'

'Aye. You do that, me lord,' said Agnes absently as she helped Meg out and wrapped a blanket around her.

'You'll stay with her tonight?' Marcus asked hesitantly. The damage was already done, but he was damned if he wanted to make things worse for the child. As it was, he could only see one solution to Meg's problems. In any case he didn't want her to wake up alone and scared during the night.

The glare which sizzled from Agnes Barlow's eyes suggested that he would have received short shrift had he attempted to make any other disposition. She softened the glare by saying, 'She'll do well enough, me lord. An' I'm sure I beg pardon if I spoke out of turn, but I'm that worritted about the lassie...an' what's to become of her now?'

She finished softly, as though speaking to herself, but Marcus found his thoughts echoing her question. What, indeed? He went down to his own dinner in thoughtful contemplation of the way in which the fates had arranged his future.

Over a meal consisting of a raised rabbit pie, a baked trout and a duckling served with a platter of vegetables and removed with an apple pie, he considered the options before him carefully.

He could settle money on Meg as he had originally planned and trust to his sister's influence to establish the girl creditably. Or he could ask Di to find her a new position if she were steadfast in refusing to accept money from him. The only problem was that if Mrs Garsby could turn Meg away, then so could others. No doubt the tale was all over Yorkshire by now that he had seduced the daughter of Robert and Caroline Fellowes. And it would travel, no doubt about that. If she had been anyone else, they might have been able to carry it off. Unfortunately her background, not to mention his reputation, made that impossible.

Which left marriage. To himself. Looked at dispassionately, the idea did not disturb him in the slightest. From the social viewpoint he had no qualms. He was Rutherford. His pre-eminence in the fashionable world of the *ton* would be sufficient to protect Meg. And as far as her background was concerned, he couldn't have cared less. People had ridden out worse scandals. And he would derive immense, if cynical, satisfaction in forcing the fashionable world to accept his choice. Especially Sir Delian Fellowes and his top-lofty wife.

On a personal level he was as happy to marry Meg as any other female. He actually respected her. Liked her gallant determination to stand alone. Liked the outrageous way she had tried to circumvent his dictatorial management of her future. His little Meg hadn't wasted time on arguing with him, she had just quietly gone ahead with her plans as though he had nothing to do with them. In which she was completely and utterly mistaken, of course, but that did not cancel the determination and courage.

As for the physical side of things…no problems there. He would positively enjoy undertaking Meg's education in her marital duties. Her beauty was not the obvious sort, but rather a subtle elegance tempered with an engaging innocence. Her face had character with its deep blue-grey eyes and the strongly marked brows. She dressed appallingly, but that was doubtless due to necessity not inclination and could be remedied easily enough. Marcus knew enough of women to be tolerably certain that she would be only too happy to be let loose amongst the fashionable modistes and milliners of London. The thought of Meg sheathed in shimmering, clinging silk had a very definite appeal to what he freely admitted to be his base masculine sensibilities.

He spared a brief thought for Lady Hartleigh and shrugged as he helped himself to apple pie. No doubt she would be a trifle disappointed, but it was not as though she needed to marry or fancied herself in love with him. Theirs would have been a marriage of convenience.

As would, of course, his marriage to Meg.

The fact that he did not know her terribly well did not concern him. Except for his mother and sister, he had never known any woman terribly well, apart from in the biblical sense, and he did not intend to start with his wife. No, a marriage of convenience, in which they would pursue their fashionable, separate lives, would suit the Earl of Rutherford to a nicety.

There was little point in pretending that he was in love. She would never believe it even if he did know how to counterfeit an emotion he was not entirely sure he had ever indulged in. No, she was an intelligent girl, to judge by the varied reading matter he had found beside her bed. Better just to put it before her as a business transaction. In return for heirs and her discretion he would give her the protection of his name and all the indulgence she had so far been denied in her barren existence. Viewed logically it seemed a fair enough bargain to him, with no danger of hurt for either of them. In addition to Fenby House, which he didn't need, it looked as though he had also inherited a bride, which he most assuredly did need.

He ignored the niggling little voice that suggested the Earl of Rutherford might be biting off rather more than he could comfortably chew, and that Marc had better look out for himself.

Later that night Meg lay on her stomach in her battered tester bed, trying very hard to cry silently into the pillow. She did not wish to disturb Agnes, snoring comfortably on the other side of the bed, did not wish to acknowledge to anyone the depth of despair and hopelessness to which she had now plummeted. Desperately she buried her face in the lumpy old pillow with its worn and darned slip. Her slight shoulders shuddered with the effort to muffle her sobs.

In the morning she would have to go to the Vicar and ask for his help in finding a job, but if Mrs Garsby's self-righteous attitude was anything to go by she thought that she might as well enter the workhouse in York immediately. Granted his lordship had offered assistance, but that was before he knew who she was. Besides, she had refused his offer and could hardly turn around now, expecting it to remain open.

The future stretched out remorselessly before her, bleak and terrifying. Now even the prospect of earning a living looked grim. Fear rose before her in the darkness, black and threatening. She fought it down before it could take control. Above all, when she saw Lord Rutherford on the morrow, he must not see how frightened she was. No one must know what a coward Meg Fellowes really was.

Except Marc, she thought as she finally drifted towards sleep. He probably wouldn't pity or despise her. He was kind and practical, dumping her into his own bath and lending her his nightshirt. She was still wearing it and she snuggled down into it, pretending he was holding her. Marc would have had some solution for her problems…

Chapter Four

Despite her exhaustion Meg awakened quite early the following morning. Agnes Barlow was bustling quietly around the room and Meg watched her through half-closed eyes. There was no need to get up yet. It was pleasant to lie quietly, later in the morning she would have to give some thought to the future, but not now. At the back of her mind loomed the knowledge that she was facing disaster, but just now she was comfortable and safe and she meant to enjoy it.

Eventually Agnes slipped out of the room, evidently convinced that she had not disturbed Miss Meg. Which was fair enough, because Miss Meg drifted back into a deep and dreamless sleep very readily. When she surfaced again the light in her room told her that it was past time to get up. Her rumbling stomach reinforced the impression that it was well past time for breakfast. She looked around for her portmanteau, but it was no-where in sight.

Frowning, she tried to recall what she had done with it, but all she could remember was that his lordship had stripped her gown off and bathed her. She blushed, not so much at his behaviour as at her own pleasure in it.

Perhaps Mrs Garsby had a point…was she a wanton? Was that how you were meant to feel? Or was there something wrong with her? She had never realised that her breasts were so sensitive, could feel as though they were on fire, sending tongues of flame throughout her body… She had better stop thinking about it…her body was starting to tingle again…

What must he have thought of her? He had done it as though it were the merest commonplace and she had made not the slightest effort to stop him! She would be well served if he did think her a bit of muslin.

And where the hell *was* her portmanteau? Glancing down at herself, she realised that she was wearing his nightshirt… Why in the world…oh heavens…of course! All her clothes had been soaked. All she had was this nightshirt, a dressing gown—belonging to his lordship—and a driving coat with about a dozen capes, also courtesy of his lordship.

Damn him! Not only did he have to strip her in that shameless way, but apparently he was also going to dress her! It seemed she was always having to be grateful to someone for their beastly charity! Furious and embarrassed, Meg scrambled out of bed and pulled on the dressing gown which was draped across a chair. The driving coat was there too, but she thought that trying not to trip over the absurdly large dressing gown would be difficult enough.

Clutching the skirt of the dressing gown around her, she made her way down stairs. No doubt her clothes were drying in the kitchen. She would go and eat her breakfast there as she had always done, while she waited for them to dry. Agnes might even have a job for her which would take her mind off what lay ahead for a brief space.

Tapping gently on Meg's door a few moments later, Marcus was surprised to receive no response. Perhaps she was still asleep. It was after ten and he had breakfasted over an hour ago but no doubt the poor girl had been exhausted. Hesitantly he opened the door and peered in.

The bed was empty, the covers flung back. She had gone down already, probably still in his nightshirt and dressing gown. Very well, he would go and find her. It was most improper, but he admitted ruefully that the situation had gone a long way beyond the proprieties.

As he went back down, he thought carefully about the best way to deal with Meg's pride and scruples. Obviously this was one female who would not submit to being ridden roughshod over as he had attempted yesterday. He suspected that had he dealt with her more gently, she might have told him her whole story. She seemed to swing unnervingly between confiding trust in him and a stiff reserve, sometimes calling him Marc, sometimes my lord or Lord Rutherford. Very well. He would have to try to encourage her to trust him, treat her gently, listen to her.

Now, where the hell was she likely to be? Probably the breakfast parlour. She must be hungry.

He drew a blank there. And in the library, the parlour and everywhere else that he looked in the next half-hour. Surely, she hadn't bolted again! Not in a nightshirt and dressing gown. She must have collapsed somewhere! Frantic, he rushed back to the library and tugged the bellpull vigorously.

When Barlow arrived in response his lordship did not mince words. 'Barlow, where the devil is she?'

Barlow blinked at the panic in his lordship's face and

voice. 'Miss Meg? Why, she's in the kitchen with Agnes, me lord. Eatin' her breakfast.'

'In the kitchen?' Marcus said. 'Why not in here? With me! Where she belongs!' Relief flooded through him. He hadn't thought of that.

'She's...she's still in your lordship's nightrail,' explained Barlow, trying not to laugh. 'Likely she thought it better to wait for her clothes to dry... Me lord, no! Agnes won't even let me in there!'

He stared in consternation as the master left the room, a steely glint of determination in his eyes. Surely his lordship wasn't going to brave Agnes's kitchen? Even if he was the master, she'd have a fair bit to say about that! Very protective of Miss Meg was Agnes, especially after yesterday. Like a hen with one chick, so she was!

His lordship was indeed going to brave the kitchen. He entered very quietly, without even bothering to knock and so came upon a scene which shook him to the core.

Meg was sitting at the big table, an empty plate in front of her and a small earthen coffee pot. Her face was buried in her arms on the table top, her shoulders shuddering with suppressed sobs. Agnes Barlow was leaning over her, holding her, murmuring gently.

'There now, dearie, just you have a good cry. Vicar will know what you should do. Never you fear! 'Twill all come out in the end.'

Marcus stood as though rooted to the floor. Never in his life had he seen a woman cry like this. As though she were desperately trying not to. Most women he knew made play with wet eyelashes quite happily in unavailing attempts to move his sensibilities. He had

seen so many artful female tears that they generally had
not the slightest effect on him. Except to bore him.

Not this time. He felt something tear deep inside him
at the sight of his little Meg's utter despair. He was
certain that she would not have allowed him to see her
fear and misery at what faced her. No, she would have
hidden it. Just as she had no doubt glossed over the full
reasons for Mrs Garsby's behaviour. Just as she had
hidden her full tragedy from him yesterday morning.

Suddenly aware of his presence, Agnes Barlow
looked up and gave a startled gasp. Meg lifted her head
and the tear-drowned eyes stared up in dawning horror.
Making a valiant effort at self-control, she stifled her
sobs, catching her underlip between her teeth.

'Meg.' He kept his voice very gentle. 'I need to speak
to you privately, if you have finished your breakfast.'

'Now?' It came on a hopeless gulp. Marcus thought
he had never heard a more despairing acceptance of
fate.

'Miss Meg's clothes...' began Agnes, frowning dire-
fully.

The look on his lordship's face stopped her. 'Mrs
Barlow, you need not have the slightest fear for Miss
Meg's safety at my hands. In any way whatsoever.' His
eyes were gentle as they rested on Meg and he came to
her side.

Reluctantly Agnes stepped back, and he swung Meg
up into his arms with easy strength. She gasped and
clung to him in shock. What was he about? He had
guaranteed her safety so he couldn't mean to...yet there
was something so tender and possessive in the way he
was holding her. Shaken, she recalled the pleasure she
had felt in his touch the previous night. Had it been

apparent to him? Did he think that with her history and after what had happened that he might as well take her?

Shame and bitter disillusionment swept through her, with anger treading hotly on their heels.

'I can walk!' Breathless and indignant, Meg wriggled as he kicked the kitchen door shut behind them. And felt those iron muscles tighten around her again.

'I dare say you can,' agreed Marcus mildly. 'But you aren't going to.'

Nothing more was said as he carried her back into the main part of the house to the library where he placed her in a chair beside the fire and tucked a rug around her. He met the nervous glance she stole up at him. Every line of her body proclaimed her mistrust. She put up a shaking hand to push her hair back.

It didn't fool him in the least. He saw instantly the surreptitious attempt to wipe her eyes and his heart clenched in his chest. Proud as the devil, he thought admiringly. Without a word he produced a handkerchief and dried her cheeks with it before tucking it into her hand.

He straightened up and asked quietly, 'May I know what your plans are now, Meg?' Take this slowly, he told himself. Don't rush her now, any more than you would in bed! And wished he hadn't thought of that particular analogy.

Drawing a shaky breath, Meg answered. 'I...I shall walk into the village and see the Vicar. He may be able to find me another situation since Mrs Garsby has...is already satisfied...' He wondered if she did that often, concentrating on the practical issues, hiding the paralysing fear behind her polite façade.

He demolished that façade effortlessly. 'Since Mrs

Garsby has accused you of being my mistress and kicked you out to walk home? Is that what you mean?'

She looked up, startled into the truth. 'Who told you…how can you possibly…? I mean, no!'

'Meg.' Despite the seriousness of the situation, a note of amusement came into his voice. 'I am not stupid. And I know my reputation and the ways of the world. No one had to tell me. It was obvious, you silly child.'

'Oh.' Plainly she hadn't thought of that. 'Well, I…I dare say it doesn't matter very much,' she lied valiantly. 'I'm sure someone will employ…'

She was interrupted firmly. 'No, Meg. They won't. Take it from me. You stand as much chance of gaining respectable employment now as you have of flying. And I am not going to permit you even to make the attempt.'

'But…I must…'

He continued relentlessly. 'Tell me, Meg. Why did you wish to be a nursery governess?'

She was silent a moment and he wondered if she were seeking another polite lie with which to protect herself.

At last she said softly, 'I thought…well…if I couldn't have children of my own…that at least I could be with children.'

'I see.' He kept his voice very light. This, he had no doubt, was the truth. 'Then you would prefer marriage and children?'

'Please, my lord…' Her voice shook with anguished intensity. 'Please don't mock me!'

He stared at her in shock. Mock her? She could think that he would mock her? Had no one ever listened to her desires before? He felt suddenly exultant that he was going to make her happy, enable her to realise her dream. But his voice was carefully controlled as he said,

'Then I think my solution to our problem will meet your approval.' He smiled down at her as she looked up in amazement.

'You...you have a solution?' Her voice was breathless.

'Mmm. You're going to marry me, Meg.'

The world turned upside down and then miraculously righted itself. Marry *Marc*? For it was Marc offering her marriage! For one mad, golden instant, joy surged through her and she nearly yielded to temptation. He would be kind to her, might even come to care for her a little, he would give her children...because he felt obliged to. At that inescapable fact, all her joy turned to dross.

She couldn't do it. Marguerite Fellowes was no fit bride for the Earl of Rutherford even if he wanted to marry her, which was patently not the case. And she could not think of one single reason why he should wish to do so. It wouldn't even be convenient. On the contrary, it would be a scandalous alliance for any gentleman, and for the Earl of Rutherford it was unthinkable. And for the kind friend who had tended her so carefully it was doubly unthinkable. She would not allow Marc to ruin himself for her.

'No.' It was said quietly but with finality.

'Will you at least listen to my reasons for offering you the protection of my name? After your refusal to accept any charity yesterday, I did not expect you to leap at my offer.'

The diffidence in his voice reassured her. He would not attempt to ride roughshod over her again. She nodded. It could do no harm. Her mind was made up. His reasons were perfectly clear. They did him honour. But she would not accept an offer made under duress. An offer made out of pity.

Or so she thought. As she listened to him she began to wonder.

'To start with, Meg, I have to marry,' he stated. 'It is my duty. The cousin who is my heir neither wants, nor is fitted, for the responsibility of the title. If he were, I would probably never have considered marriage.'

He went on. 'You are thinking that your background will be a problem. Forget it. The Earl of Rutherford can marry whom he damned well pleases!' A little strong, but his credit would certainly survive an alliance with Meg Fellowes.

'My only requirements are that my wife should be well born, reasonably attractive and should desire children. And that I can respect her. You meet all four requirements.' His words sounded cold and cynical. Hardly an encouraging proposal of marriage, but she forced herself to meet his eyes, expecting them to be hard and uncompromising.

She swallowed hard. 'N...no!' His voice and words might sound cold, but his eyes were still oddly gentle. He was offering marriage out of pity and obligation, not because he wanted to for any of his stated logical and practical reasons. She would not accept that sacrifice under any circumstances and especially not when she had nothing to offer in return.

He sighed. 'Meg, rid yourself of the idea that in marrying you I am performing the supreme sacrifice. I dare say it must look like it to you, but I assure you it is not the case.' He smiled at her widened eyes. 'Oh, yes. I know what you are thinking. And you are partially right. Marriage is the only way in which I can adequately protect you from the consequences of this business. And technically, yes, I do *have* to marry you. But believe me, I am offering you a fair bargain. In return for my name and protection, you will give me your discretion and children.'

'My discretion?' Meg was puzzled. She could not think what he was talking about. Did he mean that she must not get into scrapes all the time and must be a model of propriety? If that was what he meant, then she wouldn't have the slightest idea of how to go on. Who had there ever been to tell her? And as for his second stipulation...

'My lord—'

'Marc,' he corrected her softly.

'I *cannot* accept!' Her voice wobbled. 'You...you are offering certainties in return for something I do not know if I can...' She stopped, very embarrassed, but he had understood.

'You do not know if you can have children? Is that it?' Marcus smiled wryly. 'My dear, *that* would be a problem no matter who I married. I can assure you I have no desire to be a stepfather just to ensure my wife is fertile.'

'But...'

'Marry me, Meg.' His voice was low and persuasive.

She stared up at him. He meant it. He really did wish her to marry him. It would be a bargain between them. Suddenly she wondered what he had meant by discretion. She had to know before she answered.

'What did you mean by *discretion*?'

His amazement at the question showed in his dropped jaw and the faint flush on his cheekbones. What on earth had she said to startle him? Doggedly she faced him with the wide candid eyes of a child.

He drew a deep breath. 'I do not offer love, Meg.

That is not part of our bargain. I neither offer it nor want it. If, however, after you have provided me with an heir, you decide that you require love, then you are free to seek it. I ask only your discretion.' He looked at her soberly. 'I am no saint, Meg, and neither am I a hypocrite.'

'I...I see.' And she did see. He was giving her a *carte blanche* to embark on an affair once she had fulfilled her duty. He was telling her that she need not fear to meet the same fate as her mother. That he would consider himself free to pursue his amusements and was prepared to offer her the same freedom. He was indeed offering a straightforward bargain. Bitterly she thought that she must be almost the only woman alive to whom he could have offered such a contract openly.

Yet his eyes were still gentle. He had intimated that he respected her.

In a voice she hardly knew was hers, she asked, 'Why...why do you respect me?'

There was a pause and she looked up to find a considering look in his eyes. Then, holding her gaze with his, he said, 'I like your courage, your determination...I like your pride. You were so determined to manage for yourself, to accept no charity despite your destitution. Those are qualities I admire, that I would like the mother of my children to possess.'

It was a good answer, she thought. He had judged her on her actions as he had seen them. He was wrong, of course, it was not pride or any of those other things, just a loathing of being the despised, poor relation. But nevertheless he liked the way she had behaved, did not resent the fact that she had disobeyed him. He was just. And, she reminded herself, he has offered a bargain. A bargain made between equals. No matter what she might think of such a contract, it was still a contract in which she would be an equal partner. And, above all, he did not seem to expect her gratitude.

At last she heard herself say, 'I accept your offer of marriage, my lord.'

She shut her eyes, feeling very dizzy. Surely this wasn't happening. But it seemed that it was. She could feel his hands grip hers and draw her up to stand before him..

Trembling, she forced herself to look at him. He was very close, his tall frame towering over her. Meg was a tall girl, but she felt incredibly small and weak before him. He was looking down at her with a strange, intent glitter in his eyes.

'Shall we seal our bargain, Meg?' His voice was very soft, a velvet caress. He bent his head and touched his lips gently to hers in a featherlight kiss. She did not draw back, but stood unresisting as his mouth moved over hers tenderly. Fire seemed to ripple through her body as he released her hands, only to gather her in his arms and pull her into an engulfing embrace.

Meg was lost in a world of sensuous enchantment. His lips moving over hers evoked magic, darting fires of delight which urged her closer to his powerful body. Instinctively she nestled against him, joy exploding in her heart as she felt him pull her even closer, felt him deepen the intensity of the kiss. Here at last was someone who actually wanted her for whatever reason…someone who would care for her… She felt as though her heart would burst with happiness at the thought that here at last was someone she could care for…love…

She froze. He wasn't offering love…didn't even want it…love would not be part of their bargain. He had said quite clearly that if she wanted love, she was free to seek it...elsewhere. The question hammered in her brain— What will happen to me if I fall in love with him?

In the last ten years Meg had not dared to love. She had come to Fenby House prepared to love Samuel and Euphemia Langley, but they had made it plain that they had taken her out of duty and expected her to be grateful. They had no use for her childish affection and had never tried to comfort her confused grief over her parents.

Indeed, on the one occasion when she had given way to tears in Cousin Euphemia's presence, she had been told that her parents were a disgrace, her mother especially so, and that she must learn to control herself if she did not wish to grow up the same way. And when she had brought a posy of flowers for Euphemia on Mothering Sunday, they had been stigmatized as weeds and thrown on the fire. So she had retreated into a shell of seeming meekness...it was much safer than having your offered affection spurned. That hurt unbearably. Even with Agnes, who pitied her, she had tried to conceal her real thoughts and fears...until this morning.

Now Lord Rutherford, who by his own admission would have not the least use for her affection, threatened to force her out into contact with the world and its chill. It had been easy enough not to love Samuel and Euphemia. They had never shown her the least affection or kindness. Marc would be quite another matter. She shuddered at the thought.

Marcus released her at once, raising his head and sliding his hands down her arms to hold her hands again. He looked deep into her eyes and she dropped her gaze at once, veiling the sudden fear. 'Meg?' His voice was a little unsteady. 'Meg, am I frightening you?'

Meg stared up at him. He mustn't know what she feared! But she couldn't let him think that his embrace frightened her. It was the most wonderful thing that had ever happened to her. And if he thought she feared him, he would hold off from her. Of that she was certain. She found her voice. 'You? Frighten me? Oh, no!'

His concerned eyes searched hers. 'You're sure, Meg? I'm not frightening you...' he hesitated slightly '...physically?'

She shook her head, shaken by his concern, his consideration, his sensitivity. Her heart lurched in fear. If his lovemaking was difficult to withstand, how would she survive his tenderness?

He was pulling her back into his arms, resting his cheek on her hair and murmuring. Her already-besieged heart shuddered at the words he spoke. 'I swear to you, Meg, you will be safe with me. Always. Nothing will hurt you now.'

Except you, thought Meg in despair. She did not see how her heart's defences could possibly hold out against his unwitting assault on it. She didn't want to love anyone! And if she did fall in love with him, how would she bear knowing that he did not love her in return, did not wish her to love him? That he expected her to seek love elsewhere...as he would.

In bed that night Marcus worried about her response to his kiss. He had been very restrained with her, shackling his urge to deepen the kiss, fully taste and explore the sweetness of her mouth. Her body had trembled in his arms, whether in fear or pleasure he was not sure. Then she had pressed closer, her arms coming up to wind themselves around his neck. His arms had tightened as desire flared through him, and was ruthlessly held in check. Had he alarmed her in some way? He couldn't bear it if he had. He wanted her to feel safe with him, protected.

Something had scared her, he was sure of it. Yet her fingers had clung to his and her mouth was so soft, trembling from his kisses. He'd swear she'd wanted more. He thumped his pillow in frustration. He wanted her. But he didn't want her to submit to him out of duty.

What he did want was beginning to scare *him*.

So much so that he forced himself to think about his family's likely reaction to this unlikely match. Sheer, unmitigated outrage at first, he'd be willing to bet. Especially his Aunt Regina, Lady Grafton. He didn't doubt that he could manage Di; but Aunt Regina was another matter entirely. She'd be quite capable of scaring Meg into crying off and seeking refuge in the workhouse.

He swore. Di was going to have his hide for this, but there was only one safe option—tell her too late for a family deputation to descend upon him. Which meant he'd have to forgo having Jack as his groomsman. It would be the outside of enough to write and ask Jack to come and not tell Di. She was going to be hurt anyway; there was no need to make it worse for her.

Chapter Five

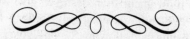

Four weeks later Marcus St John Evelyn Langley, Eighth Earl of Rutherford stood before the Vicar of the parish, listening to the Reverend Andrew Parker marry him to Miss Marguerite Fellowes. The bride, after her four weeks' recuperation in the care of Agnes Barlow under the Vicarage roof, looked to be well on the road to recovery. She had lost the dark shadows under her eyes, her brown hair was alive with golden lights and a flush of delicate colour glowed in her cheeks.

Marcus, after securing Meg's agreement to marry him, had ridden into the village to find the Vicar and arrange to have the banns called as fast as possible. He considered applying to the Bishop of York for a special licence, but on consideration thought that, since Meg needed time to recover from her illness and get used to the idea of becoming a countess anyway, he might just as well have the banns called. Besides, he could think of no better way of flinging back Mrs Garsby's insults in her teeth. To hear them called three Sundays in a row would tip her a settler she would not forget in a hurry. And a special licence would give credence to any tale that a hasty marriage was essential.

The Reverend Andrew Parker, a mild scholarly widower in his late fifties, had been extremely upset at the story Marcus laid before him and had immediately offered to house Meg until the wedding if Agnes Barlow would act as her chaperon.

'I should have taken her in at once if my wife were still alive,' he explained apologetically. He was conscious of a most unchristian desire to give Mrs Garsby one in the eye and was positively looking forward to calling the banns the following Sunday. A sermon too… Surely he could find a suitable text or two that would give Mrs Garsby pause…that old testament story of Susannah and the Elders might serve his turn…and what about 'Let he who is without sin cast the first stone…' No, probably not. Madam Garsby was so convinced of her own moral superiority that it would have no effect whatsoever; besides, he didn't want to suggest that Meg and Lord Rutherford were guilty as charged. The good Samaritan would do very nicely instead.

Once Meg was safely established at the Vicarage, Marcus flung himself into action to provide everything he thought his bride ought to have. A two-day visit to York enabled him to discover a surprisingly skilled modiste. By dint of laying down a positively shocking sum of money and promising to support Madame Heloise in every possible way in her projected move to the capital, he had succeeded in persuading her to make the journey out to Fenby in two post chaises to fit Meg for her wedding gown and trousseau. The second chaise was piled high with bolts of cloth and several awed assistants. Madame Heloise, after dismissing her first conviction that his lordship was escaped from Bedlam, had decided that lunatic or not, he was possessed of enough of the ready to make any effort expended on behalf of his bride well worth her while.

Indeed, after making Meg's acquaintance and finding out through the inevitable village channels the true circumstances of her betrothal, Madame Heloise was much inclined to regard his lordship as being straight from the pages of one of Mrs Radcliffe's romances and one whom she was more than happy to oblige.

Mademoiselle Meg, she quickly realised, was a young lady who, with a little confidence and inspired dressing, would blossom into a beauty. And not just in the common way. Her tall, slender grace, waving dark hair and blue-grey eyes with their expression of wistful abstraction would admirably become the prevailing classical modes. The raised waists and straight skirts would set off her lissom charms to perfection.

Besides, Madame Heloise liked Mademoiselle Meg. Liked her so much that in their second session, as she made some minor adjustments to the silken ivory sheath in which Meg was to be married, she dropped her French accent and told Meg, through a mouthful of pins, to, 'stop the Madame Heloise rubbish...' and just call her 'plain Louisa' since that was what her parents had christened her anyway!

Meg had stared at her in stunned amazement and then burst into a delighted peal of laughter, in which Louisa Thwaites had joined wholeheartedly. She had explained with a grin that every shopkeeper in York knew she was no more French than a bannock, but it would never do for her exalted clients to guess as much! By which admission Meg, who was rapidly gaining the aforementioned confidence, adjudged she was one of a favoured few.

Those four weeks wrought a miraculous change in

Meg. For ten years she had not known what it was to be consulted as to her wishes, deferred to and considered in every possible way. Now she was left in no possible doubt that even if her betrothed did not love her, he wished her to be happy and fully intended to look after her.

He even spent quite a lot of time with her while she stayed at the vicarage. He tooled her about the countryside in his curricle, remained to dine with her and never gave the slightest hint that she was not precisely what he had intended his bride to be. The only thing that bothered her was that he had never kissed her again after she had accepted his offer of marriage. The memory kept her awake at nights as she wondered if she had done something wrong, if his lordship had not liked kissing her. Then she reminded herself that he did not offer love and perhaps preferred to kiss her only when absolutely required to. She would do better not to dwell on the magical touch of his lips…

Instead she concentrated on his politeness, his charm of manner and his unfailing kindness to her. He seemed to take pains in remembering her likes and dislikes. She remembered clearly the first afternoon he had come to visit her and had suggested she might ring for a pot of tea…

'How do you like it, Meg?' he had asked, preparing to pour her a cup and calmly ignoring the convention dictating that she should pour for him.

Flushing deeply, she had admitted that Cousin Samuel had forbidden her to drink tea, on the grounds that it was far too expensive and he did not wish her to develop extravagant tastes.

Marcus had informed her that he would take it as a personal insult if his bride lost any time in acquiring as many extravagant tastes as possible! He had then enlarged her vocabulary with a pithy and unflattering series of remarks on the subject of their mutual relative as he poured her a cup of tea, reducing her to helpless giggles, and the very next time he had come to take her driving he had brought her a gift.

Elegantly wrapped, he had dropped it on her knees after lifting her up into his curricle to go for a drive. She stared at it in disbelief...a present...a real present.

She opened it with hands that shook as he got up beside her and set the horses in motion. It was a tea caddy, full to the brim with fragrant tea. A dainty, leaf-shaped silver caddy spoon sat on top of the tea and eight silver teaspoons were revealed when Marcus showed her the cunningly hidden drawer at the bottom. And she had found herself unable to speak, with silent tears pouring down her cheeks.

Since she had come to Fenby no one had ever given her any sort of present at all, let alone one that showed such attention to detail, that tried in an odd way to make up for everything that had been lacking in her life. True, Marcus was providing all those lovely clothes, but no doubt they were just what he felt his countess ought to have. This—this was somehow different. This was for Meg—not the Countess-to-be.

Her silence had totally unnerved Marcus. Never in his life had he bought such an unromantic present for any woman, but it had felt so right when he thought of it. At first he had just intended the caddy full of tea, but the box had that little drawer for the spoons...so he had dashed off to a silversmith...and then he had seen the caddy spoon...and all the time his heart aching to think that she had been treated as though she were one of the servants. Worse. At least they had been paid.

He concentrated on his team, not daring to ask if she liked it, until an odd sound caught his attention: a sniff, an unmistakable sniff. He steadied his horses and looked down at her…there were tears on her cheeks and she was clutching the caddy to her as though it were the most precious thing in the world. A tea caddy for God's sake! Apparently he *had* got it right, absolutely right. He shook his head slightly in amazement. Obviously he had yet a few things to learn about women.

As for Meg, she was torn between fear at the unwitting assault his kindness made on her heart, and joy at having someone to treat her as though she mattered. It was just kindness she told herself, nothing else…he doesn't care about you. Why should he? He scarcely knows you. But the mere fact that he was kind, despite his air of coldness, despite not caring for her, only tore at her all the more.

So Meg went down the nave of the village church on the arm of Dr Ellerbeck to be given into the keeping of Marcus St John Evelyn Langley in a very strange mixture of trepidation and joy.

Marcus, looking at the results of Madame Heloise's labours, had no complaints. She looked lovely, radiant. He watched her proudly as she came to him down the aisle. His bride. He vowed silently that he would be a good husband, that he would make up to Meg for the barren years she had endured.

Often cynical at weddings, no trace of cyncism tainted his response as the Vicar declared them man and wife. She was his. The fierce surge of possessiveness stunned him. Forcing back a wave of desire, he turned to her, smiling tenderly as he bent his head to feather a gentle kiss over her soft lips. For a spine-tingling instant he felt them tremble under his, parting slightly.

Again, desire seared through him and he drew back at once to offer her his arm and escort her to the vestry to sign the register. His body blazed with his awareness of her and this was definitely not the place to succumb to his inclinations. He was still haunted by the suspicion that he had frightened Meg in some way. Despite her denial, he was sure that he had upset her. And he was not entirely sure that he would be able to control his passions another time. She was so soft and sweet that he was actually looking forward to his wedding night and he did not want his bride to be in a frenzy of nerves beforehand just because he couldn't control himself. He certainly didn't want to give her a foretaste of the intimacies of the marriage bed in church.

Meg signed the enormous old register with a trembling hand. Even that brief kiss in front of the small congregation had wholly overset her intention to maintain the sort of detachment his lordship desired. She had not been able to stop herself leaning into his kiss, had actually started to kiss him back…and he had immediately withdrawn. Taking a deep breath, she turned to her husband, holding out the quill.

He took it with a slight smile and his fingers brushed hers gently as he said quietly, 'The Countess of Rutherford need fear no one. Especially not her husband.'

The velvety darkness of his voice held a world of reassurance and her eyes flew to his in consternation. Was that it? Did he still think she feared him? That she feared what he would do to her in the marriage bed? Agnes had told her last night, very gruffly, what his lordship would expect, would do. It sounded most uncomfortable, but Agnes seemed to think that he would not mind kissing her while he was doing it. In that case Meg was inclined to think she might be able to manage...that it might be rather nice to feel his body against hers... She just hoped that he wouldn't be bored and disgusted by her total lack of knowledge.

She gave him the pen and said very shyly, 'The Earl of Rutherford is very kind and he is the last person the Countess would ever fear.' She looked up into his suddenly arrested eyes. They seemed to bore into her with a burning question. She flushed, but held his gaze with her own. He must not think she feared him!

Marcus felt a strange surge of triumph mingled with tenderness as her eyes answered his unspoken question. Whatever it was that had scared her, it was not him! He signed his name with a flourish and stood back to allow the Barlows to sign.

After the Barlows had signed in witness to the marriage, Marcus escorted Meg back through the nave slowly, pleased to note that the little church had quite a respectable number of witnesses to his marriage. The Barlows, of course, but quite a number of his tenants had turned out in their Sunday best, several of them clutching bunches of primroses or violets and wind flowers. These were bestowed on Meg as they left the church, pressed into her trembling, gloved hands with smiles and muttered wishes for her happiness.

Meg felt thoroughly dazed as she changed in her bedchamber at the vicarage. And not just from the unexpected flowers. His lordship—no, she must try and think of him as Marc...he wished it—Marc was confusing her completely and there was no time to think. She had to change so that they could leave for town immediately. She had no idea why Marc was so determined to go at once, but she was only too happy to shake the dust of Fenby from her feet. It had held little but misery for her. So she changed into a carriage dress of deep blue with a matching bonnet as quickly as possible.

Agnes Barlow bustled about her, twitching her sleeves into position, handing her the York tan gloves and shaking out the white lace collar to frame her face.

'Now you look after yourself, Miss Meg…my lady…or rather let his lordship look after you!' The faded eyes were full of tears. 'There now, I'm crying! An' there's nothing to cry about…' Her tears flowed all the faster at being hugged by the new countess and soundly kissed on her withered old cheek.

'Goodbye, Agnes.' Meg too had tears in her eyes and her voice wobbled. 'I'll…I'll write and his lordship says he will need to come back later in the year, so perhaps I can come with him and see you…'

'Go on with you!' said Agnes gruffly, trying not to sound pleased. 'My Lady Rutherford to be traipsin' all the way to Yorkshire! Just to see an old woman like me!' She smiled through her tears. 'Not but what I dare say you might come to keep his lordship company!'

Ten minutes later Meg was settled alone in a post chaise, gazing out the window at the scenery flashing by. Marc was driving his own curricle. She felt a little sorry that he did not wish to be sitting beside her, but she couldn't blame him. It was a lovely day, too good to spend in a chaise. She could hear the sky larks soaring in ecstatic song over the moors and could smell the vanilla scented gorse. Perhaps when they stopped she could ask…perhaps he wouldn't mind if…

By the time they reached the first halt she had quite made up her mind that she would ask. After all, he could only say no.

He came to the door of the chaise to ask politely if she required anything as hostlers rushed out to unharness the sweating team and pole up the new one. His many-caped driving coat hung elegantly from his broad shoulders and she found herself wondering if it could possibly be true that she, Meg Fellowes, was actually married to this man.

She swallowed hard. Her voice seemed to have seized up but she finally managed to say, 'Yes, my...I mean...Marc.' She hesitated. Perhaps he preferred his privacy...she usually did after all.

He cocked his head on one side. 'Something outrageous, my dear?' His eyes twinkled kindly. 'Ask away!'

'May I...may I drive with you for a little?'

His face registered startled disbelief and he hesitated slightly before responding. 'If you are lonely I will travel in the chaise with you then,' he said stiffly as though it were the last thing he wanted to do. 'You will hardly wish to sit in an open carriage for any length of time in this breeze—'

'Yes, I would!' She interrupted him without thinking and then blushed. 'I...I mean, it is such a nice day...why waste it cooped up in a chaise? At least...if you wouldn't mind...'

Her voice trailed off uncertainly. Marcus was looking positively stunned. Oh, dear...had she stepped over some invisible line...offended against some obscure social code? She was conscious of a feeling of immense disappointment that he didn't even want her company just for a stage. She supposed he had found those drives over the last few weeks rather dull...

'It doesn't matter my lord, M...Marcus...'

She stopped. He was opening the door and holding out his arms with a faint smile.

'Come, Meg. I will enjoy some company. In fact, Burnet may take your place in the chaise and we can be quite private.' A beaming smile lit her eyes as she jumped to her feet and prepared to get down. He forestalled her, setting his hands to her slender waist and swinging her down effortlessly.

It was not the first time Meg had experienced the easy strength in his powerful frame but it *was* the first time since Agnes had explained just what her marital duties would entail and she suddenly felt shy and breathless at the pressure of his hands. Agnes had assured her that his lordship would be considerate, gentle, would understand it was her first time…try not to hurt her too much, but still… She was not frightened of him…but his strength awed her…and he was so much bigger than she was. She was stunned to feel the peculiar shivery sensation that ran through her whole body at the thought of her husband undressing her…kissing her again and—how had Agnes put it?—oh, yes…possessing her body.

Unaware of the tangle of innocent confusion rioting through his bride's thoughts, Marcus walked her over to the curricle and lifted her up into it. The exquisite softness of her body under his hands sent his imagination into a complete spin. Memories of her body nestled up against his while she was sick transformed themselves into visions of her body nestled up against him tonight…her body yielding and arching in response to his lovemaking…and she would respond…he would make quite sure of that.

He looked up into her eyes as he lifted her to the seat and his hands tightened unconsciously on her waist. That soft blue-grey gaze was wide and startled. He could feel her body trembling…

Again those delicious tremors ran through Meg's

body. Her breasts seemed to tingle and she was conscious of a feeling of inexpressible yearning which engulfed her as his hands encircled her waist. She thought dazedly that it was as though her body actually wanted him to…to possess her…despite what Agnes had said about it hurting, at least at first… And his eyes! His eyes were so compelling—it was as though he could see what she was thinking.

Then Marcus was up beside her in one easy, athletic movement and Burnet was jumping down and heading off to the chaise. His large body beside her on the seat was even more overwhelming and she gave herself a mental shake. Better not to think of it. Just enjoy the day and leave the night to the future. For now she would pretend that she was just Meg Fellowes, out for a drive with her friend Marc. Not the Countess of Rutherford being driven by her husband to the posting inn where they would spend their wedding night.

'How long do you think it will take to reach Grantham?' she asked. She rather hoped it would take most of the afternoon. It was such a perfect day. The sun was actually shining and the scents of the wildflowers in the ditches were rising in perfumed clouds. Birdsong rippled from the hedgerows and the air was full of darting birds.

Marcus glanced down at her, amused to see that she was taking such interest in the scenery. It seemed commonplace enough to him at first, but after a moment he found himself seeing it as though for the first time. The fragrances and delicate hues of flowers were suddenly apparent to him, the arching bowl of blue sky above them and the pale spring sunshine gave him the illusion of youth, of what it must be like to approach everything fresh…like that frothy lace collar framing her face. Her slender neck rose out of it swanlike…

Dammit all! What was she doing to him? He was five and thirty and a cynical, world-weary rake! Not a dewy-eyed youth about to spout poetry! There was nothing he had experienced which hadn't, on further sampling, turned out to be a dead bore. If he expected anything more of his marriage he was in for a crashing disappointment. Meg was very sweet, but she was only a woman after all and as such he would do well to keep a decent distance between them. He would enjoy her in bed…make sure she was happy and satisfied, but that would be the extent of their intimacy.

But still the thought persisted. *You could have so much more.* And he could lose it all too. Just as his father had. Every emotion congealed at the mere thought of facing that sort of pain.

It was with all this tumbling through his mind that he answered her question rather more coolly than he had intended.

'After five, I should think,' he said, concentrating on steadying his team, which had shied slightly at a hare who dashed across the road under their aristocratic noses. 'We were rather late starting.'

Meg felt crushed. Doubtless she had kept him waiting while she changed! Then a sensation of irritation seized her. It was all very well for him. He hadn't had to change his raiment! And she couldn't believe that he would have expected her to travel in her wedding gown. He couldn't be that stupid! Besides, she had taken very little time to change. She was willing to bet it had taken him longer to tie his cravat! And she was no longer meek little Meg Fellowes, poor relation! She was Marguerite, Countess of Rutherford, and she would not allow herself to be squashed like a...a...a beetle! Especially not by the Earl of Rutherford!

'Oh,' she said sweetly. 'If you had told me you were in such a hurry I would have changed in the chaise.' She gazed straight ahead between the ears of the offside leader, waiting for the inevitable riposte with an expression of complete innocence on her face.

Eventually, as the silence lengthened, she ventured to cast a glance up at her husband. He was frowning slightly but returned the look with a faint lift of one brow, before giving all his attention to his horses.

'Your trick, Meg,' he said evenly. 'I did not mean to criticise.' Little hornet! Who would have thought the quiet, downtrodden Meg had a sting like that on the end of her tongue? Plainly there was more to his bride than met the eye. For the first time he wondered just what Meg really thought of him and their forced marriage. And would she ever tell him? She had said that she would never consent to be someone's despised poor relation again. She had preferred to seek employment as a governess rather than submit to that.

Obviously the quiet façade hid an unknown Meg that he had glimpsed once or twice when her defences were down. Proud—he knew that. Courageous, certainly—although she would probably laugh at the idea. But what were her dreams? What had she wanted of life before she had learnt to hide everything behind the polite mask? And whatever it was—did she still want it? Uneasily he realised that even if he wanted to understand Meg, she might never let him close enough to do so. She was just as capable of presenting an impenetrable reserve as he was himself.

Satisfied that she had made her point, Meg sat back against the seat and settled down to enjoy the drive. At least she was out in the fresh air and on her way to London. She spared a contentedly unkind thought for the shock it was going to give her cousin Delian and his horrid wife Henrietta to find their despised cousin suddenly so far above them on the social ladder. She knew that Marcus had written to his sister and charged her to have the marriage advertised in the papers tomorrow. Meg hoped that Lady Diana had not been too shocked. There had been no reply from London. Marcus said he had told Di not to bother. By the time she had written they would be on their way and the letter would miss them.

By the time they reached Grantham Meg was extremely tired and ravenously hungry. It was well past five and she definitely wanted her dinner. It was with considerable relief that she realised that the red brick building ahead of them was the George where they had rooms reserved for the night. As Marcus guided his team through the archway into the yard she heaved a mental sigh of relief.

She was exhausted and stiff with sitting for so long and could only marvel as Marcus swung down from the curricle with unimpaired grace. Had she attempted anything of the sort, she was tolerably certain that she would have collapsed in a heap on the cobbles. It was only sheer pigheadedness that had kept her from leaning against Marcus's broad shoulder for the last couple of hours.

He came around to her and looked up with a smile. 'Tired, my dear? I bespoke dinner for six so you will have time to freshen up. It is only half past five.'

She stared down at him in consternation. Half an hour? She would starve if she had to wait so long! Her stomach, heartily in agreement, gave an audible and unladylike rumble just as Marcus placed his hands on her waist to lift her down. Judging by the lift of his brows and the severely repressed twitch at the corner of his mouth he had heard and probably felt the rebellious organ's response. The intimacy unnerved her…she tried not to think just how much more intimately he would probably know her in a very few hours.

Marcus set her down very gently, keeping his hands firmly on her waist until he was assured she was quite steady on her feet. Despite her silence on the subject he was fairly certain that Meg was utterly exhausted. Hungry too, he thought with an inward smile.

Tucking her arm in his, he strolled across the yard towards the inn door, wondering if she were so tired that it would be better not to insist on his matrimonial rights and allow her an uninterrupted night's sleep. He had booked two bedchambers to give her some privacy, so it would not be such a strain on his control as if he had to share a bed with her. Still pondering the question, he bowed to allow her to precede him into the inn. His mind on his dinner and his intentions for the night ahead, he heard a rumble of wheels and a rattle of hooves on the cobbles, but did not observe the natty gentleman who had just tooled a phaeton and pair into the yard.

Sir Blaise Winterbourne stared after Lord Rutherford in patent disbelief. Good God! How did the fellow do it? He had even found an attractive filly to mount in the wilds of Yorkshire. Must be a lively little piece too for his lordship to bother bringing her back to town and rigging her out in the first style of elegance like that. My, my, my! A pity Althea Hartleigh had been so virtuous…well, circumspect…in ignoring the lures he had cast out to her, but by the look of things this little game pullet might be even more worthwhile... She looked rather younger than Rutherford's usual fancies...no doubt she would refresh his somewhat jaded palate nicely...especially if he could have his way with her right under Rutherford's nose. That would add a certain spice to the occasion.

Humming to himself, Sir Blaise sauntered into the inn after giving his orders to the ostler who took charge of his horses. It would be as well if Rutherford did not realise that his little bit of game had been sighted. No need to put the fellow on his guard.

With not the least idea that he needed to be on his guard, Marcus dined with his bride in the private parlour he had bespoken and continued to ponder the question of how to spend his wedding night. He had no doubt of his own inclinations...he wanted to take Meg to bed and make love to her...probably for most of the night. But she sat there before him, gallantly pretending that she wasn't exhausted and trying not to look scared.

When they had finished he stood up and went around the table to her. He intended merely to assist her to her feet, but she smiled up at him with such devastating sweetness that he found himself pulling her into his arms with no warning at all.

For a moment he felt her stiffen in his embrace and then she melted against him, her soft curves moulding to the hard arrogance of his body. With a groan he lowered his mouth to hers in a searing kiss. He was gentle with her, but his passion was undeniable. He wanted her in his bed, wanted to feel her body yielding under him just as her mouth was doing now. Her lips had parted in response to the subtle command of his probing tongue and he took instant advantage, tasting and exploring her sweetness in sensuous assault. And she was responding with an innocent delight that fanned his desire to a blaze. Her tongue was curling around his in shy, untutored abandon. Small, uncertain hands crept up over his shoulders to thread themselves in his thick, tawny locks and he shuddered in pleasure.

And then confusion hit him. This was not what he had intended for his marriage. Enjoy her, yes. But this was not mere enjoyment. This was sheer intoxication. It wasn't just her body he wanted, it was her!

Time! He needed time to get himself under control. Besides, he thought in frantic justification, better not to be too eager her first time and run the risk of really hurting her.

Abruptly he released her. 'I think, Meg, that you must be very tired. You should go to bed.' His voice was distant, cold. It shocked him, but he couldn't help it. He had to think. 'I need to stretch my legs so I shall go for a walk about the town. Goodnight. I shall see you in the morning.' Without awaiting any reply he was gone, leaving a very confused bride behind him.

Meg retired to her bedchamber, uncertain whether she was relieved at his lordship's forbearance or not. Did he really think her tired, or was he just being polite? His face had given her no clue as to his real reasons for not sharing her bed. He had seemed so chilly and remote. Perhaps he just wasn't interested…found her unattractive…regarded it as an inevitable duty and one which he was in no hurry to perform. She swallowed nervously at the thought. How could she possibly share these…intimacies with him if he viewed her with distaste? It would be humiliating!

She poured water into the bowl on the nightstand and cleansed herself thoroughly, trying not to think about the way he had kissed her...the way he had possessed and plundered her mouth... Had her response disgusted him? Should she not have kissed him back? She was stunned to feel an aching, empty sensation between her thighs as she washed there. Shocked, she gritted her teeth and dried herself as quickly as possible before pulling a nightgown over her head and scrambling into bed. The soft feather mattress welcomed her weary body and she admitted to herself, with a sigh, that whatever his reasons for deciding to go for a walk, she should at least be grateful to her husband for an unexpected night's sleep.

Blowing out the candle, she settled down and snuggled under the blankets, enjoying the cosy glow from the fire. She had never had a fire in her bedchamber before...except, of course, when she had been sick and Marc had looked after her... Sleepily she allowed herself to think about Marc. He had been so kind to her...it was a pity that he kept on turning into Marcus, Lord Rutherford. Of course Marc would not have dreamed of forcing himself on her if she was tired...but then he wouldn't have to. Tired or not, Meg would have surrendered herself to his loving without the slightest hesitation...as indeed she had thought she was doing until his lordship put her from him so abruptly. Still puzzling over this, she drifted off to sleep.

She was awakened some time later by the sound of someone moving around in her room. At first she was confused—the fire had nearly died and the room was in near darkness. In her half-waking state, she thought it must be Agnes, but then a very masculine grunt, followed by the sound of first one boot, and then another, hitting the floor, woke her up completely.

She froze. All at once she knew the true meaning of the term *bride nerves*. Marcus must have changed his mind and he had come to…to…possess her body. Half-excited and half-terrified, she lay in the great bed, shaking with nervous anticipation as she listened to the faint sounds of him undressing. Even though her scared brain was trying to persuade her to panic, her body had other ideas. She could feel tingling warmth spreading through her limbs, that extraordinary feeling of weakness that was at once frightening and exciting.

A moment later she felt him get into the bed beside her. What should she do? Let him know she was awake? But if she spoke then he would know she was scared. Was he even going to speak to her before…? She could feel the hard length of his body against her and turned towards him instinctively, trustingly, her arms open, body soft and trembling, her mouth ready for his tender kisses…a world of warm, intimate darkness.

Then the world went mad. She felt a hand reach out for her, grasping, and then she was taken in a rough grip and his mouth was on hers…brutal, greedy. Frantically Meg forced herself to recall her wedding vows and lie still. She had sworn to obey him…it was no part of a bride's duty to struggle against her husband's rightful claim to her body…but it was so horrible! His gentle kisses earlier had given her no inkling of what his behaviour would be like in bed! She had expected that he would be a gentle, tender lover…at the very least considerate. Not this brute beast with his hot, lustful mouth that reeked of brandy, slobbering all over her face. His lips were cruel where once they had been tantalising…she could taste blood. The friendly dark had become a dungeon full of pain and fear.

And what was he doing now? His hands were grabbing at her breasts through the cotton nightgown, actually hurting her. She must lie still...she was his wife...it...it was his right to take her. Terrified, she schooled her body to obedience, even as she felt his hands at the neck of her nightgown jerk apart, ripping it open to the navel. Even worse than her physical terror was the feeling of betrayal, the thought that she had trusted this man, had thought he cared for her at least enough to deal gently with her virginity. His hands were now seizing her soft breasts, crushing them cruelly as he savagely forced his tongue into her mouth.

She gagged, and panicked completely as she felt his weight shift to pin her to the bed. She couldn't! She just couldn't! He could have the marriage annulled! She simply could not submit to his desires! She tried desperately to throw him off and heard a light, mocking laugh as her mouth was released momentarily. And then he took it again, even more brutally as he thrust one leg between her thighs, leaving her with no doubt that he meant to have her even if he had to force her. She couldn't believe it...that Marcus was to all intents and purposes raping her...enjoying her terror...it couldn't be happening.

But it was. She was fighting a losing battle. His weight held her down, helpless, and his powerful right hand had encircled both her wrists above her head while his left was raising the hem of her nightgown. She could feel it sliding down between her thighs, felt his fingers reaching, probing in hard, merciless lust...could feel a heavy ring scrape against her soft flesh...and then she realised... As clearly as though it were before her, she could see Marc's heavy signet on his right hand—his left wore no ring!

Her scream of protest was cut off by that hand which

The Dutiful Rake

was suddenly clamped over her mouth and a light, unfamiliar voice said, 'You would be most unwise to do that, my dear. I can assure you that he will not believe you were unwilling. Lie still and I will be on my way before he comes up.'

It was not Marc! It was a stranger! She fought with the strength of desperation to escape that iron grip on her mouth and finally bit savagely. With a curse, he hit her face a stunning blow but her mouth was free and she dragged in a breath and screamed as loudly as she could, struggling fiercely to get out from underneath him.

It was no use. He gave up trying to silence her and seemed to be concentrating his efforts on taking his pleasure as quickly and roughly as possible.

She twisted her legs together tightly and heard him mutter, 'God help me. Anyone would think you had your virtue to defend!' She could feel a hand at her throat, gripping mercilessly, she couldn't breathe…oh, God… Despairing, she could feel him forcing himself between her legs…something hard and blunt… pushing… She screamed again as the grip on her throat relaxed slightly…

And then there was a crash as the door burst open to the accompaniment of a roar of primitive, masculine rage and a blaze of light.

Marcus had taken a rather longer walk than he intended in his efforts to regain his usual sangfroid. And he felt just slightly foolish at his idiotic panic. So much did he want to hurl his stupid decision to the four winds and go back and make love to his bride that he walked right around the town a second time to cool off, before returning to the George. She was probably asleep already and it would be the height of cruelty to awaken her.

Upon his return he made his way upstairs with an oil lamp pressed on him by mine host and past Meg's door. Ruefully he thought that she must be asleep by now, it would be outrageous to go in and wake her up. Perhaps if he rose early in the morning he might go in and wait for her to awaken…

Comforting himself with this thought, he set his hand to the latch of his own door…and froze as a terrified scream rang out.

He didn't pause for thought. He knew beyond all possible doubt that it was Meg…something was wrong… she must be having a nightmare… He was already running back to her door. It was locked, but he didn't bother to knock, just hurled his shoulder at it and burst in as another agonised scream seared through him.

At first he could not believe his eyes and then with a roar of fury he surged across the room to drag Blaise Winterbourne off Meg. Winterbourne was too quick for him.

He rolled off the bed on the opposite side to the door and said mockingly, 'I did warn her not to be too enthusiastic in her excitement! Never mind. Another time, perhaps. Do let me know when you have finished with her, my dear Rutherford. A little unschooled, I must say, but I'm sure she will be worth the effort.'

Meg, half-fainting, managed to pull up the bedclothes with shaking hands. She was safe but she felt sickened, soiled by his body, his touch. What must Marcus be thinking? Would he believe what had happened? Or would he think she was truly her mother's daughter? His voice when it came was like a shard of ice, sending fresh shudders through her overwrought senses.

'Get out of my wife's chamber, Winterbourne.' Searing rage held him in its grip, but through it a cold voice counselled discretion. The last thing he wanted was the landlord up. If this story got out, there would be the very devil to pay! Very few would believe Meg's innocence. He had to protect her! She was huddled under the bedclothes, shaking visibly, her face white and dazed, her lip cut and there was a red mark on her cheekbone that looked as if it would bruise later. His little Meg...if that bastard had actually—

'Your wife!' For a moment Winterbourne was disconcerted, but he recovered his urbanity in a flash. 'Dear me! How very *maladroit* I have been. I thought her one of your little indulgences, my dear Rutherford. Do not trouble to see me out, I know my way.'

Never taking his eyes off Marcus, he pulled on his shirt and breeches, picked up his boots and edged around the bed towards the door, saying, 'Naturally I shall not breathe a word of this...unless of course you wish me to name my seconds, my lord?'

For a mad instant Marcus was tempted, but a terrified murmur from Meg recalled him to his senses and saner counsel prevailed. If he challenged Winterbourne the story was bound to leak out and Meg would suffer, even more than she had already.

Coldly he replied, 'Winterbourne, I would not care to soil my riding whip with a cur like you! Get out! But rest assured, if I hear so much as a whisper about this, I will overcome my reluctance and thrash you to within an inch of your life!'

Chapter Six

As soon as the door shut behind Winterbourne, Marcus turned to Meg. His heart contracted in his chest as he looked at her wide, terrified eyes, and saw the racking shudders that were convulsing her slender body. Her breath was coming in sobs which bordered on hysteria.

What the hell should he do? He wanted to hold her, comfort her, but when he moved towards her she flinched and cried out incoherently, cowering away from him. He couldn't blame her. After what had happened it would be a miracle if she ever trusted a man again. He was not even sure if he had been in time...had Winterbourne actually deflowered her? The thought that Meg had been raped made him feel physically ill. His little Meg...so lost and vulnerable behind her polite mask...he had sworn to protect her and he couldn't even comfort her when he had failed so abysmally!

She was speaking. 'Marc...I'm sorry...I didn't mean...I let him...'

He froze in disbelief, his eyes suddenly boring into her, an unbelievable pain lancing through his body. She had *let* him!

'I thought it was you!' She could not go on and turned to bury her face in the pillow, sobbing bitterly at the thought that she had even accidentally betrayed Marc who was now looking at her in such disgust. Then she felt a gentle touch on her shoulder, a hand warm and comforting, patting her.

A deep voice, husky with emotion, saying, 'Meg, it's all right…you're safe now. Come…let me hold you…' Those gentle hands were turning her, lifting her to lie cradled in his arms against the solid, protective bulwark of his chest. He was stroking her hair, whispering words of comfort, of reassurance. Slowly she began to relax under his touch, although her tears continued to flow unabated.

Marcus just held her, his cheek resting on her dishevelled hair, his hands stroking and soothing as he murmured softly. He could never afterwards remember just what he had said to her, but at last her terrible weeping stopped and she lay silent in his arms except for an occasional hiccough. They were quiet for a while and then Meg spoke again in a voice which cracked pitifully.

'I thought it was you…that you had changed your mind…wanted me after all…'

She had thought he didn't want her? Oh, God, no! She was still speaking and he forced himself to concentrate.

'So I…I welcomed him… He didn't say anything…just grabbed me and started…started—' She broke off, shuddering convulsively. His grip on her tightened and she seemed to gain strength. 'He…he started to kiss me…and…touch my breasts…I thought it was you… I couldn't believe it but…I thought I had to submit so I tried to just lie there…but he was so rough I panicked in the end. I tried to fight him…and then I realised…realised what I had done…that it wasn't you…'

She was crying softly again and Marcus stroked her tenderly. 'It's over, Meg. He'll never touch you again. It's over, I swear it.'

Then, to his amazement, she whispered, 'I'm sorry, Marc…I betrayed you…'

He was stunned. *She* had betrayed *him*? When he had left her alone? Not even thinking to tell her to lock her door!

'You didn't, Meg!' His voice was urgent, desperate to reassure her. 'How was it a betrayal to have been attacked?' He shied from the word *rape*. But then he thought, No, I have to know. I can't help her if I don't. How can I help her get over this if *I* fear the truth?

Hesitantly he asked, 'Meg, did he actually…?'

She shook her head, 'N…no, at least I don't think so. You came in just as…' Her voice failed at the memory of that dreadful, helpless moment when she had felt Winterbourne's body forcing itself against her in violent lust.

Marcus's blood practically congealed in his veins as he realised that in another second or two he would have been too late to save her. His voice cracked as he whispered, 'Thank God! Oh thank God! Meg…I'm sorry…I should never have left you alone. It was selfish…just because I wanted you so much…and I didn't trust myself not to…' He stopped. It would hardly reassure Meg to know he had been burning with desire for her, had wanted to change his mind and come to her room.

And what was he to do now? Should he stay to look after her or would she prefer him to leave her alone? She needed a woman to help her but there was no one he could call. If they had been in London Di would have helped, but here...he couldn't leave her alone all night.

Meg lay quietly, conscious of the comforting strength of his body. She felt safe in his arms, as though nothing could touch her there...except him. The thought came to her unbidden and she tried to force it away. It was obscene to fear what Marc would do to her...but the fear persisted; not that he would force himself on her, but that even if he dealt with her gently, she would panic in the dark, forget it was him...if he wanted her after this. Perhaps he would not want to touch her. She felt dirty, befouled as though a slime clung to her, filthy and degraded.

Marc was speaking softly. 'Listen, sweetheart, I will go to my room and change for the night, then come back to look after you, if that is what you want. I don't want you to be alone, but...' He hesitated.

'Yes, please.' She tried to keep her voice low, hiding the relief that flooded into her. He would stay! She had not dared to ask it of him. She felt that she would contaminate anything she touched.

He released her and stood up, looking down at her worriedly. She sounded so...so utterly lifeless, broken. The torn nightgown hung open, revealing her soft, creamy breasts. Dark bruises were beginning to appear and he swore softly as he realised just how brutal Winterbourne had been with her. The bruise on her cheek was stark against her chalk-white face and her cut lip was swollen. A knife seemed to slice through his heart at the thought of what had so nearly happened. Even if the bastard hadn't known she was a virgin, to force himself violently on an unknown and unwilling girl! It sickened Marc to his very soul. Even he hadn't quite realised how vile Winterbourne could be...

Swearing under his breath, he went to make up the fire and then rifled through Meg's trunk, finding another nightgown. He took the nightgown to her, saying, 'Change while I am gone. Bolt the door behind me. The lock is smashed. I'll knock when I return.'

She nodded, beyond words. Maybe it would help to change. She got up and stood shakily for a moment before following Marc to the door. He touched her bruised cheek gently and went out.

She bolted the door and stared at it, lost, bewildered; the urge to open it and beg him to come back was almost overwhelming...she was being silly—he would be back in a few minutes. In the meantime she must change.

The nightgown he had found for her was on the bed. She put it on and looked with loathing at the ripped one she had removed. It lay on the floor, its torn innocence accusing, a whited sepulchre, rotten, full of corruption. Burn it! She bundled it up and pushed it into the fire Marcus had rekindled. The flames flared up the chimney and for a moment she wished that she could be cleansed, annealed in their purifying blaze. How else could she ever be clean again?

She was still staring into the fire when Marcus came back. His knock recalled her to her senses and she almost ran to let him in. The sight of his tall figure was immensely comforting in the familiar red silk dressing gown. His arms were full of blankets and she looked at them in confusion.

'What are they for?'

'For me,' he said quietly. 'I thought you would probably prefer me to sleep in the chair...that you wouldn't want me in—'

'No!' Her voice was frantic. She could hear it and tried to control herself, but the words came tumbling out. 'Please...please...just hold me...please, Marc—' She forced herself to stop. Impossible to tell him how she felt...that if he didn't hold her that she would never feel safe... Then, looking up into his bleak face, she realised that he understood.

'If that is what you wish, Meg.' His voice was low. He felt humbled and elated all at once that she would trust him like that. Very slowly he went to her and lifted her into his arms as easily as he would have lifted a child. There was nothing amorous in his touch, just solid, protective comfort. He carried her to the bed and settled her in it before climbing in.

'Do you want the lamp, Meg?' She might feel safer that way, he thought. Then if she wakes, she can see it's me.

She shook her head. 'I don't think I'd sleep, but...' In the dark, though...

'A candle,' said Marcus. He got up again and lit one, setting it on the nightstand. Then he came back to bed and blew out the lamp. The little flame danced and glimmered, a glowing island in the encircling dark.

Marcus lay down and reached for Meg, drawing her into his embrace, settling her safely into the curve of his shoulder. He felt her body, tense at first, slowly relax against him until at last her breathing steadied and deepened into the haven of sleep. He lay wakeful for a long time, half-expecting to have to fight his own body's urges, but although he was profoundly aware of her soft curves nestled beside him, and although it would have taken very little to stir him to passion, he could hold himself easily in check by concentrating on the trust she had showed in him.

Meg awakened in a cold sweat, confused and terrified from a dream in which Marc kept turning into Winterbourne and a smothering, greedy blackness enveloped her, body and soul. There was a heavy weight across her waist, pinning her down. Marc's arm, strong and reassuring. The fire was very low but the candle flame still danced bravely. Clean, bright...she envied it its effortless purity. She wanted to wash, totally immerse herself in water to cleanse away the stains left on her, especially the stain of fear. There was water on the nightstand...if she were very quiet...

Careful not to wake him, she lifted Marc's arm and got out of bed. Perhaps if she washed she might feel clean. Stripping off her nightgown, she stood shivering in the chilly air. A flannel lay on the stand. She dipped it in the bowl and began to wash herself in the icy water, wincing as the cold bit through her. She washed and washed, scrubbing at her body until it felt raw and stinging—her breasts, her thighs...but still she felt mired.

Marcus had woken as soon as she moved his arm but he lay quietly, unwilling to intrude, trying to understand. The faint light gleamed on her white curves as he watched her, creating shadowy mysteries in the intimate hollows of her body, mysteries that he longed to penetrate, possess... He could hear her teeth chattering, but still she was scrubbing obsessively. And suddenly, with a blinding flash of understanding, he knew why she was doing it. He shut his eyes, appalled.

Never in his life had he forced himself on a woman. Ever since he and Jack had caught Blaise Winterbourne at a house party, forcing his attentions upon a terrified chambermaid, he had thought it to be the most despicable of acts, scorning those who boasted of the defenceless maidservants they had coerced.

Naturally he and Jack had stopped Winterbourne, but even so, he had never quite realised how devastating it would be for a woman—how sullied she would feel afterwards—until now, as he lay watching his bride frantically trying to cleanse the memory from her bruised and shivering flesh, a victim of Winterbourne's twisted, ongoing vengeance.

At last she stopped with a despairing murmur. 'I'll never be clean again…never!'

Marcus flinched at the dull pain in her voice, watching as she dried herself and pulled the nightgown back on. It slid down over her breasts, puckered with cold, her slender waist and those flaring hips, the long line of her thighs, all graceful, tempting curves. He shut his eyes to block out the vision but it danced before him mercilessly in all its seductive beauty, inviting him to touch, caress, burn kisses over the silken skin…show her how tender and intimate the act could be…erase, or at least counter, the dreadful memory of her near rape. It was too soon, he told himself. Perhaps if she will let me tell Di, or if I can persuade her to tell Di…

He could hear the soft pad of her feet as she came back to the bed and he lay there, gritting his teeth for control. It would be safer for her if he went and slept on the chair, but he knew if he did that she would read it as a rejection of her, a confirmation of her vileness. And he could not tell her the real reason and frighten her still further. She trusted him, had no one else to turn to. Though it killed him, he would not betray that trust.

Meg got back into the bed, shivering violently. She longed to cuddle up against Marc's warmth, feel his arm around her, holding her fear at bay, but hesitated to wake him. So she lay huddled under the blankets, trying to ward off sleep in case she should dream again. She forced herself to think about Marc's kisses, how different they had been, how tender and...exciting. She had been a little scared, but only of her own response, the wild, aching need that had pierced through her. She had not been scared of him, and when she had thought he had come to her bed to possess her, her heart had soared in an ecstasy of joy... She found that tears were sliding down her cheeks again and buried her face in the pillow to muffle her sobs.

She felt a gentle hand grip her shoulder, heard a deep voice say, 'Come here, little one.' She turned at once, wriggling into his arms and clinging to him, pressing herself against him, conscious only of the solid heat of his body, the reassuring strength of his arms. Somehow the fact that he was willing to hold her like this made her feel cleaner.

The sensation of her trembling body seared into his unruly flesh. He suppressed a groan with extreme difficulty. She must not know he wanted her...wanted her with a desire that shocked even him in its raw, primitive longing. He forced himself to stroke her hair gently, holding her against him protectively while his body screamed silently at the torture it was subjected to. It had been a physical relief when she had not nestled back up to him at first, but he could not, just for the sake of his own comfort and sanity, leave her to cry herself to sleep.

He could feel her tears soaking through his nightshirt as she wept, and said quietly, 'Tell me, Meg. It will make you feel better.'

'I...I can't.'

'Tell me, Meg.' His voice compelled in its gentle compassion.

Her voice shaking, she told him, in pitiful broken phrases that seemed to tear her apart. He shut his eyes to hold back the hot, pricking sensation. It was even worse than he had thought. She had not only thought it was him, she had been willing, pleased, had welcomed him...or so she thought...and then...she had thought it was him brutalising her. Cold horror seeped into him as he realised how terrified she must have been, thinking that she would have to endure similar acts of savage lechery regularly.

Finally she lay quietly in his arms. He held her tenderly, still burning with desire, but he managed to speak normally. 'Go to sleep, Meg. I'll hold you.'

She shuddered as he spoke and he at once released her, drew back, mentally cursing, thinking she had realised his arousal. But she clung to him in frantic terror. 'No, don't let me go!' It came tumbling out as though she could no longer contain the fear. 'I don't want to sleep. In case I dream again...'

'Dream?' She had said nothing about a dream. He should have realised. He had had nightmares after the siege of Badajoz. 'Come, Meg. Tell me everything. Trust me.'

Convulsive shudders racked her. 'No...it...it is obscene,' she whispered.

'Then it is better told and got rid of,' he said softly, his long, experienced fingers tangling in the curls at the nape of her neck, massaging the tension he could feel there. 'Told and exorcised...not hidden within where it will fester.'

So she told him.

He was silent for a moment and then he said carefully, 'One day, Meg, when you are ready, we will do something about that.'

'What? What can possibly help?' Her voice sounded hopeless, dead.

He drew a deep breath. Even saying it was enough to threaten his precarious self-control. 'By making love, Meg. When you are ready to trust me with your body, you will come and tell me. And I swear to you that I will take your gift gently.' After a minute he said haltingly, 'I want you very much, Meg, but I will not take you until you ask me to.' He could not bear that she might think he did not want her.

His fingers were still stroking her soft creamy nape, gentle and compelling, unwittingly casting a tender, seductive spell. She closed her eyes, imagining those fingers at her breast, pressing her thighs apart. And instead of black, choking horror, she felt again that wild, sweet ache…that yearning, beckoning emptiness. She already trusted him, there was nothing else to wait for. If he truly wanted to make love to her, those fiery sensations he evoked might become a blaze that could cleanse and purify her again.

Summoning all her courage, she pressed a small, shy kiss on his chin and faltered, 'Marc…would you…if you are not too tired?'

It took him a moment to realise what she was saying, for her meaning to sink in. He lay there in disbelief. He had thought it might take weeks, months perhaps, before she would trust him. He couldn't take advantage of her like this. No matter what his body thought of the idea.

'Meg…no,' he said with difficulty. 'It is too soon for you…'

She pulled away from him, numbed by his gentle

rejection. He was just being kind, he did not really want her. Perhaps he even felt as she did, that she was somehow unclean, that he would be soiled by touching her.

'I'm sorry.' Her voice was a mere thread which threatened to snap under the strain of her hurt. And then she felt his hands on her again, bringing her back into his embrace.

His voice, hoarse and shaking. 'Meg, are you sure? Quite sure?'

She was sure and turned to him, desperately raising her mouth for his kiss. She could feel his trembling hands cup her face as he feathered his lips over hers in a caress so tender, so hesitant that it brought tears to her eyes. His arms were around her, pulling her to lie against his hard, aroused body.

He had been careful earlier to lie so that she did not feel his flagrant desire. Now he held her to it, rocking his loins against her gently, whispering again, 'Are you sure?'

'Yes.' Her answer was breathed on a sigh of pleasure as he trailed light kisses over the ivory column of her throat. There was no fear at his blatant demonstration of need, only joy that he still wanted her. She felt one large hand slide down over her shoulder to tease her breast through the cotton of her nightgown, felt those darting fires under her skin as he rubbed a thumb across the nipple. It sprang to painful life, a taut, burning little bud which forced a whimper of delight from her.

His mouth was on hers again, still gentle but imperceptibly more intense, his lips warm and firm as they sipped and sampled her inexperienced sweetness. Shyly she kissed him back, opening her mouth under his instinctively, in response to the subtle pressure. She could feel his tongue flickering lightly over her lips and arched against him in unspoken longing.

With a tearing groan Marcus succumbed to temptation and slid his tongue into the soft, vulnerable recesses of her mouth. Ready to break the kiss at the first sign of fear, he explored gently and thoroughly, sweeping across the roof of her mouth in slow, sensuous strokes. Then with a surge of joy which stabbed through him like a sword, he felt her tongue, hesitant and uncertain, entwine with his in shy passion.

Endlessly patient and skilful, Marcus kissed her until she was moaning with pleasure, drowning in the sea of sensation aroused by his mouth and hands. She stroked his shoulders, astounded at the shudders of delight that racked his hard, powerful body. She wanted to feel his bare skin under her hands, wanted to feel his hands on her breasts.

His mouth was at her ear, tickling with his warm breath and then she heard him say, 'Wait, sweetheart.' He pulled away from her and got off the bed. She lay there, watching his large, dim outline as he crossed to the nightstand. A moment later there was a flare of light as he lit the lamp from the flickering candle.

He turned to look at her and said very deeply, 'I want to see you, Meg. And I want you to see me. There will be no darkness in our loving.' And with slow deliberation he drew off his nightshirt to stand naked before her, watching her reaction for the slightest hint of fear.

She stared for a moment with wide eyes and parted lips. He was so beautiful! So very powerful. So very male. Her gaze roamed over his broad shoulders and wide, muscular chest with its thick mat of hair, lower to his narrow hips…and… Her breath came in shallow

gasps as she forced herself to look at his potent, unfettered virility.

For a split second she felt fear, physical, gut-
wrenching fear as the darkness beyond the pool of light
threatened to close in and overwhelm her. She fought
it down and looked into Marc's face. Desire, concern
and acceptance were all there. If she said no, it would
go no further. He would shackle his own desire and
respect her decision. That was why he had lit the lamp,
so that he could know beyond doubt what she really
wanted.

She wanted him. Despite her fear, she wanted him.
And she knew that if she backed away now it would
become harder and harder to face her fear. Somewhere
deep down she knew that the only way forward was
straight on, through her fear and out the other side. If
he would leave the light on...if she could see it was
him...

He was picking up his nightshirt, preparing to put it
back on when she spoke. 'Can we have the lamp on
while...while we...?'

The garment slipped through his nerveless fingers. He
would have sworn that she was about to refuse, that the
sight of his aroused body had terrified her. His burning
grey eyes held her gaze, searching her face. She *was*
afraid...he could see it in the wide eyes and trembling
mouth. And something else was there, warring with the
fear—desire...and a determination to face out her fear.
Of course she wanted the light on. Then she would
know it was him...but still he was uncertain.

As he hesitated she held out her hand to him im-
ploringly and said, for the last time, 'I am sure, Marc,
please...'

Her voice trembled and he suddenly knew that if he

refused she might never be certain of his reasons, might always think that he hadn't wanted her despite the evidence of her eyes. His mind made up, he dropped the nightshirt and approached the bed. Kneeling on it beside her, he drew the bedclothes back and lifted her against him, his fingers at the buttons of her nightgown, undoing them one by one until it hung open almost to her waist.

He sat back and gazed at her partially revealed breasts, creamy, velvety flesh that his fingers ached to cup. Delectable rosy peaks, which seemed to cry out for the ministration of his tongue, peeped out shyly. With incredible restraint he set his hands to her shoulders and, looking deeply into her eyes, he slid the nightgown off, pushing it down to lie around her hips. Then he drew her very slowly into his arms.

Meg thought she would die of the sensation of being held half-naked in his arms. His hands roamed over her gently, possessively, rubbing and stroking as he explored her shape and texture. She could feel the rough hair on his chest rasping against her nipples and shuddered with delight as they burned with joyful pain. And all the time his mouth never left hers, kissing her deeply as his warm strength seduced her completely. Her eyes closed in ecstasy as he fondled her.

At last she felt him gather the nightgown into his hands and with a gentle movement slip it over her head. Then she felt his hand sliding into her hair, tangling in the soft curls as he tipped her head back to expose her throat and rain kisses on it. His other hand was at her breast, teasing and tantalising artfully, evoking little gasps of pleasure from her. Slowly his lips moved lower, and lower, into the white valley between her breasts and then with a groan of triumph he closed his mouth hotly over one tightly furled, rosy little bud.

All that had gone before was as nothing to the jolt of fire that exploded through her now as she felt his tongue rasp over her nipple in a caress that robbed her of nearly all power to think. She gasped, writhing against him in ecstasy, arching her body in frantic pleading. The only thought that hammered through her veins was how much she wanted him.

She shivered in excitement as he urged her to lie back on the pillows, following her to lie half on top of her, one powerfully muscled thigh slipping to rest with suggestive intimacy between her legs. She could feel his arousal, rock hard, pressed against her. Opening her eyes, she gazed straight into his, burning with desire.

Holding her eyes trapped with his smouldering gaze, he stroked her stomach, his fingers teasing, tickling. And then lower, to drift lightly over the triangle of soft curls. She quivered, and her eyes widened as he deliberately placed his hand over her swelling mound in a gesture of intimate possession. She lay quite still and slowly, gently, he slid his long fingers between her legs to caress her tenderly.

His mouth took hers deeply, as his fingers explored the soft, yielding folds of flesh that melted in welcoming warmth. His tongue plundered in relentless, dizzying passion as he lay beside her and loved her with consummate, devastating skill for what seemed like an eternity. She was going to die, it was so beautiful…explode with the tension that was building inside her. Someone was sobbing…crying out in longing. Dimly she was aware that it was herself and that Marc had moved, was speaking to her.

'Open your eyes.' His voice was cracking with the

effort of restraint. If he was going to take her, it had to be now. Her response was so shattering, so complete. It scalded through his veins in racking desire... But he wanted her to know it was him and he had to give her one last chance to stop him...

She obeyed and stared straight up into his flaming eyes. He was lying between her legs, she could feel him hot and hard against her quivering, virgin body. His face was hard-edged with the pain of his longing, but she heard him say hoarsely, 'Meg, little one, you know what I want...are you sure? It will hurt...no matter how careful I am...there is no help for it the first time.'

Meg's eyes filled with tears. Even now he would stop. Even now he would let her change her mind, despite his own need. In that moment, as she fully realised his tender compassion, she yielded him her heart, completely and irrevocably. She loved him and she had only one thing to give him that he wanted...

Keeping her eyes upon his face she managed to say in a choked whisper, 'I am yours, Marc...please...please take me.'

And he did. With exquisite slowness he tenderly positioned himself, parting the soft flesh with gentle fingers, and then, as she clung to him in her inevitable fear, slid into her melting heat until he found the frail barrier of her innocence. Back and forth he moved, until her tension eased, until her body softened and arched against him in need. He breached her with one powerful thrust, sinking deeply and inexorably into her body. He groaned as he fought for control, as she shuddered under him at the hurt he was inflicting. He looked into her face. Her eyes were shut and her lower lip was clenched in her teeth in an effort to hold back the soft whimper of pain. It stabbed into him...gleaming and terrible.

He remained very still for a moment and when she relaxed a little he moved gently inside her with a sigh of pleasure. She gasped and her eyes flew open. He smiled down at her tenderly and said, 'Now you are mine,' as he moved again, as if unable to control his response to her yielding softness.

She knew exactly what he meant. He held her in thrall, his gentle motions were spellbinding. She clung to him as he lowered his mouth to hers and took it in a deeply erotic kiss, plundering and pillaging in complete possession as his loins rocked back and forth in the same compelling rhythm which swept her into a whirlpool of stunning sensation as the tension mounted until at last she cried out in ecstasy as wave after wave of passion broke over her and she was conscious of nothing but his body claiming hers forever.

He couldn't sleep. Meg lay safely clasped in his arms, a peaceful smile on her face as she slept, warm and secure. She had wept in his arms after their loving, shattered by the loveliness of what they had experienced. And he had kissed the tears away, unspeakably moved by her final, unconditional surrender. In resigning her maidenhead to him, she had given him an even lovelier gift; her complete trust.

Dimly he was aware that this was not what he had expected of marriage. He had thought to take an experienced woman to wife, not an innocent who had to be cherished and protected. Even when he had decided to take Meg, he had thought it would be a relatively simple matter. Bed her with the consideration due to her virginity, teach her to enjoy her marital duties and get on with his hedonistic life while granting her every possible indulgence.

He had not expected to take her in a burning of passion such as he had never experienced. A passion that left him dazed and confused with the knowledge that he wanted her more than he had ever wanted any woman. That possessing her had only increased his desire tenfold. Certainly he had not wanted to feel this shattering urge to protect and defend his wife. He had certainly not wanted to find himself caring about her any more than any other woman he had enjoyed in the course of a long and misspent career. Jack Hamilton's words came back hauntingly: *You'll think I've run mad...find a girl you can care for...* And he had laughed, told Jack he had slipped his moorings. Had thought the notion of risking the same grief his father had suffered to be rank insanity. And yet, here he was with Meg in his arms, rapidly finding her way into his barricaded and cynical heart. His blood ran cold as he recalled the chilly bargain he had struck with her. In return for his name and protection, he had asked for children and her discretion. Nothing more. And she had accepted him on those terms. He had not the slightest right to ask for anything else. He was by no means even sure that he wanted more, never had he felt so completely out of control in his life and the sensation was not at all an agreeable one, like a ship adrift in a storm. No, the best thing Lord Rutherford could do would be to return to London and try to get on with his life while allowing Meg to discover hers.

Chapter Seven

It took them another two days' travelling to reach London. By himself Marcus would have covered it easily in a day's driving, but the chaise was far slower. Besides which Meg slept well into the morning after their wedding night, not stirring even when Marcus left her bed to go down to breakfast. She was still sleeping when he came back after arranging a basket of food with the landlord.

It was another glorious day and he thought that a picnic somewhere for lunch would be pleasant. He was tolerably certain that Meg would feel happier if she did not have to deal with the world at large just yet. It was with relief that he learned Winterbourne had left very early. He was not entirely sure that he would have had the self-control to leave the cur with a whole skin and he certainly did not wish Meg to encounter him.

They set forward just after eleven with Meg perched up beside him in the curricle. She had been very quiet since arising and seemed very shy with him. Hardly surprising, he thought with tender amusement. She was not a chatterbox at the best of times, and with Burnet up behind them there was little opportunity for any private conversation.

Meg having breakfasted late, they did not halt for their picnic until well after two, driving down a lane between high hedges and spreading a rug under a beech tree. Burnet, who had hitherto maintained a proper distance, proved to be a very agreeable companion. He had been with Marcus for years and took the opportunity to make a speech and wish the bride happy, toasting her heroically with lemonade.

'Here's a health to a bonny bride, my lady! An' wishin' you very happy!' he finished cheerfully, raising his glass to her.

Meg blushed and stammered her thanks shyly. She had thought that Marc's servants might look down their noses at her, but the genuine goodwill in Burnet's face told her she had at least one friend.

Marcus clapped lazily and said with mock severity, 'I thank you, Burnet, for your approval. But do tell me! Do I not rank as worthy of your wishes for future happiness?'

Burnet grinned at him unrepentantly. 'As to that, sir, if you ain't happy now, you never will be! I'm happy to congratulate you howsumdever on gettin' a damned sight more than you deserve! Beggin' her ladyship's pardon!'

Marcus chuckled and said, 'Well, I'm glad you only speak your mind with such beautiful frankness out of hearing of the rest of my staff! Thank you, Burnet.'

He turned, to Meg who was giggling. His heart skyrocketed in his breast to see the laughter in her eyes again. She had been so quiet and reserved during their drive that he had been quite worried. 'This is the sort of insubordination I have to put up with, Lady

Rutherford! I am counting upon you to reform my un-regenerate staff out of all recognition!'

After lunch Meg found that she was very sleepy and it did not take much persuasion to convince her to travel in the chaise. In fact, Marcus insisted.

'You may curl up on the seat and have a nap. We have another three hours before reaching our night's lodging,' he said firmly.

'But—'

He fixed her with a glare of mock severity and said, 'I have a distinct memory of you vowing to obey me yesterday morning! I'm trying to do my bit in cherishing you!' Then, very tenderly, 'Come, Meg. You will feel very much more the thing if you sleep in the chaise.'

His care for her was disconcerting and she raised her eyes shyly to his face. 'You know I am not really such a poor creature as you think, but if it will please you...'

'It won't,' he said frankly. 'I like having your company, but I will forgo it this afternoon if it means I may enjoy it tonight.' His eyes quizzed her wickedly and he touched her suddenly flaming cheek lightly, lingering at the corner of her mouth in sensuous reminiscence. Meg swallowed hard as the caress sent shivers down her spine. Perhaps it would be an idea to sit in the chaise. Even if she didn't sleep she needed to think, and sitting in the curricle with Marc's powerful body beside her seemed to disrupt her thought processes completely.

Having won his point, Marcus escorted her to the chaise and handed her up into it. She turned to smile at him, that shy, considering smile which turned his stomach upside down and made him want to kiss her senseless. He reached up and slid his fingers into the soft curls at her nape, stroking lightly and drawing her face down to him in a brief kiss.

'Until tonight, little one,' he whispered, his husky tones full of tantalising promise.

Meg sat back in the chaise, trying to collect her whirling thoughts and even more chaotic emotions. She had known from the start the danger of marriage to Marcus. Despite his occasional coldness, he had a charm and kindness that made it impossible not to respond to him. But she had not expected to succumb to it so swiftly, so completely.

It was not just his lovemaking. It was his tenderness with her, his compassionate understanding. Had he not taken her last night, she would have still loved him. The problem she now faced was that their physical intimacy would make it much harder for her to hide how she felt. And he did not want her love, had no intention of loving her. He had made that quite clear. They were not to make demands upon each other's sensibilities. And she had already made enough demands upon him. From now on she would have to try and stand alone.

Indeed, she was a great deal better off than she had been. She had a kind husband, a position in the world and a home. God willing she would have children on whom to spend her love. A tremor ran through her as she thought of how she would be given those children. She should be counting her blessings, not feeling depressed because one thing would be forever denied her! She had known the danger and had accepted it. It was just that in her inexperience she had not realised how much it would hurt.

And he must never know. Somehow she had to keep her guard up at all times to hide her secret. Perhaps leading a life of fashion would make it possible to conceal her love. She had heard much of how fashionable couples lived largely separate lives: attending their own functions, entertaining their own friends, taking lovers. She shuddered at the last. Never would she be able to bring herself to accept another. And it would hurt immeasurably to know that Marcus had a mistress.

A tear trickled down her cheek. She had agreed to it and she would have to pretend not to mind, not even to see. She would have to live the life he expected her to live. Perhaps when the children came she could be in the country for much of the year and not know what he was doing. Somehow the thought was not at all comforting.

Tired out and lulled by the rocking of the chaise, she lay down on the seat as Marcus had suggested and pulled the travelling rug over her. Perhaps she ought to sleep now. The last thing she wanted was for Marcus to decide she was too tired to share his bed.

That night, as she lay exhausted in his embrace, she wondered if she would need to have a rest every afternoon. It had not hurt at all this time. He had entered her with such gentle patience, urging her to stop him if she felt any pain. But all she had felt was wild excitement as his powerful body invaded hers and possessed it so tenderly, an excitement which had swelled and finally exploded in response to his loving. And this time he had encouraged her to join in, showing her how to please him, his delight in her pleasure and growing confidence reassuring her that in Marc she had the best of husbands.

Her body glowed with the aftermath of passion and, as she drifted towards sleep, she could feel his large, exquisitely knowing hands soothing and stroking her.

One muscular leg was thrust between her thighs in possessive intimacy. His deep voice murmured soft endearments as she pressed sleepy kisses against his
shoulder, thinking that even if he didn't love her, at
least he seemed to care about her. Half a loaf was better
than none, after all. Wasn't it?

Chapter Eight

The following afternoon the Countess of Rutherford preserved a friendly smile, as one stiffly polite servant after another was presented to her in the great hall of Rutherford House, an imposing mansion in Grosvenor Square. By the time the maidservants had been presented in a group she was wilting mentally under the glare of the staff's unspoken disapproval.

As she recalled her husband's laughing suggestion that she should reform his staff, she shuddered inwardly. It was plain enough that they held their master in the greatest awe and affection while respectfully opining that, in marrying a provincial nobody with a family history like hers, the master had taken leave of his senses. She stole a scared look up at Marcus, who looked quite unperturbed. His aristocratic countenance gave no hint that he was aware of the unmistakable outrage among his staff.

Once the ordeal was over Marcus escorted her to her bedchamber and said, 'Here you are. This was my mother's room. Why don't you have a rest before changing for dinner? I am going to go around to Mount

Street to let my sister know that we are in town. I will ask her to call on you in the morning if you wish.'

'You don't wish me to come now?' Meg asked hesitantly.

He shook his head. 'No, it is for Di to call on you.' She flushed slightly and he added reassuringly, 'Meg, I am not ashamed of you. But I think under the circumstances it might be as well if I saw Di first. Come…' he held out his arms '…give me a kiss and I will be off.'

Meg went to him, trying to hide her eagerness. Their lips met and clung briefly and then Marcus was gone, leaving Meg feeling utterly lost and quite unlike sleeping. She was so stunned by the elegance of her surroundings that her tiredness had vanished to be replaced with an overwhelming urge to explore.

She looked around her with wide eyes. Never in all her life had she seen such a sumptuous bedchamber. The wall hangings were of a delicate violet silk with a printed black border and buff silk pelmet. A very graceful chimney piece in white marble held a number of beautiful and obviously valuable examples of oriental porcelain as well as an ornate clock, with an elaborate gilt mirror surmounting all.

The bed was such a contrast to the old-fashioned and clumsy four poster she had been used to that Meg could hardly believe this fairytale confection was to be used by a mortal woman. Black with gilt mounts, it had a domed canopy, the deeply fringed, white-muslin drapes spangled with gold stars and seemingly suspended from a gilt Cupid.

Meg blinked. Was it possible one was actually meant to *sleep* in this creation? She could not, for the life of her, imagine unsophisticated Meg Fellowes doing anything of the sort! With a blush she realised that she was having no difficulty at all imagining the other sorts of things the new Countess of Rutherford might be called upon to do in this bed.

Hurriedly she fixed her attention on the rest of the furnishings. A very charming inlaid fold-over tea table stood behind a gilt sofa, and matching chairs upholstered in the same hue as the wall hangings stood grouped before the fireplace. A dainty dressing table and stool completed the furnishings. Several candelabra were scattered about, presently empty. No doubt the servants would bring the candles in later. Meg did not for one moment, in the face of all this luxury, entertain the least doubt that they would be wax, rather than the tallow to which she had hitherto been accustomed.

A respectful tap at the door distracted her from a delightful daydream in which her late and unlamented guardian totted up the bill for all this feminine froth and suffered a very gratifying seizure in the process.

'Come in,' called Meg, trying not to giggle.

A maidservant entered and said, 'If you please, m' lady, your luggage is being brought up and I am here to unpack for you.'

'Oh, how very kind, thank you so much,' said Meg with a friendly smile which was received with patent surprise by the maid. Oh, dear, thought Meg. Should I not thank her? But how rude not to, even if she is a servant. I always thanked Agnes.

The mention of unpacking made her look around for somewhere to put the unpacked gowns. A puzzled frown creased her brow as no closets or armoires met her eyes.

Before she could stop herself she asked, 'But

where…?' And then blushed with mortification as the maid silently pointed to another door.

'Oh, th…thank you,' said Lady Rutherford, feeling more and more like ignorant, countrified Meg Fellowes. A dressing room! How many more gaffes was she destined to make? Would they be talked over and sneered at in the servants' hall?

It was at this point that the previously suspicious maid realised that her new mistress was not a scheming hussy at all but, on the contrary, a young lady in a very unfamiliar and daunting situation. Without wishing to compare herself with her betters, Lucy Brown was put forcibly in mind of her first meal in the servants' hall when she had accidentally sat in the seat reserved for the head housemaid and had found herself sent to Coventry for the entire repast in consequence of this appalling solecism.

'Never you mind, m' lady,' said Lucy cheerfully. 'I dare say things is different in Yorkshire.'

'Just…just a little,' said Meg with relief at this sudden change. 'Are there any more little surprises for me?'

'Bathroom's through that other door,' offered Lucy. 'And his lordship's room beyond it.'

Meg stared at her. She shared a *bathroom* with her husband? A *bathroom*? The very idea was completely and utterly scandalous. And terribly intriguing. Had not Marcus said that this had been his mother's room? Meg was beginning to get some very interesting insights into her deceased mother-in-law.

Unable to resist, she went over to the door indicated and opened it.

And could not repress a startled squeak of shock.

A vision of subtle eggshell blue, laced with tastefully gilded mouldings, greeted her stunned gaze, hexagonal in shape with another door directly opposite hers, leading, she presumed, to her husband's bedchamber. Benches covered in more fringed white muslin stood in four niches. One side of the hexagon was taken up with a large window draped with some gauzy white material, which softened rather than blocked the light. A large alcove opposite the window was entirely taken up with an extremely elegant, canopied sofa-bed, hung with ivory silk and upholstered in silk damask the same shade as the walls. It seemed an odd item of furniture to have in a bathroom, but the bath itself was far too interesting to waste time worrying about details like that.

It was a very large, circular bath, sunk into the centre of the cream-tiled floor. In fact, it was so large that Meg had no difficulty believing that it would hold two quite easily. She cast another lingering look at that sofa-bed…and hastily returned her attention to the bath. Six small bronze lions' heads were set around it at intervals, their mouths wide open. Goodness! Did the water come out of them? How very ingenious! A lever at the side of the chamber caught her eye. She bent down to try it and sure enough water came pouring out. Meg took a deep breath as she considered the possibilities of such a bath…and the sofa-bed…

Blushing furiously at the scene her rioting imagination had conjured up, Meg turned to the decoration of the niches. Classical scenes adorned them, which seemed innocent enough until she looked more closely. The pointed oval-and-cameo decoration of the pilasters comprised dancing nymphs and satyrs, while the large central panels held scenes which even the innocent Meg recognised as well-known classical seductions.

In scarlet-cheeked fascination she examined them one

by one: Danaë and the shower of gold, Leda and the Swan, Persephone being swept up into Hades's dread chariot and, finally, Europa and the Bull. Had this room really been decorated for Marcus's mama? And did Marcus expect her to use it? Did he use it? The possibilities made her feel distinctly wobbly at the knees.

A discreet cough behind her recalled her scattered wits. She turned to see her maid with an unnaturally straight face in the doorway.

'Shall I unpack, my lady? Your luggage has been brought up.'

'What? Oh. Oh, yes. Thank you…?' She ended on a faintly questioning note.

'Lucy,' supplied the maid.

'Lucy,' repeated Meg to impress the name on her memory. 'Yes. Unpacking. A very good idea.' She marched straight back through to her dressing room, leaving that scandalous bathroom behind her. Unfortunately the equally scandalous images it had conjured up refused to remain behind, following her into the bedroom where they intruded on her thoughts with unflagging enthusiasm while she assisted Lucy to put her clothes away. Her precious tea caddy was unearthed from one trunk and Meg placed it proudly on the tea table, where she could see it from the bed. Her hands caressed it lovingly. Her first present.

By the time they were finished it was well after five. Dinner, Lucy informed her, had been ordered for half-past seven. If my lady wanted a nap she had best have it now, since she would need to dress for dinner and leave enough time to put her hair up.

Lucy explained this very tactfully, adding, 'I will come back in an hour to wake you and help you, m' lady. Mrs Crouch, the housekeeper, said as I'm to wait on you until you get a proper dresser, like all the fine ladies have.'

'Thank you,' said Meg, acquiescing in the first part of this suggestion. She was not so sure about a proper dresser. She had better ask Marcus, but personally she would far prefer the simple, kindly Lucy to wait on her, rather than a grand dresser who would probably compare her unfavourably with previous employers. Meg was reasonably sure that, despite her unexpected elevation, she could remember how to look after herself.

Yawning, she permitted Lucy to help her off with her carriage dress and snuggled down in her fantastical bed, which added extreme comfort to its aesthetic charms, in her petticoat and chemise. Silk sheets and pillow slips! Goodness! Meg wriggled against them in voluptuous pleasure as Lucy drew the gorgeously draped ivory-brocade curtains. Within minutes she was fast asleep and dreaming.

In the meantime her husband had called upon his sister and was listening patiently to a blistering condemnation of his intelligence, morals and manners.

She received Marcus in her drawing room and, once her unconvincingly disinterested butler had closed the door, glared at Marcus and asked furiously, 'What the *devil* did you mean by sending me that letter, telling me to insert the announcement of your marriage to Miss Marguerite Fellowes in yesterday's papers? Do you have any idea of the scandal broth you have whipped up? Do you have any idea of the number of people who have taken such sympathetic pleasure in condoling with me on the tragic *mésalliance* my only brother has made?

'You *idiot*, Marc! Do you realise what people are saying? That Robert and Caroline Fellowes's daughter entrapped you! How did you of all men fall for such a trick? Aunt Regina has retired to Bath in hysterics!'

'Well, thank God for that!' interjected the afflicted lady's undutiful nephew heartlessly. 'One furious female relation is more than enough to deal with at once!'

She swept on, very properly ignoring this facetious remark. 'And if you had any *notion* of the embarrassment I felt in not understanding the *commiserations* I received! It was not until Jack Hamilton enlightened me that I realised who the girl was! And not even to be invited!' She paused for breath and a perfectly genuine tear trickled down her cheek. The last thing she had wanted for Marcus was marriage to some scheming little hussy!

'Tell me, Di,' said Marcus with a faint twinkle that made her itch to slap him, 'how long did it take you to calm down this much?'

She fixed him with a sizzling glare and said dangerously, 'I'm acting, Marc. I haven't calmed down! *You* may choose to think it funny! *I* do not!'

'Very well, Di,' said Marcus ruefully. 'You have made your point. Now, would it be too much to ask you to let me explain? Meg did not entrap me in any way whatsoever. In fact, she did her level best not to accept anything from me, let alone my name! And I'm sorry about the late notice, but the last thing I wanted was Aunt Regina to appear and scare Meg into crying off.'

Di looked up at him sharply. He did not bear any signs of a man forced into an unwanted marriage. On the contrary, he looked quite cheerful and relaxed as he stood twinkling at her. And she could definitely see his point about the redoubtable Lady Grafton, since she had, on hearing the news, shrieked for her travelling chaise, saying that she would send the little hussy about her business in double-quick time. Only the realisation that the wedding would have taken place before she could reach Yorkshire had stopped her. By that stage she had been packed, so, to save face with her agog staff, she had directed her coachman to Bath.

'Very well, tell me the worst,' she said resignedly.

By the time Marcus had told her about how he had discovered Meg, she was beginning to see daylight. Marc and his overdeveloped sense of duty! Meg's flight made her blink. Was the girl mad? The tale of Mrs Garsby's inhumanity shocked her greatly and by then Marc's decision to marry had her full, if reluctant, approval.

'I see,' she said thoughtfully. 'And she accepted.'

Marcus outlined the terms of his marriage much as he had done to Meg and his sister winced inwardly. Good God! What a recipe for disaster! No matter what he might think now, Marc was not the man to acquiesce quietly if his wife took a lover. Just look at all the mistresses he had broken with after they had taken a tumble with Sir Blaise Winterbourne. Although that might simply be because he despised the oily baronet for some reason to which she had never been privy. Nevertheless, Di could not see Marc in the role of complaisant husband.

And what of the child he had married? From the sounds of it she had accepted out of desperation, having nowhere else to turn. What was her attitude towards the marriage? Did she care for Marc at all? Understand what she had let herself in for?

Di's assumption that Marc had been trapped was abandoned. Marc would know if he had been tricked. No fool her cynical, rakish brother. He might have accepted the inevitable, but it would have been with his eyes fully open and he would not have been able to hide it from her. Certainly he would not be here, championing a scheming adventuress.

Looking up at Marcus with a softened face Di said, 'Then I shall call upon your bride tomorrow morning, little brother. Be happy, my dear.'

He returned her smile and said oddly, 'Do you know, I almost think I will be.' He saluted her cheek and took his leave of her.

Di stared at the closed door, her mind full of speculation. Marc, of all men, to wear that dazed, uncertain expression on that hitherto-bored mask he presented to the world at large! Was he finally going to realise that it was not necessarily a death sentence to care for someone?

She went upstairs in a thoughtful mood to dress for dinner. Clasping her sapphires around her neck, she suddenly wondered if Marc was even aware of how different he seemed. She had never heard him speak of anyone with such feeling, never known him to express such anger. Yet he seemed to think he had acted on the promptings of duty and logic. Had he even hoaxed himself with his aloof façade?

Marcus walked home thoughtfully. Di had really taken it very well. He only hoped his formidable Aunt Regina could be won over as easily. He hoped to God she meant to stay in Bath until she had calmed down. Now he would go home and change for dinner. It was after six and he did not care to sit down with his bride for their first formal dinner together looking anything less than immaculate. He hoped that Meg had taken his advice and rested. She had looked tired, poor girl. With a twitch of his lips he wondered just what his innocent

bride had thought of her bedchamber. And their bathroom.

His steps slowed as he remembered the outrageous
woman who had designed that bedchamber and had the
bathroom installed. His heart lurched painfully and he
strode on quickly, as if to leave the hurt behind.

The tapping on her door awoke Meg after what
seemed like five minutes' sleep in her cosy, silken nest.
She yawned and stretched, then tweaked the curtains
aside to look at the clock. Half-past six! Already!

'Come in,' she called.

Lucy bustled in with a large jug of water and said, 'I
brought some warm water for you to wash with, m'lady.
Unless you'd like a bath drawn? I've had the water
heater lit so…'

Meg thought about that. It was tempting, but if dinner
was in an hour she would have to rush and she had an
uncharacteristically hedonistic desire to positively wal-
low in the steamy luxury of that bath. No, she would
have a bath before retiring for the night. Then she could
take her time.

She shook her head. 'I shall take a bath before going
to bed.'

'Yes, m'lady. Now, which dress will your ladyship
wear?'

Which dress indeed? Never before had Meg concerned herself in the slightest about her clothes since
they were all equally dowdy. Except, of course, in wishing they were not so dowdy. Now she had a wardrobe
in the first style of elegance and she had no idea what
to wear. For the last two nights she and Marcus had not
bothered to change for dinner since they were travelling.
Now she would sit down to dinner for the first time in

her new home and she wanted Marcus to be proud of her.

She went through to the dressing room and looked at the three gowns which Madame Heloise had designated for evening wear. There was really no question. A gown of shimmering blue silk with an embroidered bodice, to be worn over an underdress of ivory satin, simply begged to be chosen. The colour very closely approximated the wall hangings of her bedchamber.

'This one,' said Meg firmly.

Lucy took the gown reverently, saying, 'Oh, it's *lovely*! It will make your eyes look so blue, m'lady!' She carried it into the bedchamber, laid it on the bed and turned to her mistress.

Lady Rutherford took a deep breath and steeled herself to being waited on hand and foot.

Floating down the stairs fifty minutes later, she thought to herself that she could get used to it very easily. It was not that she had permitted Lucy to attend her like a Roman bath slave, but that it was very pleasant to have someone to make suggestions, pass things to her that she didn't even know were there…like that violet-scented soap Lucy had found. And it was lovely to have someone tell her how nice she looked! Not that she really believed it. The gown was lovely and having her hair swept up into a knot on top of her head with the soft curls falling from it was certainly very pretty, but surely she was still plain Meg Fellowes.

When she reached the hall she hesitated, unsure of where she was meant to be. Before she could panic, however, the stately individual she remembered to be the butler, Delafield, appeared from some fastness and bowed low to her.

'His lordship's compliments, my lady, and he would like you to await him in the library.'

My lady. Meg almost looked around to see if he were speaking to someone else. It didn't seem possible that he could mean her.

'The library?' she faltered.

He inclined his head. 'If your ladyship would follow me.'

He led her to a huge mahogany door which he opened to usher her in, saying, 'His lordship will be down directly. May I pour a glass of ratafia for your ladyship?'

A deep voice came from halfway up the stairs. 'No, you may not, you old villain! You may leave me to pour my lady a glass of Madeira. Ratafia, indeed! I didn't think we had any of the filthy stuff!'

The look of stern disapproval, warring ineffectually with pride, on the old man's face told Meg that Marcus, though he might be a grown man and a belted earl to boot, was still an overgrown schoolboy to Delafield.

The butler's outraged response confirmed it. 'Ratafia, my lord, is a suitable drink for a lady.'

'You go and tell that to my mother's shade,' recommended Marcus disrespectfully.

Delafield's lips twitched but he bowed and said in quelling accents, 'As your lordship pleases.'

Marcus grinned as he reached the bottom of the stairs, and said, 'Give us fifteen minutes, Delafield. I have a present for her ladyship.'

He followed Meg into the room and looked her over admiringly. The gown was cut in the classical high-waisted style, outlining the soft curve of her breasts. Alternately clinging and drifting, the filmy skirts revealed and concealed the lovely, long legs in a way that made his breath tangle in his throat. The narrow cut made them look even longer. The squared neck line with its *rouleau* was quite discreet, but it was shaped to follow the delicate curve of her breasts, coming down very subtly to a point between them, so the veriest suspicion of voluptuous cleavage was displayed. Tiny puffed sleeves left the graciously rounded, creamy arms bare. And her hairstyle accentuated the graceful line of her ivory throat.

That was quite enough, thought Marcus dizzily. Anything more and he'd be gibbering like a moonstruck halfling! As it was, all he could think of was how those arms had wrapped themselves about him, how he had pressed kisses on that lovely throat, feeling her soft moans vibrate under his lips. He had had some odd idea that the innocently sensuous siren who had shared his bed for the last two nights would be somehow invisible to the rest of the world. That no one else would see what he had seen in Meg. In the face of this celestial vision, shimmering before him in blue silk, he rapidly revised his opinion.

Dowdy little Meg had blossomed into a swan. Admittedly she had looked far more presentable in her elegant carriage dress the last three days and quite lovely in her wedding dress, but this! Any man who couldn't see what he saw was blind. Abruptly he turned away to a console table to pour her a glass of wine.

Meg watched him nervously. Something was wrong. He was staring at her as though he had been struck dumb. Was the gown ill fitting? Ugly? Was she wearing it back to front? Or was it her hair? That was it! She wished she had not let Lucy persuade her into this mode. She felt so dreadfully exposed…but wait, he was saying something.

He turned back to her and handed her the Madeira.

'Your health, my lady. You…you look quite…lovely my dear.' He had to clear his throat twice to complete the sentence. What an inadequate remark, he thought ruefully. It was the understatement of the century. And the sudden glowing look in her eyes was doing impossible and dreadful things to his heart and stomach. The two organs seemed to have got themselves inextricably confused. He had never in his life felt so wildly, gloriously out of control.

Desperately he reached for his usual sangfroid and said, with a tolerable assumption of calm, 'Yes, that gown suits you.' He told himself he was relieved to see the glow of joy fade very slightly. He did not want to feel like this! It was dangerous for both of them. They had made a bargain about how they should chart their course through marriage. He must not tip the delicate balance, not if he wanted his marriage to fulfil his expectations.

'Th…thank you, my lord,' said Meg in a low voice.

Marcus frowned slightly. He had not meant to be *that* forbidding; still, perhaps it was as well. The difficulty of maintaining the sort of relationship he had intended would be doubled if she were to look at him like that too often. Better if he saved his compliments and tenderness for the bedchamber. There at least he could be himself with her. She was too sweet and yielding in his arms, had trusted him too unreservedly, for anything else to be possible.

Belatedly he remembered that he had a present for her. 'I have a gift for you my lady,' he said politely, reinforcing her sudden formality. He walked over to the small Pembroke table which stood behind the sofa and opened the drawer, taking out a long, flat, wooden box. He turned to her and beckoned.

Shyly she went to him, wondering what he had for her. Not another tea caddy, obviously.

Then she gasped as he opened the box and drew out a long rope of shimmering pearls. She stood transfixed as he clasped them around her throat. Surely he could not mean such an expensive gift for her! It was unthinkable!

It was even more unthinkable when a moment later, after viewing with satisfaction the effect of the pearls against the blue silk, he reached into the box again and produced a pair of earrings which he screwed into her ears with surprising assurance. Another dip into the box and he was clasping a bracelet about her wrist.

'My...my lord, you cannot give me these...I...' Meg was overwhelmed. She stared at the glimmering pearls on her breasts and at her wrist.

'Why not?' he asked in surprise. 'They are always given to the brides in my family. Have been for three generations. You are the fourth countess to wear them.'

'Oh.' Meg looked up at him apologetically. 'I beg your pardon. I...I didn't understand.' She had thought he was giving them to her for her very own, and the thought was terrifying. But he was bowing to tradition, wished his bride to present a creditable appearance, no doubt. They were to adorn his bride; not a present for Meg. She stifled the longing for something of her own, not jewellery, just...something...something from Marc, rather than the Earl of Rutherford, as the tea caddy had been.

He was frowning again. Why the hell should she mind being given jewellery? She hadn't been wearing any, except her wedding ring, of course, and he'd wager if she had any it would not be the sort of jewellery that Lady Rutherford should wear. Mere trumpery, no doubt! And in his experience no woman ever minded being given jewellery. Most of 'em had any number of hoaxing ways to cajole a new jewel out of a man.

He acquitted his bride of hoaxing ways, but he did wish she looked a little more enthusiastic at the priceless articles with which he had just adorned her. Could she not see how well they looked on her? On reflection he realised that she probably couldn't.

'Come with me,' he said firmly and, gripping her shoulders, practically frogmarched her towards a console table over which hung an elderly looking-glass with a battered gilt frame.

'Now, look at yourself.'

Marcus discovered that, unlike the basilisk, Meg's wide-eyed stare did not lose a jot of its heart-stopping power in the glass. Rather it seemed to double because he was seeing her startled reaction to herself. And then he could see the disbelief on her face, the look of puzzled confusion.

'That's not me...is it?' She glanced up to meet his eyes in the mirror. He could barely hear her next words, so softly were they uttered. 'That's Lady Rutherford.'

He stared down at her sharply. 'I beg your pardon, Meg?'

An odd little tremor ran through her. 'Nothing. I...nothing.' She sounded oddly dazed, as though the mirror had shown her a stranger. 'Thank you, Marcus.' Hesitantly her hand lifted to touch the necklace briefly. 'They are beautiful.'

For the first time, as he gazed at the reflected vision of his bride adorned in the family jewels, Marcus understood why pearls were considered so suitable for a young girl or bride. Their chaste beauty was the perfect foil for Meg's unselfconscious loveliness. He had seen these jewels countless times before, since his mother had loved the set, but never had they looked more right than they did at this moment.

Forgetting his resolve to keep tenderness strictly for the bedchamber, he gave her shoulders a gentle squeeze and pressed a kiss below her ear. 'You look beautiful, my sweet. And you make the pearls look beautiful.' He felt the tumultuous pulse in her neck and released her with difficulty.

'Drink up, Meg,' he said, moving away from her. 'Dinner will be served shortly.' For God's sake! Could he not keep his hands off her for five minutes? Tonight at least he should leave her to sleep undisturbed. She could have no fears in his...their...house. He was within call if she needed to find him in the night. Theirs was to be a marriage of convenience. As such it was ridiculous to expect her to share his bed every night.

Meg sipped her Madeira and found to her surprise that she liked it. She smiled at Marcus over the glass and said, 'It's lovely, thank you. And thank you for the pearls. I have never worn jewellery at all, so...' She stopped, embarrassed. It would never do for him to think she was begging for more.

He shrugged. 'There is quite a collection of family jewellery. I selected the pearls because I thought they were bound to go with whatever you chose to wear tonight. The rest all needs cleaning, it hasn't been worn in years.'

Not since his mother had died, in fact. He flinched inwardly as he thought of the lovely, laughing creature who had gone from his life so unexpectedly... He tried not to think of her too often, but seeing Meg decked in those pearls, thinking of her sleeping in that silken apartment, bathing in that outrageous bathroom...

suddenly his mother's piquant, laughing face was before him and would not be banished. What would she have thought of her daughter-in-law? Another question struck at him brutally: What would she have thought of her son?

Not for several minutes did Marcus become aware that Meg had set down her empty glass and stepped away from him to the fireplace, where she was examining the painting of Alston Court, his principal country residence, that hung above it. He flushed slightly. How very rude of him to just ignore her like that so that she felt obliged to occupy herself! And if she had finished her wine, he must have been in a brown study for some time.

Before he could apologise the door opened and Delafield announced, 'Dinner is served, my lord and lady.'

Dinner, as Meg found, was a very formal and nerve-racking affair. Marcus described it as a neat, plain dinner, but Meg could think of no two adjectives more completely inappropriate for a meal that consisted of two courses of at least half a dozen dishes each. She found it quite bizarre to be seated at the same table as her husband with twenty feet of highly polished mahogany between them and to have a footman at her elbow every time she showed the least interest in one of the dishes before her.

This, however, was what Marcus expected of her, so she assumed an air of enjoyment and bravely lifted her voice in order to be heard when she replied to her husband's polite conversation. She wondered what he would say if she suggested removing some of the leaves from the table when they dined alone. Perhaps it might be better to wait until she was more familiar with the household before embarking upon such radical reform.

Had she but known it, Marcus was not enjoying it in the least. It had always been his custom when dining alone, or with one or two close friends, to have dinner set out on a table in the library where they could serve themselves. He had been quite taken aback when he had realised that his staff had quite different ideas now he had taken a wife. Plainly they were set on doing the thing properly with the maximum of pomp.

It was on the tip of his tongue to inform Delafield that he had no intention of changing his habits just because he had married, when it occurred to him that a seemingly endless expanse of polished mahogany was one way to keep a polite distance from his wife. If they dined intimately tête à tête in the library, it would be very much harder to hold her at arm's length.

So he held his tongue and resigned himself to the tedium of dining formally every night. He supposed ruefully that he could not expect to maintain all his bachelor habits now that he was married. Which reminded him that he had yet to make a decision about Althea Hartleigh.

Thoughtfully he accepted a helping of syllabub as he pondered this ticklish question. Should he maintain the connection or…? A slight movement at the far end of the table caught his eye. Delafield was refilling Meg's glass. She turned to him with a slight smile and soft word of thanks. The pearls at her throat shone softly in the candlelight… He had nearly asked Althea to marry him…how would she have looked in those pearls? With a shock he realised that he could not imagine her in them. He would not have even thought of giving them to her.

Conscious of his gaze, Meg looked up from her syllabub. He was frowning slightly and she lifted her chin proudly. She would not flinch before his glare. If she was doing something wrong then he should not have half a mile of dining table between them, preventing him from tactfully pointing it out to her!

Defiantly she finished her sweet and her wine and watched as the footmen began to remove the dishes from the table. She knew exactly what she had to do and rose from her seat gracefully.

'I shall leave you to the enjoyment of your wine, my lord.'

Her voice rang out clearly, taking Marcus by surprise. He hurried to his feet and went to open the door for her. She looked absolutely lovely, but so reserved, remote.

'Goodnight, my lady,' he said quietly. 'I shall leave you to your rest tonight.' It was said very softly, for her ears only. Her eyes flew to his face. For one split second he thought he saw hurt there, but it was gone instantly.

Her voice, cool and unconcerned, 'You are always considerate, my lord.'

She was gone and Marcus went back to his chair to confront an array of decanters. He stared at them unseeingly. Considerate? *Considerate?* He didn't feel remotely considerate. What he felt like was following her upstairs and showing her just how *in*considerate he could be! He heaved a sigh of resignation. He wanted a cool, uninvolved relationship with his wife. He could hardly complain when she obliged. If she had taken the hint so readily, it would save him having to explain it to her. Somehow he thought the task might have proved difficult.

After leaving the dining room, Meg pondered her options. It was far too early for bed, even if his lordship had dismissed her for the night. She had only just eaten and she didn't feel in the least bit sleepy after her nap. She would go and find a book in the library, retire to her bedchamber and read for a while, then she would have a long, luxurious soak in that bath. She might even read in it. There were all sorts of possibilities that didn't involve her infuriating husband. And why the devil should he get to sit in solitary state over his wine? Why could she not have a glass with him and chat? All these rules and formalities gave her a headache!

She had no difficulty finding a book in the library. There were several shelves devoted to novels and she selected quite a few before turning her attention to the poetry. Here she browsed happily, finding old friends and meeting new ones. Almost the only alleviating feature of her residence at Fenby House had been its library, which she had been permitted to visit weekly to select reading matter. Novels, however, had not previously come in her way and she could hardly wait to get back upstairs and open one.

Marcus spent a solitary and lengthy evening by the fire in the library, attempting to read. Never had his cosy, welcoming library seemed so utterly bereft of comfort, so empty. He wandered along the bookshelves, seeking something more entertaining than Carey's translation of the *Inferno*, noting Meg's depredations as he did so. What had she taken? Mostly poetry, but a few of his mother's novels as well. He smiled. No doubt she would enjoy Hatchard's and Hookham's. He must take her to both... He caught himself up sharply. Meg would be quite capable of finding her own way around...he was not going to sit in her pocket.

He glanced frequently at his watch and eventually, realising that he had not turned a page for the past ten minutes and that it was half-past ten, decided to retire. After all, he had been driving all day. An early night would not hurt him. He thrust away the thought that, despite retiring early for the last two nights, he was a trifle short on sleep.

In his bedchamber he found his nightshirt laid out ready, the bed turned down, everything as it should be. Yet he hesitated. The bed was enormous. A huge, old-fashioned four poster. The Earls of Rutherford had slept in it and bedded their brides in it for generations. No matter what else might be brought up to date and modernised in the London house, the Earl's bed remained, a monument to generations of feudal privilege. Unfortunately it was empty and it looked damned chilly and uninviting. Which was ridiculous, since he knew perfectly well that his valet would have passed a warming pan through it as soon as he knew his master was on his way to bed.

Marcus swore fluently. The only thing that was going to warm that bed to his satisfaction in the foreseeable future was Meg. And the thought infuriated him. He did not wish to be held in thrall by his wife's charms. Surely he could control his desire for at least one night! He had shared her bed for the last *two* nights, for heaven's sake. What more did he want? And she had seemed happy enough with his intimation that he did not wish to avail himself of his…rights—he found the word *rights* rather unpleasant…as though he could take her when and as he pleased without any regard to her wishes. No doubt Winterbourne had thought he had the *right* to force himself on an unknown girl.

He should at least check that she was comfortable

and happy in her room, and know that he was within call. No doubt she was sound asleep by now, but if she wasn't, he could just tell her that...that he was near by, would come if she needed anything.

He pulled on his dressing gown and padded on bare, silent feet to the bathroom door, finding it slightly ajar. He pushed it open and stopped dead, his eyes almost popping out of his head in shock.

It was not dark as he had expected. A brass oil lamp set on a stand cast a golden glow over the chamber, creating mysterious shadows within the sofa-bed and glinting on the gilded mouldings. But that was not all. It shone with a tender radiance on something much softer, something infinitely alluring and utterly desirable...

His bride was lazing in the bath with her back to him, her hair tucked up on top of her head with a tortoiseshell comb, one ivory arm outstretched as she languidly soaped it. Her head was resting on the edge of the bath as she half-sat, half-floated in the water. Her breasts gleamed as the lamplight slid over her wet skin, which shimmered between pink-tinged ivory and gold. Steam drifted upward from the surface of the water, catching the light as it twisted and wreathed in the draught from the door.

Marcus found that he was scarcely breathing and he would not have been at all surprised to find steam escaping from his ears. Never in his entire life had he been confronted by anything so incredibly, so deliciously erotic. He watched in something approaching agony as Meg, all unknowing, soaped her breasts, her stomach and then lifted one slender leg out of the water and casually soaped that.

His mouth was absolutely dry, his tongue practically

cleaving to the roof as his body registered what he was seeing. All his noble and unconvincing waffle about leaving her to sleep peacefully was incinerated in the volcano of desire that erupted inside him.

He licked his lips and, striving to sound matter of fact, said, 'May I join you, Meg?'

She spun around with a shocked exclamation, sending water swirling across the floor. Her dark eyes were wide and the blush on her cheeks did not stop there, he noted with wicked satisfaction.

'J...join me? In the bath, do you mean?' Her voice was a breathless squeak.

'Mmm,' said Marcus with a lazy smile. 'I understand that was what my mother had in mind when she persuaded my father to have it installed...' His smile held her captive as he shrugged off his dressing gown and tossed it on to one of the benches.

Meg could not tear her eyes away as he slowly removed his nightshirt. Even though he had shared her bed for two nights, she still caught her breath at the sight of his magnificent, naked body. It seemed so impossible that such strength could be allied to such gentleness, such tender skill. And his desire was so obvious, so flagrantly and potently obvious! She trembled as he lowered himself into the water beside her. Somehow this was far more frightening than the intimacy of bed. There at least she knew roughly what to expect now!

He was reaching for the soap and sponge. She watched him nervously. Was he just going to wash himself? She relaxed slightly and then gasped as he reached for her, a seductive twinkle in his eyes.

'But I...I washed already...' she faltered as she felt him begin to soap her arm. Surely he wasn't going to...he couldn't be!

'Did you?' he asked politely. 'Are you sure you washed…everywhere?' The sponge slid over her breasts, his fingers teased over the rosy peaks as his free arm slipped around her to draw her closer, silencing her half-hearted murmur of protest with a gentle kiss. Meg shut her eyes and gave herself up to the exquisite sensations he aroused as he washed her with intimate thoroughness. First her breasts, with slow, circling strokes, grazing over the suddenly taut nipples with agonising delicacy, then her shoulders and arms and back across her breasts to the gentle swell of her stomach, sensuous, sweeping motions that left her gasping and dizzy.

She felt him ease her across his lap and lay unresisting in the curve of his arm as he reached down and began to soap her legs. So lightly, so possessively, in some strange way she felt that he was cleansing the last faint traces of Winterbourne's vile touch from her body. Her eyes were closed, her lips slightly parted and she could only marvel at the riot of sensation he was evoking in her body. Her mind had long since ceased to function.

Marcus gazed down at his wife's blissful face resting against his shoulder, the dark, curling lashes lay softly on her cheek and damp curls clung to her brow. He kissed them away. God, she was so lovely! The lamplight gleamed on her soap-slicked body, gilding it rose-gold. He rinsed the soap off and, with a groan of pleasure, lowered his lips to her waiting mouth.

His senses seemed to explode as he tasted her sweetness, felt the soft lips part in willing surrender. He deepened the kiss as he tangled his fingers in the wet curls at the base of her stomach, teasing, probing her melting warmth in possessive intimacy. Her body arched in shuddering response, leaving him in no doubt of her desire.

Controlling his immediate, instinctive response with difficulty, Marcus continued to tantalise and caress until she writhed in his embrace, turning in his arms to cling to him, her body pressed against his in flagrant need. Her small hands moved over his heavily muscled shoulders and back in shy exploration, tangled in his hair as she gave way to the inferno he had ignited within her.

At last he could stand no more. His body, white hot with desire, was screaming for release, to feel her lissom body under his, arching, pleading for his possession. He broke the kiss and stood up, drawing her with him, the water pouring off them as he assisted her from the bath and scooped her up in his arms.

Her mind completely drugged by his mouth and hands, Meg barely registered that her suspicions about the sofa bed had been quite correct as she was laid tenderly on the silken covers. She reached for him with a smile as he lowered himself to her. He hovered over her for a moment and pulled the comb from her curls, releasing them to tumble in chaotic abandon over the bed. And then his mouth was on hers again, fierce and demanding as he pressed her thighs apart and joined them with a single thrust of his powerful body.

His harsh gasps entwined with her soft cries in the tender counterpoint of passion, finally reaching an overwhelming crescendo as they soared together in the ecstasy of their joy.

When Marcus could at last bring himself to draw away from his wife's body, he wrapped her tenderly in a towel and carried her through to his own chamber where his bed awaited them. He had no intention of having to come looking for his bride in the middle of the night. That would be far too revealing.

Chapter Nine

Returning to her own room at an advanced hour of the morning, Meg blushed to find her maid there already. With an inward groan she remembered that she had asked Lucy to come up at nine. In future, she would arrange to ring. To her relief the maid did not appear to notice anything amiss and made no comment about the fact that her mistress was enveloped in nothing but a very masculine, red-silk dressing gown that threatened to trip her up at every step.

'Good morning, m'lady. What are you going to wear this morning?'

Trying to act as though nothing out of the ordinary had occurred, Meg gave a reasonable part of her attention to this important consideration. After all, she was to meet her sister-in-law for the first time and it would not do to look a fright. But as she dressed in a morning gown of soft fawn muslin, her confused thoughts persistently turned to her husband, to his tender, passionate lovemaking which contrasted so oddly with the polite formality he had assumed as soon as she had left his bed half an hour ago.

He had draped his dressing gown around her, inform-

ing her politely that he had business to attend to for the
rest of the day and would see her at dinner. Almost as
an afterthought, as she had been leaving, he had warned
her that his sister, Lady Diana Carlton, would pay her
a morning visit, doubtless to plan her presentation to
society at large. Meg had simply nodded, clutching his
dressing gown around her with trembling fingers.

How in the world, she wondered, could a man be so
cold and formal when twenty minutes earlier he had
been making love to her with a slow, sensuous passion
that had brought tears of joy to her eyes? It seemed that
in bed he was Marc, infinitely loving and tender. Out
of it he was my lord, the Earl of Rutherford, with eyes
like shards of ice.

Perhaps, she thought, as Lucy dressed her hair, this
is what it means to have a marriage of convenience.
Not for the first time she wished she were a little more
experienced, knew what was expected of her. If Marcus
wished to be very formal at all times except in bed,
then she could hardly ask him. It seemed that the protective mask which had sheltered Meg Fellowes from
the world for the last ten years was still needed.

Lucy obligingly conducted her mistress to the drawing room after breakfast, which she seemed to think was
the right place for Lady Rutherford to receive her expected caller. As the very imposing mahogany door
closed behind Meg with a soft *thunk*, she gazed around
the apartment in wide-eyed awe. She had thought the
library very elegantly appointed after the shabby and
comfortless state of Fenby House. Now she realised
that, in comparison to the neo-classical opulence and
grandeur of this salon, the library was a mere private
sitting room, relatively cosy and informal.

Wondering what she was supposed to do while she awaited morning callers, Meg occupied herself by exploring the room. An enormous and very soft carpet cushioned her sandalled feet as she moved about examining things. Gilt chairs, luxuriously upholstered in crimson silk brocade, stood against the wall. None of them looked terribly inviting, but the sofa set at right angles to the fire looked as though it would be reasonably comfortable. An Argand lamp stood on the sofa table behind it, and there were numerous other lamps scattered about on occasional tables.

A rectangular pedestal table with claw feet stood near the window, its crimson drapery matching the upholstery of the chairs and the tasteful swathes of fabric adorning the windows. An empty candle stand stood in one corner.

It was a very polite room, Meg thought as she examined a painting. You could not imagine anyone raising their voice, or feeling upset or indeed feeling anything in here except a respectful admiration for the wealth and taste that had created it. She did not dislike the room, but it was not a room for living in. It was, she realised suddenly, a room in which it would be easy to wear the polite mask of Lady Rutherford, which would have to disguise and protect Meg Fellowes and her foolish heart.

She looked around again. Seen in this new light the room appeared much less daunting. Its splendour was only a stage for her masquerade, a protective colouring like that fawn she had stumbled on once, its dappled coat rendering it practically invisible until she had nearly stepped on it. In this room and others like it she would be safe. No one would try to see behind the mask in these surroundings. No one would even realise that there was anyone there.

Just as she was laughing at herself for these fanciful thoughts, the door opened and a confident, feminine voice said, 'Don't be so idiotish, Delafield! You are not going to announce me to my sister as though I were Royalty! If his lordship has had the unmitigated gall to go out and leave the poor girl to receive me alone, then I'm sure we will manage!'

Meg braced herself for the ordeal and turned to greet her visitor with a polite smile firmly pinned in place.

Her visitor stopped dead inside the door, saying, 'Good heavens! Marc didn't tell me how lovely you are! How very typical!'

Whatever else Meg had expected, she certainly hadn't expected that! She was horrified to feel a wave of crimson wash over her face. How stupidly gauche this elegant creature would think her! And how like Marc she looked!

A friendly chuckle rippled from Lady Diana as she swept forward to enfold Meg in a scented embrace. 'Oh, dear! I am sorry! I didn't mean to put you to the blush literally. Now do come and sit down and we shall ring for Delafield to come back and bring us some wine and cakes! Poor lamb, it will give him something to do!'

Meg allowed herself to be drawn to the sofa and said weakly, 'Won't you sit down, my lady?'

Her sister-in-law shook her head. 'My lady won't. Di will.' She smiled at Meg. 'Don't be formal with me, my dear. Marcus has told me all about it, you know. And while it is not what I would have chosen for him, frankly I am so relieved that he has in the end married a girl of character, rather than the alliance he had in mind, that I vow I could kiss you!' She continued with disarming candour. 'Don't feel that you have committed a social crime in marrying him, my dear! From what he has told me, you will do very well. With Rutherford to protect you, your family scandal does not matter in the least. We have quite enough of our own to cancel yours out.'

'It...it is not a love match, you know,' said Meg shyly. She didn't want this kind new sister-in-law to be under any misconception about the marriage.

'I should be surprised if it were,' said Di gently. 'Marc prefers to hold aloof from caring too much, you know. But he will look after you well, of that you may be sure! Now tell me, where is the wretch?'

She frowned slightly at Meg's explanation and said, 'Men! They're all hopeless, even Marc!'

Then she determinedly led the conversation into happier topics, telling Meg that once the staff got over the shock they would be fine, and if they weren't then they had only to resign. Marcus would never tolerate any slight to his wife, so she had only to carry on as normal.

Hesitantly Meg explained that she was quite unused to any sort of staff. Di listened in disbelief and then gave it as her considered opinion that Samuel Langley had been all about in his head.

'For you may depend upon it, my love, it must have greatly reduced his own comfort and that is something most men will go to any lengths to preserve!'

'Even Marc?' asked Meg with the rare smile that lit up her whole face.

'Especially Marc,' affirmed Di, noting the smile and proceeding to impart a great deal of excellent advice on how to deal with her new status.

'Above all, my dear, don't pretend to be other than what you are!' she said wisely. 'The servants here are all devoted to Marc. Once they see that he is happy with you then they will be your staunchest allies. Why, they even adored our mother and *she* was a Frenchwoman! Papa always said jokingly that it was a mark of the respect in which they held *him* that they accepted her, but I think it had as much to do with herself in the end. And I am sure they will accept you!'

'Oh, I didn't know your mother was French,' said Meg, resolutely ignoring the suggestion that Marc would be happy with her. He had made it quite obvious that while he was happy to enjoy her company and charms in bed, he would pursue his own course independently.

Di chuckled mischievously. 'What did you think of your bedchamber and bathroom? You don't think any self-respecting *Englishwoman* would have installed that shameless bathroom! Maman followed *all* the French fashions and took great delight in scandalising society with them!'

Meg blushed again as she recalled my lord's reaction to finding her in the bath. Had she been shameless in using it? Should she not, in future?

Before she could stop herself she asked, 'Should I...?'

'Yes,' said Di firmly. 'As often as you like! London has long since recovered from the scandal of Lady Rutherford's shocking bathroom.' It would do Marc good, she thought, to find Meg in there. Shake him up a bit. God knows he needed it!

Having set Meg's mind at rest, she outlined her plans for Meg's social life. She would hold a select assembly next week to launch her. Rather late notice, but people would come, never doubt it. Marc had a box at the opera, Lady Rutherford must be seen there. Marc would make up a party. Almack's, of course: she had already secured a promise of vouchers from Sally Jersey, who had a soft spot for Marc. He would escort her there, the first time at least. After that she could choose to attend under the escort of any number of unexceptionable, single men.

It all sounded quite dazzling to Meg. The only aspect which concerned her was Di's unquestioning assumption that Marc would be willing to have so many demands made on his time. She did not doubt he would do it, but she did not think he would like it and she had no wish to tease him.

Very hesitantly she explained to Di that she did not think Marc would wish to do all this.

'Why in heaven's name not?' asked Di.

'We...we promised not to interfere with each other,' said Meg, awkwardly. 'He only married me for an heir and because he...he had to.' She met Di's searching gaze proudly. 'So we are agreed to lead our own lives, not to tease each other.'

'Marc,' said Lady Diana Carlton, ominously, 'will do his duty to *my* satisfaction and that is all there is to it. Don't you worry, Meg. I'll deal with my little brother!' She snorted indignantly.

After promising to return to take Meg up for a drive in the Park at the fashionable hour of five, Lady Di took her leave, perfectly satisfied with her brother's wife. The child was quite lovely, she thought approvingly. Rather shy, but that would do her no harm—quite the opposite. She was not at all farouche; on the contrary, she had a certain dignity.

It would do very well. Unless Marc were more inhuman than she would credit, he would at least have to become fond of the child. And that would be a great

deal better for him than the marriage he had been contemplating, which was exactly the sort of thing he had
been so cynical about for years. Di didn't pretend to
understand the logic behind her brother's conviction
that he would only be married for his money and therefore might as well go into it with his eyes open.

All she knew was that, in marrying Meg Fellowes,
he taken on quite a different sort of relationship. She
wondered if he were entirely aware of just what he had
done. Meg was not the sort of girl to embark lightly on
anything, let alone marriage. Di had known perfectly
well that Marc had been prepared to offer his wife a
carte blanche to take lovers as long as she were discreet. And Meg had married him on those terms. Did
he expect her to take him up on it? And how would he
react if he thought she was doing so?

Di was willing to wager that her cynical brother
would be quite surprised by his own jealousy if his
bride so much as glanced aside at another man. She
would wait with interest to see what Jack Hamilton
made of the situation. Perhaps he would join them in
the park this afternoon. She must send a note around to
his lodgings.

Dressed in a modish, Turkey-red walking dress, Lady
Rutherford was handed up into Lady Diana Carlton's
glossy barouche that afternoon with an air of confidence
that she was far from feeling. The thought of braving
London society terrified her but it would never do for
anyone to know that. Not even Di, who was being so
kind. And it would certainly never do for Marc to think
she could not bear her part in his world.

Besides, she was damned if she'd sit around the
house all day doing nothing, hoping against hope that

his lordship would come home early and be a little less chilly. No, she would go out and enjoy herself and find out from Di exactly how she was meant to entertain herself in London. And if Marc did happen to come home before dinner then it would do him good to hear that his bride was out making her own way in the world.

Accordingly, when Marcus came home fifteen minutes after her departure, with a small box nestling in his waistcoat pocket and a feeling that he had been rather cowardly niggling in his conscience, he was greeted with the intelligence that Lady Rutherford had just gone for an airing in the park.

Marcus paled slightly. Meg? Alone in the park? At this hour? Dear God! He should have warned her! If anyone realised who she was...that he had not bothered to escort her on her first appearance! Without waiting to be told that his bride had gone in the unexceptionable company of Lady Di, he turned on his heel and strode out the door, fully intent on showing his world that Lord Rutherford was more than happy with his bride.

Rather to her surprise, Meg did not have to exert herself to enjoy the outing. People were actually very kind. It seemed Lady Di knew everyone, and the high-stepping bays which drew the carriage became quite fidgety at being halted so often in response to greetings and demands to be presented to Rutherford's bride.

Lady Jersey and her friend and fellow patroness of Almack's, Lady Sefton, both promised vouchers independently of each other. If Lady Gwdyr was cold and haughty that was nothing at all to tease oneself about, Lady Di assured Meg. She was always thus! Even when she had merely been Mrs Drummond Burrell! And so it went until Meg's head was in a whirl and she could scarcely remember the names of all the grand people who had been presented to her.

Lady Di, it appeared, was looking for someone in particular. She muttered to herself, 'Now where is the wretch? Not like him to fail…ah!' With an exclamation of satisfaction she indicated a tall, dark-haired gentleman on a dapple-grey horse approaching the carriage. Meg's heart plummeted straight into her kid boots. For one joyous moment she had thought Diana had seen Marc approaching. Sternly she told herself not to be such a sentimental little pea goose.

'Jack Hamilton,' said Lady Di. 'He is one of the Leicestershire Hamiltons, their head actually, and Marc's closest friend. We have known him for ever.'

The tall man brought his horse up beside the carriage and said easily, 'Hullo, Di. Thanks for your note. I'm honoured. Not but what I have observed that most of the world has been before me.'

Lady Di chuckled. 'Sad, isn't it? Here's poor Meg, fresh from Yorkshire and the ordeal of marrying Marc; and all people can do is come and stare at her as though she were a rare beast at the Royal Exchange!' She turned to Meg and said, 'You must allow me to present Jack Hamilton, my dear.'

'I am happy to make Mr Hamilton's acquaintance,' said Meg with a shy smile. She held her hand up to him and he leant down from his horse to clasp it warmly.

'Lady Rutherford, the pleasure is mine, I assure you,' he said with obvious sincerity.

Lady Di opened her mouth to deprecate this formality between two who were bound to become good friends, but shut it again as she caught a warning look from Jack. Instead she turned to Lady Wragby, who was riding on the other side of the barouche, and left Jack and Meg to further their acquaintance.

Jack was in no hurry to rush his friend's bride into familiarity. He had seen the unmistakable reserve in her eyes. She was not a girl to be rushed into anything, this one. Had Marc had the brains to see that? She was not at all what he had expected. Di's hurried note to say that it was all for the best and Marc's appalling *mésalliance* a godsend, had not prepared him for this. He was not quite sure what he had expected, but it had not been this vision of shy, dignified loveliness.

Accordingly he confined his conversation to topics of general interest, and, finding that she had an ardent desire to visit Hatchard's as soon as possible, promptly offered to escort her there as soon as she liked. 'Tomorrow, if you care for it, Lady Rutherford. Just name the day.'

She blinked up at him. 'But won't you find it rather dull? I can very easily go with my maid, you know.'

Hamilton gave her to understand that he had never been dealt such a setdown. Her maid preferred as escort!

'I didn't mean that!' said Meg indignantly. 'You know I didn't!'

Jack laughed. 'I assure you, I am too well known at Hatchard's myself for my going in there to occasion the least remark. And who knows? If I take them a new and wealthy customer, they may even give me a handsome reduction!'

'What's that?' asked Lady Diana, turning to them after promising Lady Wragby a card for her forthcoming assembly and accepting in turn a vicarious invitation for Meg to attend a ball. 'Hatchard's? Are you going to take her there, Jack? How thoroughly typical of you. I vow if you ever fall in love, it will be with a girl who can help you catalogue that overstocked library of yours! Oh!' She broke off with an exclamation of annoyance. 'Would you look at that? How odiously provoking!'

Marcus had looked in vain for Meg at first. The park was crowded and people kept on coming up to him with words of congratulations and sly comments about keeping his intentions very *sub rosa*. He fended off his well-wishers with practised ease, but they delayed him and it was hard to keep an eye on all the strolling ladies while still being polite.

It was not until he met Maria Sefton, who told him that she had just had the honour of being presented to his bride by Lady Diana, that he realised his mistake. What the devil was he about, charging into Hyde Park for all the world like Perseus rescuing Andromeda, when the wretched chit was apparently sitting up in Di's barouche being presented to the world? He'd been imagining her bogged in all sorts of social quagmires requiring his protection, and it was no such thing.

With a polite murmur of an urgent appointment, Lord Rutherford bade Lady Sefton farewell and turned for home. Far too late.

A delicate hand was laid on his sleeve and an arch voice said, 'Is this the future you mentioned, my lord?' Wincing inwardly, he turned to confront Althea Hartleigh's peridot-green eyes, which held his in mocking challenge.

'Good afternoon, Althea,' he said politely.

'Is it?' she responded. 'I understood, my lord, that we were to discuss the future when you returned to town. No doubt we can still do so?' There was the very faintest of questions in her light voice.

Marcus's lips firmed in a hard line. Not at Lady Hartleigh's shameless advance to a newly married man, but at the shocking realisation that he had not the least inclination to avail himself of her offer. Plainly she was willing to swallow his marriage with a good grace, equally plainly she assumed that he wished to continue their connection as though nothing had changed. A week ago he would have said she was perfectly right.

Little though he might relish the thought, things had changed, himself not least of them. It was not merely that he felt it would be insulting to Meg and, in view of their circumstances, unwise to pursue the liaison; it was simply that he no longer had the slightest interest in Lady Hartleigh's experienced expertise. Meg's innocent passion had seared itself into his senses, making the thought of taking his pleasure with another woman seem ridiculous.

'No, Althea,' he said quietly. 'I am afraid that is not possible now.'

He attempted to lift her hand from his sleeve, but the green eyes blazed and she gripped hard suddenly, hissing, 'How dare you dismiss me like a common whore!' Then, seeming to regain control in a flash, she glanced past him, and said blandly, 'Why, I do believe you are right, Marcus. It *is* a delightful afternoon. Is not that Lady Diana? How very pleasant! I wonder who her charming companion can be?'

With a feeling of impending doom, Marcus turned slowly to encounter his sister's furious glare, Jack Hamilton's disbelieving gaze and, by far the worst of all, his wife's look of shocked hurt, which vanished instantly in calm, indifferent acceptance.

And this pattern card of wifely correctitude said in

the lightest of voices, 'Good gracious. It is my lord! How very singular!'

Jack Hamilton's head snapped around in amazement. The little devil! He wouldn't have thought she had it in her. But there she sat with cool composure, just as though Marc had not exposed her to ridicule and contemptuous pity. Perhaps she didn't understand, he thought. But a glance at her hands, clenched tightly in her lap, assured him that Lady Rutherford understood only too well. He found himself wishing heartily that he could be privy to Marc's thoughts right now.

They were indeed worth being privy to. His wife's reaction to his supposed misdemeanour aroused all sorts of conflicting emotions in Marcus's breast. Anger that she thought him so base that he would intentionally compromise their situation further was mingled with pain that he had hurt her. For he had. For that split second he had seen the truth in her eyes. And then she had withdrawn behind a mask of well-bred indifference. She had turned a blind eye, just as he had wanted his wife to do. What he hadn't counted on was seeing it happen. Seeing transparent, trusting Meg whisk herself out of sight, leaving behind a lovely, elegant stranger, who sat in his sister's carriage making polite conversation to Jack Hamilton.

Damn it all! She was smiling up at Jack as though she hadn't a care in the world. And he, the unprincipled rake, was smiling back in a way that made Marcus long to tear his throat out!

Lady Di instructed her coachman to pull up.

With a silent commendation for Meg's attitude, she opened fire. 'Good afternoon, Marcus. You see I persuaded dear Meg to take a little carriage exercise with me. Lady Hartleigh, how delightful to see you! I believe you have not been presented to my brother's bride yet. Meg, dear, permit me to present Lady Hartleigh.'

The two ladies exchanged the friendliest of acknowledgments while Di calmly watched her little brother practically grind his teeth in suppressed fury at the impropriety of presenting Althea to Meg in this way. Propriety, thought Di savagely, could be a two-edged sword!

She continued with her rifle fire. 'May we take you up, Lady Hartleigh? I'm sure it would be no trouble to deposit you where you belong!' A strange sound from Jack Hamilton made her say, 'Dear Jack, I do hope you are not feeling unwell. That sounded very like a cough.'

'Just some dust in my throat,' explained the afflicted Hamilton, still spluttering.

'Yes, do take Lady Hartleigh home, Di,' said Marcus, in what was obviously an attempt to take control of a situation that was fast deteriorating. 'You will be a trifle crowded with three, so I will escort my lady home.'

His hitherto biddable bride raised her dark brows at that. Get out of this nice comfortable barouche and walk home with *him* just so he could appease his conscience and silence the *on-dits*? When snow lay in hell, she would!

'How very kind of you, my lord,' she said sweetly. 'But I should not like to put you to so much trouble. And, indeed, if Lady Hartleigh does not mind a little crowding, I should like to further our acquaintance. I feel sure we have a great deal in common.'

Diana nearly broke her jaw keeping a straight face as Meg rolled up her husband, horse, foot and guns. Short of ordering her out of the carriage, he could do nothing but accept this masterly dismissal.

Biting back all the things he would have liked to say,

Marcus inclined his head, saying ironically, 'I am my lady's servant to command. I will see you at dinner, madam. Good afternoon, Di, Jack. *Au revoir*, Lady Hartleigh.'

He stalked off, wondering what on earth had possessed him to farewell Althea like that. Now she would think he intended to maintain their relationship! As would Meg, Diana and possibly even Jack. And he had no intention of doing anything of the sort! Not even to put his impertinent bride in her rightful place!

By the time Meg left him to the enjoyment of his wine that night Marcus was about ready to strangle her. It was not that she had said anything she should not have, or indeed given him the slightest reason to suppose she minded in the least if he had an affair. On the contrary, she had spoken cheerfully of how unexpectedly kind everyone had been, of whom Diana had presented to her, of the prospect of visiting Almack's and the opera. All in all she gave a convincing impression of a young bride intent upon cutting a dash in the world of the *ton*.

It was just that; an impression. By the time she left Marcus, Meg had a splitting headache and wished only for the privacy of her bedchamber. Accordingly she went straight upstairs, summoned Lucy to assist her and went to bed. She didn't even feel like reading. Her headache was making her slightly dizzy so she blew her lamp out and snuggled down in the silken sheets. For a few minutes she managed to pretend that everything was perfectly fine, that she had not a care in the world, that Marc was welcome to take his pleasures elsewhere. And then she dissolved into tears.

Despite having gone into her marriage with her eyes

wide open to what he intended, despite knowing the danger of caring for him, she realised that she had completely underestimated the pain involved in knowing he had another interest and the sense of betrayal in suspecting he had spent all, or part of, the day in Lady Hartleigh's no doubt experienced and expert embrace.

What chance did naïve, inexperienced Meg have against a sophisticated beauty like Althea Hartleigh? Oh, he had enjoyed her, had been kind enough to ensure her pleasure, but after seeing her rival, Meg could not believe that he would rate her charms above that green-eyed beauty. In fact, it did not even cross her mind that such might be the case.

Her shock, when she heard the door into the bathroom open and saw the light of her husband's candle, was intense. Surely he was not going to come to her bed now! Not after spending the day with… With her cheeks still wet with tears, Meg knew if he touched her now she was lost, would end up sobbing her heart out in his arms, revealing how deeply she had fallen in love. And he would resent it, would feel trapped by his pitying kindness. She didn't dare. His rejection she would not be able to bear. And pitying forbearance would be even worse.

'Meg? Are you asleep?' His voice was very soft, a velvet growl in the faint glow of his candle.

Lie still! Pretend to be asleep! She lay unmoving, hoping he might go away.

But the candle came closer, was set down on the night table and blown out as she felt her husband's large, naked body slide into bed beside her.

Unfortunately, since Marcus had not spent the day or even part of it in the enjoyment of Althea Hartleigh's charms, he did not go away. Since he had, in fact, spent a very large proportion of the day in pleasurable contemplation of his wife's enthralling passion, he was in no way minded to do so. If Meg were asleep, he would be content to snuggle her into his arms and hold her until she should chance to awaken, but he fully intended to spend the night with her, one way or another.

He wanted to reassure her somehow that he had not been so cruel as to betray her so early in their marriage. Short of telling her outright that he was innocent, the only way he could think of was to bed her and tell her that he wanted no one else.

So he gathered his supposedly sleeping wife into his arms with the utmost gentleness.

And felt her freeze and then jerk herself away from him to the other side of the bed.

Shocked, he lay still and then said reassuringly, 'Meg, sweetheart, it's me, Marc.' Perhaps, after her experience on their wedding night, he should not have just slid into bed with her in the dark.

'I know,' came the devastating response. 'I...I have the headache. Please, my lord, not tonight.'

For a moment he was stunned, and then he thought that despite her chatter she *had* looked rather pale at dinner.

'Then cuddle up and let me hold you,' he said gently. 'I promise I won't pester you.'

There was a moment's charged silence, during which Meg summoned up all the icy reserve of which she was capable. In the face of his tender consideration it was a daunting task.

Thankful that the dim light made her face unreadable, she said very politely, 'No. Thank you, my lord.'

Marcus felt as though a sword had passed straight through his guts. And then he lost his temper.

Swinging himself off the bed he said coldly, 'Then I will relieve you of my unwelcome presence, Madam Wife!' And in tones of brutal indifference, 'No doubt I can find amusement elsewhere!'

He waited a moment for Meg's response, but she was struggling with tears and remained silent so he turned on his heel and stalked out in a mixture of hurt and affronted male pride.

Hearing the door slam behind him, Meg buried her face in the pillow and cried herself to sleep, a proceeding which took over an hour and did absolutely nothing to help her headache.

Chapter Ten

A week later the Countess of Rutherford, exquisitely gowned in clinging, shimmering blue silk, stood between her sister-in-law and husband, being formally presented to society. Lady Diana's idea of a select assembly turned out to mean that she had not invited above two hundred or so people to have the honour of meeting Rutherford's bride.

Sir Toby commented on this with gentle satire and told Meg with a grin that he would quiz her on names later in the evening.

Meg was fairly certain that she would not remember a quarter of the names she had heard, although many of the people she had already met while driving with Diana. These she greeted with genuine relief as being lifelines in a sea of frothing, gossiping humanity. So confused was she by all the noise and new faces that she would have even greeted Lady Hartleigh with relief.

Lady Hartleigh was conspicuous by her absence, a fact which confirmed Meg's belief that there was some connection between her and Marcus. Why else should Di have been so annoyed at seeing them together? Perhaps he had even contemplated marriage with her.

Di had intimated that he had considered a marriage she disapproved of.

Trying to concentrate, she responded to Lady Castlereagh's gracious compliments on her looks with a shy 'thank you' which did her no disservice in that lady's eyes.

Lady Castlereagh had already been pleased to approve of Rutherford's choice and she confirmed it now, saying, 'I must wish you happy, Rutherford. I shall look forward to seeing the two of you at Almack's.' She passed on regally to inform her acquaintance that Rutherford's bride was just what she liked in a girl, dignified and with no simpering nonsense about her. Attractive too, trust Rutherford for that!

Despite his continuing hurt at his bride's rejection, Marcus swelled with unspoken pride in her composure. To anyone who did not know her she appeared perfectly happy with her surroundings, delighted to meet one curious stranger after another. Only Marcus suspected that she was finding the whole business somewhat of an ordeal and he could not have said why he had that impression. Certainly she did not shrink towards him, or cling to his arm. Her voice held no tremor and a friendly smile curved her soft mouth.

It was just that he had the oddest feeling that he was watching a play, in which a very talented actress held the stage. Which would have been all very well if she had ever relaxed and cast off her mask. But she didn't. In the last week he had seen very little of Meg. At first he had been too angry to trust himself near her and by the time he had cooled and approached her with overtures of friendship it had been too late.

She was caught up in a whirl of social engagements, fittings with Diana's dressmaker, visits to Hatchard's and Hookham's. And when he did see her she held him at arm's length with her chatter about her doings, how kind Diana was being and how much she was enjoying London. In short, he had lost Meg and acquired Lady Rutherford.

Even when he gave her a betrothal ring, which he had meant to do on that ill-fated day they had met in the park, she had maintained her barricade. Oh, she had thanked him prettily enough, put it on at once and turned her hand so the enormous diamond blazed. But he could not flatter himself that she was in the least moved by it. And he had not made the least attempt to enter her bed again or woo her into his. Never in his life had he been rejected by a woman and it had stung unbearably.

Had he but known that Meg had been hard pressed not to burst into tears when he gave the ring to her and went to sleep each night with her cheek cuddled against it, then he might have felt appeased. But he did not know these things; although he was observant enough to recognise the mask which Meg wore, he could not see past it to what lay underneath.

So Meg stood at his side, bitterly unhappy, and utterly determined that no one, least of all Marcus, should know it.

The throng of people flocking up the steps had died down and Di turned to Meg. 'Well, my love, I think it is time Marc took you to mingle with our guests.' Narrowly observing the slightest of shadows in the depths of Meg's dark eyes, 'And a glass of champagne too, I think! Oh, dear! Who is this arriving? I'm sure I didn't send out this many cards!' Then she fell silent as she saw who was coming through her front door.

Marcus beside her swore softly and said, 'What the hell did you invite them for, Di?'

'I didn't, you idiot,' she informed him with sisterly directness.

'Well, well, well,' said Sir Toby in detached interest. 'Your call, I'd say, Marc.'

Very puzzled, Meg gazed at the vaguely familiar couple ascending the stairs towards them.

She was sure she knew them, but couldn't remember having met them in the last few days with Di. Yet the red face of the corpulent gentleman puffing his way up to them was familiar, as was the hatchet-faced lady on his arm. Somewhere deep inside she began to shake. Who on earth could they be? She was aware that Marcus at her side was absolutely rigid with fury.

'My dear little cousin!' gushed the gentleman. 'I dare say Lady Diana did not realise we were in town! But really, we could not ignore you, dear Marguerite.' Then, as she continued to look at him blankly, 'I am your Cousin Delian, Marguerite!'

Her jaw dropped. Looking down at her, Marcus saw, for the first time in a week, a genuine reaction from his wife. Hurt, shock and disgust at this undisguised hypocrisy were all there for a fleeting moment. And something else which clawed at his heart. Briefly he had a glimpse of the frightened, grieving orphan, confused and alone. And then the mask slipped back into place.

But Marcus had seen enough. 'How charming, Sir Delian. But you did manage to ignore Marguerite for ten years very satisfactorily. You really needn't do such violence to your feelings now.' His silken tones cloaked a murderous rage at a man who could throw a ten-year-old child out of her home and not even settle money on her.

Sir Delian blustered ineffectually and his wife took over. 'How is this? Do you tell me that we are not welcome here, my lord? At our cousin's coming-out?'

'About as welcome as you made her ten years ago,' said Marcus with deadly emphasis. 'We, however, shall not be so ungracious as to turn you away. Unless Marguerite would prefer me to do so.' He turned to Meg. 'Well, my dear?'

She stared up at him. What was she supposed to say? Those icy grey eyes gave her no clue. The decision must be hers. It had been the dream of her life to one day repay Delian and Henrietta for casting her out and now she had her chance. She looked at them uncertainly. Sir Delian was obviously upset, his weak chins quivering as he passed a handkerchief over his florid countenance. Lady Fellowes looked as proud and disagreeable as ever.

Meg had a blinding flash of memory, recalling the day they had arrived at Thornaby, summoned her and pronounced sentence of exile from her home. Lady Fellowes had spelt out, in words the frightened ten-year-old had not understood for years, just why she was to be sent away. Sir Delian, she recalled, had protested a little but had been overruled. Now was her chance. She could refuse to acknowledge them and word would get out that she had done so. It would ruin them socially.

She couldn't do it. It was not in her nature to return evil for evil.

'No, my lord,' she said quietly. 'I will be pleased to acknowledge my only family.'

Sir Delian gasped, 'My dear child! I am so delighted! You must know we have been meaning forever to have you on a visit! Perhaps now that you are—' He fell silent before the searing scorn in the light grey eyes before him. They were like chips of ice, hard and implacable.

'Lady Rutherford has acknowledged you, Sir Delian,' interposed Marcus. 'It will be for her to determine what, if any, friendship should develop.'

With her head held high, Lady Fellowes towed her spluttering husband past them into the house.

'Really, Marc! Was that necessary?' expostulated Di.

Marcus looked down at Meg, a curious expression in his eyes. 'Yes, Di. It was.'

Meg returned his gaze, wide-eyed and defenceless. Just for a moment he was her Marc again, protective and caring.

Shyly she put her hand on his and said, 'Thank you, Marc.'

Her touch seemed to scorch through her kid glove, searing his fingers which longed to clasp hers. Instead he shrugged and said, 'I can't stand hypocrites. Shall we mingle?' And felt a strange pang of dissatisfaction as he saw Meg's barriers crash down, leaving him confronted with the polite and obliging bride he thought he wanted.

'Certainly, my lord.' What a fool she was to think he had responded to her need! He had merely found the Felloweses distasteful, for which she could not blame him in the least.

For the rest of the evening Meg circulated through the pressing throng and found herself feeling more and more at ease. People were kind and did not, thank God, expect her to remember all their names. Indeed, they were only too happy to present themselves to her notice.

'Dear Lady Rutherford. You won't remember, but Di presented me in the park...'

'We met in Hatchard's, Lady Rutherford…'

'You must have met so many people this evening, dear Lady Rutherford…'

And so it went on. Marcus, after an hour or so, had drifted away, satisfied that she was launched safely and could manage for herself. There was no danger of her being ignored or finding herself at a loss. So he brought her a glass of champagne and excused himself gracefully, leaving her deep in conversation with Lady Wragby on a sofa.

Meg rather liked Lady Wragby, who was fat and comfortable with absolutely no pretensions to fashion or beauty, but was possessed of an abundant good nature which ensured that she was everywhere welcome.

Lady Wragby was obligingly pointing out various persons of note and telling gently scandalous stories about them when an urbane voice from behind them said, 'How delightful. I have longed to renew my acquaintance with Lady Rutherford.'

As her veins congealed to solid ice, Meg turned to face the mocking eyes and thin lips of Sir Blaise Winterbourne. He had possessed himself of her hand and was raising it to his lips. Meg could barely repress a shudder as he kissed it. All at once she felt tainted, defiled, and sickeningly, shamefully afraid.

Regardless, she gave him back stare for stare and said, 'Have we met? Oh, of course! Mr Winterbourne. In Grantham, was it not?' She had the queerest feeling that Meg was standing a little distance away, quaking with fear, admiringly watching Lady Rutherford deal with an awkward situation.

Winterbourne laughed gently. 'I am flattered that you remember me, Lady Rutherford. But Rutherford made wretched work of presenting me! It will be more appropriate for you to call me Sir Blaise.'

He lingered beside the sofa for a while, chatting to Lady Wragby and idly quizzing Meg.

'Such an elegant gown, dear Lady Rutherford. But then you are always exquisitely garbed for the occasion, are you not?'

Meg deflected his barbed gallantries with increasing coolness until to her relief she observed Jack Hamilton approaching through the crowd. He had his head on one side and was regarding her with one cocked eyebrow.

As he drew closer Winterbourne excused himself and sauntered off. It would never do to give Hamilton of all people the least suspicion that he was sniffing around the Countess of Rutherford.

Hamilton bowed low over Meg's hand and greeted Lady Wragby with pleasure.

'How nice to find people I actually want to see. Didn't Di say something about a select assembly? Remind me not to come to a squeeze.'

Lady Wragby chuckled. 'Never mind. Should you like to come to a nice select card party next month? I'll only send out a hundred cards.'

Hamilton shuddered. 'Thank you for the warning. I believe I have a prior engagement that evening!'

'Why, you wretch!' protested Lady Wragby. 'I haven't even told you the date!'

In their relaxed and cheerful company Meg recovered slightly, laughing at their teasing and responding in kind. Yet, observing her, Jack thought she was rather pale. He could not say what it was that had told him she was upset, but he would have sworn that she was frightened by Winterbourne. Racking his brains, he could think of no reason for her to be so, unless of course Marc or Di had warned her that he made a habit of bedding Marc's mistresses and might think it amusing to seduce his Countess. He resolved to keep a brotherly eye on Meg. He thought she was the best thing to happen to Marc in years and he did not want anything to go wrong.

By the time Lady Fellowes sailed up to claim the privilege of cousinship, Meg was feeling thoroughly at ease again.

'My dear Marguerite,' she said, as she contrived to draw Meg away from Jack and Lady Wragby. 'I do trust there is no resentment on your part for your cousin's very understandable decision to protect his children from any breath of scandal. As a mother and dutiful wife I could only concur with his opinion.'

Holding herself proudly, Meg said steadily, 'My memory of the occasion is perfectly clear, *Cousin* Henrietta. I hold no resentment where it is not due.'

'Then we may be comfortable,' said Lady Fellowes with a sublime unawareness of the edge to Meg's response. 'Naturally, now you are so advantageously married, no one will give a thought to your past.'

'*My* past?' queried Meg. 'I was under the impression that it was my parents' past that was the problem.' She could not quite believe this bare-faced hypocrisy. 'I am still their daughter!'

'How you do take one up, dear Marguerite,' said Lady Fellowes with a tinkle of laughter. 'Now, you must know I am bringing out dear little Sophia this spring. She is presently recovering from this dreadful flu, so I have left her at home this evening. The most fragile constitution! But I am sure you will be pleased with her. Such a dear child. She is quite longing to meet her long-lost cousin.'

Since Meg's only memory of Sophia Fellowes was of a seven-year-old who had marched into her bedchamber and announced that it was hers now, as well as all the toys, and Mama wished to see Cousin Marguerite in the drawing room at once, she was not unnaturally startled at this announcement. But she did not wish to harbour a grudge so she said quietly, 'I am sure I will be pleased to make the acquaintance of my cousin.'

'It will be of the first importance to arrange a suitable match for her,' went on Lady Fellowes. 'I am sure Lord Rutherford has so many amiable friends—'

Meg interrupted at once. 'I beg your pardon, Cousin! I can see someone I wish to speak to most particularly. Pray excuse me.' With a charming smile she took her leave and looked around desperately for someone she knew.

A deep voice at her elbow said, 'At a loss, my dear?'

She stared up into her husband's enigmatic grey eyes.

He possessed himself of her hand and placed it securely on his arm. 'Never, my dear, make your escape before you have the route thoroughly planned. You may find yourself out of the pan and into the fire.'

'I don't know what you are talking about!' she snapped, furious that he should have been listening and seen through her ploy so easily.

'Did you not wish to escape from your hypocritical cousin?'

'Certainly not,' lied Meg, without the least hesitation. 'My cousin is perfectly amiable. I merely saw someone I wished to speak to!'

'Oh? Who is it?' asked Marcus. 'I will engage to escort you to your unknown friend.'

'That, sir, is none of your business!' Her eyes blazed at him. 'We have a bargain, do we not?'

'We do,' agreed Marcus. 'Are you bent on fulfilling your side of it?' Steel-hard eyes bored into her.

She met them bravely, shuddering inwardly at what he was suggesting. 'Again, sir, it is not your business if I am.'

Grey ice chilled her to the bone. 'I would point out, madam, that there is a little matter of an heir to be settled before you emulate your mother's career.' He bowed and left her.

Jack Hamilton, watching this exchange from an alcove, winced. He could not hear what was being said, but he didn't need to. He knew Marc well enough to know that he was hellbent on digging his own grave. And, to judge by the stricken look on Meg's face as he bowed and left her, he was doing a first-class job.

Casually he strolled out and greeted Meg. 'Come and have a glass of champagne, Lady Rutherford. You cannot possibly spend the evening chatting to your cousin and husband!'

He winced again as Meg turned to him and treated him to a brilliant smile. It was as though the hurt child had never existed.

'How kind of you, Mr Hamilton,' said Lady Rutherford. 'I'm dreadfully thirsty. Such a squeeze!'

It was dark…a myriad of greedy hands grasped at her breasts, her thighs…smearing a filthy slime over her…a hard, lustful mouth was forcing itself on hers…smothering her screams…choking her…

Meg awakened, sobbing and sweating in her terror. The fire was nearly out, but it cast enough light for her to avoid the furniture as she unthinkingly headed for the safety and reassurance of Marc's room. Despite the coldness between them, she did not think he would deny her the security of his arms.

She stumbled around the edge of the dark bathroom and found the door, groping for the latch. Unhesitatingly she headed for the bed, still shaking with fear as she scrambled in, reaching for Marc.

It took her a moment to realise that the enormous bed was empty, that Marc was not there. At first she could not think. Shock held her in its grip. And then the implications of his absence burst upon her like an exploding shell. He had gone out to seek consolation elsewhere as he had told her he would do. She lay there in his cold, empty bed and wept as though her heart would break until she slept again.

Coming up to bed half an hour later, slightly befuddled from all the brandy he had consumed in his library since he brought Meg home, Marcus stared in amazement at the sight of Meg in his bed. What the devil was she doing there? He cursed the brandy. Better go back downstairs. He was damned if he was going to get into bed with his wife in this disgraceful state! Be an insult to the poor girl.

Accordingly he wandered back downstairs and stretched out on the library sofa where he finally fell into an uncomfortable slumber.

Awakening from another nightmare in the early dawn, Meg found that she was still alone in her husband's bed and crept back to her own room. Bitter despair held her in its grip. She had driven Marc away and had no idea how to call him back without betraying her love for him. She eventually drifted into an uneasy sleep.

When she finally arose, not in the least refreshed,

Meg dressed herself in her prettiest morning gown and pinched her cheeks to force some colour into them. Lady Rutherford must not show the world a pale face if she were to protect Meg. Resolutely Meg left her chamber in the forlorn hope that breakfast would be of assistance in maintaining her façade.

By the end of her solitary breakfast she had made several decisions. Firstly, she must go to Marc and somehow let him know that she had not meant to refuse him her bed, that she had been feeling unwell, which had the merit of being at least partly true. Secondly, she had to tell him about Winterbourne. Ask him what she should do when she met him, and tell him about her nightmare. She felt cold at the thought of confiding so much to anyone but surely, surely to her own husband...

Accordingly she asked Delafield to inform her when his lordship was up and about and repaired to the drawing room to read. She had not been there more than an hour when the door opened and Marcus came in. He was his usual immaculate self, if a little pale, in buff breeches and a dark blue coat. His riding boots were polished to a shine which made Meg blink a little as she absorbed their splendour.

'Delafield mentioned that you wished to see me, madam.' He was feeling distinctly scratchy this morning. He had a stiff neck from the night on the sofa and a devilish head from all the brandy. If Meg were about to reproach him for his absence last night, he would have something to say about undutiful wives! He had absolutely no intention of confessing that he had spent the night on the library sofa since he had been far too under the weather to share a bed with her. Especially since the reason for his condition had been his frustration over her.

In the face of his formality, Meg completely lost sight of the course she had charted for herself and started in the middle. 'Y...yes. Did you know that Sir Blaise Winterbourne was there last night?' she asked, keeping her voice as steady as possible.

Marcus softened slightly, his tone gentler. 'I did know it. I should have warned you. He is everywhere received. Since I had not told Di anything, I could not strike his name from the guest list. It will be impossible to avoid him, I am afraid, but since he is not a friend of mine, you need not fear that I would expect you to receive him.'

Meg nodded. 'I see.'

She seemed collected enough, thought Marcus. He reverted to his former tone. 'Is that all you wished to speak to me about?'

She flinched inwardly. Could he just dismiss it like that? She felt cold and sick, as though the nightmare still rode her.

'No, my lord.' She drew a deep breath and again started in the wrong place. 'I...I came to find you last night—'

He interrupted at once. 'Might I remind you, or perhaps I should say, inform you, that it is a husband's right and privilege to indicate when he wishes to have congress with his wife.'

She stared up at him, stricken into silence and he went on coldly. 'You, of course, have the right of veto.' *Which you have exercised.* The words hung unspoken between them. His final comment set the seal on his fate. 'I would suggest, Lady Rutherford, that you adhere to this convention. You will thus be spared the humiliation of knowing that you are not the only desirable female in London. Our bargain, you may remember.'

Meg wondered if she were going to be sick. She had meant nothing to him, then. He cared as little for her as Cousin Euphemia had done, had dismissed her just as coldly. All his kindness and tenderness had been nothing more than a ploy to get her into his bed willingly. And even that had probably been to expedite the begetting of an heir. No doubt he found the more experienced Lady Hartleigh far more to his taste. Well, she was welcome to him! Lady Rutherford could stand alone!

'I beg your pardon, my lord,' said Lady Rutherford sweetly. 'You have made your position perfectly clear, for which I thank you. I shall endeavour to keep to my side of our bargain.' Bitterly hurt, she searched for the worst thing she could possibly think of to say to him. And found it with disastrous ease. 'You need not fear that I shall again refuse to do my duty. I am perfectly aware that my *right of veto* as you term it, is one that not many husbands would allow me. I would not like you to think that I am ungrateful, or taking advantage of your chivalrous nature.'

She rose gracefully and left the room with her head held high, praying that she would make it safely to her bedchamber before the scalding sensation behind her eyes became a torrent of tears. She had been a fool to think that it would be possible to confide in him, ask for his help. He had made his attitude quite plain. She was nothing to him, less than nothing, and it was as well to know it now, before her foolish heart imagined otherwise.

Marcus stood and watched her go, absolutely

stunned. Was that how she had seen it? Duty? Nothing more? Damn her! She was as cold-hearted and mercenary as any other woman and it was as well to know it now!

Chapter Eleven

Over the next month Meg hurled herself into the social gaiety of London. She attended Almack's, danced the night away at innumerable private balls, attended the opera, collected a court of devoted admirers and succeeded in persuading her husband that he had indeed made a marriage of convenience.

She made innumerable friends, mostly through Diana's introductions. She found that the people Di presented to her as her own personal friends were kindly, unpretentious and delighted to welcome her to their circles for her own sake.

The same could not be said of her Cousin Henrietta. Meg had no doubt that, had she married a man of lesser consequence, Henrietta would have refused to acknowledge her and would have ensured that Cousin Delian did the same. She actually found herself feeling sorry for Sir Delian. It was plain that he was ruled by his wife and that, left to his own devices, he would not have thought to turn his orphaned little cousin out of her home.

He had tried to explain and apologise to her one morning in the park when he had taken her driving. The morass of half-sentences, as he attempted to tell Meg he had never meant to leave her destitute, without revealing his wife's ascendancy, was utterly pathetic.

In the end she stopped him gently. 'Cousin, there is no need for all this. You acted as you thought best. No one can do otherwise.'

Sir Delian Fellowes swallowed hard. That was exactly the problem. He had *not* acted as he thought best. He never did if Henrietta disagreed. And now he felt guilty, ashamed of his cowardice. Especially since Meg seemed disposed to forgive what had been done to her and include them in her circle of friends despite the obvious disapproval of her husband.

He tugged at his neckcloth with one hand. 'You are very kind my dear. It…it is more than—'

'Oh, fustian!' said Meg cheerfully. 'I sent Cousin Henrietta a card inviting you and Sophia to join us for dinner and then go on to the opera next week. It is to be my first visit! Do say you will come! I am so looking forward to it. Lady Diana and Sir Toby are to come, as well as Mr Hamilton!'

'Jack Hamilton?' asked Sir Delian, suddenly intent.

'Why, yes.' Meg was a trifle surprised over his evident approbation.

'Henrietta will be most obliged,' said Sir Delian delightedly.

'Obliged?'

Sir Delian explained. 'You see, she has been trying for ever to introduce Sophia to his notice.'

'Oh,' said Meg hollowly. This was something she hadn't thought of. She had pondered over whom to invite. To keep the numbers even a single gentleman had been required. Jack Hamilton was the only one she could think of and she hoped devoutly that he would

not think she was attempting to match him with Miss
Sophia Fellowes. As far as Meg could see, Sophia was
not so very much changed from the arrogant little girl
she remembered.

'Yes, indeed,' continued Sir Delian. 'I think I may
safely say that we shall all three be delighted to accept
your kind invitation, my dear.'

'How…how lovely,' achieved Meg, thinking that the
opera had better be good if she were to enjoy what
promised to be an unexpectedly embarrassing evening.
If Sophia made an obvious play to engage Jack's interest, Marcus would be utterly furious, she thought miserably. She was perfectly aware that he disliked her
cousins, and scorned Sir Delian.

She was still worrying when Jack Hamilton approached the phaeton and hailed them.

'Good afternoon, Lady Rutherford. Sir Delian, your
most obedient!' He smiled up at them lazily. 'I'm going
to steal your fair companion, Sir Delian. Will you walk
with me, Lady Rutherford?'

She glanced hesitantly at Sir Delian, not wanting him
to think she wished to quit his company, but in truth
she found it difficult to think of what to say in the face
of his overwhelming guilt.

Sir Delian, however, was perfectly ready to oblige a
man whom he definitely did not wish to antagonise. 'A
theft indeed, Hamilton! But I shall forgive you and look
forward to seeing you at my cousin's little opera party
next week. Lady Fellowes and I shall be pleased to
present our little Sophia to you.'

Meg suppressed a curse with difficulty as she caught
Jack's glance, brimming with laughter.

He helped her down, saying, 'The pleasure will be
all mine. Good afternoon.'

Meg met his eyes ruefully as Sir Delian gave his pair the office and said, 'Oh, Jack, I mean, Mr Hamilton, I am most dreadfully sorry!'

'Jack will do very nicely,' he said laughing. 'And as for the rest, don't give it a thought. 'Tis an inevitable part of being an eligible bachelor. Just ask Marc, he can tell you all about it.'

'I did *not* mean to expose you to that!' said Meg indignantly, ignoring the reference to her husband's erstwhile status as society's most sought-after *parti*.

'I never thought you did,' replied Jack with a chuckle. 'Tell me, how is Marc? I thought he was a little out of sorts when last I saw him.'

Meg hesitated. She hadn't actually seen Marcus for three days. Well, not to speak to, at all events. She had seen him at a ball the previous evening. He had greeted her politely and then gone on his way. He had next been seen dancing with Lady Hartleigh. A casual inquiry an hour or so later had elicited the information that he had taken his leave early. As had Lady Hartleigh.

Aware that Jack was watching her closely, she said unconcernedly, 'Oh, Marcus is well enough, I believe. He is always very busy.' Adroitly she changed the subject. 'I am so glad you are to come to the opera with us. I shall be able to ask you all sorts of questions.' Determinedly she kept the conversation focused on opera until Jack had escorted her home.

Jack was deep in thought as he left Meg. He'd noted her slim fingers clutching the dainty pink reticule and the slight firming of her lips, the gallant tilt of the chin as she lied to him. He'd had the impression that Marc was not spending much time in his countess's company. What he hadn't been sure of was how the countess felt about it. He had his answer. And there was not a damn thing he could do about it, except extend a hand of chivalrous friendship to her.

A slight smile curved his lips. That, of course, might be enough to bring Marc to his senses! If he thought his best friend was after his wife... Jack felt a twinge of unholy amusement at the prospect of Marc's outrage. The only difficulty would be how to mislead Marc without Meg, or indeed anyone else, getting the wrong idea—Meg especially. Marcus might have offered his bride a *carte blanche* to conduct discreet *affaires*, but Jack was morally certain she would never do so and would shrink from such a thing, and anyone who suggested it, in horror.

This little expedition to the opera should serve his turn very nicely. He spared a moment's compunction for the false hopes he was going to raise in Miss Fellowes's breast and in the more ample bosom of her mama. Oh, well! There must be some casualties in a war.

Just as Meg had feared, her first appearance at the opera was not an unalloyed pleasure. To begin with, it was plain that Marcus viewed the inclusion of the Fellowes with extreme disapprobation. It was not that he was rude to them or even inattentive. Quite the opposite. He was extremely polite. Nothing could have exceeded his civility to Sir Delian and Lady Fellowes, or to Miss Fellowes. But it was such a contrast to the easy, unceremonious manners he used towards his sister, Sir Toby and Jack Hamilton, that Meg wanted to throw something at him. Especially since he was equally polite to her!

To her immense surprise, it seemed that Jack

Hamilton was quite taken with Miss Fellowes. He certainly spent a great deal of time flirting with her in the most unexceptionable way. Meg began to feel rather nervous since it was plain that Marcus was viewing this with a rather jaundiced eye.

He took advantage of an appallingly long and dull anecdote related by Lady Fellowes to draw Meg aside and say, 'If you are attempting to fulfil your cousins' hopes by introducing Miss Fellowes to an eligible bachelor, might I request that you leave my close friends off your list of victims?'

For a moment anger blazed in those expressive eyes, but she dropped her lids swiftly to veil her fury. 'Oh? Do you not think Mr Hamilton can take care of himself? It appears to me that he is very well pleased with his company.' Her tone was light and unconcerned and her eyes, when she raised them to Marcus's face, betokened only innocent inquiry.

Marcus's temper slipped its leash somewhat. 'That's because he's too damned polite to appear anything else!'

Meg seemed to consider this for a moment. 'Really? What a pity it isn't catching. Do excuse me, my lord. I must attend to our guests.' She favoured Marcus with a glittering smile, calculated to make him want to wring her neck, and went to speak with her cousin Sophia. How dare he! To think that she would hatch vulgar, hateful schemes like that! He ought to know her better! Meg conveniently ignored the fact that she had been doing her level best to ensure that Marcus did not know her, that of late weeks he had seen only Lady Rutherford.

There was a snap in her step as she approached her

cousin and Jack Hamilton, her flushed cheeks and over-bright eyes a clear sign of temper.

Jack looked up at her approach with an encouraging smile that insensibly soothed her ruffled emotions. 'Ah, Meg. Come and add your voice to mine. I am trying to persuade Miss Fellowes to walk in the park with me one day. Perhaps you would care to join us as her chaperon?' His eyes quizzed Meg mischievously.

'A chaperon? Me?' Meg chuckled. 'What do I have to do?'

'Oh, just walk with us. Lose yourself at a prearranged signal. Feign deafness, blindness and generally act as though you aren't there!'

Miss Fellowes simpered in a sickening way, batting her lashes at Jack's outrageous parody of the duties of a chaperon. 'Dear Mr Hamilton, you are the most dreadful flirt!'

'Am I?' A tone of surprise crept into his voice. 'Good God! I thought I was doing quite well. It just shows how you can be mistaken! Meg, my sweet, I shall have to practise on you.'

This casual endearment smote on Marcus with stunning effect. He couldn't quite believe his ears. That Jack Hamilton of all men should be flirting with the Countess of Rutherford stunned him. He turned slightly to see how Meg had reacted and nearly choked on his Madeira. She had laid her hand on Jack's arm and was laughing up at him in the most natural, unaffected way. As though she were used to such over-familiar endearments!

The emotions that ripped through Marcus were utterly overwhelming. The urge to drag Meg away from Jack forcibly blazed in his heart. A remark from Lady

Fellowes, who was claiming his attention, recalled him to his surroundings.

'Dear Sophia is enjoying herself so much, Lord Rutherford. So kind of you to invite us. But then, we are family, are we not? You must give us the pleasure of entertaining you and dear little Meg very soon.'

Rutherford returned a civil, if automatic and uncommitted reply. Meg and Jack? Oh, surely not! Jack wouldn't do a thing like that! *Would he?* And Meg? He couldn't quite believe it. We had a bargain, he reminded himself. I told her she was free to seek love elsewhere, that I would not give it. That I didn't want hers.

So why the hell was he feeling as though he wanted to give Jack a leveller and wring Meg's elegant creamy throat? At the thought of touching Meg's throat a surge of pure desire roared through him. His fingers tingled at the memory of the soft skin, that deliciously skittering pulse that throbbed below her ear. With an internal curse he tore his mind away from the primitive and wholly discreditable visions it was conjuring up.

'Such a charming gentleman,' Lady Fellowes was saying. 'So much address. I vow he is quite a favourite of mine.'

Marcus smiled rigidly. Address? Jack? Too bloody much for his money! About the only thing he wanted to address to Jack right now was a cartel of war.

At this inopportune moment Delafield announced dinner and Marcus practically ground his teeth in rage as he watched his best friend take his bride into dinner. Which was all perfectly acceptable and above board, of course; if only Meg hadn't looked at him so glowingly, hadn't seemed so utterly content in his company.

It was probably just as well that the length of the table made it impossible for Lord Rutherford to hear much of the laughing conversation which flourished between Mr Hamilton, Miss Fellowes and Lady Rutherford. To judge by Lady Rutherford's laughing eyes and sparkling smile, not to mention Miss Fellowes's rather frequent recourse to her ivory brisé fan, it was excessively entertaining to both of them.

Unavailingly Marcus told himself that Jack would never serve him such a turn. That he was flirting with Meg to cover his attentions to Miss Fellowes. But why on earth would he bother flirting with Miss Fellowes? She was just the sort of arch, simpering, society virgin that Jack detested. Which left the unwelcome possibility that Miss Fellowes, not Meg, was the stalking horse.

By the time they left for the King's Theatre his temper was in a lamentable state. They went in two carriages and somehow Jack had managed to arrange it so that he went in one with Meg, Di and Miss Fellowes, while Marcus ended up with Sir Toby, Sir Delian and Lady Fellowes. Upon their arrival in the Haymarket it was perfectly plain to any observer that Lady Rutherford was entirely happy with her escort.

Marcus drew a deep breath as he politely offered his arm to escort Miss Fellowes to the box he rented. He had made a bargain with Meg. If she chose to act according to the terms he had set, then he would have to accept it. No matter how much it hurt. But Jack? Surely it was just flirtation!

As they entered the box Meg gazed about in wonder. The theatre was full. The boxes reserved for the wealthy shimmered and glittered with silks, satins and jewels. Below in the pit the less well-off milled about, awaiting the rise of the curtain.

'Goodness,' exclaimed Lady Fellowes, peering across

the theatre. 'There is my cousin Winterbourne! Now who is he with? Oh, yes! That's Lady Hartleigh's box. Hmmph! It's a mystery to me how that woman contrives on her jointure. That box must have cost above five hundred pounds!'

Since he had paid for the box shortly before his visit to Yorkshire, Marcus could have told her exactly how much above five hundred pounds. He chose, however, to ignore the comment, looking sharply at Meg to see if she were panicked at the presence of Winterbourne.

Meg merely said innocently, 'Perhaps it was a present. After all, if she likes music it would be a very good present.' She must not, she told herself, make a cake of herself. Winterbourne could not possibly distress her from the other side of the theatre. And she supposed he had to have *some* relatives. But it was a dreadful shock to realise that he was connected to her family, however tenuously.

Jack was moved to comment, 'It would, of course. But I fancy Lady Hartleigh finds the entertainment of her peers quite as fascinating as the stage.'

Marcus glared at him. Jack, damn his eyes, knew precisely which of her *peers*, as he had so delicately put it, had made Lady Hartleigh a present of her most expensive box.

A choke from behind them caught their attention. Sir Toby, finding all eyes upon him as he spluttered, waved his hand excusingly. 'Just a crumb in my throat. Don't mind me. I shall be better directly.'

Eyeing the very elegant pair of opera glasses in his wife's hand, Marcus hoped devoutly that she would not think to turn them on some of the boxes opposite during the performance. Otherwise she would be bound to discover just why so many members of society, who could not so much as carry a note in a bucket, let alone a tune, chose to patronise the opera with its convenient private boxes full of discreet shadows.

'Now, what is it tonight?' asked Lady Fellowes brightly.

Meg turned an enquiring gaze upon her. Surely she had mentioned on the note that it was La Cenerentola? She reminded her politely.

'Oh, of course! Mozart! I dote on Mozart.' She beamed at Jack. 'Dear little Sophia is excessively musical, Mr Hamilton. She takes after me, you know.'

'Er...I believe Signor Rossini to have written this opera, my dear.' Sir Delian sounded a shade apologetic. He smiled deprecatingly at his wife as she glared at him.

'Dear me,' Marcus cut in smoothly. 'How very inconsiderate these foreigners are. They can't even manage to compose their own operas. It would never happen in England!'

'True,' said Lady Diana drily. 'Since we import all our operas and don't have any written by modern English composers. Ah, they're starting!'

'Di,' said Sir Toby apologetically to Meg, 'is most unfashionable in that she comes to the opera in order to enjoy the music.'

'Why, whatever else would anyone come for?' asked Meg innocently. Sir Toby's jaw dropped ludicrously. A glare from his brother-in-law warned him that he had said quite enough and he muttered something incoherent, which was common enough not to have aroused Meg's curiosity had not her cousin Sophia Fellowes looked so scornfully knowing. Realising that she had somehow made a fool of herself, she made a mental note not to ask any more questions unless it were possible to address them very quietly to Jack.

She sat expectantly in her seat as the orchestra swept into the overture. There had been so little opportunity to hear any music in Yorkshire. Uncle Samuel had never engaged any sort of governess for her so she had never learnt to sing or play the pianoforte. She heaved a sigh of pleasure as the music ebbed and flowed around her. By the end of the first act she was entranced. Despite not knowing a word of Italian she knew the tale of Cinderella well enough to follow the action, and the music, she found, told her exactly what the characters were feeling.

She had always thought that opera must be a silly sort of thing where people got up and sang in the most unlikely way. Now she discovered that on the contrary the music somehow took the story and added an extra level of emotion to it. That the music could somehow twist itself around her very soul. And she knew how poor little Cinderella felt, lost and vulnerable, dazed that anyone, let alone a prince, could possibly love her.

And sometimes, she thought sadly, Cinderella's luck is quite out. How would she have felt if her Prince had only married her because he had to, because society and his own sense of honour demanded it? That, far from returning her love, he regretted his chivalrous action in marrying a poor little nobody? Meg bit her lower lip hard. She had wanted so much to be a good wife to Marc, even if he didn't care for her. And now they could barely converse without trying to hurt one another. There was a hot pricking behind her eyes and quickly she raised her opera glasses in defence. The last thing she needed was to be caught crying in the middle of the King's Theatre.

Slowly she became aware of the oddest sensation of being watched. Puzzled, she lowered her opera glasses and stole a glance around the box. Sir Toby looked as though he were sound asleep…yes…that was definitely a snore! Diana was watching the stage and Marcus was trying to, albeit distracted by Cousin Henrietta's arch comments. Jack was leaning on the rail, his attention on the performance, seemingly unaware of the languishing glances being cast in his direction by Cousin Sophia, and Cousin Delian looked to be in a fair way to joining Sir Toby in the arms of Morpheus.

She must be imagining it. Then, as she swung her gaze back to the stage, a movement in the box opposite caught her eye. Startled, she looked more closely. And felt a rising wave of sickness.

Sir Blaise Winterbourne had his opera glasses trained directly on her. Suddenly Meg was appallingly aware of the low-cut gown she was wearing… Fear flooded her as the music receded, giving way to nightmare panic that surged up from the darkness to choke her, drag her down into the yawning pit… A simpering giggle from Sophia dragged her back from the brink of the abyss.

She still felt cold and sick, but at least she was in control of herself again, able to think and quell the terror. Casually she reached for the Norwich silk shawl on her lap and slipped it around her shoulders. At least she didn't feel naked to that lecherous gaze.

Jack turned to her. 'Cold?' he murmured.

'A…a little,' she returned, aware that her voice was shaking.

Meg had managed to regain control of herself before the interval, but she sat rather quietly during all the chatter. Marcus had ordered champagne to be served and she sipped hers dubiously, not entirely certain she liked it.

Jack leaned over and said softly, 'Now, whatever you do, don't pour it over the edge.'

'Pour it over the edge?' Meg tried not to giggle. 'Why on earth should I do that?'

He chuckled at her near slip. 'Well, that's what my sister tells me she did here once! Caused quite a commotion down below. Roars of protest about the decadent aristocracy, threats of insurgency. If you ask me, it was a miracle Barraclough was induced to offer for her after that.' He changed the subject. 'Are you enjoying yourself on your first visit to the opera?'

'Oh, yes!' Her enthusiasm was thoroughly unfashionable. 'But I don't know anything about music. I…I wish I did. My Cousins Sophia and Henrietta sound so knowledgeable.'

'But you must have learned to sing and to play the pianoforte.' He sounded amazed and she shook her head, blushing slightly.

'No. My guardian did not engage a governess for me.' She blushed. 'I…I have no accomplishments at all. I fear I'm not much of a bargain for my lord.'

It was said with a gallant attempt at humour, but Jack could hear the underlying pain in her voice. Several things clicked into focus for him at that point. Lady Rutherford was scared, scared that she would betray her ignorance and shame to Marc, scared that she would not be able to hold her own in the strange new world into which she had been pitchforked. None of which would matter very much if things were all right between her and Marc. But they weren't. And Meg's lack of confidence in herself would not help. He had the queerest notion that some other fear was making it all worse, undermining her natural courage and gallantry.

He cocked his head and said gently, 'Then we must do something about that.'

Her eyes flew to his in startled query.

He smiled back. 'First, engage a singing master. You have a lovely speaking voice. Learn to sing. As for the other accomplishments, talk to Di. You can learn to draw, paint in water colours, embroider, whatever you like. I'm sure if you wished you could go and join her daughters and their governess.'

'Jack,' she breathed. 'That's a wonderful idea! I feel such an ignoramus at times and I don't wish my lord to…to feel—' She broke off in embarrassment.

He nodded sympathetically. 'May I give you more advice, Meg? Or, rather, a clue about the admittedly base propensities of the male sex.'

She nodded.

'Most of us don't really give a damn about a woman being able to embroider prettily or draw or paint. Some don't even care if she's intelligent or not. Marc, I can safely assure you, will not be concerned if you have all the feminine accomplishments or none of them. On the other hand, I know he appreciates your intelligence. So, if you decide to acquire a few accomplishments, choose the ones that really appeal to you. You enjoy reading, so learn French and Italian. Learn to sing. For your own pleasure and satisfaction.'

Their soft exchange was interrupted at this point by Sophia Fellowes, who had watched Jack's attentions to Meg with ill-concealed annoyance.

She fluttered her lashes at Jack and said, 'Are you enjoying the performance, sir? I vow I have never seen so many modish gowns!'

Jack and Meg exchanged a speaking glance, full of

laughter, even as he responded politely to this revealing exclamation.

This, then, thought Meg, striving to control her incipient choke of laughter, was why people came to the opera whether they were musical or not. To see and to be seen. Very well. She would conform. And in the meantime she would allow the music to ravish her senses and comfort some of her loneliness. No one need know. To the world it would appear as though Lady Rutherford was obeying the dictates of fashion.

Still chuckling inwardly, she turned away from Jack and Sophia. And found her husband's cold grey eyes resting on her enigmatically. A faintly sardonic smile played at the corner of his beautifully cut mouth. Meg felt her throat close up and her mouth go dry as she imagined, remembered the skill of those firm lips and the long fingers, negligently holding the stem of his wine glass. Determined not to betray herself, she bit her underlip hard to stop its trembling and then gave him her most brilliant social smile. The grey eyes, that had once held tenderness, hardened slightly as he inclined his head in acknowledgement. And then turned away.

Marcus felt devastated. Adrift. He had seen Meg in action for over a month now and knew that she was playing a part for the benefit of society. Even for him. He thought he could have accepted that. But to see her lower her guard for Jack hurt unbearably. The way she had looked at him! Friendly, relaxed. Damn it! She was his! Or she had been, before he drove her away.

The music began again but Marcus heard little of it, lost as he was in his own worries. What the hell had he got himself into? He had never expected to suffer agonies of jealousy over the inevitable infidelities of his countess! Infidelity…the very word grated on him. It was the last word he would have associated with Meg, he realised. It just didn't fit. But he had set the terms of their marriage himself, and he would have to acquiesce...

A faint movement caught his eye. Sophia Fellowes leaning over to address some coy remark to Jack. Fury welled up in him. It was no more than Jack deserved if Meg did foist that simpering woman on to him, but he was damned if he'd let her get away with it! As soon as they got home he was going to have a long overdue chat with his wife.

'I should like to speak with you privately, madam,' said Marcus ominously as Meg started up the stairs towards her bedchamber with her candle.

She turned, concealing a yawn. The late nights were beginning to exhaust her and she had been feeling rather unwell recently. 'Could it not wait until morning, my lord? I am rather—'

'Now.' His voice was coldly inflexible.

Fury blazed in Meg's eyes. How dare he address her thus! 'Since you ask so charmingly, my lord, naturally I am delighted to comply.' The dulcet tones were strangely at odds with the simmering rage in her eyes. 'I shall await your pleasure in the drawing room.

She did not have long to wait. Marcus joined her almost immediately.

He stated his grievance with disastrous promptitude. 'I must demand, madam, that you do not subject my friends to such obvious matchmaking efforts. In particular, I object to Mr Hamilton being a victim of such schemes! Especially in connection with Sophia Fellowes.'

Meg thought it entirely likely that she might explode,

but she held on to the edges of her temper with difficulty. 'Pray, tell me, my lord, have you some specific objection to my cousin?'

'She is a mercenary little bitch!' said Marcus, not mincing words. 'On the catch for a husband and with not the slightest shred of feeling for anyone save herself! Besides which, I do not like her family!'

Meg felt as though he had stabbed her. Hurt mingled with rage. 'And what is left for her if she does not marry?' she stormed. 'A life of dependency! Poverty, perhaps! Do you think any woman wishes to marry for those reasons? Because she must?'

Belatedly Marcus realised that he had been tactless in the extreme. Furious with himself, he lashed out, 'She would be marrying for money alone! Do you think any man wishes to be married for his money and social position? If she cared in the least for Jack...'

Cared? Her own pain exploded inside her into coruscating fury. 'Care? Why should she care? What man looks for that in his marriage? I was under the distinct impression that *love* was to be sought outside marriage! That marrying for money, position and social security was all one could expect!'

Marcus's brows snapped together. 'Meg, I am well aware that your position and Miss Fellowes are vastly different. You had no one to care for you—'

'Damn you!' The words burst from her uncontrollably. 'I don't want your pity! Do you think I *wished* to play the beggar maid to your King Cophetua? I...I should never have accepted your offer!' She whirled and fairly ran from the room, slamming the door behind her.

Marcus slumped into a chair, his head in his hands. Hell! What on earth was he to do now that she was regretting their marriage?

Chapter Twelve

A week later, Marcus sat frowning as he watched his wife pick uninterestedly at her breakfast. She had eaten very little and seemed, in his opinion, to be existing on a diet of dry toast and tea. It was her business, of course, but he was conscious of a nagging, barely acknowledged worry that she was not looking her best. Faint shadows showed like bruises under her eyes and she looked so pale in the mornings, which was about the only time he saw her, here in the library having breakfast. She always came down, no matter how late she had been the night before. And he sat there absent-mindedly consuming sirloin while longing to consume her instead.

And there she sat, pushing her egg around her plate with a look on her face that suggested it exuded an unpleasant odour. What the hell did she come down for if she were just going to sit there playing with her food? Except, of course, for the tea and toast.

'Is there something wrong with the egg?' He had not meant his voice to sound so harsh and mentally kicked himself. Frustrated desire was doing absolutely nothing for his manners.

Sure enough her face froze into an expression of indifference. She would not willingly allow him to see anything of her feelings, he realised. Not even that she didn't like her egg.

'I am not terribly hungry,' she said, with a cool detachment she was far from feeling. In fact, she felt thoroughly nauseated, a normal state of affairs for her in the mornings just now. The smell of the egg was revolting and the sight of Marcus gobbling beef in that odiously insensitive way made it worse. About all she could face was tea and toast. And she had no intention of telling her husband. It was none of his business!

'Then why come down to breakfast?' inquired Marcus, before thinking how that might sound. His tact was suffering along with his manners, he thought with an inward groan.

Meg flushed. Why, indeed? The only reason she came down was to see him. They rarely dined together now, except in company. If they found themselves at the same social engagements, it was more by coincidence than design and on more than one occasion she had suspected that he had left a ball early after finding her there. No doubt he wished to avoid having to dance with her.

So she came down to breakfast each morning to see him, even if not to speak to him since he was invariably buried in the paper and returned the briefest of monosyllabic grunts to anything she said.

This query about her egg had engendered the longest conversation they had had in days. And she was certainly not going to tell him the truth. Not after he had made it quite plain that her presence was unwelcome.

She summoned up a brittle smile and said, 'I beg your

pardon, my lord. I didn't realise that I was expected to be fashionable at breakfast time.'

'What the devil do you mean by that?' A note of anger resonated in the deep voice. The little baggage was possessed of an uncanny knack of wrongfooting him!

Good! I've stung him out of that maddening self-control, thought Meg with undutiful relish. Aloud she said, 'Merely that I will in future breakfast in my room. I am not stupid, my lord. I can take a hint.' Despite her best efforts, a note of bitterness crept into her voice.

Marcus noted it at once. 'Meg, I did not intend—' He stopped. How long was it since he had called her Meg? Since he had spoken to her gently? He went on with difficulty. 'I only thought you looked pale and wondered if you were feeling quite well, getting enough sleep…'

Meg wavered for a moment. The urge to tell him everything was almost overwhelming, the nightmares about Winterbourne, the tiredness, feeling sick in the mornings. And most of all she longed to tell him she had not meant to refuse him her bed, that she missed him, did not wish to take advantage of their bargain, that she loved him, wanted only him. But the habit of years held her back. After being taught so brutally not to confide, not to let anyone know what she was thinking, she hesitated fatally.

Misinterpreting her silence, Marcus said stiffly, 'I have no desire to interfere with you. I merely wished to exercise my duty of care as your husband.' He forced back the words he longed to say. She obviously did not wish to be pestered.

Duty of care? Duty? Damn him! Why did he have to say that? I don't want to be a duty! It was all Meg could do not to burst into tears of frustrated despair. Fool that she had been to think that marriage could remove the hated stigma of being a poor relation, a charity case, that she would be able to live with Marc and not care how he regarded her.

Her voice commendably steady, she said, 'Then you have done so in asking after my health. Now, if you will excuse me, I have an engagement with my cousins.' She rose to her feet, trying to ignore the fact that he had risen as well to escort her to the door and open it.

Marcus moved to her side and was overwhelmingly aware of her slender body as he walked with her to the door. She haunted his dreams at night until he could barely control his desire to march into her bedchamber and get into her bed, overpowering her resistance with his body, silencing her protests with kisses. He wanted her so badly, it was physically painful, and the sight of her each morning alone at breakfast was almost more than he could bear.

Dammit all! She was his wife, wasn't she? With a muttered curse he grasped her shoulders and swung her around to face him. For a bare instant his scorching gaze seared into her startled eyes and then with another curse he dragged her into his arms and brought his mouth down on hers in unrestrained passion.

Meg was stunned. His mouth crushed hers mercilessly, holding her captive as surely as his arms. And she felt herself melt against him in unthinking surrender. Never had he treated her so before! He had always been so gentle, so considerate in bed. He had aroused her to passion without once allowing her to feel threatened by his own desires.

Now his mouth was ruthless, daring her to resist. She could feel his hands at her hips as he moulded her against him, forcing her to feel his arousal. His loins were grinding against her soft belly in flagrant, undisguised need. And his tongue, possessing her mouth in brutal, plundering intimacy, told her exactly what he wanted of her body. And she wanted it too! Her brain screamed feebly that she ought to be terrified but her treacherous body was useless, trembling, her knees shaking, her thighs dissolving into heated, melting desire.

And then she felt dizzy as the nausea she had been holding at bay threatened to overcome her. For one dreadful moment the room tilted and swirled into blackness as she went limp in his arms.

Marcus felt the change at once. She sagged against him helplessly as his arms tightened instinctively to support her. Horrified, he raised his head to see her eyes shut and her face appallingly, accusingly white. Shaken with remorse, he lifted her into his arms and carried her to the sofa where he laid her tenderly.

How could he have done that? Allowed his frustration and desire to ride him so that he abused her trust! Dear God, he was no better than Winterbourne to treat her so! Lashing himself with scorn, he stood waiting for her to recover for what seemed an eternity.

When at last her eyes opened, they stared up at him in unspoken hurt, shimmering with tears.

'Why—?'

He cut her short, unable to bear her accusations. 'I agree. Most distasteful. A regrettable interlude. You need not fear that it will happen again.'

'I...I needn't...' Meg's voice shook uncontrollably. He had found her distasteful. *That* was why he had stopped kissing her...no doubt why he had never attempted to share her bed again, why he had told her so brutally not to come to him.

'No.' His voice was icily uncompromising. He ought to hold her tenderly and comfort her, but after this he could not trust himself to touch her. For one insane moment he had thought she was responding to his passion with equal abandon. And now, as he looked down at her, all he wanted to do was to take her in his arms again and continue what he had started even if it meant he took her against her will. Swearing savagely, he turned on his heel and walked out of the room, slamming the door behind him.

When next he saw Meg it was at an evening party two days later. She greeted him coolly as though nothing had happened. So he shrugged to hide his pain and buried himself in most of the amusements he had enjoyed before his marriage. The only problem was that he didn't enjoy them any more.

One amusement he eschewed completely. Lady Hartleigh cast out her glimmering lures in vain. Not even to ease the frequently painful frustration he felt would Marcus avail himself of her charms. He wanted Meg and no other. But they had made a pact not to interfere with each other and, even if he told himself that she owed him children to fulfil her side of the bargain, he would not force himself on any woman, least of all her. So he greeted his wife politely when their paths crossed socially and held his tongue about the increasing air of fragility she wore.

'Ah, good morning, cousin.' Sir Delian greeted the elegant Countess of Rutherford cheerfully as he descended the steps of his Mount Street mansion. 'You will find Sophia and Lady Fellowes within. A stroll in the park, is it?'

'Yes,' said Meg, heartily wishing she had not agreed to it. True she did not feel as sick as she had done at breakfast, but she would have given much to be tucked up on a sofa with a book right now. Or practising her drawing. Her new master seemed to think that she actually had some talent and, judging by the way he had ruthlessly castigated and torn up her first efforts, she did not think he was indulging in flattery.

The butler escorted her to the drawing room and announced her in regal accents. The Countess of Rutherford. Meg shook herself mentally. Would she ever get used to it? Stop feeling like an impostor? She stepped into the elegantly appointed room. And stopped dead. An immaculately clad figure was rising to bow gracefully.

'Dear Lady Rutherford, such a pleasure to meet you in my cousin's house. I had no idea, when I first met you, how closely we are connected!'

Meg felt sick and giddy as Sir Blaise possessed himself of her hand and kissed it. It took all of her self-control not to snatch it back. She repressed a shudder at his touch. All at once the sense of degrading foulness came flooding back into her soul. And this time there was no Marc to turn to for comfort and protection.

'I understand you are well acquainted with my cousin, dear Meg,' interposed Lady Fellowes smoothly. 'Sir Blaise has offered himself as your escort this morning.'

'Such an honour,' said Sir Blaise. 'To escort two such charming young ladies.'

The ensuing conversation eddied around Meg, who was experiencing waves of nausea and blind panic.

Somehow she had to control herself, let no one see her terror. He could do nothing in the park. There was nothing to be afraid of. Except fear itself.

Sir Blaise insisted on having a lady on each arm as they strolled to the park. Every nerve in Meg's body was shudderingly aware of his touch, the loathsome proximity of his body. And she could not escape, leaving Sophia to be escorted alone. Not that she had the slightest fear for Sophia's safety, but Cousin Henrietta had made it quite plain that she regarded Meg as Sophia's chaperon. She would be furious if Meg left Sophia alone. Meg set her teeth and thanked God for Sophia's giggling, simpering presence. At least it saved *her* from being alone with Winterbourne.

They had not proceeded far into the park when even this dubious protection was withdrawn. Lord Atherbridge strutted up to them.

'I say, Winterbourne! Two lovely fillies! Demned greedy, dear boy! Demned greedy!'

'You wound me, Atherbridge.' Sir Blaise was all conciliation. 'What can I do to atone? Ah, I have it! I shall relinquish my dear little cousin to you. Dear Cousin Sophia, you will not mind exchanging me for poor Atherbridge?'

Since Lord Atherbridge was possessed of a handsome fortune and was blessedly single, Sophia had not the least objection. 'Oh, no, Cousin.' She smiled up at his lordship meltingly. 'It will be such an honour for me!'

Meg nearly gagged at this blatant toadeating. How could she? Never would she resort to flattering Marcus like that! And to do him credit, Marcus would be just as revolted as she was. They drew ahead, Sophia gossiping and giggling girlishly. Meg clenched her teeth. Her disgust went some way to dissipating the fog of fear enveloping her, but she was drawn back to reality all too easily by Sir Blaise.

Not having Sophia on his other arm left his hand free to press Meg's, captive on his arm. She shuddered noticeably and he smiled urbanely.

'I am so delighted that we may continue our interrupted acquaintance, Lady Rutherford,' he said, continuing to pat her hand. 'Allow me to compliment you on your appearance in the fashionable world. You looked charmingly at the opera the other night! My companion Lady Hartleigh agreed with me heartily! '

Suddenly furious, Meg glared up at him. 'Perhaps you should limit your attentions to your companion! And the stage!'

He laughed softly. 'Dear me, how very unfashionable! Coming from a lady whom I observe to be most fashionable.' His eyes raked her suggestively, 'From her gowns, to her...marriage.'

All of a sudden Meg felt that she could scarcely breathe. She managed a polite smile for Lady Castlereagh who waved to her from a barouche.

Winterbourne continued smoothly, 'And I always like to be fashionable, my dear.'

The oily endearment mocked her. Marcus had once called her that. She took a shaky breath at the remembered tenderness in his voice...he hadn't meant it either. Oh, God, that was Lady Gwdyr, looking dreadfully haughty. She must pull herself together, she'd nearly cut the icy peeress.

'We could be fashionable together, don't you think, Lady Rutherford?' From his voice you'd have thought he was suggesting an outing to Almack's, thought Meg dazedly. Instead of which his eyes, roving over her body, were suggesting something quite different, some-

thing of which the mere thought sent shudders of re-
vulsion through her very soul.

Help came from a most unexpected quarter.

'Why, Lady Rutherford! How delightful. I have been
longing to further our acquaintance.' The arch tones of
Lady Hartleigh were as welcome as manna from
heaven. No doubt, thought Meg ironically, as her brain
started to function again, she is annoyed with me for
purloining another of her lovers.

Lady Hartleigh showed all the skill of a prize collie
bitch as she cut Meg out neatly and appropriated
Winterbourne's arm. She chattered without ceasing of
this person and that, of the scandalous price of candles
and the outrageous way in which her dressmaker was
dunning her.

'Too dreadful!' she said mournfully. And flashed a
quick glance at Meg. 'Tell me, do they dun you, Lady
Rutherford?'

'Er...no,' admitted Meg. There was no opportunity
for that. Cousin Samuel's training had been far too thor-
ough.

'Outrageous,' said Lady Hartleigh. 'Here am I, a poor
widow, who cannot in the least afford to be dunned,
being pestered to within an inch of my life, and the
Countess of Rutherford, with one of the wealthiest men
in the land to husband, doesn't get a single one!' She
shook her head sadly at the injustice of such a thing.

Meg stared at her suddenly. Why, she was mocking
herself! Why should she do such a thing? Then, as Sir
Blaise stepped away momentarily to respond to the
greeting of a friend, the green eyes flashed towards
Meg. 'Stay away from Winterbourne, Lady Rutherford.'
Nothing more. The brilliant eyes were veiled instantly

and Meg could not decide whether she had been given a warning or a threat.

Later that evening in the privacy of her carriage Lady Hartleigh said casually to her escort, 'The Countess of Rutherford seems to be making quite a hit in certain quarters.'

'Quite so, my dear,' he responded suavely. 'One must grant that Rutherford's taste is, on the whole, impeccable.'

She nodded thoughtfully. 'And, of course, it coincides so neatly with your own.' There was a faint hint of speculation in the lilting voice.

'But of course, my dear.' Sir Blaise smiled. 'No doubt you are feeling his unexpected marriage to be an unfortunate lapse of taste.'

She shrugged her slim shoulders, elegant in their low-cut gown. 'What should I care?'

'Oh, merely for the loss of a fortune and a title.'

A mocking laugh rippled from her. 'You forget, Sir Blaise. I have a title and...sufficient money for my wants.'

'It is always pleasant to have a little more than is sufficient,' he suggested.

'Very pleasant,' she agreed. 'But what is done is done. I see no way of altering the facts. Do you?'

'It is *always* possible to alter the facts, my dear Althea,' he assured her. 'Perhaps you might like to give me some assistance. For which, of course, you would be suitably...er...rewarded.'

Another ripple of laughter eddied through the darkness of the carriage, this time laced with triumph. 'Behold me, Sir Blaise. All ears, I do assure you!'

Chapter Thirteen

Lady Rutherford gazed nervously around Almack's crowded assembly rooms as she waltzed with Jack Hamilton and wondered why she had ever let Marcus persuade her that she would enjoy London. True she had made friends and met with more kindness than she would have believed possible. Yet she felt totally alone. Of all her acquaintance only one seemed to suspect that Lady Rutherford was merely a disguise.

Jack Hamilton would not let Meg hide when they were alone. He was the one person she could relax with slightly, but not even to Jack could she explain what was the matter. She could have told Marc, but she had not seen him for a long time. Only Marcus, Lord Rutherford, who greeted her politely, bought occasional gifts to adorn his countess, and had never attempted to come near her again after that dreadful morning in the library. Meg told herself proudly that she didn't care. Every single night as she cried herself to sleep.

But that wasn't the only problem. The reason she was scanning the rooms so anxiously was because Sir Blaise Winterbourne, ever since escorting her in the park, had made her the object of his attentions. He never missed a chance to approach her, soliciting her to dance in situations where she could not possibly refuse him. Only when Rutherford was present did he avoid her, and, as Rutherford so rarely escorted his countess to parties, Winterbourne had ample opportunity to further his pursuit of the lovely Lady Rutherford.

So Meg hid behind her mask, never allowing him to see her fear, deflecting his gallantries as she did those of a dozen others. And dreaded sleep. Sleep, which should have been a haven of respite from her growing unhappiness, but had become a nightmare in itself. Night after night she woke terrified, longing for Marc, but having found him missing that first time and having been informed that it was not her place to come seeking him, she forced herself to remain in her own room. If he were not home, but had gone to take his pleasure with a woman he did not find distasteful, she did not wish to know it. And besides, she had sworn never to be in the position of poor relation ever again, never to beg for anything. Especially not from her own husband with whom she had made a very clear bargain.

Through the silken swirl of dancers she caught a glimpse of Winterbourne's mocking eyes. Every muscle in her body seized and she stumbled slightly as Jack whirled her through a turn. The feeling of dizzy sickness that had swept over her without warning so often in the last two or three weeks was worse than ever as panic ripped through her. She felt Jack's hand tighten on hers, his arm like iron about her waist as he steadied her.

'Whoops,' he said unemotionally. They continued back up the room, Meg deathly pale and Jack thoughtful.

He made it a practice never to interfere between a couple but he was sorely tempted to break this rule and take Marc by the scruff of his immaculate neck and shake some sense into him! Meg, he thought, was starting to look like a ghost. And, unless Jack missed his guess, it was not just the unsatisfactory state of affairs between Marc and Meg. Winterbourne had something to do with it.

There he was now! Watching her through the swirl of dancers. And, judging by the way Meg had stiffened in his arms, she had seen him too. No doubt he would claim Meg for the next waltz, after which she would be as glittering and unapproachable as ever. Well, this time he was going to do something about it!

Staking everything on one throw, he said softly, 'You know, you don't have to dance with him, Meg. When he approaches you, tell him you have the headache and that you are about to leave. I'll escort you home.'

She stared up at him in shock. 'What...what are you talking about, Jack?' she faltered.

'I don't know, Meg,' he answered honestly. 'You will not confide in me. Which is fair enough, I am not your husband. But whatever is wrong between you and Marc, you should tell him about Winterbourne.'

'There is nothing to tell,' she said. Her heart quailed at the thought of confiding in Marcus. Belatedly she realised that she had not denied Jack's assumption that she and Marcus were at odds.

'Just that he upsets you and will not leave you alone when Marc is not present,' said Jack, tightening his arm as he whirled her around.

She rallied. 'No more so than half a dozen others. All of whom, Di warns me, are husbands who would dearly like to be able to serve Marc as he served them!' There was a sting of angry contempt in her voice.

'True enough,' he said with a chuckle. 'But don't

blame it entirely on the philandering of Marc's bachelor days. With most of 'em, your own charms have just as much to do with it!'

She snorted, ignoring the last part of his comment. 'You speak as though my lord's philandering days were all in the past!'

The bitterness in her voice got through at once. Jack stared down at her. At last! The mask had dropped completely. He said slowly, 'Take my word for it, Meg, they are. And believe me, I would know if they weren't!'

Aware that she had slipped, Meg recovered quickly. 'My dear Jack, you are Marc's closest friend. I would not expect you to betray him. Nor should you think I mind. It is a marriage of convenience, after all.'

Deliberately he said, 'I might not betray Marc, but neither would I tell *you* an outright lie by assuring you that if Marc has sought any other woman since marrying you, then he is keeping it very dark. And, if you are refining on that unfortunate meeting in the park weeks ago, then I think you have between you made a mountain out of a molehill.'

Shaken, she said, 'But he said—'

'Meg, I don't know, or wish to know, what damnfool things Marc has said in a temper,' said Jack firmly as the music drew to a close. 'But Marc has no more sought consolation elsewhere than you have. Unless you count sparring at Jackson's, engaging in more curricle races than ever before, consuming far too much brandy and generally behaving like a bear with a sore head!'

'You mean I'm making him unhappy?' Meg was horrified. She had thought Marc was entirely happy to be free to pursue his own hedonistic life. He must be! He had exactly what he had asked for.

Jack nodded, adding, 'But no more so than he's making you unhappy. You're just better at hiding it from the world.' She was, too. He was willing to bet that, if it hadn't been for Winterbourne, he might never have realised that she was unhappy. Her next words, though, stunned him.

'But he finds me distasteful!' It came out in a stricken whisper.

Jack stared at her and said, 'Meg, he's really not *that* stupid! If he gave you that impression it was in sheer self-defence. You two are as bad as each other!'

She would have protested further but Lady Jersey came up just then, full of wickedly malicious gossip, and Meg was claimed by Sir Toby. He never danced, but often claimed Meg to sit out for the more energetic reels on the basis that she was family and would afford him protection from actually having to perform.

He was quite open about this as he steered her to a chair and, when she threatened teasingly to make him dance, he simply said, 'No, no, my dear! Think of the scandal if I expired on the floor in your arms! And Di is far too young for widowhood!'

Truth to tell, Meg was only too happy to sit out with him for half an hour. He was kind and undemanding to converse with and she was finding that she tired more and more easily in the last couple of weeks. And she felt sick so often; throwing up in the mornings and feeling queasy at the sight of food. Doubtless she was not getting enough sleep, but even the appalling paroxysms of vomiting with which she was afflicted were better than nightmares.

So she acquiesced to Sir Toby's plan for her entertainment with a certain relief. Apart from a chance to rest, it gave her the opportunity to think. Something she had resolutely avoided for some time.

Jack's blunt advice had cleared her head appreciably. If he said Marc was not…amusing himself elsewhere, then he probably wasn't. Jack wouldn't lie to her. But the question remained, why wasn't he? She had, albeit accidentally, refused him her bed. It would have been fair enough if he had sought consolation. Then that morning in the library…had he thought *she* was disgusted with *him*? If that were so he would never approach her…

Oh, God! What a mess she had made of everything! If only she had had the courage to tell him how she felt and assure him that she would still abide by their agreement, then it would all be much easier. At least they would have understood each other.

She bestowed half of her attention on Sir Toby's description of the excellencies of his favourite spaniel bitch and the litter she was nursing.

'Lovely dog, Meg. Must ask Marc if he'd like one of the pups…'

By the end of their peaceful half-hour Meg was feeling much better and Sir Toby was wondering just what Meg was thinking about. Something was bothering her, but he rather suspected that Jack had the matter in hand. Probably safer if he didn't interfere.

'Ah! A family affair! How cosy. My dance, I believe, Lady Rutherford.' Winterbourne's smooth tones broke in upon them. Sir Toby looked at him disapprovingly. Couldn't stand Winterbourne. Oily sort of chap. You practically skidded every time he opened his mouth. Still, the ladies seemed to like him and it was no business of his who Meg danced with. He might just mention it to Jack, though.

So he bowed gracefully to Meg and said, 'Thank you,

m'dear. Let Marc know about the pup. He can have one if he's a mind to it.'

He was gone into the crowd, leaving Meg to face Winterbourne.

Made bold by Jack's advice Meg went on the attack, ignoring the choking fear. She had run for long enough! 'Really, Mr Winterbourne, I am at a loss to explain your predilection for my company.'

Seeing his raised eyebrows, she said, 'Oh, dear! How clumsy of me. I have so much trouble remembering your high degree.'

'I'm sure you do, Lady Rutherford. I always thought that given a little schooling you would turn out quite creditably. And as for my predilection, as you call it, for your charming company…let us say that I always finish what I set out to do.'

White with anger now more than fear, Meg said sweetly, 'How sad not to know when to give up. Especially when someone else has already achieved the goal ahead of you.'

'My dear Lady Rutherford, I am not one to measure my…er…achievements against those of another man.'

'Just as well!' she said with a glittering smile.

'Quite so,' he said. 'Ah, here is our dear Cousin Henrietta.' He acknowledged her with a sweeping bow. 'How do you do?'

'Dear Sir Blaise, and Marguerite. I am very well,' cooed Henrietta. 'How charming a couple you make. I was just saying to Lady Jersey how much pleasure it gives me to see my two cousins so happy in each other's company.'

Meg's nausea rose and she forced herself to breathe deeply. Jack was right—she had to tell Marc. What was Sir Blaise saying now?

'A moment earlier and I should not have known whom to solicit to dance. As it is, I am promised to Lady Rutherford for this waltz. Pray excuse us, Cousin.'

'But of course, dear Blaise. Good evening, Marguerite. I shall call upon you in the next day or so to arrange a little alfresco entertainment. Perhaps to Richmond with Sir Blaise. Just a family affair, of course.'

Meg murmured a polite rejoinder, all the while vowing mentally to have a full calendar for the next month. Head held high, she permitted Winterbourne to lead her towards the dance floor. Glancing back at her cousin, she saw that Lady Fellowes was watching them go with a faint smile twisting her thin lips. A smile of triumph. Meg's dark brows snapped together as a sudden suspicion flickered through her head. Could Henrietta possibly know what had happened? Could she be egging Winterbourne on? Hoping that Winterbourne would ruin the Countess of Rutherford and justify her refusal to house her husband's orphaned cousin? No! Surely not! It was too base! She shook her head to clear it. There was a more immediate problem to deal with. She had to get rid of Winterbourne.

She was damned if she would submit to his persecution any longer! Going on the attack had given her courage and she was on the look out for an opportunity to turn the tables on her persecutor. It presented itself in the large form of Jack Hamilton who strayed into their path with seeming innocence.

Meg took her chance at once, saying clearly for all to hear, 'Ah, Jack, here you are! Mr Winterbourne...I mean, Sir Blaise has been good enough to escort me to you. I have the headache and would be vastly obliged if you would take me home.' She turned to

Winterbourne. 'I thank you, sir, for your escort and your most informative conversation. Be sure I will bear it in mind. Good night.'

'The biter bit,' said Winterbourne, acknowledging her appropriation of his own method of forcing her compliance.

She met his eyes and said, 'As you see, sir, I am an apt pupil.'

He bowed and said smoothly, 'You relieve my mind enormously, Lady Rutherford.'

Meg placed her hand on Jack's arm and allowed him to lead her away, heaving a sigh of relief. She should have turned on Winterbourne weeks ago instead of trying to avoid him and dodging him through the fashionable crushes of London's hostesses. It never paid to run away from your fears, she reflected. And that was precisely what she had been doing, both with Winterbourne and Marc.

Jack had forced her to voice her unhappiness about Marc and by doing so she had found out the truth. Now that she had faced Winterbourne and served him with his own sauce, she no longer felt as though he were dominating her life. She was still afraid of him, but she was not afraid of being afraid, which had been crippling.

Jack called a chair for her and walked back to Grosvenor Square beside it, conversing with her companionably. He did not allude to their earlier conversation and, although tired and a little abstracted, Meg found his presence very soothing.

Meg opened the front door with her latch key, saying, 'Shall you come in, Jack? I don't doubt that the servants are abed but there will be brandy in the library if you would care for it.'

A discreet cough informed her that Delafield at least was not in bed. 'Good evening, my lady, Mr Hamilton. Can I fetch you anything?'

'Oh, Delafield, how nice,' said Meg. 'Yes. Some tea in the library for me if you please. Jack?'

'The brandy will be enough,' he said, preceding Meg to the door.

Marcus, arriving home early from Cribb's Parlour, headed straight for the library as had become his habit. He tended to put off going to bed these days. He was not sure if he dreaded more finding Meg in his bed or not finding her in his bed. Not that there was much chance of finding her in his bed again. His own curst pride had ensured that. It bothered the hell out of him.

And her growing friendship with Jack continued to terrify him. He couldn't bear to think that they might…fall in love. The unspoken words seared themselves into his soul. And the thought of Meg giving herself to Jack as she had to him. It appalled him but he had made a bargain. A contract. And he hadn't given her much cause to wish to renegotiate the terms of their marriage. But that was what he wanted. To cancel that sordid transaction and start again. Offer her his love. His adoration. And pray to God that she would forgive him and accept it.

His hand was on the latch when he heard voices within. He stopped dead, listening. A delightful ripple of feminine laughter bubbled up…that was Meg… followed by deeper tones… Good God! It couldn't be! Surely Jack would not…had he behaved so badly to Meg that things had already gone this far? The thought was like a knife twisting inside him. For a moment he hesitated.

And then scorching, jealous rage ignited inside him. He had told Meg that she was welcome to her amusements, need not fear his wrath…so long as she was discreet—and there was no discretion about this, dammit all! And then, on a blinding flash of realisation; he would not permit it anyway! She was *his* wife and it was about time she was reminded of it!

He flung open the door and stalked in, expecting to find them in each other's arms. Instead of which he found Jack standing in front of the fire, nursing a glass of brandy and Meg at the sofa-table, pouring herself a cup of tea from a very elegant basaltware teapot. He had to admit that if this *was* a seduction, then it was like none that he had ever participated in. Brandy, yes. But *tea*?

Neither did their reaction remotely suggest that they were concerned at his unexpected entry. His wife, damn her, simply smiled and offered him brandy, which Jack moved to pour. All of which served to make him even angrier.

Despite the fact that he didn't really believe they had been intending to betray him, he said coldly, 'I'll thank you to conduct yourself with more discretion, my lady. Entertaining a gentleman alone at this hour is not at all the thing.'

Meg was silent as colour flooded her cheeks and drained away, leaving her strangely white. For a long moment their eyes held and Marcus could see the wound he had dealt her reflected in them. He couldn't speak. Horror that he could have said something so despicable to Meg held him speechless. How utterly brutal he had been! And she was looking as though he had struck her! What the hell was wrong with him these days? He couldn't remember ever feeling this bad tempered for so long at a stretch. It had to stop!

At last she broke the silence. 'No doubt my lack of discretion bothers you more than my supposed infidelity.' For all its soft tone her voice shook with suppressed pain and the cup and saucer rattled in her hand as she set it down.

He didn't quite know what to say but Jack saved him the trouble. 'Meg, why don't you take that cup of tea up to bed with you and leave me to chat with Marc? It was good of you to offer to wait with me but, since he's home now, you need not scruple to go up. Goodnight, my dear.'

Marcus flushed. If he could see that look of frozen pain on her face, then so could Jack. No doubt he was trying in his chivalrous way to protect her. From her own husband! Shame lashed him that his best friend could possibly think Meg needed protection from him. Suddenly he was flooded with relief that she had had Jack to turn to in her misery. But enough was enough. He had to reassure her, could not let her go thinking he believed her capable of betraying him.

He went straight to her and picked up the cup and saucer. 'I beg your pardon, Meg. That was infamous of me. And quite unwarranted.' He eyed her closely. 'You look exhausted. Go to bed, my dear. I'll see you in the morning.' She nodded and held out her hand for the tea cup, again the calm Lady Rutherford who had held him at bay for the past month. He winced. She had accepted the apology at face value, but every line of her body was tautened to breaking point. She would not willingly drop her barriers again. And he could not force the issue in front of Jack.

So, shackling his urge to sweep her into his arms and

kiss her into surrender and oblivion, he smiled. 'I'll take it for you.' And he escorted her to the door, opening it for her before giving her the cup. 'Goodnight, Meg.'

He bent to kiss her gently on the cheek.

Her eyes widened in shock and instinctively her hand lifted to touch the spot lingeringly, as revealing as the sudden vulnerability in her eyes. Marcus felt an iron band tighten inexorably around his heart. Was that all he had needed to do? Could it possibly be as simple, as difficult, as that? Had he only needed to show her a little unashamed tenderness to breach her defences?

'Goodnight my lord…M…Marc.' Her voice was little more than a whisper and then she was gone.

Steeling himself, he shut the door behind her and turned to face Jack.

'Very well. You don't need to say it. I insulted both of you comprehensively. Your intelligence! Our friendship! Her virtue! You name it, I insulted it!'

'You forgot your own intelligence,' said Jack mildly. 'I had not thought you could possibly be such a codshead!' He didn't think it was the moment to admit that he had been aiming for this outcome. 'You really are a sapskull, Marc!'

Marcus groaned and said, 'For God's sake, give me that brandy! What brings you here at this hour? I'll accept that it wasn't Meg's charms.'

'I escorted her home from Almack's,' said Jack. He hesitated and then said, 'Since you are here, there's something I wanted to say. Ask you actually.'

'Mmm?' Marcus took a reviving sip of his brandy. He supposed Jack was going to tell him what a fool he was making of himself.

'Why is Meg so scared of Blaise Winterbourne? Did you or Di warn her about him? Because if you did, I think you overstated the case a trifle. The poor girl is terrified of him. And surely he wouldn't dare—?'

'What?' Marcus practically dropped his brandy. 'Did she tell you she is scared of him?'

Jack's amazement was writ large in his stunned demeanour. 'She didn't have to tell me, Marc,' he said. 'It's obvious every time he approaches her or dances with her. At least it is to me. Probably would be to you too—if you were ever there, that is.'

Marcus felt sick. 'He's been dancing with her? And she let him?'

'How can she refuse?' asked Jack reasonably. 'Although I think he makes quite sure she is in no position to do so, without calling attention to herself. She managed it tonight—that's how I came to bring her home. And I hate to say it, but his attentions are beginning to be noticed. That cousin of Meg's is doing her best to draw everyone's attention to it.'

'That bastard!' Marcus exploded. 'I swear I'll kill him!' His eyes narrowed to slits of icy rage, his fists clenched as though ready to strike. He began to pace like an enraged tiger. Raking strides took him back and forth across the room, his whole body alive with a searing anger not even Jack had ever seen.

Eventually he calmed down enough to say, 'This must go no further, Jack. I'd prefer Meg didn't even know I've told you.' Briefly he told Jack what had happened on his wedding night, finishing with, 'I let him go because I thought the risk to Meg of any scandal was too great.'

'He tried to rape her?' Sick horror sounded in Jack's voice.

'Came damn close too,' said Marcus, shuddering as he remembered how close.

'My God!' said Jack. 'It's miracle she hasn't collapsed from the strain! Why the hell didn't she tell you?'

'Because,' said Marcus evenly, 'I impressed it upon her that we were to lead separate lives, were not to tease each other and we have been doing just that. But not any more.'

'Well, thank God for that!' said Jack in relief. 'You two have been at cross purposes for quite long enough. I was getting quite depressed at watching the pair of you make a mull of your marriage.' He added thoughtfully, 'Interfering did give me something to do, though.'

Taking himself upstairs half an hour after seeing Jack out, Marcus castigated himself for not realising that Meg's façade hid unhappiness, for not forcing the issue when he had seen she looked unwell. He felt shamed that she could possibly have tried to carry such a burden alone, that she had been too hurt by his coldness to come to him. Never again, he vowed as he changed into his nightshirt. I'll see her in the morning and put this right.

He would have liked to go to her then and there, but she was probably asleep. And if he got into bed with her he would not answer for his behaviour…still, it would do no harm to peep through the door quietly. If she were asleep he could go away again…if not…

Accordingly he took a candle and padded through the bathroom, trying not to think about the night he had found her in the bath. He tapped very gently on the door. She would hear it if she were awake. There was no reply.

He was halfway back to his bedchamber when a muffled cry of fright pierced through him. In a flash he was across the bathroom and through the door.

A small lamp was burning on the nightstand and by its light he saw Meg sitting up in bed, obviously dazed and shaken, clutching the bedclothes in trembling fingers as she shuddered convulsively.

'Meg!'

She turned to him, her eyes wide and unseeing as the nightmare held her in its lingering grip. For how long, he wondered, had she been having these nightmares? Days? Weeks? No wonder she had been looking ill! He strode across the room and sat down on the edge of the bed to take her in his arms. She was not really awake, but she seemed to settle as he held her and murmured comfort in her ear. He silently cursed his pride that had blinded him to her sadness. He had thought she looked unwell because she was indulging her social ambitions, when all the time she had probably been plagued by nightmares.

He had let himself believe that she was, after all, no different from any other woman who would have married him for his money. Despite the fact that she had refused to accept his charity and had only accepted his name when he persuaded her that it would be a fair bargain. No doubt if he could hide his hurt under a surfeit of pleasure-seeking, so could she. He should have gone to her the morning after she had refused him her bed and had it out with her. Instead he had indulged his pride and left the hurt to fester, in both of them, it seemed.

She moved slightly in his arms, murmuring in distress.

'Meg, sweetheart. It's just me, Marc,' he soothed her. 'You're safe now. Nothing can hurt you. Go to sleep.'

'Marc?' She sounded barely awake.

'Yes, love.' The endearment slipped out unconsciously. He froze as he heard it on his lips.

'Not Lord Rutherford…just Marc.' And with an odd little sigh she suddenly relaxed completely in his arms and fell deeply asleep.

What the hell did she mean? *Not Lord Rutherford…just Marc.* It made no sense. They were the same person, weren't they? Or were they? He thought about it as he climbed over her and settled down with her in his arms. She had called him Marc when she was ill, when she was relaxed with him, when he had made love to her. Ever since their quarrel he had been *my lord* and she had been *madam* or *my lady*. It did make sense. The man she had called Marc was a far cry from Lord Rutherford. She hadn't even tried to tell *him* about Winterbourne.

Then it dawned on him. That night he had found her in his bed—she had asked to see him the next morning. She had started to say something about Winterbourne, about coming to find him. The realisation of what he had done exploded through him. She *had* come to him. And he had turned her away, had not bothered to listen. Instead he had indulged his pride again, spouting arrogant nonsense about his rights, making it impossible for her ever to confide in him, or indeed approach him at all.

With the result that she had suffered a month of sheer hell that would have broken most other women. Not only had she had to endure Winterbourne's attentions, but she had endured them in the belief that the one person whom she might have expected to protect her, was the one person she could not tell. She had endured it in the belief that he would not, in fact, give a damn.

She stirred slightly as his arms tightened unconsciously. A small sigh of content breathed from her. Marcus rested his face against the silken locks. His little Meg. Somehow he would have to make quite sure she knew that Lord Rutherford was gone for good. Somehow he had to convince her that Meg was safe with Marc and would not need to hide within Lady Rutherford any more. Not with him, anyway.

Chapter Fourteen

Meg woke quite early feeling more refreshed after her night's sleep than she had in weeks. She lay in a contented doze. Her dreams last night had not been so terrible as they usually were. Somehow, at the last minute, the vileness that was Winterbourne had transformed into Marc, whose strong arms had banished the strangling terror, whose voice had comforted her.

Gradually she became aware of a heavy weight across her waist and another one pinning her legs to the bed. Puzzled, she turned her head and encountered her husband's sleeping face, strangely relaxed and gentle in slumber, with the cold eyes hidden. Fascinated she stared at it. The straight aristocratic nose, the square chin with the veriest suspicion of stubble. With a delightful shiver she remembered how sensuously it had rasped across her tender breasts when he made love to her. He had chuckled at her shocked reaction the first time, a deep seductive rumble and had promptly done it again...and again.

Somewhat belatedly she wondered why he was in her bed. Did this mean that he had come to claim his rights and had been too considerate to awaken her? Suddenly she remembered her dream, that Winterbourne had been transformed or rather had been banished by Marc. Had it been a dream? Or had Marc heard her? She knew she had woken up crying out several times in the past weeks.

His eyes opened, putting an end to her speculations. For they were warm and tender and he smiled at her, a glorious, beckoning smile as he whispered, 'I'm a bloody fool, Meg. Will you forgive me?' The arm lying over her waist tightened, an iron band drawing her to him.

She went willingly, her soft curves yielding to the hard strength of his body and felt him stir against her.

'Forgive *you*? Oh, Marc, I'm so sorry!' Tears trickled down her cheeks. 'I didn't mean all those awful things I said!'

He kissed the tears away and said in a light tone belied by the depth of tenderness in his eyes, 'Didn't you? Well, you should have, because I deserved the lot of them!' And then desire took over for both of them, rendering all the extended apologies they had intended utterly obsolete.

Over a month's abstinence had Marcus straining at the bit like a half-wild stallion and Meg discovered that her hitherto gentle husband could be fiercely possessive and demanding in his lovemaking and that having her nightgown ripped off by the right man was really quite exhilarating. And Marcus found that his shy, inexperienced bride could, with the right encouragement, become quite inventive in her efforts to please him.

Afterwards they slept again, wrapped in each other's arms in the blissful exhaustion of utter fulfilment.

* * *

Meg woke again later to find herself alone and a note on her pillow.

> Dear Meg,
> I have something to see to this morning. It will not take long. If you like, after that I could take you for a drive or stroll in the park. Which reminds me, we have not yet arranged a riding horse for you or a suitable carriage if you would like to drive yourself.
>
> Marc

With a happy sigh Meg sat up and swung her legs out of bed. Only to be assailed with a wave of dizzying nausea. In her joy at being reconciled to Marc, she had quite forgotten to get up carefully and slowly, ring for a cup of tea and get straight back into bed before the nausea could really take hold. Frantically she dived for the nightstand and was copiously and comprehensively sick into the wash basin.

Feeling extremely plain and quite unlike the seductive siren who had so thoroughly pleasured, and been pleasured by, her husband an hour or so earlier, Meg rang the bell and got back into bed to wait for Lucy.

Meg had in the end decided to keep Lucy as her maid without asking anyone's advice. She liked Lucy and didn't give a damn what anyone thought anyway. But she did wish Lucy did not seem quite so delighted by her puzzling bouts of sickness. She even seemed to think Meg ought to be delighted. Oh, well, as long as she brought hot water to make a pot of tea, Meg was prepared to overlook her ill-concealed delight at this fresh evidence of Lady Rutherford's weakness.

Perhaps, thought Meg hopefully, now that she and

Marc were sharing a bed again, the nightmares would stop. She was sure the sickness was only because she hadn't been getting enough sleep. Even when he was cross with her, Marc had said she would make herself ill if she didn't let up.

It turned out to be one of her worst mornings. The cup of tea helped only marginally and the thought of breakfast revolted her. Lucy, more than usually heartless, brought up some dry toast and insisted that she eat it. Mrs Crouch, she said, had insisted it was just the thing for a lady who was feeling a mite poorly and the mistress was to eat it up and no nonsense.

Meg did as she was bid, thinking that Di had been quite right in her prophecy that the staff would accept her. Lucy and Mrs Crouch were as kind as Agnes Barlow could have been.

Marcus whipped through his accounts that morning with only a cursory blink of amazement at the trivial nature of the bills with which Meg had presented him. Despite Di's encouragement, Meg had spent very little on herself. Except, he noted with a rueful grin, at Hatchard's. The bill from there did make him raise his eyebrows a trifle. Obviously Jack, whom he knew to have taken her there the first time, had been far more successful than Di in persuading her to extravagance.

He already knew that she kept a careful eye on the household accounts. Mrs Crouch had indicated that the mistress was doing just as she ought, learning the ways of a fashionable London household and then making shrewd suggestions where necessary. He snorted. No doubt Great-uncle Samuel would be proud of her now.

When he had finally ascertained that he had dealt with all the bills for the last month he gave his secretary directions for settling them and ordered his curricle to be brought around.

He returned an hour later with an oddly shaped parcel under his arm and a spring in his step as he went in search of Meg. Delafield informed him that he believed the mistress to be in the drawing room.

Upon entering the drawing room, Marcus thought that either Delafield must have made a mistake or that Meg had left the room. It appeared to be empty at first glance. He was about to leave when an odd circumstance caught his eye. The crimson drapery on the pedestal table was half off. Startled, he went to investigate.

And found Meg lying unconscious behind the table, half-covered in the drape, her face white. For a moment he was frozen in shock and then with a strangled groan he dropped the parcel on the table and knelt beside her, gathering her into his arms. He lifted her effortlessly and carried her to the sofa to lay her down upon it as though she might break.

Chafing her hand, he said, 'Meg, sweetheart. What's wrong? Meg?'

Her eyelids fluttered open. 'Where…what happened?' She looked completely dazed, her eyes unfocused.

'Are you all right, Meg?' He held her comfortingly against his shoulder.

'Y…yes. I felt so strange…and then…I was looking out the window and I turned to hold on to the table…' She sounded very puzzled.

'You must have fainted,' he said worriedly. She just wasn't getting enough sleep, he thought. And what about the nightmares? 'Meg…' He was very hesitant. After all, they had only just made up their differences—

at least, he hoped they had. 'Meg, how much sleep have you been getting? Have you been having nightmares, apart from the one you had last night?'

Her sigh of relief breathed through them both. 'Every night,' she whispered, with an involuntary shudder.

His arm tightened protectively as his eyes closed in pain at the thought of her waking up alone and scared, unable to come to him for comfort. 'The night you came to find me—'

'Yes. That was the first one.' She began to cry softly. 'I tried to bear it, Marc. But in the end I was so frightened to sleep that I just tried to avoid it as much as I could. Put off coming home…read…anything… anything but sleep…'

'You'll sleep in my bed from now on,' he said quietly. She stirred in his arms. 'No, don't argue. There is nothing for *you* to be ashamed of. If I hadn't been such a bloody fool that morning, this wouldn't have happened. In fact, if I hadn't been too top-heavy to think straight when I came up to bed that night I would have just got into bed with you. Instead of which I went back down to the library and spent a damnably uncomfortable night on the sofa!'

She twisted around to look at him. 'You did *what*?' Stunned disbelief echoed in her voice, all her tears suspended.

Shamefaced, he nodded. 'Told you I was a bloody fool. The crick in my neck lasted for days!'

'You mean you didn't…you just let me think…'

He nodded again. 'So, you see, I did deserve all the things you said to me. Even if not for quite the reasons you thought I deserved them for.'

They sat quietly for a while until Marcus bethought himself of the forgotten parcel and fetched it.

With a teasing smile he said, 'I have something here for you, my sweet.'

She stared up at him, her heart pounding. He had something for her, for Meg. With hands that trembled, she took the package and unwrapped it on her lap. The coverings fell away and she sat dazed, staring at a silver teapot.

Lifting her eyes to his, she said huskily, 'But we have lots of teapots…' Her voice cracked with emotion.

His sounded wobbly too. 'But this is for you, Meg. Just for you.'

Tears flooded her eyes. 'For Meg? Not for Lady Rutherford?' she whispered. And flushed scarlet. He'd think she'd lost her wits.

But with a groan he caught her into his arms, teapot and all, and said harshly, 'It's for Meg—from Marc.' She could feel his lips on her hair, his arms warm and hard, holding her safely. It was just for her—for Meg, from Marc. Not something the Earl of Rutherford thought his countess ought to have to present a good appearance. She would not need to hide any longer.

As if he had read her thoughts he said, 'Lady Rutherford may throw as much dust in the eyes of the *ton* as she can, but I want Meg.' He held her at arm's length and looked deep into her eyes.

'Oh, Marc! I…' Her heart nearly tore apart with the torrent of love that poured through it. The words were nearly out, when she remembered. He didn't want to love. And despite all he'd said, he hadn't said he loved her. She choked the words back. Forced them into submission. He was her friend again, her lover in only one sense.

'Meg?' His fingers had tightened on her shoulders. His eyes burnt into hers.

She forced herself to smile. 'Then...then we are friends again?'

In his turn Marcus forced a smile. 'Friends.' He pulled her back into his arms and stared despairingly over her head. *Friends.* For a moment he had thought, had hoped, that she loved him. But she had drawn back. As he must. It was too soon to tell her how much he cared. He'd have to show her first, regain her trust.

Belatedly he remembered he'd suggested a drive in the park and reminded her of it.

'Just the thing to bring some colour back to your cheeks,' he said firmly, overriding her protest that she really didn't feel at all the thing. 'Fresh air will help,' he insisted. 'We'll go to the Park. If we take Burnet, he can look after the horses while we have a gentle stroll.'

Meg argued no more. The thought that Marc wanted to spend time with her out of bed was too wonderful to be gainsaid. She vowed that this time she would do nothing to disturb the happiness she had been granted. It was too fragile.

Half an hour later in Marcus's curricle, Meg was regretting profoundly that she had not been more assertive over her qualms about taking carriage exercise that morning. The rocking of the well-sprung vehicle on the cobbles was making her dreadfully queasy. Her stomach roiled in protest and she felt cold and clammy. Determinedly she gritted her teeth and tried to think of something, anything else. Marc, thank God, had his eyes on his horses and had noticed nothing amiss. If they could but reach the Park so that she could get down!

Finally, just as they turned into the Park, she could

control herself no longer and gasped, 'My lord... Marc...stop! Please! I must get down...'

Marcus glanced down at her and swore. She looked about as green as the grass. There was a barouche directly behind them; he could not possibly stop in the gateway. Frantically he drove in and pulled his team over.

Before Marcus could so much as open his mouth, Burnet had let go of the straps, leapt from his perch and was at the wheelers' heads. But Meg was even faster. The horses's hooves had not stilled before she was on the carriageway, retching violently.

Marcus was beside her in a trice. 'Meg! Why did you not say you felt so unwell?' Dear God, was she really ill? Was it more than just a lack of sleep and unhappiness? And she had not told him!

Recovering slightly, Meg said, 'Oh, Marc! I'm so sorry...in front of everyone!'

'Damn and blast everyone!' he said, to the intense delight of the Ladies Castlereagh and Sefton, who passed by in a barouche at that moment. 'It's *you* I'm worried about!' He dragged a handkerchief from his pocket and wiped her mouth gently.

Despite looking distinctly green, she smiled at him radiantly. 'I shall be all right. I am always much better after lunch for some reason.'

He stared at her in disbelief as the implications of what she had said crashed in on him. *Always much better after lunch.* He could remember his mother being affected the same way—when she was increasing!

'How...how long have you been feeling sick in the mornings, Meg?' he asked very quietly.

She thought carefully. 'A couple of weeks, maybe three.'

'And you didn't think perhaps you should mention this to me?' He couldn't believe that she would not have told him something of *this* magnitude. Even if they had been at odds! Exultation warred with shame that she had not told him.

'Tell you I felt a bit sick in the mornings? Why?' Meg was puzzled. Belatedly Marc remembered; in her experience, gentlemen were never interested when one was unwell. Samuel had never bothered with her, even when she broke an arm, and now she raised questioning eyes to his face. But it went further than that…she was not in the least flustered, just puzzled. Puzzled, for God's sake!

And Marcus realised, with a lurch of his heart, that his innocent, uninformed bride had absolutely no idea of the significance of her bouts of sickness. That she had never had anyone to tell her these things, had never thought that she would need to know them. Instead of her coming to him, beaming with shy pride in her news, *he* was going to have to tell *her* she was probably pregnant. Looking around wildly for help, he caught his tiger's sapient eye.

'Took my old ma the same way, every blessed time,' offered that worthy in a helpful spirit that made Marcus long to brain him. 'Goes off after a bit usually.' He seemed quite unsurprised.

'Thank you, Burnet,' said Marcus drily, wondering if everyone in the household except himself and Meg knew the truth. He hoped to God his staff was as discreet as he had always thought. If this got out, they would be twitted by their entire acquaintance. He pushed these thoughts to the back of his mind. For now he had to get Meg home, preferably without further mishap.

'I think, my dear, that I had better take you home,' he said in as restrained a tone as he could manage. He wanted to explode with his joy, to shout his triumph to the blue skies with their lamb's-wool clouds. A child! His child! Meg's child! He didn't give a damn if it were a boy or a girl! He had better tell Meg first. Privately!

'A baby?' Meg could not believe her ears. 'You think I'm having a baby?'

Marcus nodded. 'It's quite likely you know, sweetheart. It is a common result of sharing a bed...or—' his eyes twinkled wickedly '—a bath, for that matter.'

Meg would have blushed had she not been scarlet already. After marching her into the library and settling her on the sofa, Marc had proceeded to ask her a series of the most embarrassingly intimate questions imaginable, on a subject she had never dreamed a gentleman would know anything about.

He had actually asked her when she had last had her monthly courses, and upon hearing that it was before their wedding, had asked her how long before. Flustered at such a personal question, she had had to rack her brain for ages before remembering that it had been about a fortnight before. As if that were not enough, he had actually asked her if she were generally regular.

Upon being informed in an embarrassed mutter that she was, he had told her very gently that he thought she was going to have a baby.

A baby. A baby of her own. Marc's baby. She sat in stunned silence, unable to speak for the wave of joy that flooded her heart. She would have a baby to love and nurse. Someone who would love her, depend upon her. Someone who needed Meg. And Marc had given her this priceless gift.

Concerned at her long silence, Marcus spoke her name very softly. 'Meg?' What was she thinking? Was she frightened at what lay before her. Childbirth? Suddenly Marcus was frightened. It overwhelmed his joy. Women died in childbirth…frequently…as his mother had done. His guts twisted into a hard knot of fear at the memory. What if he lost Meg? Resolutely he thrust the idea away.

'Meg, are you all right?' She was so silent, her head bowed. He put a hand under her chin and lifted it gently and met such a blaze of joy in the blue-grey eyes that his own knot of fear began to dissolve in the face of it.

'All right?' Her voice was breathless. 'All right? Oh, Marc! Thank you!' She flung her arms around him and hugged him. He held her tightly, stroking the nape of her neck, his fingers teasing and seductive, and felt her quiver responsively. Not quite the usual way of doing things, he thought ruefully. She should have told him! Come to think of it, shouldn't he be thanking her? Nothing, he realised, absolutely nothing about this marriage fitted in with his expectations.

After a light meal Meg retired to her room for a nap and Marcus headed for the library to do some much-needed thinking. All this was more than he had bargained for. He had glibly told Meg that he was marrying for children. Expected her to produce an heir or three.

With a sickening sense of shame, he realised that in making his cold-blooded bargain, he had accorded her less respect than he would one of his brood mares. He had not expected to feel this chilling, bone-shaking fear at the thought of Meg in childbirth.

Or had he? Was that why he had tried to choose a wife he would not care about? Except, of course, in a friendly, detached sort of way. Women died all the time in childbirth. Vibrant, affectionate, *loving* women. Women like his mother, for example.

For the first time in years Marcus allowed himself to think about his mother's death and the baby brother who had died with her. He knew that the one unhappiness in his parents' marriage had been that they only had two children. It had not been a desire for a back-up heir that had worried them. They had simply wanted children and there had been several miscarriages in the fifteen years between his own birth and the pregnancy that had killed her.

He remembered his parents' happiness during those last school holidays. The buzz of excitement in the household. They were ecstatic. The pregnancy had gone so well. And five weeks later he'd been summoned to his housemaster's study where the news had been broken to him. He remembered thinking that the gods had been jealous of so much happiness, and he determined to guard against it. What you didn't have, no one, not even the gods, could take away. His father's agony of guilt and remorse had only confirmed him in his opinion. Better not to care if loss could destroy a man so totally.

And now he cared. Without ever intending such a thing, he had fallen in love with Meg after making a bargain with her that now shamed his soul with its sordid assumptions. And she had accepted it. Not because she was after his money or title, but because she had been desperate and had had nowhere else to go—and because she had been too innocent and unsophisticated to see it for the insult it was. With a groan he realised that he had taken advantage of her as surely as Winterbourne had attempted to.

And now she was pregnant, radiant with joy. Had thanked him as though he had bestowed a priceless gift upon her, when what he had given could prove to be a death sentence. He wanted to go to her and tell her he loved her. Beg her to start over with him. Let him court her and woo her as he should have done.

But even if it now revolted him, they had made a bargain. He had promised not to make demands on Meg, not to interfere with her. Just because he no longer wanted the freedom he had reserved for himself was not a sufficient reason to break his word. She had accepted his word in good faith. How was she supposed to understand that his proposal had been an attempt to hide his own fears, when even he had not realised that?

And even if she did agree, even if she did come to love him in return…it would be to tempt the gods, make them look too closely at his joy, make them look with jealousy on his little Meg. The thought stabbed through him like a cold, shining lance, piercing his entrails with chilly, merciless terror. To voice his love would be to offer Meg as a hostage to fortune.

But he could not go on the way he had been. Even if he did not dare to ask for her love, they would have to be friends if she were to be happy. He could not bear to think that she might ever be too proud, or scared of him, to ask for his help. And perhaps if the gods could see his despair, they might think he was already miserable enough and overlook his little Meg.

As she dressed for dinner Meg was conscious of a warm glow of happiness. She was having a baby and she was going to see Marc at dinner. He had tucked her up for her nap and said so.

Until dinner, my sweet.

The endearment rested safely in her heart, a buffer against all possible harm. She was going to see Marc. Even if it was across fifty feet of over-polished mahogany. All right then, twenty feet! But it might as well be fifty for all the conversation you could have down its length. Still, if that was how Marc preferred it... It was his house, after all, and she had promised not to tease him.

She floated down to dinner, far happier than she had been in weeks. Marcus was awaiting her in the library and smiled as she came in. She felt her heart leap in a wild dance of joy as he came to her and kissed her tenderly.

'Did you sleep well?' he asked as he released her.

'Oh, yes,' she said, rubbing her cheek against his shoulder.

Marcus felt a stab of joy. She looked so much better, less pale and wan. And her eyes had lost that haunted look he had seen in them lately. She was again the confiding, trusting woman he had married. Just what he had done to deserve such a blessing he didn't know, but he was damned if he'd endanger it again.

And he was definitely not going to risk exposing her to Winterbourne again. Which brought him to a problem. He really had to go to Yorkshire to oversee some of the improvements that he had set in train and he was definitely not prepared to leave Meg alone in London. But how would she cope with the journey if she were feeling unwell?

As he escorted her to the dining room, he asked, 'How would you feel about a trip to Yorkshire in a couple of weeks?'

Her eyes flew to his. 'You'd take me?'

He nearly died. She could still think he'd leave her behind? After what she'd told him?

With Delafield in the hall he couldn't do a thing except press the small hand on his arm and say, 'I won't *not* take you. We'll travel in easy stages, any way you like, by chaise or my curricle. And we'll stop as often as you like. I need to go up to see to a few things, but there's no hurry. We'll go when you feel you can manage it, not before.'

He wanted her with him. It took a moment to sink in, that he didn't want to be without her, even for a short time. Her heart swelled. Surely, even if he never loved her as she loved him, she could be happy with what she had now?

To her surprise at the end of dinner, when the covers had been removed and the footmen dismissed, Marcus beckoned to Delafield and said, 'Now that you have demonstrated to your mistress that the staff can provide a formal dinner, do you think we could have it set out in the library when we dine alone or just have one or two intimate guests?' It was said with the sweetest of smiles, but there was no mistaking the authority in that voice.

Delafield seemed shocked. 'My lord, what is suitable for a bachelor establishment cannot be right for my lady—'

'My lady,' said Marcus inflexibly, 'would prefer not to have to shout across twenty feet of mahogany to address a simple remark to me. You know what Shakespeare says..."Her voice was ever gentle, sweet and low, an excellent thing in a woman"...I do feel, Delafield, that we should preserve your mistress's excellences where possible.'

Meg practically choked in her napkin in her efforts to stifle her giggles. Master and servant turned their attention to her at once.

'I beg your pardon, my lady,' said Marcus. 'I hope this meets with your approval.'

She nodded, the lower part of her face still hidden behind the napkin, bright eyes gleaming with fun. It was so lovely to have her tender, caring Marc back. To be able to share a joke…and a bed.

'Good. Bring your wine glass with you and we'll both go to the library.' He rose and held out his arm with a very wicked smile. A smile which suggested he was pleased to be sharing a bed again. Blushing, she went to him and placed her hand on his arm.

As they left the room she was moved to inquire, 'Why *do* women have to leave the room for the gentlemen to finish their wine?'

Marcus grinned as he caught a warning glare from Delafield who was holding the door for them. 'Tradition, my dear, dictates that the gentlemen are supposed to sit over their wine and recount…er…stories in somewhat dubious taste…if you follow my meaning.'

He observed his wife's comprehensive blush with marked satisfaction.

'Oh,' said Meg weakly.

Marcus promptly pressed his advantage. 'Dining alone with one's wife, of course, has obvious benefits,' he pronounced urbanely as he allowed his gaze to rest appreciatively on Meg's low-cut neckline.

'It does?' Meg was only sure of one thing. He was going to say something absolutely outrageous.

'Mmm. I always prefer to follow up such stories with action!'

Chapter Fifteen

Sitting before a roaring fire in the cosy library of Rutherford House, wrapped in what appeared to be every cashmere shawl in London, with a hot brick at her feet on a very fine day in late spring, Meg was wondering if she could deal with another seven months of this nearly terminal boredom. She was seriously considering telling Marc that it was all a false alarm and she had had her monthly courses after all. According to Mrs Crouch it would be a while before she started to show. Perhaps by then Marc would have calmed down a trifle.

Even being back in the same bed was driving her insane, because he wouldn't touch her! Not since the night he'd told Delafield to reduce the dining table. After telling her a couple of what she suspected were relatively tame post-dinner stories, he'd seduced her on the library floor in front of the fire and since then he'd behaved as though he'd taken a vow of celibacy! He just about had a seizure if she so much as sneezed and she had not been allowed to attend a single party in the last week. He had given it out that she was indisposed and unable to see anyone. And unfortunately Di had been out of town for a few days.

Meg had been understandably shy about telling anyone she was pregnant. But in the face of Marc's overreaction she had to do something! Which was why she had meekly acquiesced in his plan for her morning: to whit, sitting in front of the fire doing nothing except wait for Di, who had returned last night. The moment Marc's back had been turned she had scribbled a quick note and dispatched one of the footmen with it.

There was something odd about Marc's reaction to her pregnancy. At first she had not doubted that he was delighted, but increasingly he looked worried. She had caught him looking at her as though he were guilty of some heinous crime. And when she asked him if something was wrong, he lied. Badly.

And he was cosseting her to death. Sending her to bed early. Keeping her in bed late, which would have been fine if he had joined her. But the wretched man came to bed long after she was asleep and was invariably out of bed by the time she awoke. She usually awoke to discover him making her a cup of tea, having shamelessly intercepted Lucy at the door in his nightrail.

In the face of his behaviour, she could not doubt his concern, could not doubt that he cared for her personally, but she could not break through his iron control. And she wasn't quite sure what to do about it. Or even if she should do something about it. Perhaps Marc was afraid that if they made love the baby might drop out or something. After having been told by her husband that she was pregnant, Meg was not prepared to confess to even more ignorance of her bodily functions to him.

So, when in doubt, ask an expert. Di had four healthy

and mischievous children and that made her the obvious choice.

She came in unannounced. 'Goodness, Meg! Are you really sick? It's simply boiling in here.'

Her keen glance took in the voluminous shawls and the look of resignation on Meg's perspiring face as she sat down on the sofa beside her. 'Whatever is the matter? You know, dear, if you're a trifle warm, I should take off one of those shawls. Or maybe even five of them.'

Meg hesitated for a moment and then said baldly, 'Marc seems to think I'm increasing.'

'Marc! What the devil would he know about it?' asked Di.

'Well, he certainly knows more than I do!' confessed Meg shamefacedly and told Di what had happened.

To her everlasting credit Di succeeded in maintaining a straight face until the end of Meg's recital.

'You were sick?' There was an expression of respectful awe on her face as she regarded her sister-in-law. 'In Hyde Park?'

'On the carriage way.'

'During the morning promenade?'

Meg nodded.

At first it was just a twitch at the corner of her mouth, which rapidly progressed to a broad grin. Finally Di gave up the unequal struggle and succumbed to peals of laughter. Meg, who had spent the entire week cooped up with a husband in low spirits, joined in heartily.

'Oh, dear,' gasped Di, when she could speak. 'I should love to have seen his face! His high and mighty lordship, the Earl of Rutherford! How utterly splendid! Why, oh, *why*, did I have to be away? But tell me, why is Marc looking so glum? I saw him from the carriage as I drove up and he doesn't look happy at all. And why on earth are you sitting tucked up in front of the fire on such a lovely day? Are you feeling sick?'

'Not now,' said Meg. 'I'm always fine by late morning. As for why I'm sitting here—Marc won't let me so much as set foot out of the house. He was delighted at first, I think, but now he seems…I don't know… pleased, but…angry.'

'Oh.' Di was silent for a few moments. 'Maman. I never thought of that.'

'Pardon?'

'Maman. Our mother,' said Di slowly. 'Did Marc never tell you anything about her?'

Meg shook her head. What on earth could her mother-in-law have to do with it?

Di told her. 'Maman died in childbirth when I was twenty and Marc was fifteen. No. He wouldn't tell you. Stupid question. He never talks about her much. He was shattered by her death and our father's reaction didn't help. You see, Papa blamed himself and his desire for more children. He spent the rest of his life flailing around in his own guilt. Which was silly, because Maman wanted the baby as much as he did.'

She sighed and then went on, 'So Marc, while doubtless *aux anges* in one respect, is also shaking with terror in case you should suffer the same fate. At least, I suppose that is the problem. And it certainly explains his over-protectiveness. He practically drove me crazy the first couple of times I was increasing, so I hate to imagine how he'd feel about you.'

The thought of death had not occurred to Meg. She had been so excited at the thought of a baby that the risks involved had not sunk in. She had just thought Marc was concerned about her feeling sick.

Swallowing hard, she turned to Di and said, 'But do you think—?'

Di interrupted her briskly. 'What I think is that Marc is making a cake of himself! Now, get rid of these ridiculous shawls and come and take a stroll in the park with me. It will be very much better for you if you stay active and healthy. Take my word for it, giving birth needs lots of energy and if you sit around worrying about Marc's idiocy for the next six months you'll go mad. Come along, I can tell you all about it as we go.'

'There's just one other thing, Di.' Meg definitely didn't want to ask this question either on the way to, or in, the park. 'Is it safe to…to…well, to make love when you are increasing?'

Di simply stared at her. 'Is it safe? Why ever wouldn't it be?'

Meg blushed. Maybe Marc just wasn't interested. had only ever wanted her because he needed an heir. 'I just thought…well…Marc won't touch me!'

'Marc,' said the absent Earl's sister, not mincing matters, 'is the biggest idiot I know!' She stopped just short of informing Meg that, although he might not have used such stratagems himself, Marc Langley certainly knew there was nothing to fear in making love to a pregnant woman. A pregnant wife, in fact, was one of many a rake's preferred targets.

Instead she opted for practical suggestions. 'Now, here's what you should do…' And she proceeded to give a piece of scandalously detailed advice that brought a very naughty twinkle to Meg's eyes, and an even naughtier smile to her lips.

'*That* should settle *him*!' concluded Lady Diana confidently.

Lady Rutherford thought there could be no doubt of that.

By dint of some extremely devious questioning of the servants, Meg had ascertained that Marc was taking his bath during the late afternoon when she was supposedly tucked up safely in bed. No doubt he thought he was being excessively clever, she mused with unbecoming smugness, as she nestled down into her silken bed-clothes for a sleep after her stroll with Di.

Her sister-in-law had been full of information and advice about pregnancy, childbirth and babies. She hadn't bothered about toddlers. 'Time enough for that. They are revolting little angels. That's all you need to know about them for now.'

And, 'Once you stop feeling quite so sick, get Marc to take you down to Alston Court. Fresh air and gentle walks in the country will be much better for you than town... He's taking you already? After going to Yorkshire? Humph! At least he's showing *some* evidence of rational thought!'

Meg had felt as though she were being advised by a loving mother or elder sister as they walked.

'Of course women die, my love. I can't deny that. But to be worrying about it now is nonsensical. You can do nothing about it except stay as well and happy as you can.

'Wet nurses may be fashionable, but you feed him, or her, yourself. Marc won't mind and it is the loveliest feeling you can imagine. So cuddly!'

And later, 'I'll come down to Alston Court for your confinement naturally—' She stopped short as Meg stared in amazement. 'Well, only if you want me to...'

'Want you?' Meg's eyes were shimmering with tears.

The one thing really scaring her had been facing the ordeal without a mother or sister. The thought of Cousin Henrietta attending the birth was not to be borne. 'Would you really come? Oh, Di!'

'Of course I'm coming!' said Di indignantly. 'Now dry your eyes. You can't possibly *cry* in the middle of Hyde Park. Throwing up here was outrageous enough!' Then, in tones of inspiration, she added, 'You know, dear, if I were you, I should bring that nice, sensible Mrs Barlow you told me about, back from Yorkshire. I'm sure Marc would think it a good idea.'

Now, as Meg dozed off, she clung to the idea that Di was treating her as though she were truly family, not just Marc's accidental bride. Briefly she thought of the dangers in childbirth. Di was right. She should concentrate on staying happy and healthy. And Di had promised to have a tactful word with Marc. Tactful for Di, anyway. So she went off to sleep, content in the knowledge that Lucy had promised faithfully to awaken her at four o'clock.

Marcus relaxed back in his bath and shut his eyes with a sigh of relief. He'd had a busy morning and Di's message demanding his immediate presence had taken him completely by surprise. She didn't do that often, so he had gone and received an earful of sisterly candour that had left him stunned.

He really hadn't meant to scare Meg with his behaviour, but he could see now that he had been just a shade over-protective. And of course he didn't think she needed to spend the next seven months incarcerated on a sofa…it was just that—

Just that he was an ignorant, addlepated male, who

shouldn't be allowed out without a leash, Di had finished for him.

He had apologised and promised to atone. And she'd had one or two brilliant ideas; such as taking the Barlows down to Alston Court. But when it came to his own sister informing him that making love to his wife would not cause the baby any harm, he drew the line. Frostily he had told Diana to mind her own business. He had left almost at once, but the dignity of his grand exit was totally ruined by Di escorting him downstairs and shamelessly telling him, in front of her fascinated butler and two openly amused footmen, that reformed rakes were all the same—the world's biggest prudes when it came to their own wives.

She was right, of course, he admitted to himself in the sanctity of his bath. He was being an idiot. He couldn't help himself where Meg was concerned. His erstwhile cynical and rational brain seemed to dissolve into a liquefied mess of panic just thinking about her in childbirth. And of course he didn't think that making love would endanger the baby, or not in the way Di meant. It was just that stupid, illogical idea that to be too happy was courting disaster. That he was terrified to tell Meg that he loved her. And that he knew he would never be able to make love to her again without telling her. He hadn't explained that to Di. It sounded mawkish in the extreme, even to him and he didn't dare think what Di would have to say!

Perhaps, he thought, it would be better to accept the joy he had now and leave the future to take care of itself. It made far more sense really. He wondered why he hadn't thought of it before. Probably because you don't think at all when Meg's around, an annoying internal voice informed him. Any fool who could think that she and Jack would have had an affair is clearly unhinged!

His decision made, he stretched, luxuriating in the warmth of his bath and in the delightful intention of taking his wife to bed. Early. For the express purpose of having his scandalously wicked way with her. His loins tightened painfully at the thought. After which he was going to tell her just how much he loved her. If he could find the words…if they even existed…

A faint click behind him informed him that he was not alone. Startled he swung around and there was Meg, draped—dressed would definitely have been an over-statement—in a flimsy silk peignoir. Its shimmering, pink folds clung and shifted in the most tantalising way, affording glimpses of long silky limbs which made him wonder if the incendiary heat charging his body would cause the bath to boil over. His mouth suddenly dry, he stared at her, noting the darker pink of her nipples which peeped shyly through the diaphanous fabric and that darker shadow at the top of her thighs… He swallowed hard. Hell! She looked like a siren in that thing, ripe, seductive.

'Oh, hullo, Marc. Am I disturbing you?' The slight curve at the corner of her mouth told him that she knew perfectly well he was extremely disturbed. In a very basic, male way. And her voice! It sounded so husky. What the hell was she thinking of? The answer came at once. His sweet little Meg was thinking of exactly the same thing he was.

As if in confirmation of this, she smiled at him with heart-stopping slowness and glided across the floor to one of the niches. Unhurriedly she allowed the peignoir to slither with a seductive hushing off her shoulders on to the bench and, wearing nothing but that smile and her rippling, tumbling curls, she came and sat down on the edge of the bath beside him. Ostensibly to trail her legs in the water.

'Will you be long in the bath?'

Marc looked up and met the blandest query in her eyes. The hunter, he realised belatedly, had become the hunted...and was enjoying it immensely. His shy bride had turned out to be an unprincipled little hussy.

'How long would you like me to be?' he drawled. Two could play this game.

'Oh, take your time,' she responded.

That went without saying, thought Marc, as one silken leg grazed his shoulder in seeming innocence. He would be only too pleased to take his time with her. Within reason, of course, he amended, as that leg slid past again.

Casually he stretched and slid one wet, powerfully muscled arm behind her bottom to scoop her off the edge and into the bath. She came unresistingly and met his fiery gaze with a becoming blush. He smiled wickedly. So, she was not quite as calm as she was pretending to be. Good.

Keeping his voice light, despite the screaming demands of his body, Marcus enquired, 'Just what do you think you are doing?'

'What do *you* think I'm doing?' countered Meg, a trifle breathlessly as he manoeuvred her with one compelling hand in the small of her back to straddle his hips. The other hand was lazily caressing one puckered and aching nipple. She gasped in pleasure, her eyes widening in shock at the novelty of her position.

Marcus did not reply at once. Her response was so spontaneous, so lovely, he just wanted to watch her, adore her with his eyes and hands.

But at last he said, 'Seducing me?' The hand at her breast trailed down her stomach, leaving a track of fire, and slid between her thighs. The hand at her back drew her closer and she felt his mouth close possessively on first one breast and then the other. She pressed small, moist kisses on his nape, under his ear and sobbed with desire as he loved her, gently, thoroughly.

In a voice husky with passion she asked, 'Do you mind being seduced?' She had a feeling that the tables were well and truly turned now anyway.

A little laugh shook him as he lifted her to ease her against his throbbing body. 'Does it feel as though I mind?' He gave her no chance to reply, reaching up to tangle his long fingers in her silken tresses, and taking her mouth in a kiss of raw, unfettered passion as he brought her quivering body down to meet his possessive thrust in absolute mastery.

Meg's last coherent thought was that if he did mind, he was certainly going to a great deal of effort to disguise the fact. They hadn't even made it to the sofa-bed this time.

Meg lay nestled safely in Marc's arms, wondering dreamily if they ought to get up and dress for dinner. It felt so lovely just to lie here with his hard, warm body pressed against her, his gentle, knowing hands caressing her shoulder and the occasional pressure of his lips as he dropped a light kiss on her still-damp hair.

Marc had dried her so tenderly after they had finally left the bath and somehow they had ended up in his bed making love again. And now they lay together in a tender intimacy which nearly broke her heart. At times like this it was so easy to pretend that he loved her, know that she loved him… The words welled up in her heart, straining, desperate to escape. She held them back, not wishing to destroy the fragile joy of the moment. Instead she turned her face slightly and pressed a kiss on the hard wall of his chest, revelling in the contrast of smooth skin and underlying steel of muscle, drinking in the warm, musky scent of his body.

His arms tightened to iron around her and she heard a soft groan deep in his throat. And then his voice, inexpressibly tender, 'Meg, dearest, loveliest Meg. My little love...'

She couldn't bear it. The endearment shattered her joy into fragments which pierced her heart like a storm of arrows. For a moment she just froze, trying to ignore her pain, but it was impossible to pretend any longer. Her eyes filled with tears which spilt over in a flood of grief. 'Don't...please, Marc...don't say that,' she whispered.

The words nearly tore his heart out. It was too late, he thought despairingly as he turned her gently to face him. She didn't want his love. He had hurt her too badly, confused her with his contradictory behaviour. Then, as he saw the tear-drowned eyes and the trembling mouth, hope surged in him. *'Don't say it?'* he asked. 'Why not, my darling?'

She saw him through a blur of tears. 'I can't bear it,' she said brokenly. 'Not...not unless you love me.' Oh, God, what had she said? He didn't want her love. No one had ever wanted her love. Numbly, she waited for the inevitable rejection, for him to tell her gently that he could not love her, that he was sorry, but he was just fond of her. His very kindness would make it the worst rejection of all.

His voice was barely recognisable, tearing with emotion. 'Then you love me, Meg?'

'Yes,' she whispered. 'I'm sorry, Marc...I can't help it.' She tried to pull away from him, but found that his arms were drawing her back, cradling her against him as he kissed the tears away.

'I think we need to renegotiate our bargain then, my little love,' he said, shakenly. 'Something along the lines of *a heart for a heart*. Mine was yours long ago, even if I was too proud to admit it and ask for yours in return. As I do now.'

Her heart completely overflowed in its frantic joy. 'Oh, Marc,' she sobbed. 'It was always yours. I knew when you asked me to marry you that I would love you. You were always so kind to me...looked after me, but you never seemed to *pity* me. Even when you offered to marry me, you offered a bargain between equals. Always before people either despised me or pitied me. You were the only one who ever accepted me and didn't care about my family.'

A surge of shame ripped through him. That vile bargain he had struck with her! All these weeks it had kept them apart, tormenting him, nearly destroying Meg. Yet she had continued to love him and he, fool that he was, had never seen it.

'And you never told me.' He kissed her gently. 'Because of our stupid bargain. And because I shut you out.'

She shook her head. 'No. Not just that. I was too scared anyway. You see, when I went to Yorkshire I thought that Cousin Euphemia and Cousin Samuel had sent for me because they cared about me. But they...they didn't. And Henrietta had told me I was a disgrace. So...I...I couldn't tell you. Why on earth would you, of all people, want me to love you? No one else did.'

'Because I can't live without it, Meg,' he said passionately. And lowered his mouth to hers in a kiss of total possession and dedication.

Chapter Sixteen

Gala Night at Vauxhall Gardens was always enjoyable, thought Meg. She had attended several times before in company with Di and Toby, who included her in their parties as a matter of course. Jack Hamilton had been her escort on these occasions. Handsome, kind, attentive to her every need, he was an escort any lady might preen herself on. But nothing, thought Meg, could possibly rival the delight of wandering the groves in the company of her absurd and over-protective husband. Unless it was waltzing with him, pressed to his body in a way that made every nerve tingle as his powerful thighs moved intimately against hers as they danced.

Her eyes, raised to his, shone with her love and Marcus had to bring every vestige of self-discipline to bear not to bend and accept the invitation of her softly parted lips. His arm tightened appreciably around her, drawing her even closer. He was aware that quite a number of persons were watching them in scandalised amusement. He couldn't have cared less. She was his! And he wanted the whole world to know it!

And in a couple of days he'd have her all to himself. Her morning sickness was so much better, now she was getting enough sleep, that they were leaving for Yorkshire. After that he'd take her straight down to Alston Court. The thought of seeing Meg in the place he'd always thought of as home sent a warm glow right through him. She'd never had a proper home, one full of love and happiness. And of late years, he'd known deep down that Alston Court was crying out for a mistress, to be the happy home it had been in his mother's day. Seeing Meg there would finally lay that ghost to rest as well.

Watching them as he chatted casually to Di, Jack thought that, until now, even he had never seen the real Meg. Oh, he had seen past the glittering façade of Lady Rutherford, but he had never seen the glowing, adoring girl who was circling the floor in Marc's arms.

Di was saying something of the sort about Marc. 'Such a change in the pair of them! Oh, Jack, I've not seen Marc like this since he was a boy.' Consideringly she said, 'Not even then! No boy could look like that!'

She was right, thought Jack. Finally surrendering to love in his mid-thirties, Marc was mature enough to know the value of what he had been granted. He had seen Marc with enough women to recognise the difference. For the first time ever Marc was letting his feelings show and obviously didn't give a damn who saw it.

'And Meg!' continued Di, with an almost maternal pride. 'I vow she is lovelier than ever. Such a bloom!' She stopped short, and Jack waited with a slightly quirked eyebrow.

Taking pity on her sudden embarrassment, he said smoothly, 'Better start thinking of christening presents, hadn't we? I understand you and Toby and I have to do our duty early next year.'

'Oh, good!' said Di, in relieved accents. 'I'm so glad they asked you as well. Now I must get back to our box. Aunt Regina will be grilling poor Toby mercilessly.' She rustled away after giving him an affectionate pat on the arm.

Jack stayed to watch the dancers as they swirled past him in a scented whirl of silk and superfine. A discreet cough at his elbow drew his attention. He turned and blinked in surprise. Lady Hartleigh stood just behind him, her gaze fixed on a tall, tawny-headed figure as he whirled his laughing partner through a turn.

Without looking at Jack, she said in amusement, 'He never danced with me like that.'

'Did you want him to?' asked Jack curiously. And then thought, what a tactless question!

But Althea Hartleigh gave a genuine laugh. 'No, Mr Hamilton, I did not. Heavens! Only think of the *scandal* had he done so!' Then with a faint smile she added, 'As you so rightly thought, I wanted Rutherford's money and his title.' She paused for a moment and added, 'And his, shall we say, physical prowess.'

Whatever answer he had expected, it hadn't been that! 'You're very honest,' he said gently, wondering if she had been hurt by Marc's defection.

She shrugged. 'Not my worst enemy could accuse me of deluding myself. And it did not occur to me that Marcus wanted more. Well, he didn't, did he? Not from me.' She was silent for a moment and then said deliberately, 'Any more than I wished to give it.'

'I'm sorry—' began Jack.

He was interrupted at once. 'Don't be. We would not have been happy. I thought Marcus as cold and calculating as myself. Had I known he could be like this, I should have run a mile!' There was no mistaking the sincerity in her voice.

There was a moment's silence and then she said, 'Tell Marcus to watch his bride. Winterbourne is out of town at the moment but when he gets back... I have heard some things that worried me about Lady Rutherford and Blaise Winterbourne. And he watches her all the time. Both he and Henrietta Fellowes are out to do the chit a mischief.'

Jack stiffened and she laughed harshly. 'Don't be a fool, Hamilton! I can see what's under my nose. That child is as much in love with Marcus as he is with her. But that would not deter Winterbourne. As a woman, I cannot stand by and acquiesce in what he would do to her. And I have as much affection for Marcus as for any man—I do not wish to see him hurt. Warn them for me. I cannot approach either without causing trouble.' She smiled up at him with something of her old glimmer in the green eyes. 'As I did that day in the park! Add to your kindness by apologising to Lady Rutherford for my tactlessness and wishing her happy for me. I took a liking to her that day. Unlike most wives, she was furious with her husband, not me. I found it a refreshingly honest perspective.' She drew a sharp breath. 'The dance is over. I must rejoin my party.'

Before Jack could do more than nod in assent she was gone, lost in the fashionable crowd coming off the dance floor.

Marcus had Meg's hand tucked securely in his arm. He felt as though he were still floating in a haze of music and silk. Slanting a glance down at her, he found her soft eyes raised to his face. This was the real Meg, warm, giving, vibrant. The mask was gone for good.

Thank God he had finally had the sense and courage to accept the joy he had been offered.

'I love you, sweetheart,' he murmured.

'I...I...' Her breath failed her totally. Despite the fact that he hadn't lost a single opportunity in the last week to tell her how much he loved her, it still reduced her to jelly. And the last thing she had expected was that he would say it in the middle of a crowded dance floor. Dammit all, she couldn't even speak! The words she longed to say could not make it past the lump in her throat, but lodged there quivering, useless. But her eyes, shimmering with sudden tears, said enough for Marcus.

Understandingly he caressed the small hand clutching his sleeve. 'A terrible place to make a declaration, my darling. I'll make it again later in more appropriate surroundings.' Probably several times, he mused. Now that the words were out, he suspected that he might never be tired of saying them. Especially if they were going to bring that look into her eyes.

'Time to rejoin the others for supper,' said Jack as they came up to him. He would have to try to get Marc alone to pass on Althea's message. No point in alarming Meg. Not in her condition. He grinned at her, 'Come and draw Lady Grafton's fire, Meg. She's grilling Toby at the moment, apparently.'

Marcus grinned. 'Poor chap must be exhausted. Aunt Regina won't just sit there and let him chunter on about his dogs. Come along, Meg. Do your duty!'

There was a teasing twinkle in his eye, which deepened as Meg said naughtily, 'Dear me, how is it that such a small word as *duty*, can encompass such a *varied* multitude of tasks?'

'You, my lady, are a baggage!' her husband informed her. 'Furthermore, you are embarrassing Jack.'

'Behold my blush,' said Jack laconically.

Back at the box Marcus had hired for the evening, Jack found it worse than impossible to drop a quiet word in his host's ear. The formidable Lady Grafton was intent on giving both Meg and her iniquitous nephew the once over. Persuaded by Di to return from Bath and give the union her blessing, she was determined not to do so without first enjoying herself.

And after supper she insisted that her nephew escort her for a brief stroll and then to view the fireworks, taking as an insult his suggestion that she might find it too much.

'Hmph! I'm not in my winding sheet yet, Rutherford. Nor likely to be after a stroll around the gardens.' She paused to consider. 'Not but what the scandalous behaviour of most of your generation is enough to send anyone to their grave!'

The party, accordingly, got up. Sir Toby claimed Meg's escort, saying to Jack in an undertone, 'Exhausted, dear boy! You take Di. Couldn't cope with any more of the Langley women tonight.'

The fireworks were magnificent and Meg, who never tired of them, was utterly entranced. But she found that standing still for so long was far more tiring than walking. In fact, she began to feel slightly unwell due to the warmth of the crush of people and an overpowering aroma of scent.

Before she could say anything, Sir Toby, experienced in the ways of ladies in delicate condition, remarked, 'I say, m'dear, it's getting a trifle crowded. Shall we take a stroll?'

Marcus heard this and turned around in time to see Meg's relieved face as she assented. He cocked his head at her in an unspoken question and she smiled back reassuringly. A stroll, she thought, would be lovely. No need to annoy Lady Grafton by dragging Marc away.

There were innumerable walks in the gardens, which were lit by well over thirty thousand lamps. Meg and Sir Toby wandered up and down, meeting very few other couples. Those they did see seemed perfectly content to lose themselves in a fashion Meg did not doubt Lady Grafton would label as scandalous with unconvincing righteousness.

As they strolled in companionable silence Meg reflected on her new happiness. During the past week since their reconciliation she and Marc had gradually come to a full understanding. At last Meg could see why he had been so confused. Why, even when he fell in love, he had been so reluctant to tell her. Their bargain had just been an excuse, for both of them. He had hidden his fear and pain over his mother's death behind its terms and she had used it to disguise her fear of rejection.

Now the pretences were over, leaving them free to acknowledge the truth. That they loved each other and would take the joy offered with both hands.

Her mind was brought back to earth by an audible snap as her garter gave way.

'Oh, bother!' she said, as, with a disconcerting slither, her silk stocking came down.

'Eh?' Sir Toby was rather startled.

'My garter,' she said with a blush. 'It's broken... Would you mind...could you...?'

'Oh, certainly, m'dear,' said Sir Toby cheerfully. 'I'll just pop around the corner and wait for you.' He bowed elegantly and took himself off.

Meg battled with the garter for several moments before deciding to give up and just stuff the offending item, along with her stocking, into her reticule.

Just as she straightened up an amused voice said, 'How very convenient. That will be one less article to strip from you. And I don't even have to draw off that dolt Carlton.'

She whirled to meet Sir Blaise Winterbourne's cruel eyes. Shock rendered her speechless for a moment and then she opened her mouth to scream.

Sir Blaise was too fast. He moved like lightning and had one arm twisted behind her back while his free hand was clamped mercilessly over her mouth. She could do nothing as he forced her away, the pain in her arm was making her dizzy. She barely noticed the pearl bracelet she had been wearing snap and drop to the ground.

'Do not think that Rutherford will be able to save you this time, my dear,' he mocked. 'He is at the other end of the gardens. And even if you tell him you went with me unwillingly, our dear mutual cousin Henrietta will assure the world that she saw us leaving together via the water gate, a most happy couple.' His voice was light as he continued. 'So you see, you are ruined anyway. It remains only to be seen whether you will drag your husband's name in the mud or submit to your fate quietly.'

Sheer terror held Meg in its relentless grip. She had been right, then, that evening at Almack's. No doubt Henrietta would be delighted to see her ruined and be able to say, *Like mother, like daughter!* And if Marc, knowing the truth, stood by her, then his proud name would be ruined as well. Not for one moment did Meg doubt that he would stand by her.

The pain in her arm grew worse as Sir Blaise, enjoying his triumph, twisted it harder. The dim walk seemed to swirl and tilt before her eyes. They had reached an unfrequented part of the grounds. He turned her to face him, still with her arm twisted cruelly. She could not doubt that he meant to ravish her, but suddenly her terror and pain scorched into sheer flaming rage. She would *not* tamely submit and let him destroy her and Marc. Furiously she began to squirm and wriggle, stamping at his feet, striking at him with her free hand.

He caught it and laughed. 'Remember, my dear, if you scream, your cousin will swear you came willingly.'

And then she remembered something: Agnes Barlow's gruff tones as she advised Nellie Bates, one afternoon in the kitchen at Fenby, on how to deal with a suitor who'd become too forward for Nellie's liking. She couldn't for the life of her see what use it would be, but Agnes had seemed quite sure.

She jerked her knee upwards—hard.

After some ten minutes Sir Toby succumbed to his concern about the inordinate length of time his sister-in-law was taking over a mere broken garter. Strolling back around the corner, he was most surprised to find her gone.

'Extraordinary,' he said to himself. It was most unlike the chit. She ought not to be wandering about alone. If Marc found out he'd be fit to be tied. Or had Marc come to find her? Just as he was pondering the likelihood of this, his eye was caught by something half hidden under a bush. Pink and shiny, it shimmered in the lamplight.

Suddenly his air of languor dropped from him as he strode over to pick it up. Meg's reticule! At least it looked like hers. He opened it and, sure enough, there was a silk stocking with a broken garter on top.

For a moment he was undecided, but then he saw something else on the ground a few yards away. With an oath he sprang forward. Meg might have dropped her reticule and forgotten it, but she would not have dropped that bracelet! Without the least hesitation he began to run back towards the boxes.

'She said *what*?' Marcus had gone absolutely white at Jack's information. He felt as though someone had just ripped out his heart. Looking around frantically, he said in a shaking voice, 'Where's Meg?'

'Calm down, man!' said Jack. 'She's with Toby. He's quite capable of looking after her. And Althea Hartleigh says that Winterbourne is out of—'

'Hamilton!'

They swung around to see Lady Hartleigh.

She gripped Jack's sleeve. 'Winterbourne is here! Have you told—?' She glanced at Marcus's face. 'You did. He chatted briefly to Henrietta Fellowes and then disappeared off after Lady Rutherford and Carlton. You'd better hurry. That bitch looked as though she'd been left with a juicy bone.'

Marcus was gone, running in the direction taken by Toby and Meg half an hour ago. The thought that Winterbourne might try to abduct Meg terrified him. The fury he had felt on his wedding night was as nothing to the rage and panic he felt now. Then he had scarcely known Meg. Now she was his, the most precious thing in his life. No fear of scandal would save Winterbourne this time. Marcus would kill him if he tried to lay hands on Meg!

Dimly he realised that Jack had come with him. He slowed down—they were at the junction of the Grand

Walk and the Grand Cross Walk and he had no idea where to go.

'Marc, this is crazy!' expostulated Jack. 'She's safe enough with Toby. He'd never leave her alone here, you know—'

He stopped abruptly as a relieved yell came to their ears.

'Thank God!' Toby was running towards them from the Dark Walk. He came up, panting. 'Meg's disappeared. Garter broke, so I stepped away to let her deal with it. You know, just around the corner. Came back and found these!' He held up the reticule and broken bracelet.

Marcus took them in hands that shook uncontrollably. His eyes met Jack's in anguish. 'Winterbourne. This time I'm going to kill him.' The deadly quiet of his tones startled Jack and Toby more than an explosion of rage would have done.

'What?' Sir Toby was considerably taken aback. In the twenty years he had known Marcus he had never seen him like this. Had never suspected that he could feel anything this deeply.

'Where were you, Toby?' Marcus forced himself to act logically. He could not help Meg by running in circles.

'Follow me.'

Meg felt her knee crash into her tormentor with satisfying force. And stared in stupefaction at the result.

Winterbourne's hands dropped from her, all their brutal strength dissolved as though it had never been. He doubled over with a wheezing moan and collapsed in a shuddering heap, practically sobbing in agony.

Agnes's voice echoed in her memory. *That'll settle 'im an' give you time to run.*

Meg ran blindly. She had no idea where she was going precisely, but she knew she didn't want to be there. What she wanted was Marc…his arms around her, secure and warm, banishing her fear. She had not taken more than a dozen strides before she hit a solid wall.

A solid wall with arms that tightened around her and a voice that broke as it said, 'Meg! Oh, thank God! Are you safe?'

She'd never felt safer. And Jack and Toby were there as well, patting her shoulders and reassuring her.

At first Marc felt as though nothing mattered but having Meg back safely in his arms, apparently unharmed. He held her to him tightly, his cheek pressed to her hair as she clung to him. His hands stroked her gently, soothingly until he felt her shuddering ease, felt her relax against him. Then he spared a glance for Winterbourne, still wheezing painfully on the ground. Dimly he was aware of surprise—surprise that he could feel not the slightest twinge of masculine sympathy for a man in that situation.

Then rage took over. He caught Jack's eye and said, 'Look after Meg for me, Jack. There is something I have to do.' He put her into Jack's arms very gently, saying, 'Stay with Jack, my love.' He caught Jack's eye. 'Try not to let her watch.'

He strode over to Winterbourne's gasping form.

'Get up, you cur!' he snarled. 'This time I'm going to give you what you deserve.'

Winterbourne stayed where he was.

Marcus waited a moment, and then said in biting accents, 'Toby, go out to the carriages and borrow a whip.

If anyone asks what you want with it, you may tell them, with my compliments, that I need it to thrash Winterbourne, who is too cowardly to stand and face me. He has only enough courage to assault a woman!'

Winterbourne staggered to his feet, still clutching his midriff. 'Think…scandal,' he gasped.

'*Your* scandal,' said Marcus. 'There are enough witnesses, including Lady Hartleigh, to prove that you assaulted my wife! And if you try it, I'll have nothing to lose by putting a bullet straight through you! I don't think either the law or society will find my actions unforgivable. You can tell Henrietta Fellowes that with my compliments.'

He waited a moment, taking a savage satisfaction in Winterbourne's pain. 'If you have that flask of yours, Toby, give him some. You can always have the scullery maid boil it before you drink from it again. Or I'll buy you a new one.'

Toby obliged and Winterbourne gulped at the brandy gratefully. Slightly recovered, he looked around uncertainly, all his urbanity fled. He glanced at the flask and then at Sir Toby.

'Keep it,' said Toby coldly. 'I've too much respect for my scullery maid to soil her with anything you've touched!'

'Now,' said Marcus, from between clenched teeth, 'now, Winterbourne, I have something to say to you.'

The right hook he delivered to Winterbourne's nose sent the baronet reeling. He followed it with a savage uppercut which snapped his head back and Winterbourne staggered backwards into a tree. Marcus followed him, but Winterbourne slithered to the ground again with a moan.

'Good God! What on earth has Rutherford done to

Winterbourne?' A startled, feminine, voice brought Marc up short.

Coldly and deliberately, Marc turned his head. Lady Jersey and her lord stood staring in rampant curiosity.

'Really, Marc! Do you think this is a suitable venue for you to pursue your quarrel with Winterbourne?' Lady Jersey appeared to feel deeply over this unseemly fracas.

'Good evening, Sally,' said Marc, very politely. 'While it may not be the venue I would have chosen, since Winterbourne considered it a suitable venue for attempted rape, I was, shall we say, constrained?'

'What?' Sally Jersey's eyes flew to Meg, still supported by Jack. 'Dear God. Meg, are you all right?' Horrified sympathy rang in her voice as she rushed across to Meg.

The Earl of Jersey spoke thoughtfully. 'Sorry to interrupt you, Rutherford. If your arm gets tired, let me know. Be happy to take a turn.'

His wife turned sharply from comforting Meg. 'Oh, for goodness sake! What if someone else comes along? The last thing Meg needs is for anyone to know about this. Not that anyone will blame her, but for such a thing to get about…it would be intolerable for the poor girl!'

She cast a contemptuous glance at Winterbourne and spoke in tones of shuddering disgust. 'Rest assured that if he ever attempts to enter Almack's again, he will be thrown out. Trust me. And I'll make it quite plain that he is not to be received by anyone!' Her eyes glittered venomously. 'I won't need to say why. No one will question me.'

No one, least of all Winterbourne, doubted her. The Countess of Jersey's word was law. If she decreed that

Winterbourne could not be received, then he was finished as far as the ladies were concerned.

'I'll deal with the clubs,' offered Lord Jersey, sealing Winterbourne's ruin. 'Better if you keep out of it, Marc. Someone might guess the truth. Leave it to Sally and myself.' He held out his arm to his countess. 'Come along, my love. Before I am tempted to assist Marc in murdering that filth. Evening, all.' He led his wife away inexorably.

Disgustedly Marcus stepped back, throttling the temptation to send Toby for a whip. Sally was right. If anyone else appeared...

'Marc? Could we...could we go home now?'

He turned and looked at Meg. She still stood in the circle of Jack's arm, but her eyes said clearly that she wanted him. He cast a lingering glance down at Winterbourne. There probably wasn't much point in sending for the whip. After what Meg had done to him, he wouldn't even feel it.

He walked over to Meg and took her from Jack, dragging her into his arms. 'Oh God, Meg! Will you never do anything the way you're meant to?' His voice was rough with passion. 'I expected a fashionable wife who would run up astronomical bills at the dressmakers. The only bill you have run up is at Hatchard's! I thought I wanted a marriage of convenience and fell in love with you instead! Now I come racing to rescue you and find that you have rescued yourself!' He held her tightly.

'Do you you mind?' asked Meg as she nestled against him. Here in his arms she was safe from everything.

A strange sound, half-groan and half-laugh, was ripped from deep inside Marcus at her question. Mind? *Mind?* How could he possibly mind having his life